CASTAWAY DREAMS

HIGH SEAS #2

DARLENE MARSHALL

…"What is your favorite color?" he barked.

"Pink! Oh, I need some water!"

He gave her the flask and she swallowed, and while she looked a bit pale, she kept her stomach's contents intact. His distracting question had done its job.

She took a deep breath.

"I did it, Doctor. I ate the—"

"Do not say it, do not think about it."

"It was not so bad. We may be onto something here."

"No one is going to eat raw fish if they can possibly help it, Miss Farnham. Now, close your eyes."

She did, obediently opening her mouth like a fledgling in the nest, and he fed her more tidbits. His fingers brushed against her moist lips as she took the food from him, her warm breath caressing his sensitive finger tips. Now he was trying not to think about it, what it felt like to have this beautiful woman take his fingers into her mouth, lightly sucking at them as she pulled in the firm, salty morsels, her delicate throat working to swallow, her eyes closed and an intense look of concentration on her sweat-dewed brow.

"One—" He cleared his throat and tried to speak again. "One moment, please—no, do not open your eyes!"

He grabbed his coat and pulled it across his lap, even though the day was hot and growing hotter. The last thing he needed was for her to open her eyes and see him sitting inches away with his compass pointing north.

"What are you thinking about, Doctor?"

"Involuntary responses…"

you! The romance is hot, the writing is smart, and the plot is just plain fun"--Reading to Penguins

Castaway Dreams
High Seas #2

DARLENE MARSHALL

ISBN 978-0-692-81973-9

Ebook ISBN 9781370859627

PUBLISHED IN THE UNITED STATES OF AMERICA BY: EVE D. ACKERMAN

❀ Created with Vellum

DEDICATION &
ACKNOWLEDGEMENTS

To all the medical personnel—MDs, EMTs, RNs—who read various scenes and said I didn't screw it up. Any mistakes are mine, not theirs.

To Ms. Erin Speer for checking my geometry info. Math teachers rock! Kids, listen to your teachers! They're right, you will need this stuff someday.

To Raphi, who complained about my burdensome requests, but did translate one line of French for me.

The librarians at the Alachua County Library District.

Compuserve Books and Writers Community. After all these years, still the best.

Thank you to my beta readers: Connie, Janice, Amarilis and Jayne, and to my editor, Catherine.

Love, as always, to Raphi (even though he wouldn't read my geometry scene), Micah (who played banjo when I needed a boost), and of course, to Howard. Happy ever after doesn't just happen in fairy tales. Thanks, guys!

CHAPTER 1

1817

*A*lexander Murray spent his lifetime dissecting bodies, trephining skulls, and seeing gray matter splattered across the decks of warships. He knew one could not exist without a brain. Nonetheless, Miss Daphne Farnham appeared to be the living, breathing example of a brainless existence.

Perhaps he'd write a paper on it for the medical journals, he mused as he poured himself more coffee.

He was unsure why he found Miss Farnham so irritating. It wasn't their being in close quarters. If anything, the *Magpie* was roomier than the *Caeneus*. Maybe it was simply after living for years at sea, higher-pitched voices grated on his nerves.

No, that wasn't it, he thought as he sipped the harsh brew and listened with half an ear to the conversation around him. Some of the warrant officers had their wives aboard ship, and it was not as if he disdained the company of women. No, it was purely about Miss Farnham, a fellow passenger traveling from Jamaica to England.

Just now at luncheon she asked Mr. Carr if he had in his

possession the latest issues of *La Belle Assemblée*. She *desperately* needed to know if her Oldenburg bonnet was still fashionable enough to wear while walking along the Serpentine.

The war was finally over, England was at peace, and the best thing this woman could find to talk about was hats.

Alex looked at the others through the steam rising from his cup. The gentlemen at the table didn't mind Miss Farnham's breathy little voice and fatuous conversation. They weighed in with their opinions, all of them agreeing, naturally, that she would look lovely no matter what bonnet she wore. Mrs. Bertha Cowper, Miss Farnham's companion, ignored the byplay and continued to shovel plum duff into her mouth, her florid coloring not helped by the heat.

Miss Farnham looked as fresh and winsome as if she'd just stepped off the pages of her journal of fashion. She sat across from him, giving him an opportunity to observe her whether he wanted to or not. Her dog sat on her lap, his beady black eyes glaring at Alexander over the edge of the table. The cur had a rose-colored ribbon tied around its neck, a ribbon that exactly matched the one threaded through Miss Farnham's curls, curls glowing a sunshined gold in the dim cabin light. Her large eyes twinkled at a comment from her shipboard swains, eyes one crewman swore were violet, while another said they were the blue of bluebells washed in the dew. Her dainty mouth was bracketed by two deep dimples highlighting her white and even teeth when she smiled, and her nose was exactly the complement needed to her other features—not too long, not too short. Her form was all that could be desired, the men swore, slim where a woman should be slim, rounded where it mattered.

The first mate, Mr. Carr, was bright enough to recognize an opportunity when it was dangled in front of him and now did his best to make a positive impression. Alexander had seen women flock to him in Jamaica, drawn by his smooth conversation, well- tailored coats, and vapid handsomeness.

But he was a competent mate, which was all that mattered on a voyage like this. Besides, Carr's interest in their passenger was no concern of Alexander's.

"It is all about the blunt the girl will bring with her," Carr said over breakfast that morning, where none of the passengers were about and it was only the senior officers and the surgeon.

"Tyndale's bad luck could be my good fortune, Mr. Murray," he smirked. "With her reputation in tatters and Tyndale dead, it's a grand opportunity for me."

"Her father's a nabob," Captain Franklin said repressively, reaching for the plum jam. "He'll be looking to buy a title for her, boy, not wanting to marry her off to a sailor. There will be some lord with pockets to let or gambling debts who will take her, you mark my words. Farnham's money can cover all of her sins, especially with her looks!"

The only child of a gentleman who'd made a fortune in India, Miss Daphne Farnham would make someone an acceptable wife, save for two things, and Alexander acknowledged only one of those mattered to most of his peers.

George Tyndale ran off with her to Jamaica, then like so many other Englishmen newly arrived in the tropics up and died of yellow fever. Even Alexander heard the rumors and questions about whether Tyndale had indeed married the young lady.

The fact that everyone continued to refer to her as Miss Farnham, rather than Mrs. Tyndale, gave credence to these rumors and Miss Farnham did nothing to correct that impression. Perhaps the captain was correct. Enough gold could buy an understanding husband and return one to society. It was only poor women like Janet Murray and her bastard son who had to suffer the indignities of life on the fringes of the community.

The other problem with Miss Farnham apparently was only an issue to Alexander. Her purpose in life, as far as he could determine, was to be ornamental. Even her most common fashion accessory was ornamental rather than useful. There was no place aboard ship for little dogs unless they were ratters, and any proper ship's rat would sneer at her white puffball of a bichon.

That animal was another source of irritation and had been ever since the first day he'd come aboard with his mistress. Within an hour of sailing, Miss Farnham was frantically knocking at Alexander's cabin door.

"There is something wrong with Pompom, Dr. Murray!"

The dog shivered, its tail tucked between its legs. Before Alexander could share with her the most obvious conclusion, she thrust the animal into his arms. He immediately pushed the heaving dog at arm's length, but it was too late. The little beast cast up his accounts all over the front of Alex's coat. Pleased he didn't drop the creature to the deck, he set him down, whereupon the dog vomited again, this time on his boot. However, he did look more chipper after purging his system, and Miss Farnham swept him up into her arms.

"Oh, Pompom, you had an upset tum-tum! But now my puppy-wuppy's all better, isn't he?"

Miss Farnham looked at him, her brilliant blue eyes filled with admiration. "You are the best doctor. You cured my precious Pompom."

"Your animal is seasick, Miss Farnham. Feed him dry biscuit and water for a few days and keep him away from me."

She had appeared startled that Alexander didn't find her odious little animal as adorable as she did.

"Come, my darling. Dr. Murray is being a big old

grumpywumpy." She'd stuck her retrousse nose into the air, and turned on her heel, offering the surgeon a flash of a neat ankle before exiting his cabin.

Now back in that cabin after luncheon, Alexander was engrossed in one of the many journals he'd accumulated during his tenure on the *Caeneus* but had not had time to read. The war brought advances in surgery and medical techniques, some he'd experienced firsthand, but it was time to catch up on those other innovations uncovered by his brother surgeons. He hoped to observe them in London, but study now would prepare him to discuss them.

So when there was a timid knock at his cabin door he was less than pleased at the interruption and set the journal aside with a sigh. His fiercely negotiated passage to England included being available to the crew of the *Magpie* should they need his services. When he was not feeling put out by interruptions, he had to agree staying busy at his craft was better than boredom.

On the other hand, boredom could be better than more time spent in the company of Miss Farnham. But there she was, standing in his doorway, clutching the front of her dress. Her animal was not with her, so maybe this time she would not need veterinary services.

"Yes?"

"Oh, Dr. Murray, I am having trouble breathing!"

"Come in," he said to her. He looked down the passageway but did not see her chaperone.

"Where is Mrs. Cowper?"

"She wanted a 'lie down' after luncheon. She says it helps her digestion."

With as much wine as Mrs. Cowper consumed at lunch, it was a wonder she hadn't fallen down the companionway headfirst to have her "lie down."

"Sit down, please," he said, gesturing at his bunk. "Now, tell me what the problem is."

"When I climb the ladder it feels like I am choking and not breathing enough air!"

Her slim hand fluttered to her shapely bosom and he studied her critically.

"Does this happen if you loosen your stays so they are not too tight?"

"Dr. Murray! Such a thing would never occur to me, to loosen my stays."

"It should occur to you," he said mildly. "I have seen this before with so-called ladies of fashion—and a few men as well. You are so tightly laced that you cannot give your lungs enough room to expand. I will demonstrate."

He pulled her to her feet by that slim hand and instructed her, "Now, take a deep breath, as deep as you can."

She tried, but it was obvious to his eye that her corset constricted her to the point where it was impossible for her to fully pull air into her lungs.

He grunted.

"My prescription is this, Miss Farnham: loosen your stays and give your body room to do what it is meant to do. Nature did not intend for you to be swaddled like an Egyptian mummy." She stared at him.

"I cannot loosen my stays, Dr. Murray. If I do that my clothing will not fit properly."

"I am a surgeon, not a man-milliner. You asked for my medical advice, I gave it to you. What you do at this point is entirely up to you."

He opened the door for her to leave so he could return to his reading, but she paused in the doorway.

"Thank you, Dr. Murray, I will consider what you said, even though it sounds like silliness to me."

"I am addressed as Mr. Murray, Miss Farnham."

"But the sailors call you 'doctor.'"

"Aboard ship a surgeon also acts as a physician and an apothecary, so some sailors and seaman have that habit."

"I believe I will call you Dr. Murray also. Someone of your many years of experience deserves a more exalted title than an ordinary 'mister.'"

"Someone of my many years?"

She nodded vigorously, golden curls bouncing, and other parts of her bounced as well, which distracted him for a few seconds from the bizarre conversation.

"You cured my lovely little Pompom when his tummy was upset, and now you cured me, so you must be a truly talented medical man! After all, you just said you are experienced at physicking people, maybe even more than my physician at home. And you look like you have been doing this just forever and ever."

"There are days, Miss Farnham, when I feel I have been dealing with the minor complaints of silly people for, as you say, forever. Good day to you, ma'am."

Alexander was still mulling over her fatuous remark about his age as he strolled the decks after supper. He knew his strong feelings about her would stun his former crewmates. More than one ship's officer and seaman claimed Alexander Murray was the most phlegmatic, abstemious and least passionate individual ever to serve in the Royal Navy.

"In the middle of a hurricane, you would find him calmly taking notes between patching up men hit by tackle or thrown to the deck by the force of the waves," Captain Thomas Doyle of the *Caeneus* had remarked at the farewell dinner for Alexander in Jamaica. "We were all praying like Jonah's heathen shipmates, and Murray could be down below, sleeping like Jonah, oblivious to it all. I know, because I have seen him do it,"

He hadn't thought much about how people viewed him

during his service with the navy, but now with his changed circumstances he found himself doing more self-evaluation. The weather across the Atlantic had been so cold and miserable this past summer of 1816 that he stayed a year longer in the islands. But the letter tucked into the back of his journal called him home, and this voyage gave him time for introspection.

He paused when he heard his name mentioned as he stood in the shadows, the speakers unaware of him.

"Mr. Carr, when Dr. Murray fixes those grim eyes of his upon me, I feel I am standing in front of St. Peter awaiting admission to heaven! What makes him act so dour and disapproving? Does he never smile?"

Maybe Miss Farnham was not so foolish after all, Alexander thought, if she could assess his character so well based on her brief interaction with him.

"I have never seen Murray smile, Miss Farnham, but do not fret your pretty little head over that old stick," said the *Magpie*'s mate. "And you should not worry about being allowed into heaven, for I vow, you are the veriest angel!" her young gallant swore.

Naturally, the very vapid Miss Farnham giggled at this bold declaration. It was a noise that had the exact effect of putting Alexander's teeth on edge.

He stepped out and observed the couple. Their heads were close together as they talked, and her chaperone was nowhere in sight. Feeling every bit the elder they thought him, he cleared his throat. Of course, they jumped apart as though he'd caught them in Carr's bunk together. Carr mumbled something and hurried off, leaving poor Miss Farnham to face him, alone and unprotected.

She surprised him then. Instead of running after her swain, she only watched him go, then turned back to Alexander. He could swear he saw a rueful gleam of humor in her eye, but the light was poor in the evening dusk.

"Dr. Murray," she said in her light voice. "How do you find the weather this evening?"

He gave the chit points for daring to strike up a conversation with dour, judgmental Dr. Murray, even if it was only banal niceties regarding atmospheric conditions. He took a step closer and she almost flinched back but held her ground. He never suspected he had a propensity for trying to terrify young women, which just went to show one could learn something new about oneself every day.

"The weather, Miss Farnham, is warm. And wet. Just as it is most days in the tropics."

"La, I am aware of that." She reached up to pat the hair elaborately arranged over her shell-like ears. "I vow, this wet air makes my hair just curl and curl until I cannot do a thing with it!"

She stood there, a silly smile on her face, no doubt waiting for him to make a comment on her bountiful curls. Perhaps comparing them to buttercups or golden coins or sunshine or something equally nonsensical.

"It is well known, Miss Farnham, that wet air makes hair curl. You are no different from many other people in that regard," he said repressively.

She stared at him a moment, then those large eyes blinked. He couldn't help but notice her eyes were shielded by thick and dark lashes, a setting contributing to their attraction. To other men, certainly not to him. It took more than eyes like sapphire velvet to affect him.

"Why do you dislike me, Dr. Murray? You do not even know me."

If he felt a twinge of discomfort at being put on the spot by this chit, he repressed it. It was an honest question, so the least he could offer was an honest answer.

"I am not sure," he said thoughtfully. "I suppose it is because I spent most of my life surrounded by people who are useful. On a frigate, boys as young as eight years old carry powder in the midst of battle. I have never known anyone whose existence was without purpose. You, however, seem to me not a very useful person."

Alexander regretted his honesty and his blunt words as soon as they left his mouth. It was not the girl's fault she didn't have two thoughts rattling about in her head. She could not help it, and at least she had her beauty—and wealth —to compensate for it.

"Useful," she said in a low voice. "Is that how you evaluate people, Doctor?"

He looked at her with greater interest. Perhaps she was not as dim as he thought.

"Yes, Miss Farnham, that is how I evaluate people. In the natural world everything serves a purpose and is useful, from the animals we hunt and the plants we harvest to the maggots eating dead flesh."

"But what of young ladies? Must they be as useful as," she swallowed, "maggots?"

He stepped closer to her, intrigued now. She smelled of lavender, and the part of his brain connected to certain anatomical functions registered this and woke up. It had been a long time since he'd relaxed in port with hired companionship. Then he remembered young ladies were not in a class of women where one could dally without conse- quences, even young ladies of questionable reputation.

But he was still intrigued.

"I do not deal much with young ladies. I can tell you though all the women I do know have been, in one fashion or another, useful." He thought back to a certain young woman who ran off with an American and added, "Some are extremely useful, and competent in a crisis, and yes, that is how I judge people."

Her eyelashes lowered, shading her thoughts from him. She wore something ruffled and pink, of course, and he noted that women's gowns were now so high-waisted it brought their bosoms into pronounced prominence. She had a shawl of flowered silk wrapped about her against the evening breeze and the light wind whipped strands of hair out from under the frilly and completely non-utilitarian bit of lace atop her head.

"Dr. Murray! Such a harsh assessment of the ladies! La, sir, you would find yourself shunned from the most entertaining drawing rooms for such a puritanical outlook."

"Since it has never been my desire to be a success in entertaining, I will not fret over it, Miss Farnham."

She seemed to be mulling over his words, then her face brightened. "I do have a useful skill."

He looked at her.

"I am quite talented at picking out just the right hat or gloves to complement an ensemble."

She smiled, waiting for his praise.

"I would hardly term that a useful skill."

"Oh, but I beg to differ, sir. Knowing which accessories make an outfit complete is what makes us civilized, and attractive to look upon."

He found his mouth opening to argue this and then shut it. What was the point? But now, with her mind engaged, she was prepared to defend her claim. She came closer then and lightly laid her lilac-gloved hand on his arm.

"What is life without some color, some entertainment, Doctor? Should our days only be filled with work and useful functions? What of…" She thought for a moment, and since he suspected this was a rare event, he did not interrupt her.

"Butterflies! Butterflies spend their days flitting from flower to flower. They live to entertain."

"You are mistaken, Miss Farnham. Butterflies are useful creatures, as are other members of the Lepidoptera family. Butterflies and moths spread pollen amongst plants. Even the ugliest and plainest moth can do that job, just as a butterfly does. They also make a meal for birds."

"My dear Dr. Murray! Do you see butterflies floating through a meadow on a summer morning and only think of them as food for larger creatures?"

He would have told her how long it had been since he'd seen a summer meadow, with or without butterflies adorning it, but he was too aware of the feel of her hand on his arm. She was not applying any pressure at all, but it drew his senses. That butterfly touch, even muted by her gloves and his coat, made him aware of how alien she truly was, how soft and clean and fragrant, so different from the men with whom he spent his days and his nights.

"Miss Daphne Farnham!"

Mrs. Cowper's grating voice broke his concentration, and he looked up from the soft lips of his interlocutor to see her chaperone bearing down on them like a ship of the line. Even in the near dark he saw how pale the older woman's face was. She was also short of breath but given her size that was to be expected. One could not haul that much weight up and down between decks without strain.

"Mrs. Cowper, are you well?"

She looked at him disdainfully.

"I am well enough, Mr. Murray! I just need to sit down and drink my cordial to feel tip-top again. As for you, miss, you should not be out here. What would your father say?"

Bertha Cowper's jowly cheeks were aquiver with indignation, and small wisps of hair that had dared to escape her tightly pulled bun were sticking to the sweat pouring down her forehead. He started to speak again, but she was still going on.

"And if I need medical attention, I will wait until we are in England and I will consult a proper physician." She punctuated this by grabbing Miss Farnham by the arm in a grip that made Alexander wince for the young woman's sake, and pulled her charge behind her, still talking.

"You should not be speaking to the likes of Mr. Murray. He's only a ship's surgeon. You are in enough trouble, young lady, you do not need to be looking for more…"

"But the sailors call him doctor."

"They are common, and ignorant. You are above him in station and it will not help your reputation to be seen spending time with him or with the other riff-raff aboard this vessel!"

But then an odd thing happened. Even as she was being hauled away, Miss Farnham turned. She smiled at Alexander, a smile of such surpassing sweetness he was struck dumb by the gesture. He could see all too clearly now how even a reasonable man could lose his composure over a cloth-headed young lady.

CHAPTER 2

*D*aphne stood outside the door to Dr. Murray's cabin, chewing on her lip. She did not want to knock on that door. A shiver ran down her spine as she pulled her wrapper tighter and shifted her weight from foot to foot. It was dank and dark in the narrow ship's corridor, and it was oppressive. She was tired of the smell of mildew and damp, tired of life in a boat that never stood still, tired of water that tasted like old sweat.

Most of all, she was tired of being judged. Everyone looked at her and found her wanting. The mate looked at her with speculation in his eyes, thinking her fast. The captain looked at her and saw her as a passenger likely to cause trouble. Mrs. Cowper looked at her and saw a girl who was no better than she ought to be, but whose father paid well for her to be transported home.

Dr. Murray looked at her with the most condemning visage of all. She could understand how Mr. Carr and the captain and Mrs. Cowper might judge her based on the stories that had spread like fever through Jamaica and England, but Dr. Murray found her very existence an affront.

When he looked at her with those changeable eyes of his, sometimes gold, sometimes a mossy green, it felt like he was peering deep into her soul, diagnosing her, and not liking what he found. She did not know what purges he would prescribe for her supposed moral ailments and intellectual shortcomings, but she knew the cure would not be pleasant. He was the closest thing to a physician on this ship though, so there was nothing for it. She knocked on his cabin door, resisting the desire to knock and run.

The door opened while her hand was still half raised to knock again, and he peered out at her. He was in his shirt-sleeves and seeing him undressed startled her into silence. He always looked so formal, so proper. Now though he was half unbuttoned, and his silver touched hair was mussed, as if he'd been running his fingers through it. It made him look human for a change.

For a brief second, Dr. Murray looked as startled at seeing a woman in a wrapper standing outside his cabin as she was by his appearance, but then he composed himself.

"Miss Farnham?"

"It is Mrs. Cowper," Daphne said in a rush. "She went to the privy and has not returned, and when I knocked she did not answer."

He frowned at her words but did not look surprised.

"One moment."

She looked at the closed door, but before she could wonder he returned, a lantern in his hand. He led the way to the tiny room at the front of the ship, the direction the sailors called "forward," though Daphne had never figured out why they could not say "front" like regular people.

Following behind Dr. Murray gave Daphne a view that surprised her. Given his years she would expect a belly or a spreading form beneath his conservatively cut coat. Instead, what she saw was solid but not padded. Broad shoulders and back, average height, and he seemed remarkably preserved for his age. His linen shirt was mended at the collar and at the seam behind his arm, but it was clean. She'd noticed that about the surgeon. He kept himself scrupulously clean, and unlike many of the other men aboard ship—or Mrs. Cowper —smelled mostly of soap, not stale sweat.

The hair that was not silvered in back was a warm russet and it curled at the nape of his neck. From the wet air, she thought, no different from others in that regard. Somehow, she thought he'd be distressed if he knew his hair was out of place, normal though it might be.

They were at the privy now—"head," he absently corrected her—and Dr. Murray rapped sharply on the door.

"Mrs. Cowper, are you ill?"

There was no answer, and he pushed on the door, but it was stuck and would only open scant inches.

"Hold the lantern over my shoulder please, Miss Farnham."

Daphne rushed forward to make herself useful, that quality Dr. Murray prized above all others. Her view inside was restricted and the odor was strong, but she held the lantern up, steadying it with one hand beneath. Mrs. Cowper appeared to be slumped over against the wall. He put his hand inside and rested it on the older woman's neck, pulling his hand out a few minutes later.

"Mrs. Cowper is dead."

"Dead? That is not possible! Are you certain?"

He looked at her. "There is no heartbeat. I have long observed that when there is no heartbeat, people cease living. So yes, I am quite certain that she is dead."

Daphne knew she was blushing, and she was angry, more at him than at herself for saying such a foolish thing. Of course an experienced ship's surgeon knew when someone was dead, but this was not a normal occurrence for her!

"Return to your cabin, Miss Farnham. I will inform the ship's officers of what has happened."

"Is there…is there something I should do?"

"What do you suggest?"

What she wanted to do was burst into tears. Not because of any fondness for Mrs. Cowper, who'd been her jailer more than her companion, watching her, criticizing her constantly and writing notes for her report to Daphne's father. But this was another complication in her life, a life that had had far too many complications lately to suit her.

Dr. Murray was still observing her, unfazed by being a foot away from a corpse. These things must happen to him all the time. His craggy face was lightly stubbled with the day's growth, but he looked alert and not at all as if being up in the middle of the night was an issue, or a new experience.

"I will write a letter to her family expressing my regret at Mrs. Cowper's passing," Daphne finally said. There. That was something useful she could do.

"You are the only other woman aboard ship. Did it occur to you, Miss Farnham, that you might be useful laying her out for her burial? Do not drop that lantern, it would start a fire."

He took the lantern from her nerveless fingers as Daphne stared at him.

"I could never do that! How you could even ask—"

She knew from his expression that she'd fallen even further in his esteem, if such a thing were possible.

"It was more in the nature of a suggestion, Miss Farnham. I knew better than to ask," he sighed. "Return to your cabin. I will see to it."

Daphne turned and walked blindly back to her cabin. Pompom greeted her and jumped into her lap when she sat on her bunk, staring at the empty covers of the bunk across from hers. He licked her hand and she put her head down next to the warm body snuggled into the crook of her arm.

"At least you love me just the way I am, Pompom," she whispered to the bichon.

~

Alexander logged the time of death, then woke Captain Franklin with the news that one of his passengers was no longer among the living.

The captain was not happy.

"You are a surgeon, couldn't you have done something for her?"

"Certainly. I could have told her to stop drinking port, eat a more moderate diet and try not to have heart failure, but I doubt she would have listened to me."

Captain Franklin scowled at him and ran his hand over his bearded face. "Send Mr. Carr to me. And I will want to see you in the morning—later in the morning, after breakfast."

Alexander did not want to volunteer, but he felt obligated. "Do you need me to lay her out?"

"Would Miss Farnham be willing to help? No, I thought not." Captain Franklin sighed. "Mrs. Cowper won't keep in this heat. Yes, do what needs to be done when the sun's up. The sailmaster will sew her up and we will do the burial service later today."

"Miss Farnham did say she would write to the woman's family."

Captain Franklin grunted.

"It will be logged here as well, and that should satisfy everyone. Good night, Mr. Murray."

Alexander returned to his cabin, and made some quick

notes in his own journal, then dropped off to sleep, a skill perfected over years of being awakened in the middle of the night. A passing thought almost kept him awake: Miss Farnham did not have hysterics or swoon over Mrs. Cowper's death. That was the only bright spot in this evening's events.

The next morning, or later the same morning, depending on how disgruntled one was over interrupted sleep, Alexander sat at breakfast with a subdued Miss Farnham. They were the only ones left at table, the ship's officers busy at their tasks, and the steward in the galley. He observed her over the rim of his coffee cup.

"You are not eating. Starving yourself will not bring Mrs. Cowper back."

Miss Farnham's head jerked up. She did not look as neatly put together as she usually did, and it occurred to Alex that without another woman in the cabin she had no one to help her dress in the mornings.

"Why do you not have a maid?"

He didn't know why he asked. He really did not care.

"We had a girl hired to come with us. She became ill the day we were to sail, and Mrs. Cowper would not wait for another ship. She said she was under strict orders to fetch me back to England on the first ship out, and she was worried she would not be paid her full amount if she delayed."

"You are not mourning Mrs. Cowper then."

The ghost of a smile hovered around her mouth. She needed no cosmetics to add color to her lips or cheeks. Only someone in close contact with her might notice the slight shadows beneath her eyes. Oddly, the small flaw did not detract from her appearance, but made her seem more human and less like a china fashion doll.

"Mrs. Cowper and I were not on good terms, but she is

dead now, and I lost an opportunity to become friends with her."

Alexander set down his coffee cup. It was clear to him why this chit needed a keeper. Anyone who was such a poor judge of humanity would be as easily led astray as her yappy little animal, wagging its tail and doing tricks in the hopes of a treat.

He almost said something but stopped himself. It was not his concern. In a few weeks, maybe less if the weather held, they would be in England and he could move on with his life. Miss Farnham, now crumbling a ship's biscuit between her manicured fingers, would no doubt be whisked off to her proper social setting and he need never give her a thought again. A baseborn Scotsman who labored as a ship's surgeon was not going to cross paths with the likes of Miss Daphne Farnham.

"If you will excuse me, there is work I must do before the burial service today."

"Burial—Mrs. Cowper isn't going to be buried in England?"

"No. There is no way to preserve her body for burial, and in the tropics it is best to deal with these situations as quickly as possible. The heat and the humidity bring on rapid decomposi— "

He stopped. She'd gone slightly green, and while up to now Miss Farnham had proved herself a hardy sea voyager, he had no desire to put it to the test.

"There will be a burial at sea." he finished up. "Captain Franklin will ensure that all is handled properly."

"Oh!" She looked intrigued. "I will include the information about the burial in my letter to her family. It will ease their pain to know all was done in accordance with the customs of the sea."

"You do that, Miss Farnham."

She dipped her dainty little chin in farewell, then resumed eating her breakfast with more appetite. Alexander hesitated at the door because she looked so alone, but he had matters to attend to, the deceased Mrs. Cowper being chief among them.

Late in the morning the crew and passengers assembled as Captain Franklin read the service for burial at sea, four sailors standing by the larboard rail where the canvas-wrapped body awaited its final destination.

No one wept, though Miss Farnham sniffled a time or two and wiped her eyes. Mrs. Cowper had not endeared herself to the crew with her constant complaints about the rigors of sea voyaging. Alex studied the faces of the men. Most were bored, but some were intrigued, as a break in routine was always a welcome diversion. Some looked at the girl. He resumed listening to Captain Franklin, who was wearing his best coat for the occasion. This was the point where he'd seen things go horribly wrong in the past, so he paid attention.

"We therefore commit her body to the deep, to be turned into corruption, looking for the resurrection of the body, when the sea shall give up her dead and the life of the world to come, through our Lord Jesus Christ, who at his coming shall change our vile Body, that it may be like his glorious Body, according to the mighty working, whereby he is able to subdue all things to himself."

Captain Franklin nodded to the sailors standing by at the plank where the body rested. The sailors picked up the inboard end, and the body smoothly slid off its platform and into the cold waters of the Atlantic, sinking out of sight. Alex let out a breath. He'd seen more than his share of burials at sea and knew without proper preparation, the body could end up bobbing after the ship, an unpleasant *memento mori*.

Miss Farnham had shown a modicum of common sense

and left her small dog in her cabin. Mr. Carr came over to speak to her, and she smiled wanly at him.

"Mr. Murray!"

Alexander turned to find Captain Franklin at his side, scowling at his mate and at his passenger.

"Come to my cabin. We must talk."

Alex cast another glance at Miss Farnham, then followed the captain below. The captain went to a sturdy chest, unlocked it, and pulled a bottle of rum out. He poured himself a tot, and after a slight pause, poured some for Alexander.

Captain Franklin did not offer him other refreshments but seated himself at the mahogany table serving as his desk. The captain's cabin was only slightly larger than that of the senior crew and passengers, but Captain Franklin was not parsimonious when it came to his own comfort. The seats were generously cushioned and the bunk was commodious, far better than the furnishings the passengers enjoyed.

"I will be blunt with you, Murray," the captain said. "Having that Cowper woman drop dead like that, it's not good. Not good at all."

"I am sure Mrs. Cowper would agree with you, were she able to."

"Do not try my patience!" Captain Franklin leaned back in his chair and eyed his passenger.

Alexander thought they'd had a reasonable rapport on this voyage. Still, after a near lifetime in the Royal Navy, the laxness of the merchant ship chafed at him like clothing rinsed in saltwater. The *Magpie* was a 220-ton brig and a solid vessel, making good headway after a successful venture to the West Indies. With the war over and Napoleon banished to St. Helena, shipping in the Caribbean resumed with a vengeance. The Americans and British were back to competing in the marketplace rather than with guns, and ships plied the sea lanes at will without having to wait for convoys and escorts.

He never thought he would miss the navy, but it had its standards and he was already missing that. His last posting on the *Caeneus* was an especially sharp contrast to his current situation. Captain Doyle ran a tight ship and the men in his command served with zeal and dedication. Aboard the *Magpie* there was always a slight air of sloppiness, of items not squared away, and Alex suspected there was more concern about the cargo and profit than about maintaining the ship and its crew. He'd already had an argument with Captain Franklin in Jamaica over conditions aboard the *Magpie*. The sailors who'd served in the past with the tight-fisted Franklin knew they had the surgeon to thank for their heavy weather gear and better victuals on this voyage. Alex wondered if his good deed was about to be punished as the captain took a drink of his rum and scowled into his glass.

"This has created a problem for me, Murray. With that Cowper woman dead, Miss Farnham is alone and unattended. This is not a good situation."

"I cannot imagine what your concerns have to do with me, Captain." He set his untouched glass on the table and rose to leave.

"Take that seat, Murray, or I will have you confined to your cabin for the rest of the voyage."

"On what grounds?"

"Do not be tedious. You have been at sea long enough to know I can do whatever I damn well please aboard my own ship."

Alexander sat. He almost picked up the rum but forced his gaze back on the captain.

"I will come right to the point. For the duration of this voyage, I am making you responsible for the Farnham chit."

The silence in the cabin was deafening. "You cannot make me the chaperone for a young woman."

"I just did," Captain Franklin said with an unpleasant smile. "And while I do not need to explain myself to you, I will anyway."

He began ticking points off on one hand, a hand whose ring finger was missing the last two joints. But he was still able to count. "You are the only other passenger. The crew have their own duties and cannot be spared to play nursemaid. You are a surgeon and agreed to be responsible for the health of all aboard this ship. All means all, and I assure you my mental well-being is an issue here if that girl is not under control. Finally, your age makes you less of a threat than youngsters like Mr. Carr, who I guarantee would have that girl's skirts tossed over her head in about the amount of time it takes Stubbs to play 'Fiddler's Green' on his fiddle. How old are you anyway, forty-five? Fifty?"

"Thirty-five."

"What?"

"I am thirty-five years old, Captain Franklin."

"Truly?" the captain peered at him. "I never would guess that. Regardless, it is all to the good."

Alexander's palms were sweating. Odd, that never happened during surgery. He had to make one more effort at stopping this madness. "What about my well-being?"

"I do not care about that," Franklin said bluntly. "You already paid your passage, and if the girl drives you into an apoplexy, that is your problem. When it becomes my problem, I shall deal with it. As I am now."

He stood, putting an end to the discussion.

"Good luck, Murray. You will need it."

CHAPTER 3

$\mathcal{A}$lexander wanted to run to his cabin, bar the door, and not emerge until the docks were in sight. Miss Farnham was nominally an adult and could see to herself.

But then he remembered her bedraggled and lost look at breakfast. She'd reminded him of the kitten he'd brought home when he was eight or so. His mother had glanced up from the barley soup she was stirring, took one look at the ragged patch of fur clutched to her son's chest, and shook her head.

"That is all we need, Alexander, another mouth to feed. A useless one at that."

"I will take care of him, Mama," he promised, holding the kitten so tightly that it mewled in protest. "I will teach him to be useful. He can hunt for us."

Janet Murray put her work-roughened hands on her hips and looked down at him. Her russet hair, the same shade as her son's but liberally streaked with white, was coming down from the tight knot at the back of her head. She squatted down in front of him on the scrubbed flagstones and rubbed one finger along the kitty's head.

"A hunter, hmmm? Will he bring me a nice deer, do you think?"

Alex looked down skeptically at the gray bundle in his shirt.

"I do not think he will grow large enough to bring down a deer, Mama, but he might grow large enough to hunt mice."

One of Janet's rare smiles creased her cheeks. "That was a jest, Alex. Such a solemn little man! You must not be so serious about everything."

He had just looked at her. Boys whose mothers never married, those boys knew from the first time they heard the word "bastard" that life was serious. When his father's agent brought his mother her quarterly payments for Alexander's maintenance, he knew from the remarks the oily little scrub made, the way he looked at Janet, that life was serious.

Alex set down the kitten. Janet ruffled the curls atop his head, and said, "Fetch your wee kitty a drop of milk, son. If he's going to grow up to be a hunter, he will need his strength."

The kitten grew into a fine mouser named Robby, after Robert the Bruce, of course. If such a small scrap of nothing could become useful, perhaps there was hope for Miss Farnham on this trip.

He knocked at her door and her little dog commenced yapping.

Then again, perhaps not.

She opened the cabin door without asking who was on the other side. Alex resisted the impulse to run his hand through his hair in frustration.

"Dr. Murray! What a pleasant surprise."

"Is it?"

She blinked up at him. "That was conversation, Doctor. It is what one says…" her voice trailed off and she looked befuddled.

"We must talk, Miss Farnham."

He stepped past her into the cabin. Trunks were open, and there was an explosion of fabrics in the small cabin, festoons of feathers and lace and ruffles and ribbons, mostly in pink, every shade from the faintest blush of dawn to a deep sunset rose.

Now he was really tempted to run back to his own cabin and bar the door, but he had never yet shirked his duty, no matter how unpleasant.

Something crunched under his foot as he stepped into the cabin. He bent down and retrieved a book, which to his eye looked forlorn and out of place amongst the fripperies. Miss Farnham fluttered by him, closing the door behind her. He almost told her to leave the door open, but he did not want their conversation to be overheard.

"Have a seat…oh…" her voice trailed off as she realized every available surface was covered with furbelows.

"It is no matter, I will stand." Alex dropped the book on her pillow and took an armful of fabric off the one chair for her to be seated. The clean fragrance of lavender floated up to him. He resisted the temptation to bury his nose in it and breathe more deeply and piled the frocks atop another mountain on the now empty bunk where Mrs. Cowper had slept.

Miss Farnham sat, looking up at him with an inquiring expression on her face. For a moment she reminded him of Robby, but then he remembered how canny the cat was and the image was lost.

Alex pulled down the edges of his waistcoat, did not run his fingers through his hair, and gazed at his new charge.

She was wearing a frock that was, of course, pink, a particularly bilious shade. Or maybe it was just the circumstances. Regardless, the garment was askew and he suspected it was misfastened. Her hair was loose around her shoulders, though some attempt had been made to bring it to order, a sad attempt evidenced by the trail of pins filtering down from a spot above her ear. The dog made a final "yip" at Alexander, then settled into a pile of cloaks, watching him with its beady eyes.

"I have come from a meeting with Captain Franklin."

"Was it a pleasant meeting?"

He stared at her. "No. No, it was not a pleasant meeting. It concerned you."

The animation drained from her face and she looked down at the deck. He clasped his hands behind his back, forcing himself into stillness. He refused to feel sorry for her. He was feeling sorry enough for himself. But looming over her probably wasn't helping the situation.

This time Alex swept the fabrics off the bunk onto the deck, and while Miss Farnham stirred, she did not protest.

"Here is the situation," he said bluntly. "Captain Franklin made me responsible for your welfare for the remainder of this voyage. I need not tell you that your situation is precarious, a single woman aboard a ship full of sailors. The captain believes this is the best possible solution. If you cooperate, then nothing more will be said of this when we reach England."

"Do you really believe that?" she asked, raising her eyes from her tightly clasped hands.

"Do you have another choice, Miss Farnham? Because if you do, I would like to hear it."

She made a noise that in a less elegant person might be termed a snort. "Choices. No, I do not have a choice, do I?"

There was something about her that struck him then, but the moment was lost when she looked around her at the fabric filling the small cabin and said, "Then you will need to help me out of my clothes, Dr. Murray."

All those years of listening to the ship's guns pound out their charges must have affected his hearing.

"I beg your pardon?"

She looked at him, a vapid smile on her face. "My clothes. They fasten in back. Ladies are dressed by their maids."

"You do not have a maid," he said stupidly.

"No. I only have you, Dr. Murray."

He realized his mouth was hanging open, and he closed it with a snap.

"That is ridicul—"

"And you must help dress my hair," she said, waving at the mess atop her head.

"See here, Miss Farnham, I cannot spend my day being your maid."

"I do not expect you to do *everything*, I can do my own mending."

Alex wanted to refuse, but he knew enough about women's clothing to acknowledge the dress fastenings might be a problem.

"Your hair, you cannot dress it yourself?"

"We come from different worlds, Dr. Murray. All my life I have had maidservants. It was their job to be useful. I never brushed my own hair, nor have I pinned it. That was always someone else's task."

Alex knew his interaction with ladies was limited, but this woman was nothing more than a pretty parasite, living off the efforts of others.

"Then the first thing I shall do is teach you how to be more self-sufficient. Give me your hairbrush."

She was not put off by his brusque tone but rose unhurriedly and Alex stood as well. She smoothed down her skirts and, brushing past him, located a silver-backed brush beneath a pile of hats.

"And a ribbon, Miss Farnham. Something sturdy."

"La, Doctor, I do not believe 'sturdy' and 'ribbons' are two words that go together," she simpered, but she located a pink satin length beneath some shoes and passed it to him, along with the hairbrush.

"Sit!" he ordered, and the dog barked.

"No, Pompom, I believe the nice surgeon meant me," she said, seating herself again.

Alex seethed as he stood behind her chair and pulled the wandering pins from her messy coiffure. This was *not* part of his arrangement with Captain Franklin, and he was tempted to storm back to the captain and allow him to manacle Alex for the duration of the voyage.

Even as he was thinking this, his mind registered the feel of the silken strands gliding between his fingers. So much of his day was spent with his hands in unpleasant or noxious substances, it was a tactile awakening, feeling the curls wrap themselves around his hands, making him itch to...

"Dr. Murray? Are you ready?"

His mind snapped back to the task. It was a job, nothing more. No different than bandaging a wound or rolling pills. He took the brush from her soft fingers and pulled it through, starting at the crown, working his way back to the ends, gently unsnarling the inevitable tangles.

From this angle behind her he could see the rise and fall of her chest. Her dress was misbuttoned at the neck and a patch of skin at her collarbone peeked through, paler than the soft pink of her garment, and flushed with life.

Wonderful. Now he was not only in this humiliating position, but he had to step back from the chair or Miss Farnham would realize he was not in control of his body. He concentrated on the task, but it did not help. Not at all. It did not matter that she had nothing but air between her ears. She was still a young and nubile woman and he had a good imagination. He envisioned these curls loose around her shoulders. Not like now, when she was dressed in her badly fastened gown, but falling over her naked shoulders as she sat astride him, her hair curtaining her ample breasts, breasts whose form he could make out from this angle above her. She would look good riding him…

"You have done this before, Doctor."

That was exactly what he needed to bring himself back to the present. The memories her comment evoked were of a different girl, one whose brown hair was straight and long.

"Yes, I know how to brush and braid a woman's hair."

"Your wife?" her voice was a touch lower and huskier.

"No. I am a bachelor, Miss Farnham. Pass me the ribbon." He efficiently braided the mass of gold and tied off the end tightly.

"This will do for you for while aboard ship, a simple means of keeping your hair in place. Do you know how to make a braid?"

She looked up from where she was examining the rope of hair falling over her shoulder. "I think so."

"Bring me three more ribbons. I will demonstrate."

In short order he'd braided together ribbons of pink, yellow and violet.

"Ooooh, how colorful! I believe I shall wear that braided ribbon today."

"I made that to demonstrate for you how to braid, Miss Farnham, not as an adornment."

She looked up at him, a smile dimpling her cheeks. "But even instructional materials can be pretty, Doctor. And do you not think that now you can call me Daphne?"

"No. Stand up and I will adjust the fastenings in your garment."

She sighed, but stood, obediently as a child. But she was far from being a child. He adjusted her tapes, all the while itching to unfasten them. Purely the natural reaction of a man too long at sea, and he reluctantly saw the wisdom in Captain Franklin's arrangement. If he was tempted by her charms, how much worse would it be for the crew, who were not medical men but sailors used to women of easy virtue?

"There. Your task until suppertime is to go through your wardrobe and find those garments most practical. Look for items that can be fastened with a minimum of effort on both our parts."

"Oh dear. I imagine this means I will not be dressing for supper."

"If it involves me, no, you will not. Stay in your clothes until I return to undress you tonight."

His words hung in the air between them, and Alexander felt heat rise up his neck.

"Of course, Dr. Murray."

Alexander gave her a stern look, but her blank face showed no understanding of the double meaning of his words.

It was all to the good, her not being very bright. If she were intelligent, she might be dangerous.

~

The cabin door closed behind him and Daphne buried her face in a pillow, biting it to keep from bursting into laughter. The look on poor old Dr. Murray's face! Really, as if she would have anything to do with a stick like him!

As soon as she'd thought the words though she remembered the feel of his strong hands in her hair. The way he stroked the hairbrush through, with just the right amount of pressure and no tugging made her want to purr like a kitten —or wag her tail like Pompom.

It also made her wonder who the woman was for whom

he had performed this task in the past. A sister? A lover? She could almost imagine a younger version of the curmudgeonly surgeon, one whose face was unlined and less careworn.

Almost. It was too difficult to imagine that man ever being carefree enough to enjoy brushing and braiding a woman's hair.

She fluffed the pillow, smoothing it with her hand. It was simply proximity. The man had no address at all and must have had his sense of humor surgically removed. George, for all his faults—and dying and abandoning her in Jamaica loomed large in her mind—at least made her laugh and feel she was special. He did not care if she was "useful," beyond her ability to bring thousands of pounds with her.

Daphne shook her head, pushing back thoughts of George's betrayal. The younger son of a younger son, George had worried about how he would make his way in the world. No wonder eloping with her seemed like the opportunity he'd waited for all his life.

She picked up the braided ribbons. It seemed simple enough. Once she saw something demonstrated for her, she remembered how to do it. But there had been no need in the past for someone to show her how to braid. There was a nanny, or a maidservant, or Mrs. Cowper to do it for her. That was their job. Hers was to look good when they finished. If Dr. Murray did not understand that was how the world—her world, the only world that mattered—worked, then it was simply too bad.

Daphne looked around the tiny cabin. Practical garments — what exactly did that mean? Something drab and dull, no doubt, with nothing in the way of a ruffle or a bow to liven it up. She chewed on her lip as she thought. She'd start with shoes. Some of the many pairs Mrs. Cowper had brought from England when dispatched after her were lovely to look at but would not be comfortable for long walks. Not practical.

There! Now she had a goal, and she would show mean-spirited Dr. Murray that she knew how to fend for herself.

At least until it was time to undress.

~

Alexander re-wrapped Lowry's wrist, sprained in a fall the ship's carpenter took earlier in the week.

"It is good for us to have a surgeon aboard, Doctor. You and the young lady are ideal passengers, cooperative and helpful."

Alexander noticed the late unlamented Mrs. Cowper wasn't mentioned.

"Miss Farnham is helpful?"

"She needed a sandbox for that little pup of hers to use as a head. I built it for her, and while I told her she didn't have to pay me, she insisted on doing some mending for me if I wouldn't take her gold."

"I am surprised the girl did not simply expect you to wait on her like her other servants."

Lowry twisted and turned his hand, checking the range of its motion, and seemed satisfied when he could make a strong fist without difficulty. He had an off-center nose, the souvenir of some long ago tavern brawl—probably more than one—and intelligent eyes he now focused on Alexander.

"There is nothing snobbish about Miss Farnham, Doctor. She's a high-spirited lass, no doubt about it, but she has a good heart. Once she finds a proper man, one who will give her a home and young ones, she'll settle down."

"Ladies of her class do not spend their days and evenings taking care of their homes and children, Mr. Lowry. They are too busy flitting from the dressmaker to the glovemaker and then off to the theater or some card party."

Lowry stood, and shrugged his wiry arms back into his coat. The carpenter was a small man but his arms and back were roped with muscle from years of working to keep ships whole and afloat.

"You are harsh, sir. Give the young lady a chance and she may grow on you."

"A fungus grows on you, Mr. Lowry."

The older man chuckled, but he did not pursue the conversation, shaking the doctor's hand and returning to his duties.

Alex cleaned up his tiny sick bay. He did not want to think about Miss Daphne Farnham as anything but an empty-headed fashion doll. A doll—or a patient—could be handled briskly and efficiently. But a young woman who did mending for an old carpenter, that made her all too human to him.

It was going to be a long voyage.

He finished writing his notes. As he stepped to the cabin door he paused, looking into his shaving mirror on the chest. It was no wonder everyone thought him a graybeard. Life at sea during wartime had tested him and weathered him as it weathered the ships he served on. Hair once a rich copper was now streaked with gray, just as the ship's brightwork dulled if not tended properly. His eyes were still a clear hazel, but the deep lines at their corners came as much from care and worry as from squinting into bright sunshine on the ocean. Janet Murray's red hair had also whitened at an early age so it did not surprise him to see his hair fade, but he had not considered how others viewed him. Normally this would not concern him, but he thought with the war over he might take a wife when he returned to Britain and settled his affairs.

He knew what he needed. A woman who would be a good housekeeper. Someone who would be frugal and know how to live within the earnings of a surgeon who had some prize money but was by no means a rich man. He wanted her to be attractive, of course, but not so beautiful that she only cared about her looks.

He wanted someone like Moira.

Setting aside the mirror Alex turned and went to the chest that held his instruments. It was over two feet long, carved of fine cedar and lined in velvet. He lifted the lid and the tools of his trade gleamed in the light, oiled and polished. Sharpened. Ready to be called into action, so much a part of him they were an extension of his arm, a fixture in his hand as he wielded his lancet and his saw.

Beautiful tools. He'd used them to save lives. He lifted the top tray. There, tucked into a tiny pocket at the bottom of the chest, he saw the outline of a miniature.

It was the effort of a traveling limner, one with more enthusiasm than skill, but he had managed to capture something of his subject. Moira's gentle eyes, her long nose, the chestnut hair gleaming when the summer sunlight hit it.

The artist had lightened her browned skin because he thought his subjects wanted to be seen as ladies, not Scottish farm girls.

Moira surely laughed at that, her round cheeks with their sunkissed rosiness as much a part of her as her soft burr when she sang while working, milking her father's cows, barefoot in the yard as she fed her chickens.

Alexander told her he would return, first from his schooling, then from the sea. He would return and she would marry him, and they would live together and raise children and chickens. She had the miniature painted and gave it to him on his first visit after joining the navy, on one of the soft summer evenings when they lay out in the fields away from prying eyes.

"My father wishes me wed, Alexander," she said in her gentle voice.

He stroked his hand through her hair, the hair he loved to brush and braid for her, and then she would weave chains of flowers to wear in it and insist he wear one, too, just to make him laugh.

"I will speak with him tomorrow. I have a little put aside now, and he'll listen to me."

But when he arrived at the McDonald house the next day, Mrs. McDonald told him Moira was ill.

"I am sure she will be able to visit with you tomorrow, Mr. Murray," she said, but the next day Moira was still abed, and Mrs. McDonald reluctantly allowed the young surgeon to see her with the girl's watchful mother standing in the room.

"Moira?"

Her face was near as pale as her bedding. She opened her drowsy eyes and gave him a weak smile. "Good morning, Alex."

Ignoring her mother's harrumph of disapproval, Alex sat on the bed beside Moira and took her wrist. Her skin was warm, her pulse rapid, and she winced when she shifted herself to accommodate him beside her.

"Do you have pain, my dear?"

Mrs. McDonald made a small movement behind him, but Alex ignored her to focus on Moira. Her eyelashes lowered, veiling her eyes.

"I have a griping in my bowels, Alex," she whispered, embarrassed. "Ma gave me a purge and I am sure it will be over soon."

"Where is the pain?"

She whispered again that it was down in her belly,

gesturing with her hand at her right side. Alex did not frown, for he was already becoming better at keeping his emotions veiled from those he treated, but he was worried. He'd seen a case in Edinburgh where a man with a similar pain low in his side expired after fever set in.

But that patient was an older man, and Moira was young and healthy. He patted her hand and said, "I will return tomorrow to check on you, my dear. In the meantime, do as your mother says, and you will be up and about in no time."

But the next day her pain was worse. She was still fevered so he bled her and promised to return to check on her. When he saw her again the pain was gone, and his heart rose, but it was a false comfort.

Within a day the fever raged again through Moira's young body, alternating heat and chills and Alexander could only watch helplessly as she sank into delirium, then unconsciousness, and then finally slipped away from him forever.

A year later his mother was dead and Alexander never returned to Scotland. He looked down at the fragile porcelain portrait, all that was left of a vibrant young woman. That, and his memories of the scant hours when they'd held one another, and the dreams they'd shared, dreams that went with Moira into the grave.

A young man believes love, and people, will last forever. He believes he can save the world, that his bright instruments can stave off the inevitable. Alexander no longer believed in either love or forever, but he was a practical man and thought a wife, and the comfort she would bring him might be worth the effort.

He would look into it once this voyage was over.

～

*B*eing awakened in the middle of the night was nothing new for Alexander but when he opened his cabin door, he had an uneasy feeling of *déjà vu.* Miss Farnham stood there, again barefoot, looking over her shoulder.

"Come in, Miss Farnham," he said, not bothering to add *before the entire ship knows you are here.* "What can I do for you?"

She was pale, and he saw the pulse at her throat beating fast. She looked over her shoulder again at her closed cabin door, then back at him, her eyes wide as she stepped into his cabin.

"I had a nightmare. I dreamed Mrs. Cowper was still with us, following in the ship's wake."

He looked at her sharply. She barely spoke above a whisper and twisted her wrapper in her hands.

"I overheard the sailors talking, Doctor. People follow the ship after they are thrown into the ocean, trying to return."

"Sailors are a superstitious lot, you must pay them no heed. I helped prepare Mrs. Cowper for burial, and I can assure you she is dead and has gone to her rest at the bottom of the Atlantic Ocean."

"I understand. That makes sense, but my heart is racing." She put her hand on her bosom, maybe thinking he might not know where her heart was. "Is my heart going to stop as hers did?"

Alexander knew he could dismiss her fears and tell her nothing would come of them, and he certainly knew her heart was not about to fail. So he did not fully understand why he stepped closer and rested his hand on her neck.

At one level, the answer was obvious. He could see the beat, faster, yes, as her agitation sped her body's reactions to stress. Measuring her pulse was a perfectly logical thing to do. It had nothing to do with wanting to feel the silken skin of her throat, to experience the warmth of her, the fragrance of a clean woman.

Her hair had come loose from its night braid, the curls framing her face, and he idly brushed a curl away from where it rested against his hand on her throat.

"You are agitated, but you will not die, Miss Farnham. Were you reading your lurid novel before you fell asleep?"

She looked puzzled for a moment. "Mrs. Radcliffe's book? Yes, but what does that signify?"

"Reading novels can contribute to a disordered mind. You should stick to more edifying literature before sleep."

"Oh," she mulled that over, then shook her head. "It is not my mind that is disordered, Dr. Murray, but my heart that is fast."

She gestured, to make sure he understood the difference between her head and her heart.

"Don't you want to listen to my chest? Dr. Drummond at home always puts his ear on my chest to listen to my heartbeat and reassure me it is strong."

"Very well. If it will help you fall back to sleep."

She followed his instructions when he told her to sit on his bunk.

"Unfasten your garments please."

Instead she clutched them tighter and looked at him wide-eyed. "I did not think you liked me, Dr. Murray!"

He was dumbfounded for a moment, then the penny dropped.

"Miss Farnham, this works best with only a thin barrier between your skin and my ear. Just do as I say so I can return to sleep. You only need to unfasten your nightdress partway."

"Oh."

She loosened her wrapper and shrugged it off her shoulders. Her nightdress was plain, which surprised him, but it was of fine linen and had a pink satin ribbon that she untied, leaving the neck to gape open. The outline of the form beneath tantalized him, but he forced himself to concentrate.

He pulled out a thin and worn handkerchief from his sea chest and shook it open.

"Lie down on my bunk, on your back."

She followed his instructions, and he sat next to her. He eased the night garment open, exposing the upper mounds of breasts that he could say, with perfect accuracy, were some of the finest he'd ever seen. Lush and pink, rising and falling with her breathing, like rosy-tipped meringues. He draped the cloth over her, then bent his ear to her chest to listen, and learn, as he had done so many times in the past.

If he lingered there with his cheek on her bosom longer than was clinically necessary, it was hardly his fault when her skin was so warm, and soft, and fragrant, and completely hairless, unlike so many of the other chests he'd listened to. To be honest, he did not need to put his ear on her bosom at all. She was already looking better since he'd distracted her from her thoughts about the specter of Mrs. Cowper following in their wake.

However, if it brought her a measure of comfort, who was he to argue with her? So he listened to her strong, healthy heartbeat, pronounced her lungs clear, and helped her to her feet.

She looked down at her bare toes as she refastened her garment and he folded up the handkerchief. "You must think me a silly ninny, to bother you this way."

He did not seize the opportunity to agree with her that, yes, he absolutely thought her a silly novel-reading ninny.

"You are not the first person to suffer a nightmare after a shocking event, Miss Farnham. You did the right thing in coming to me."

"I do feel much better now. I believe I can go back to

sleep," she said brightly. She moved to exit the cabin and had her hand on the latch when she turned and looked at him.

"Thank you for not laughing at me, Dr. Murray."

She gave him that smile that made him feel slightly disoriented. No doubt it was only that so few people he encountered in the course of a day's work had any reason to smile at him.

After putting up his handkerchief and making a brief note in his journal regarding her visit, Alexander climbed back into his bunk. He couldn't say why he took his pillow, where her head had lain moments before, and brought it up to his nose. Lavender. A soothing scent, calming for the nerves.

Which was, of course, the only reason why he fell asleep with his arms wrapped around his pillow.

CHAPTER 4

The sun was low in the sky, under clouds looking like anvils poised to fall on the horizon. Alexander heard a familiar "yip" as he was spotted by Miss Farnham's little dog, straining at its leash to reach him. Recalled to his duty at the sight of his charge deep in conversation with Mr. Carr, Alexander walked over to where the couple chatted at the starboard rail.

"Oh, Dr. Murray!" Miss Farnham chirped, waving her free hand in the air. "Mr. Carr was admiring my ribbon, and I told him you gave it to me."

She wore a pale gold straw bonnet with an explosion of lavender roses and greenery, the braid snaking over her left shoulder, its end now tied off by the tri-colored braid Alexander used for his demonstration.

Carr leaned forward to pick up the ribboned end of the braid where it rested on Miss Farnham's bosom. A noise sounding suspiciously like a growl welled up from Alexander's chest, startling the younger man so much he took a step back.

It startled Alexander, too, who finished on a throat-clearing gesture. "No doubt Mr. Carr has duties to see to and little time for admiring your attire."

"Not at all, Dr. Murray," the mate said with a satisfied smile. He took Miss Farnham's hand gloved in rose-colored leather and placed it on his arm. "I am at liberty to stroll with Miss Farnham before supper."

He, too, looked at the clouds on the horizon and frowned.

"We may be in for a blow tonight or tomorrow, so it is good to take advantage of this opportunity while the weather is still fair."

"Perhaps Dr. Murray would care to join us as we walk around the deck?"

Carr looked dismayed, and Alexander was sure he had never met a young woman so ignorant of human behavior and motivations. She appeared completely oblivious to the mate's attempts to court her but putting a spoke in the younger man's wheels was part of a chaperone's task. He bowed in her direction and said, "I would be pleased to join you."

"Mr. Carr, do you truly think the weather will change? Are we in danger?" she asked.

The deck was not wide enough for the three of them to easily walk abreast, so Alexander was to the rear and couldn't see their expressions. He knew he was not an expert sailor, but he had been at sea long enough to recognize trouble signs. The thunderheads building to the southeast were like black boulders piling one atop the other. Remembering previous encounters with bad weather gave him an idea.

"Miss Farnham."

The couple ahead of him stopped walking and Miss Farnham turned to look over her shoulder, knocking Carr in the head with her oversized bonnet, which immediately started a chorus of apologies between the two of them.

Alexander stood with his hands behind his back, waiting for them to stop twittering like starlings.

"Tomorrow morning, report to sick bay after breakfast. You will roll bandages and help me organize my supplies. If we encounter rough weather then I can expect men to show up with sprains and contusions at the very least, and possibly more serious injuries."

"See here, Murray, you can't order Miss Farn—"

"Will that make me useful?"

She'd ignored the mate's protests and was looking at Alexander, her eyes reflecting the color of the late afternoon sky.

He watched her for a heartbeat before answering.

"You will be performing a useful task. It is not the same as being a useful person. But it is a beginning."

Carr still protested, but Alexander was not listening to him. He watched the play of expression on Miss Farnham's lovely face and found her small smile oddly unreadable. And challenging.

"Yes, Doctor, I will be in your sick bay after breakfast. To perform a useful task."

"You have no business ordering a passenger about, Murray!"

"Do not scold poor Dr. Murray," Miss Farnham said, patting the glaring mate on the arm. "He cannot help himself, I am sure. After all, he has spent years and years ordering people to take their medications even when they taste unpleasant, or to suffer through some procedure which will improve their condition. Ordering people about is his nature."

Alexander was startled. "Are you now my champion, Miss Farnham?"

"A man of your age and experience does not need me to champion him, Dr. Murray. But, Mr. Carr, do you truly believe the weather will turn rough? I would so hate for my poor little Pompom to be sick again."

Without another glance at Alexander she turned to her swain, who glared one last time in his direction and then resumed strolling with her.

"We will know more as the night progresses. But do not worry your pretty little head over it. Captain Franklin and the crew are all experienced hands, and we will ride this out without difficulty."

A shiver ran down Miss Farnham's delicate spine and she clutched her escort's arm with one hand while the other kept a tight hold of her pup's leash as the dog sniffed at the chicken coop, setting up a squawking inside. After another glance behind to confirm Alexander was still following like an albatross, Carr resigned himself to simply strolling and not doing anything further that would advance his case with the attractive heiress.

Normally Alexander would have had at least a dozen other places he'd rather be, but this thwarting of Young Lochinvar entertained him, so he kept his countenance severe and his steps steady as he walked along.

Sadly for the younger man, he was called back to his duties and Miss Farnham and her dog were alone on deck. Alexander stepped up to her side.

"I would offer my arm as your escort, Miss Farnham, but two things occur to me. One is that you do not appear in any danger of falling down if you do not hold on to me. The other is that I risk becoming entangled in that animal's leash."

He did not think he had said anything to amuse, but those dimples that surely had other men tripping over their own feet without the danger of the dog's leash punctuated the smile flashing on her face.

"How very logical you are, Dr. Murray. By all means, do

join me on my walk, but do not take any unnecessary risks. At your age a sprain or a broken bone is no small thing."

Was the chit *baiting* him? Alexander had not thought she possessed the intellectual skill or the intestinal fortitude to cross verbal swords with him. Of course, he was above such petty irritations, so he clasped his hands behind his back and strolled alongside her.

"Why rolling bandages?"

"I beg your pardon?"

"Why do you wish me to roll bandages for you?"

He looked at her, her face mostly shaded by the flowers flopping around her hat brim. It was an impractical piece of headgear, but when she turned her head and looked him full in the face it acted as a perfect frame for her features, making her eyes appear more amethyst than clear blue. It was an interesting trick of the light and hues, nothing more.

"Bandages must be rolled to be ready for use. It is one of the constant tasks one finds in a surgery and if I must do it, it takes time away from more important tasks."

"Ah. So my time is less valuable than yours, Dr. Murray?"

He paused in his steps, looking at her. "Are you prepared to argue that it is not less valuable?"

"I would lose, wouldn't I?"

He did not bother to dignify that with an answer.

"Since Mr. Carr was called away, what do you know about this weather, Doctor?"

He did not want to send her into a panic, but it was good to be prepared for any happenstance. "Weather is a constant concern aboard ship. This is the storm season, and Captain Franklin must be especially vigilant."

"I have been through some strong storms in England."

"But you did not experience a hurricane in Jamaica, did you?"

She stopped and looked at him. "Is that what is coming?"

Now he had gone and done the very thing he said he would not do. "I do not think so. I am not a sailor, but those storms are rare. More likely it is a typical blow and will be over without mishap."

They completed another circuit of the deck in silence, each lost in thought, and then she went below to wash for supper.

~

"This may be our last hot food for a while, lady and gentlemen."

Daphne looked up from her plate of boiled beef and questionable objects that might be root vegetables. The captain served himself a hearty portion, and the others followed suit. Except for Dr. Murray. She had noticed that about him. He was as spare in his table habits as in his attire and his conversation. He did not drink to excess, as some of the officers did, nor did he eat to where his clothes strained at the seams, as they did on Captain Franklin.

Did the man have any passions at all? Nothing that drove him to act foolishly or take risks? Daphne thought sometimes during the tedious days aboard ship that she would be willing to dance a hornpipe if it would produce for her a cup of chocolate. The thought of the treat for which she lusted had water pooling in her mouth.

Oh well, at least it made the salt beef easier to chew.

"Do you not agree, Miss Farnham?"

She stopped chewing and swallowed, brought back to her surroundings by the question from Mr. Carr.

"I am so sorry, sir, but I was woolgathering and did not hear your question."

"Thinking of the beautiful shops awaiting you in London?"

His question was innocent enough, but Daphne caught the doctor's eye at that moment and the sardonic expression on his face tempted her to say that she was thinking about passion and lust.

However, that would open up a hornet's nest given her past, and her current precarious and unchaperoned circumstances, so she refrained.

"La, Mr. Carr, what would a lady be thinking of if not fashion and the upcoming season? I fear my wardrobe will be sadly out of date by the time we dock, and I will exhaust myself replenishing it. It is all too fatiguing to dwell on, but I shall do what I must."

Daphne punctuated this by pushing her plate aside to take to Pompom, and pulled out her fan, for the air in the captain's cabin where they took their meals was close and heavy, hotter than usual even for the tropics. She wished again for a ladies' maid or someone who would help her dress for dinner, because while her walking dress of merino cloth with its delightful lilac satin bands at the hem was *a la mode*, the high neck and lace ruff did not bare as much skin as the lightweight silk evening gown she would have worn for such a humid evening.

She'd managed to fasten a white satin bandeau to keep her hair from falling across her face and sticking to her skin and wrapped her braid into a twist and pinned it atop her head, all by herself.

She feared though that if she moved her head quickly the entire mass would come undone and billow out in a disorderly mess. That would no doubt make old Dr. Murray raise one of his heavy eyebrows at her, using it in place of a sneer or a biting comment to illustrate how he felt about her general uselessness.

The man understood nothing about ladies and their lives. It took time and effort to arrange one's hair, to apply a bit of rose lip salve or brush a touch of pink on cheekbones just so, disguising that one was indeed wearing cosmetics. Being laced up, fastening garters, picking just the right chapeau, these were time-consuming tasks. And one did not do it once in the morning, oh no, there were separate outfits for riding and walking and morning calls and evenings in with family and evenings at the theater. He had no idea how many pairs of shoes and boots and slippers alone that took. It was a wonder she was not more exhausted at the end of each day!

Now, Mr. Carr appreciated her. He did not judge her, he admired her face and form. He never thought about whether she was useful.

But Daphne had to admit, she found Dr. Murray's forthright disdain intriguing. He was one of the few men she'd met, of any age, who made no effort to charm her. His verbal provocations made her want to respond in kind. While their encounters too often left her feeling like she was lacking in some fashion, at least they made her feel alive and stimulated.

"Captain Franklin, why did you say this may be our last hot meal?"

Captain Franklin paused from lifting his overloaded fork to his mouth, looked at the food he wasn't about to chew with a moment of regret and answered her.

"We're in for rough weather, Miss Farnham. Nothing the *Magpie* cannot handle, but when we're tossing about, we can't risk a fire in the galley. As soon as we're past it, though, Cookie will put something on the boil for us, you can be sure."

"I will be ready for your men, Captain," Dr. Murray said.

"You are making me glad I brought you aboard as a passenger," the captain said with a genuine smile. He shoved his food into his mouth and spoke around it. "I wish I could carry a sawbones on every voyage and save myself from the chore of tending the men."

Dr. Murray said nothing to this, carefully cutting his beef into small bites. Daphne had not thought about a voyage without a medical man. On her journey to Jamaica she'd been too busy dealing with the violently ill George. The ship's officers and crew were full of helpful advice, so she did not miss having a physician or surgeon about.

There was always a physician or surgeon available when she was growing up, whether in the country or the city. Her father's wealth guaranteed a fast response and her every need was attended to promptly and diligently. She paused, thinking about Dr. Murray as one of those men. She could not see him dropping everything and neglecting his other patients to leap at her father's commands, as she suspected Dr. Drummond did when called to treat Mr. Farnham's gout or Daphne's occasional childhood ailment.

He glanced up and met Daphne's eyes across the table. It was an interesting face, she thought, broad and well-made, with a blade of a nose. His forehead was high, the rufous hair neatly swept back and kept short, a style more suited to practicality than fashion. Not a handsome face like Mr. Carr's, and one could easily overlook it, focusing instead on the surgeon's gruff demeanor. After all, when one was having dealings with a surgeon, what his face looked like was generally the last consideration, wasn't it? You looked at his hands, the strength in his arms for bone-setting or bone-sawing. Daphne broke the glance and looked down at those hands, finely shaped, with long fingers holding his fork and knife in a delicate manner, handling them like instruments, no motion or effort wasted.

Then she remembered that those hands would shortly be on her, helping her out of her clothes, and she felt the warmth flow across her cheekbones. Startled, she looked up again at Dr. Murray. He was still watching her face, but now his eyes were darker, more brown than the blend of forest colors she saw when he was in the sunlight. Unaccountably nervous, Daphne licked her lips and his eyes grew darker still at the motion. He set his silverware down on the rough table and appeared about to speak.

"Excuse me, gentlemen," she said, rising to her feet, and there was a wave of motion as the men jumped up, Dr. Murray the last to rise as he watched her still.

"Are you well, Miss Farnham?"

"Yes, indeed I am, Mr. Carr, but I just recalled some tasks I must see to in my cabin before it becomes too late. If you will forgive me, I will say goodnight now."

Daphne paused outside the captain's cabin, holding her tinware plate for the dog, and took a deep breath. She could still hear the rumble of voices within as the men finished up their supper and port.

There was nothing to be nervous about. Dr. Murray would be brisk and efficient, as he always was, and he would look at her as if she had a brain the size of Pompom's.

~

There was nothing to be nervous about, Alexander mentally chided himself. The chit had a brain the size of a walnut, and all he had to do was enter her cabin, undo her tapes, and bid her goodnight.

The fact that her looking at him earlier this evening had caused his body to stir to life was simply proximity and her undeniable physical attractiveness. He could have taken care of these needs in Jamaica, but between the rather dubious wares offered in the dockside brothels and his efforts to wrap up his work aboard the *Caeneus*, the opportunity passed, and he was bound for England.

With the delectable Miss Farnham.

He wiped his palms against his thighs and took a deep breath. As soon as his knuckles touched the door, it was flung open, and it helped clear his thoughts.

"Miss Farnham, you must ask who is on the other side of the door before opening it," he said sternly. "What if it were one of the sailors standing there, a man with no business being at your cabin?"

"Why would a sailor be rapping at my door, unless he had an important message?" She blinked up at him, those long, lush lashes shading her eyes. "Oh dear, do you have indigestion?"

"The pain I am experiencing at the moment has nothing to do with supper. May I come in?"

"Of course," she said, opening the door wider. Some order had been restored to the cabin, and there were fewer furbelows blocking movement. Miss Farnham beamed at him.

"I did as you said, Doctor, and pared down my wardrobe. I also packed up Mrs. Cowper's belongings and had them put in the hold. I am certain her family will be glad to receive them when we dock."

Alexander looked at her.

"Did you find more appropriate attire for yourself?"

"Yes. I found a stomacher-front walking dress that I can fasten, that one there of rose-striped muslin." She gestured at a white frock draped over a chair. Alexander could see nothing that distinguished it from other women's garments, but that was not the issue.

"It is last season's style, but I am willing to make do and wear it."

"I am cognizant of what a great sacrifice it must be for you, Miss Farnham."

"Indeed," she sighed. "But if it aids me in being more useful, Doctor, I will do what I must."

He looked at her, but the girl seemed completely serious. "Is that the only useful garment you own?"

She put one finger to her dainty chin as she thought. "I think there are dresses in a similar style in my trunks in the hold."

"You have more trunks than these?"

She smiled at him as if he were the one with diminished mental capacity standing in the cabin.

"Of course I have more trunks. But it sounds to me as if the men will be busy tonight and tomorrow with this storm, so I will wait before asking them to haul them up so I can look for additional garments."

She'd removed the headpiece she wore earlier, and her thick braid snaked down her back, more disheveled than the neat construction he'd made earlier in the day. Wisps of hair curled around the tops of her ears and across her forehead, drawing attention to her eyes and her delicate cheekbones.

The silent cabin seemed too warm to him. He was anxious to leave and return to his own quarters, so his voice came out gruffer than he intended when he said, "It is time you were abed. Turn around and I will unfasten you."

Without waiting for her assent he stepped behind her. She stood with her hands at her side, like a fashion doll. Chinaheaded, stuffed with sawdust…

…smelling of lavender and the slight tang of a woman's body sweating in a warm, moist environment, the skin at the back of her neck dewy and shining in the lamplight. When a swell caused the deck beneath his feet to shift, he grasped her waist to steady her.

"Thank you, Dr. Murray," she said in a low voice. He pulled his hand back as if burned and grunted in response, concentrating instead on the ties at the back of her frock. Ridiculous, the way women's garments were fashioned. He'd heard tales of fops who needed to be squeezed into their coats by their valets and who were incapable of tying their own cravats, but he'd never thought about an entire class of humans reduced to the status of dressmakers' dummies by their need to be fastened in and out of their own clothing.

Such thoughts should distract him from the feel of the soft skin beneath her nape, the area above her chemise and corset revealed by the fabric falling away beneath his fingers. Fingers he'd always prided himself were steady and sure, but now seemed swollen and clumsy, fumbling with a knotted string.

"Your hands are warm, Doctor. My maid at home always had hands like icicles."

"Good circulation."

"I beg your pardon?"

"The strong flow of blood beneath the skin keeps my limbs warm, Miss Farnham. Your maid might benefit from a modest amount of brisk exercise each day to keep her blood circulating."

"I have no doubt, Doctor, if I were to suggest such a thing Hattie would remind me she leads a busy enough life caring for my wardrobe, not leaving time or desire for additional exercise."

He paused from the string he was undoing. It was above a corset that distracted from his task, the boning pulled tight at the bottom and reminding him her hips were scant inches from his own, and it would only take a sweep of his hand to bring that pert backside up against him. Her chemise of fine lawn edged over the top of the corset, one strap slipping down a rounded shoulder. The garment was nearly translucent, the fabric so soft that if he kissed her through it he would feel the warmth of her rosy skin against his lips.

"What was that noise? Did you say something?"

"Nothing." But perhaps conversation would distract him. Even conversation with Miss Farnham.

"You are concerned about your maid being overburdened with additional responsibilities?"

"Of course. Poor Hattie has to work hard to see to it that I am properly turned out and fashionable. I do not want to make her life more difficult."

The string he worked on unraveled from its knot. Slim as she was, she could wiggle out of her own clothes the rest of the way.

And there was a mental image he could spend the entire night doing without.

"I am finished. You can do the rest on your own."

She turned, clutching her dress to her bosom. Alexander carefully kept his eyes on her face.

"Thank you, Dr. Murray. You are a most useful person."

"Indeed, I am, Miss Farnham. Since I will be busy tomorrow and you will be assisting me, I will bid you goodnight."

"I understand. I remember my grandfather would retire early after supper to rest."

For one brief moment Alexander was tempted to haul the half-dressed chit into his arms and show her how far he was from being incapacitated by age or infirmity, but sanity imposed itself on him. He bowed and left her standing in the middle of her cabin looking like a pink package of temptation.

Mr. Carr was standing outside the cabin, in time to catch a brief glimpse of Miss Farnham and hear her say, "Goodnight, Doctor. Thank you for undressing me."

Alexander adjusted the cuffs on his shirt and turned to the smirking officer.

"A word of advice: Miss Farnham is my responsibility, and it is a responsibility I do not take lightly. If you attempt anything that might damage her reputation, I will introduce you to some of the more dramatic methods I use to treat the pox. You will find the experience educational, but not enjoyable."

The younger man paled and his eyes grew large.

"I am always glad when I can clarify these medical procedures for my patients—or potential patients. Goodnight, Mr. Carr."

CHAPTER 5

"*R*ed sky in the morning, sailors take warning..." Daphne looked at Dr. Murray. "Is that true?"

He looked up from where he was compounding something, a salve or an ointment. Daphne was not sure which, but it had a sharp smell in the small cabin, filling the air with the scent of mint.

"Yes, Miss Farnham, oftentimes a red sky at sunrise means rough weather ahead."

Daphne frowned down at the clean, but worn cloth strip she was rolling for bandages. The sea rocked this morning, the waves having an oily look to them as they swelled beneath the *Magpie*. She felt the tension in the crew as they worked at their tasks, all of them looking to the southeast where black clouds piled up in an ominous wall. The sky at sunrise had a sullen reddish cast and the air was oppressive and heavy. Yesterday sea birds followed them, but the skies were now empty of life, only high, scudding clouds moving as the wind picked up.

Dr. Murray was already at work when she arrived, and his eyes skimmed over her neat braid and the muslin dress she wore. It was one of her favorites even though it was out of fashion, and she thought the doctor's braided ribbon a nice complement to the dusty rose stripes in her skirt. There was a rose flounce at the bottom, the higher hemline showing off her wonderful kid halfboots that laced behind, the ones she'd fallen in love with when she saw the design in the shoemaker's.

"Why such a sad sigh?"

"I love these shoes, and I fear when I return to London they will no longer be fashionable. Then I must give some serious thought as to whether I should continue wearing them."

Dr. Murray paused from his labor and looked at her.

"Miss Farnham, I am going to pretend you just walked into the cabin and we did not have this conversation. It makes my brain hurt when you say things like that."

"That is odd. My brain never hurts."

He looked about to remark on this, then stopped himself and gave his head a small shake, returning to his task.

"What are you mixing? It smells"—she thought for a moment—"pungent."

"An ointment for sprains. That is one of the more common injuries the sailors suffer during storms. I am also making a salve for treating rheumatism."

"Rheumatism?"

"A sailor who spends his time in a cold and wet environment is prone to aches and diseases of the joints."

Daphne grabbed a fresh strip of cloth and paused. She'd never thought about the details of doctoring. What had these bandages been used for in the past? Had they wrapped broken ribs on a sailor falling off one of those sticks that jutted out and held up the sails? Covered a nasty gash after an encounter with pirates? Who had the unpleasant task of washing out the bandages when they were unwrapped?

She was about to ask when voices were heard outside the cabin. Daphne paused to listen, shamelessly eavesdropping on the conversation between the captain and the mate.

"Barometer still dropping," she heard the captain say. "Our best option is to try to run before the storm."

Daphne could not hear Mr. Carr's reply, and when she glanced at him she saw Dr. Murray also had stopped to listen to the conversation, but the two officers moved off.

"It is going to be a bad storm, isn't it?"

He looked down at the ointment, his fingers shiny in the shifting lamplight with the grease from his preparations. Then he looked her in the eye.

"Yes, Miss Farnham, it will be a bad storm."

Oddly enough, his stark words eased the tension from Daphne's shoulders. Dr. Murray may not like her very much, but his answers to her were always bluntly honest, if rudely phrased. He did not smile at her and tell her not to worry her pretty little head as the other gentlemen did.

"What should I do to prepare for the storm?"

He still watched her, and his eyes changed. He didn't smile at her—she could not imagine that happening. Instead, his look was, if not approving, at least less censorious.

"A very good question." He straightened up from his labors, wiped his hands on a cloth and then covered the bowl with it.

"The *Magpie* is a sound ship, and the captain and crew are experienced. But if I were you, I would pack a valise. It should be a bag you yourself can carry. In it, only put those things that are absolutely necessary, or those things you would preserve at all costs."

"One bag?" Daphne stared at him. "But…but it is impossible, Doctor. I could not pack everything necessary to me into one bag!"

He cocked one of those accusatory eyebrows at her.

"Impossible? That is too bad. Let me tell you what will happen if the worst occurs and we have to abandon the ship: you will grab the first thing at hand and cling to it. It might be a book, it might be a scarf, it might be one of those shoes you are wearing now that will soon be unfashionable and unwearable. It will not be those items most important to you, I can guarantee it."

"You have been shipwrecked before?"

"I have, and I will be prepared. Whether or not you are prepared is your concern and entirely up to you."

Daphne almost said, "You won't help me?" but she feared that other eyebrow would be brought into play at her expense. She was silent as she rolled the last of the bandages. When she turned back to him, Dr. Murray had a chest of instruments open, and was examining them.

"Is that what you will take with you?"

He held up a lancet, wiped it on his coat sleeve, then examined its edge in the light.

"My chest is the most valuable item I own. If there is time to take any one thing with me, this is what I will take." He put the blade down and looked at her. "Again, abandoning ship is a last resort and I do not expect that to happen. It is always best to be prepared for the worst situation, though. If it happens, you are ready; if it does not happen, you can count yourself pleasantly surprised."

As if to punctuate his words, the *Magpie* rolled as the seas grew heavier. Daphne heard rain falling now, and Mr. Carr yelling something about hatches. She grabbed hold of the table to steady herself.

"If the captain orders us to abandon ship," she said, her voice barely above a whisper, "Will you come for me?"

He stopped what he was doing and looked at her, his own stance steady with the roll of the ship.

"I will come for you, Miss Farnham."

"Promise me!" Daphne gripped the table edge. She hated to hear the pleading note in her voice, but the idea of being forgotten in the turmoil of a sinking ship terrified her.

"I promise I will come for you. You will not be alone." His hazel eyes were calm as they watched her, and his wide shoulders, the solidity of him standing there comforted her, and she took a deep breath.

"Then I will be in my cabin, packing a valise."

"Do not leave your cabin so I know where you are."

"Yes, Dr. Murray."

Daphne turned to leave, but his voice stopped her.

"Wait a moment."

He was looking through the jars in a chest, rummaging around until he reached deep inside and pulled out a tin about the size of a deck of cards.

"Take this. You might need it."

She looked down at the tin, then raised the lid. A fragrance of spices, strong and sharp, filled her nostrils.

"It is candied ginger. Until now you have been a sturdy sailor, but in this weather even the most stable of travelers is tested. Eat a small piece about once an hour or two and it will help keep your stomach settled."

"This is thoughtful of you."

"Nonsense. I simply do not want you expelling your supper onto my boots later on."

Daphne swallowed, the image his words raised not helping her as the ship rolled again. She hurried to her cabin, sailors moving past her intent on their tasks, not stopping to exchange a word or a smile as they normally would.

Inside her cabin Daphne closed the door and sat on her bunk. Pompom poked his head out from beneath the covers and whined, licking her hand.

"You know something's amiss, don't you, boy?" Daphne whispered to him. She could hear the wind above her whistling and humming through the rigging of the ship, the rain pounding against the hatches fastened tight against the water. It was a stout ship, she told herself, one which had made the Atlantic crossing many times.

But the rain and wind continued to pound the *Magpie* through the day and into the night, and the ship bucked like a wild horse as it rode the waves. No one brought her supper, and she did not miss it. She was not yet sick, but the constant rolling of the vessel tested her. Clammy sweat stood out on her brow and darkened her armpits, and she clenched her teeth and thought of calm meadows and sunny days. Pompom huddled next to her, his small body shaking. He'd made a mess earlier and she had cleaned it up and disposed of it in the covered pot, making sure the cupboard was latched so it would not come rolling out across the deck. On her other side sat her valise, close at hand and giving an odd sort of comfort. If they had to leave the ship, she would not be grabbing a shoe or a hairbrush in the confusion.

Daphne must have dozed, because she awoke to a pounding at her cabin door. She made her way carefully, the deck rolling beneath her feet. When she opened the door, clinging to the frame, Dr. Murray stood there with a flask and a cloth-wrapped parcel.

"You have not eaten, Miss Farnham." He pushed his way past her into the cabin and Daphne released her grip on the door frame just as another swell pitched beneath her feet.

She lost her balance and fell against Dr. Murray, and he grabbed her, his stance widening to take their weight against the storm-tossed movement of the *Magpie*.

Daphne knew she should move, she wanted to move, but it felt so safe standing there in his grasp, his strong arms wrapped around her, the flask in his hand hard against her shoulder blade.

"Oh, Doctor, please do not mention food! I have been so careful, but you will ruin it."

Her head came up to his neck, and she saw the pulse beating there above his collar. Odd, she thought, his neck was firm and muscled, not at all slack and wattled as was usually the case with older men. His voice rumbled in her ear when he spoke, and he made no move to remove her from his embrace.

"On the contrary, I know best in these cases. You must eat a small amount of biscuit—just nibble at it if you like—but it will help keep you steady. This is watered wine, and it, too, will help."

"If you say so," she said in a small voice, but she made no move to push herself away. The doctor smelled minty, of oil of wintergreen, like the salve he'd been compounding earlier. Only a shameless hussy would take advantage of this serious and practical man's proximity to huddle in his arms like Pompom, but it felt so good after a day of being tossed like a cork. She knew he would not let her fall, and that reassurance warmed her as much as did his body next to hers, the rough wool of his coat scratching beneath her cheek.

And it occurred to her as she stood there that for some reason, Dr. Murray did not seem to be in a hurry to push her away and return to his physicking.

But as the deck slipped again beneath her feet, Daphne released her hold on the doctor and lurched to her bunk. She took the food from him and he stood there and watched her as she unwrapped the biscuit, breaking off a small piece for herself, and another small piece for the creature whose black nose stuck out from beneath the covers, sniffing the air suspiciously.

They both chewed in silence, and she washed down her bite with a sip of the water, giving Pompom a taste from her cupped hand. To her surprise, she did feel better after consuming the food.

"Your color is returning. I will check back on you later."

"Dr. Murray."

He paused, looking back at her over his shoulder.

"Thank you. I know I am a trial sometimes…and not a very useful person…but I appreciate all you are doing for me."

He did not say "You are welcome," or "Think nothing of it," or "Of course you are useful," or "It is my pleasure, to be of assistance to you" as Mr. Carr would have done. He only looked at her a moment longer and said, "Good night, Miss Farnham."

When the door closed behind him Daphne removed her boots and lay down on her bunk, Pompom cuddled close. She did not think she'd sleep with the tossing of the *Magpie*, but she must have dozed again, for the next thing she knew she was hurled to the deck as the ship heeled sharply.

The deck was wet. The lantern was still lit, and as she looked over at the door she saw water trickling in, and the ship stayed tilted and off center. She grabbed hold of the bunk and pulled herself to her feet, soothing a whimpering Pompom.

As if in a dream Daphne sat on the bunk, holding her pup. She wanted to flee the cabin and find answers, but she was too afraid to move.

And Dr. Murray promised he would come for her.

She no sooner thought that than her door flew open. Dr. Murray stood there holding a dark cloth bundle, his surgical chest suspended from a strap that went across his shoulder over his heavy weather gear. At the sight of that worn wooden box, Daphne swallowed.

"She's taking on water fast. Come with me," he said, turning to the passageway.

"Wait!" She grabbed her valise, stuffing some last-minute items into it and fastening it.

"There is no time, we must leave now." He took the valise from her and grabbed her, shoving her arms into a heavy coat that smelled of tar and sweat. Ragged sleeves hung down past her wrists, and Dr. Murray rudely threw her valise back to her and grabbed her arm, pulling her along. The deck was tilted so severely that she would have lost her balance if not for his strong hand hauling her with him like so much baggage. Around them there was a strong odor of spirits and she saw sailors passed out, bottles rolling beside them.

"Wha—"

He barely gave them a glance. "They would rather die senseless than be aware when the sea takes them."

Daphne was horror-struck and her feet wouldn't move. He rounded on her, his face grim, his voice low. "We will survive this, Daphne Farnham. Do not give up!"

"Yes, Doctor," she whispered, and clutching her valise with one arm, she held onto the back of his coat with the other. She followed him past the lanterns swinging crazily in the listing ship, their light illuminating scenes from hell and the smell of smoke and saltwater and vomit strong in the air.

He pushed her up the ladder, following so closely behind she knew if she slipped he would stop her from falling. As her head broke through she was struck with a blast of water, not the sea but the rain pounding sideways into them as the gale whipped it into a maelstrom. The force would have knocked her off her feet if not for the steady arm of the man by her side. Heads down, they inched their way to the rail where Mr. Carr was waiting for them, holding fast to a line. In the muted light of the black morning he was barely recognizable beneath his oilskins, but he grinned at Daphne.

"Good to see you walking the decks, Miss Farnham."

He had to shout to be heard above the wind and the rain, and his voice was hoarse from commanding the men all night.

"Oh, poor Mr. Carr! You are soaked through!"

"I have had better days." He laughed, then his face grew grim. "Go now into the boat, miss."

Daphne blinked water out of her eyes. Her hair was plastered against her head and she felt water trickling down her neck but the coat Dr. Murray had forced her into kept her warm.

"Give Captain Franklin my thanks, Mr. Carr."

He exchanged a look with the doctor and turned back to her. "That is much appreciated, Miss Farnham. Now, you must climb into the boat with the surgeon here."

She started to turn away, but he said, "Wait!" and grabbed her by the arm. As Daphne turned back to him, Mr. Carr took her face between his hands and kissed her full on the mouth. Dr. Murray stirred beside her but said nothing.

"That was a lovely memento of our voyage together, Miss Farnham. Thank you."

"Mr. Carr!" Daphne smiled at him, raising her voice over the rain pounding her. "I should slap your face for taking liberties, but I will wait to scold you until I see you again and we are both dried out."

He looked at the doctor again, then looked back at her.

"I look forward to that meeting," he said hoarsely. "Now into the boat with you."

Daphne was hustled to the stern of the ship where a bosun's chair was rigged for her, and a sailor waited in the boat below to assist her. Dr. Murray tossed him her valise, then climbed down into the boat as the rain pounded against him, and her heart rose in her throat. Once he was in the boat, she was lowered in, the rough rope chafing against her ungloved hands. She picked up her bag from where it sat in the rain and seawater awash in the bottom of the small craft and held it tight on her lap. Dr. Murray sat aft of her, his chest alongside him, listening to the commands from above.

The sailor, whose name she could not recall at the moment, grinned at her and said, "Sit tight, miss, we'll take a few more aboard and we'll be safe."

She smiled back at him and he turned at a shout from above, just as another pounding wave threatened to swamp the boat. The sailor grabbed at the line securing the boat to the *Magpie*, but with a jerk the line snapped, flinging him into the turbulent waters.

In an eye blink Dr. Murray stripped off his coat, tied a rope around his waist and dived into the water after him while Daphne clutched the seat, alone in the boat.

"You swore you would stay with me," she whispered.

She could still hear shouting from above but could not make out the words over the storm. She scanned the sea anxiously, wiping the water from her face, but there was nothing. Nothing except rain pounding down, and churning waves.

"Move to larboard!"

She whipped her head around and saw Dr. Murray in the water, holding onto his lifeline. He was on the far side of the boat hollering at her, but she understood, even if she still didn't understand larboard and starboard. The small craft would be overset if the weight was not balanced. She braced herself as Dr. Murray heaved himself into the boat, tipping it dangerously close to the waterline.

He was alone. Daphne grabbed the surgeon's coat and put it around the shivering man, then she looked around her. They were both alone out on the ocean. If the *Magpie* was still there, it was hidden behind a wall of thundering water.

Dr. Murray worked in the bottom of the boat, hauling out a piece of canvas and yelling to be heard over the rain.

"We will cover ourselves to keep the rain out of the boat. Use that bucket to bail out the bottom!"

He ran rope through grommets on the cloth and tied it down over the boat while she bailed. Within minutes her arms were aching and blisters were rising on the soft skin of her hands, but she dared not stop, not when there was still water in the boat.

Dr. Murray took the bucket from her and began bailing, more quickly than she'd been able to do. At his direction, she ducked under the cloth awning. It cut off most of the light but kept the rain from pounding on her bare head. She opened her valise and made herself as comfortable as she could in the dimness and the damp, shivering inside her coat. It was not freezing out, she thought they were still in the tropics, but even so she was chilled from her exposure to the elements. She had no way of knowing how much time passed while the doctor bailed, but finally he stopped and crawled under the canvas with her.

"The sky is lightening and it appears the rain is tapering off," he said hoarsely. It was too dark to see his expression, but she saw the movement of his hands flexing. Then he glanced at her and in the dim light his eyes honed in on her skirts.

"What is *that* doing here, Miss Farnham?"

She refused to be intimidated, even though with Dr. Murray around that was no small feat.

"You told me to pack those things that are absolutely necessary, or what I would preserve at all costs. Pompom is very necessary to me and I will not abandon him." She looked down at the wet dog shivering in her arms and clutched him closer. "Pompom loves me and needs me. How could I leave him behind?"

"He will eat and drink our supplies."

"Pompom is a tiny scrap of a thing, Doctor, and I will share my ration with him."

"He is a useless burden."

"To listen to you, *I* am a useless burden, but I will not let you heave me over the side either," she said firmly. "Pompom stays."

She looked down at the smelly bundle of fur in her lap and removed his pretty red leather collar, the one where his name was spelled out in brilliants. The leather might tighten as it dried and hurt his little neck. He shivered less now as she petted him, and after some time she realized the doctor was correct. The rain was not coming down as fiercely as it had, and eventually it tapered off almost completely while the boat's two occupants sat in their own silence.

Without speaking to her, Dr. Murray moved back out into the air, rocking the boat, but Daphne held onto her seat with one hand and Pompom with the other.

"If you can put that pup down for a moment, I need your assistance."

Daphne found an area at the edge of the small craft that seemed less awash than the bottom, and opened her valise, popping Pompom inside. The dog was content to rummage through the damp clothes and make himself a nest, settling down with a sigh. She wished she could join him, but the doctor needed her help.

She poked her head out from under the canvas and blinked. The rain was now just a smattering, more of a heavy mist, and the black clouds that loomed on the horizon yesterday appeared to be behind them. She had no inkling of where "behind" them was, where they were, or where they were going. At least they seemed to be moving away from the storm.

But the sea around them was empty. No sign of the *Magpie*, no sign of life at all.

Dr. Murray sat in the bow waiting for her.

"We need to take stock of our supplies and talk about our situation. Moving around will be better for you than sitting." She must have looked confused, because he continued speaking. "If you sit with your feet in the water and do not move around, you will develop immersion foot. Your limbs will swell, your skin will become ulcerated, infection and gangrene will set in and you will die. Take off your boots now while you still can pull them off your feet."

This was said in the same calm voice that he used when asking for the coffee to be passed to him at supper. She knew she was staring when he sighed and said again, "Your boots, Miss Farnham."

Daphne sat on the wet bench, hastening to remove her boots and stockings. In the meantime, the doctor cautiously moved around in the boat, examining the water butt stowed there. His own feet were bare and his trousers rolled up. She tried not to stare at his muscular calves, but they were there, and they were well-shaped. The doctor would not be padding his stockings with sawdust when he wore knee breeches.

The image of this blunt-spoken surgeon gaining admittance to a venue like Almack's made her smile. She could imagine him telling the patronesses a thing or two about their health or habits without pausing to weigh the consequences.

"We are fortunate the crew of the *Magpie* prepared the boat before the storm," he said now. "It would be better if we had a sailing craft, but at least there is some water."

"What about food?"

"No food, but that is less of an issue than drinking water,

at least initially. Let us take one crisis at a time, Miss Farnham."

Daphne could see the wisdom in that, but then another issue occurred to her. "Um, Dr. Murray?"

He stopped doing whatever he was doing with the rope he held and looked at her.

"What do we do when we need to…when we have to go…" She stopped, unable to put it into words.

"Are you asking what to do when you need to relieve yourself?"

She nodded, her face burning. She almost thought he smiled, but it was only a lessening of the tension around his mouth.

"I will tell you, but you are not going to like it. If you were one of the sailors you would just aim over the side. Not into the wind, of course. However, since you are not equipped to do that, and for other requirements, I will rig the lines for you to hold onto while you perch in the bow, hanging out over the water."

"I never could! With you sitting there?"

He raised a damp, but still effective, eyebrow.

"I am a surgeon, Miss Farnham. Are your parts the same as any other woman's? Then you will not be showing me anything I have not seen before, so it need not worry you."

Daphne was still certain she'd never be able to do what she needed to do with him sitting there, but that, too, was a worry for later.

"The rain stopped," he said, looking about them. "Give me the bucket and I will bail some more."

Not knowing what else to do, she passed him the bucket, then sat sideways on the seat that stretched across the boat, her legs thrust out before her. Her gown was ruined, sodden and torn from her exertions, but it was an older gown anyway and she did not let it fret her. Her stomach growled, and she put a hand over it.

"I am afraid you will go to sleep hungry tonight, Miss Farnham. Though I'm told in China they eat small dogs…"

"Dr. Murray!"

"Tomorrow we will see about catching some fish, provided this weather holds."

She looked about her at the sun low in the sky, red tinged clouds passing before it and coating the ocean with a deep color. The rest of the sky was clear and untroubled, and stars were already glinting in the east. It was a sight Daphne would have enjoyed more from the deck of a large, stable vessel. Or, even better, from shore.

But it could be worse. She had Pompom. There was water. And best of all, she had someone with her who would make sure all turned out well.

She could not help but contrast Dr. Murray with poor George. George knew everything about the latest fashions, he knew all the gossip, he was a popular and witty dinner guest, and he would have been a total disaster in this disaster. Where Dr. Murray was calm and thoughtful, he would have been panicking, looking for someone to save him.

Daphne frowned. She was not much different. She had already been branded not useful, and she knew right now, in this situation, it was a true statement. She had to depend on Dr. Murray to keep her alive, for without him she would not know how to do anything to save herself. She did not even know how to open the water barrel that he was examining now.

But perhaps she was not so useless after all…

"Dr. Murray?"

He looked at her, his normally neat hair disheveled and curling around his face. She wiped her hand against her torn skirt, because she had been tempted to reach across and smooth the hair back from his forehead.

"There is something in my valise that may help."

He cocked one of those brows and waited for her to continue. Instead of speaking, Daphne pushed aside Pompom from inside the bag. He grumbled in protest, but she needed to hold him over the side—or something—before they settled in for the night, so it was just as well he woke up.

"Look!"

Daphne held up her treasure, and Dr. Murray reached out for it.

"Why, Miss Farnham, how very useful."

She preened under his praise. The doctor's compliments were rare, but all the more appreciated. Then a frown pinched between her eyes. He was praising the item, not her.

Dr. Murray turned the wine flask he'd given her on the *Magpie* over in his hands.

"We can use this instead of the bucket to get drinking water out of the water butt. This will be the perfect solution."

"As you said, it is useful, Dr. Murray."

He looked at her, his face hard to read in the gathering dusk. "Yes, but you did a useful thing bringing it along, Miss Farnham."

"Does that make me a useful person?"

"Perhaps it depends on what else you thought worth stowing in your valise?"

Oh dear. Daphne bit her lip, not at all sure he would approve of her choices. She quashed the impulse to wring her hands together.

"I have an idea. Let us wait until morning, when there is more light, and I will share with you what I packed. Just as you are waiting to tell me the tale of your shipwreck."

"Fair enough. In the meantime, we are both exhausted, and hungry. Take care of yourself and your animal, then we will open this flask and drink some of the restorative watered wine and settle in."

She took care of Pompom, who'd already anticipated her and lifted his leg against the side of the boat, but he was a small thing and there was already bilge awash in there so she did not think about it. But to her amazement, when he made to squat, he allowed her to perch him in a tight hold at the bow of the boat and managed to do what he needed to do, earning a great deal of cooing praise from his proud mistress.

"If you two are quite done, Miss Farnham."

"What a good boy you are, Pompom. What an intelligent boy! I am sorry, my little puppy-wuppy, there is nothing for you to eat. Tomorrow, Dr. Murray will find you food."

"Not if you call that animal 'puppy-wuppy' again I won't."

Daphne ignored this and washed her hands in the ocean before taking the flask, Pompom still perched on her lap. As the cool liquid flowed down her throat she thought nothing had ever tasted so good, even though normally the ship's drinking water was a necessary evil, but nothing more. She poured some into her hand for the dog, and he lapped at it eagerly.

"That is enough," Dr. Murray said, reaching for the flask. "You will make yourself ill if you drink too much. You can have more water tomorrow."

He did as he had promised—or threatened—and rigged a line for her to hold onto while she sat off the front of the boat—the bow, he reminded her—and necessity finally drove her to do what needed to be done. To her relief, she was dampened, but not dunked, and survived the experience.

Her eyes were adjusting to the night darkness, helped by a half moon that cast a soft light over the empty ocean. A breeze picked up, nothing like the earlier wind, but enough to make her huddle in her damp coat. Thank goodness Dr.

Murray had thought to force it on her. He was a stiff and curmudgeonly old man, but right now there was no one she would rather have sitting across from her.

She shivered in her coat, and he noticed the movement.

"We can conserve body heat by huddling close together, Miss Farnham. Stay where you are."

So saying, he moved across the small space separating them until he was close to her side. He arranged the canvas into a bundle stretched across the benches in the stern, leaving a flap he could lift. He sat next to her and opened his coat.

"Inch yourself over here. And yes, bring that animal. He gives off heat."

If it had been anyone else Daphne would suspect it a ploy to woo her, but it was Dr. Murray, so she snuggled up against his left side, Pompom in the crook of her arm. The pup seemed quite content to be close to the two humans, and with a sigh kneaded his front paws into her skirt, then settled down. Daphne wanted to sigh herself as she put her head on the surgeon's chest. He took the edge of his heavy coat and pulled it over her, told her to grab the canvas and pull if over them, too, then stretched his legs across until his feet were perched on the far bench. Daphne followed his example, her feet just making it to the improvised footstool.

"Put your legs across mine, Miss Farnham. I can support you as you sleep and your feet won't fall into the water."

"Can you sleep sitting up?"

"I have done so far too often, and I can lean back against the canvas. But you should try to rest now. In the morning, we will take stock of our situation."

"Yes, Doctor," Daphne murmured, her eyes already closing. She could feel the strong beat of the surgeon's heart beneath her cheek as she drifted off to sleep between the two warm male bodies.

CHAPTER 6

Miss Farnham slept the sleep of the innocent and the ignorant, but Alexander lay with his eyes open, looking at the stars above him. For the first time in his life, he wished he was a sailor, not a surgeon. He had always depended on others to handle the mechanics of sailing because he was too busy with his medicine and his studies to bother learning how to navigate at sea.

He had a vague idea where they were. Somewhere near Bermuda. He could only hope they would drift to an island or be spotted by a ship.

He also knew, to his regret, that despair killed shipwrecked men. He had seen it happen with the wreck of the *Syrinx* back in '08. Lieutenant Havers was the senior officer among the survivors in the boat, but it soon became clear he was a liability to their survival. His emotional outbursts and conflicting orders led to a rapid breakdown in authority. Havers's despair at their situation drove him to slip over the side of the boat into the ocean's unforgiving embrace.

It was Alexander the men looked to, his phlegmatic demeanor and his calmness in the face of disaster pushing him into a leadership position he neither wanted nor thought himself suited for, but it was his, nonetheless.

"We knew we could trust you," a seaman named Smith said after their rescue. "You would listen to us, and you would make the right decisions, Dr. Murray, just as you do when you decide whether a man needs his leg chopped off."

Alexander looked down at the two helpless creatures that were now his responsibility. Out of the thousands of people with whom one could choose to be marooned, Miss Daphne Farnham would be at the bottom of his list.

No doubt there were men who would be thrilled at the idea of being castaway with a nubile young miss, but Alexander would gladly have traded her for a tough old salt who knew how to navigate and rig a sail. He would not be so pretty to look at, but he would be much more useful.

He sighed and adjusted her beneath his arm. She murmured something and went back to sleep, not knowing how close they were to disaster.

To her credit, she'd brought supper. He looked at the annoying animal in her lap, who farted in his sleep, growled, and settled back down.

Alexander followed the dog's example—at least so far as to close his eyes and settle down—and tried to snatch what sleep he could before dealing with the next problem.

~

"But I do not understand, Dr. Murray," Daphne Farnham said the next morning, looking like a sleep-tousled kitten, her rosebud mouth pursed. "Surely someone will realize we are missing and come after us?"

"We can hope that will happen, but the reality of life at sea is ships sometimes sink. No one knows when this occurs unless they happen to be cruising nearby."

He was trying to rig a line to dangle over the side and see if he could catch them some breakfast. He'd seen a school of silver fish swim by that he thought might be sardines or sprats, or something similar. Alexander raided his medicine chest for line but found nothing to put at the end of it.

Miss Farnham had taken care of her morning business, and the dog's, and was watching him.

"What are you doing?"

Alex suppressed a sigh. He did not want to chat with her, not when there was food to be sought, but he paused. If he was going to be stuck in a boat with Daphne Farnham for the foreseeable future, he needed to work harder at being pleasant, because the last thing he wanted to deal with was a moping, maudlin miss.

Though to her credit, he had to acknowledge, she'd been even tempered so far.

"I saw some fish swim by earlier. I hoped I could find a way to hook one, but I need a hook to do that."

"Wouldn't a net be better for small fish?"

"Of course it would!" he snapped, his temper frayed by the ridiculous question. "But I do not have a net."

"I do."

"What?"

"I have a net."

She smiled brightly at him, as if what she just said made sense. When he found himself still speechless, she dragged her valise over to her and began rummaging through it, pulling out a length of pink fabric.

It was indeed a net, made of tightly knotted silk. He took it between his hands and pulled, but the powerful silk cord didn't tear.

"It is a hair net. It's not a large net, of course, but maybe you could catch a small fish in it?"

"Miss Farnham, you are amazing," he said, and he meant it. "What else is in that bag of yours?"

Daphne Farnham had not eaten in over a day, she was sitting in a boat somewhere in the Atlantic, her nose was turning the same shade as her rosy hair net, but she glowed at his words. Alexander remembered all the times his mother had patted his head and told him what a good boy he was, what an intelligent boy, what a capable boy, and he'd grown to take her praise for granted. Did no one ever praise Miss Farnham's qualities beyond what was reflected in her looking glass?

Now she was pulling items from her valise, her voice apologetic.

"A shawl, my hairbrush, ribbons to tie my hair, salve for my lips, a mirror, hair pins..." She paused. "I do not know why I packed them because I cannot pin my own hair. Oh well. I also have stockings"—she blushed at mentioning such an intimate item—"a night rail, extra corset strings, tooth brush and powder, hand cream, a sewing kit, and some, um, rags. In case I need, um, rags. Oh, and this. Oh dear."

The last item she pulled from her valise was a straw bonnet, sadly chewed at the edge of the brim. She looked accusingly at Pompom, who ignored her as he licked himself. Alexander marveled at the treasures spread out before him.

"Miss Farnham, you are the heroine of the day."

"I am?"

"Do not sound so surprised. The items you packed are wonderfully useful. For example, that lip salve. You can put it on your lips, your nose, your cheekbones and your chin. It will help keep those areas that are most vulnerable to sunlight from being badly burned. And your hat may not be fashionable enough for Mayfair, but it will keep you from sunstroke. Put it on now, please."

She did, asking him to hold her mirror while she concentrated on tying her ribbons. Then she followed his instructions, putting rose-tinted salve on her face, though the end result left her in giggles.

"I look like a red Indian from America!"

He put the mirror in his coat pocket. "This mirror will be useful in signaling a ship if we spot one. Your hairpins are about to become fish hooks, the corset strings are fishing line, and your net will, I hope, allow us to gather the fish that we will use to bait those hooks and give ourselves something to eat."

"But how will we cook the fish in the boat, Doctor?"

"Do not worry about that yet. First, let us catch the fish. Give me the bucket."

He filled the bailing bucket a third full with seawater and then set to his task. Boredom was the enemy when cast adrift nearly as much as lack of food and water, and Alexander looked at the morning with a new enthusiasm. He leaned over the gunwale dragging his net while Miss Farnham shifted to starboard.

"Come here, ye wee buggers," he said beneath his breath.

The sun beat down on his bare head, but he knew patience was the key to success, the net drifting in the water like an unthreatening clump of seaweed, until the school of silver fish came by, closer, closer, and….

"Caught them!"

He pulled his small net up and a dozen, maybe fifteen, of the fish were caught and dumped in the bucket, where they swam in confusion. The others darted in the water, but not too far, and soon he had a second catch, and there were plenty of nourishing fish shimmering in the morning light as Miss Farnham clapped her hands and the dog barked, jumping back and forth on the thwarts next to his mistress.

"Well done, Dr. Murray! You caught us some food." She looked in the bucket, and her smiles changed to a frown of puzzlement. "But how will we eat them? There is no fire and no way to smoke them like kippers."

She wouldn't like what he was going to say next, but just as she'd learned to perch her bottom off the bow, she'd adjust to this, too.

"We are going to eat them raw."

She gulped, and put her hand on her throat.

"Raw fish?"

"Needs must, Miss Farnham. We have to obtain sustenance, and they're here for us." He didn't tell her the water butt was not as full as he'd hoped. If they were desperate enough and caught a seabird, they'd be eating its raw flesh and drinking its blood for liquid. And then there was the dog…

"I do not know if I can—"

"You can and you will. Now, let me prepare them."

Alexander pulled a folding knife from his pocket and quickly beheaded, deboned and cleaned the fish, leaving some swimming for bait. The small pieces of seafood gleamed in the sun when he was done, and she held back her dog, who was lunging at them with no qualms at all about raw fish.

"See? Your dog knows they are safe to eat."

"My dog would eat cat droppings if I let him," Miss Farnham said with asperity as she wrestled with the hungry animal. "Let me feed him first, then he will settle down."

She scooped up a handful of fish, checked it for bones, then let the dog eat from her palm. He did, with an intensity that Alexander could only admire. Then the animal thoroughly licked his mistress's hand and would have leapt up to give her fishy kisses had she not restrained him.

"A little water for you, Pompom, and then you go lie down."

After the dog was finished, she rinsed her hands in the ocean and looked at him. Alexander had to keep from snickering at the oh-so-fashionable Miss Farnham. Her hair was a tangled mess, red paint was streaked and smeared on her face like a doxie after a particularly busy night, and her lucent eyes were narrowed as she waited for him to explain how she was going to eat raw fish.

He felt almost…he hesitated because it was so odd as to defy description…almost lighthearted. Then her stomach growled in a most insistent fashion.

"Now, this is what we are going to do," Alexander said firmly. "Have you ever eaten oysters on the shell?"

She blinked. "Yes, of course."

"Then you know how it is done. You sip the oyster off its shell, taste it, chew a bit and then let it slide down your throat."

She looked down at the fish pieces on the bench.

"I generally eat my oysters off of fine china with a silver fork, a squeeze of lemon and plenty of champagne."

He scooped up some of the fish in his hand and said, "Close your eyes, Miss Farnham."

She did, sitting still as their boat rocked gently on the silent water.

"Now, imagine you are dining with friends. Perhaps it is after an evening at the theater. You have arranged for a late supper and there are oy—"

"There should be music." Her eyes popped open and she looked at him accusingly. "If we arranged for a late supper, we would arrange for musicians. You could hum, perhaps?"

"Close your eyes. Now."

"Oh, very well," she grumped, but she closed her eyes. And started humming.

"Miss Farnham."

One eye popped open.

"You cannot hum and eat at the same time. No, do not even think of trying it."

She sighed resignedly and settled herself back down, eyes closed, lips pursed.

"Open your mouth."

Her mouth with pink salve darkening her already luscious lips opened, just a sigh's worth, and Alex brought the fish to her lips. She nibbled it off his fingers, swallowing rapidly, then her eyes flew open and she put her hand over her mouth.

"Daphne! What is your favorite color?" he barked.

"Pink! Oh, I need some water!"

He gave her the flask and she swallowed, and while she looked a bit pale, she kept her stomach's contents intact. His distracting question had done its job.

She took a deep breath. "I did it, Doctor. I ate the—"

"Do not say it, do not think about it."

"It was not so bad. We may be onto something here."

"No one is going to eat raw fish if they can possibly help it, Miss Farnham. Now, close your eyes."

She did, obediently opening her mouth like a fledgling in the nest, and he fed her more tidbits. His fingers brushed against her moist lips as she took the food from him, her warm breath caressing his sensitive finger tips. Now he was trying not to think about it, what it felt like to have this beautiful woman take his fingers into her mouth, lightly sucking at them as she pulled in the firm, salty morsels, her delicate throat working to swallow, her eyes closed and an intense look of concentration on her sweat-dewed brow.

"One—" He cleared his throat and tried to speak again. "One moment, please—no, do not open your eyes!"

He grabbed his coat and pulled it across his lap, even though

the day was hot and growing hotter. The last thing he

needed was for her to open her eyes and see him sitting inches away with his compass pointing north.

"What are you thinking about, Doctor?"

"Involuntary responses."

He managed to cram more fish into Miss Farnham, then ate some himself. It was far from the worst thing he'd ever eaten, and it did the trick, making his body behave. It wasn't enough to satisfy, but it was enough to let him focus on bending the hairpins into hooks and setting out with bait fish to catch something more substantial for their supper.

"If you would stop twitching, I could do this more easily."

She stopped her squirming on the seat and sighed. "I am sorry, but I am not used to sleeping in my corset and now…" She rolled her shoulders and frowned. "It is not comfortable. I am itching."

He stopped what he was doing. The sun beat down full on them, and it was unlikely he'd catch more fish in the heat of the day. Better to try again late in the afternoon when the sun was setting. For now, it made more sense to have shade to rest in during the hottest part of the day, and to give Miss Farnham some relief. He needed to keep her out of the sun as much as possible. Her skin was not leathery like his from exposure to the elements, hers was soft, and white, and so delicate he could see the tracery of veins in her neck where her dress was torn and her skin showed through above her shift—

"Dr. Murray? Are you going to help me out of my clothes like you did on the *Magpie*?"

He put up his line and said, "Take off your hat and turn around."

She did, and Alexander began to undo the tapes of her dress.

"You will want to put your dress or some other garment

back on when I am finished, otherwise you will be sunburned."

"My night rail has been drying in the sunshine. I could put that on."

He made a noise of assent as he worked on the corset strings, knotted and stiff from their soaking. He did not want to cut them, knowing they might need the string, so it took longer than he wanted, his fingers brushing against the fine linen of her shift, the skin beneath it warm and rosy with health. She had a tiny mole just beneath her shoulder blade, which made him wonder if there were other interesting marks on her body. At that point, the knot came unraveled and he loosened the strings while she took a deep breath.

"That feels so good."

She arched her back and stretched, and he looked steadfastly out to sea, trying to think of the woman with him as just another collection of skin and sinew, bone and organ, no different from any other human he'd had his hands on over the years.

It wasn't working. Here he was, in the middle of the ocean, and his unruly body was sending him urgent messages. He knew why, he'd seen it before with men after battle. When you come close to death, there is a drive to procreate, to prove yourself alive. It was not that he was attracted to Miss Farnham *per se*, simply that she was here, with him, and she was the right gender to bring his more primitive urges to the fore. That's all.

"Do you know what would be perfect, Dr. Murray?"

Yes, as a matter of fact he did, he'd seen it demonstrated at a brothel in Naples…

"If you would scratch my back, because it is so itchy."

And that wasn't it. But it was probably a better idea than what he was fantasizing about, so he said, "Lean forward and I will loosen this some more."

She did, and he pushed the sides of her corset apart, the shift beneath looking bedraggled as it clung to her skin in the tropical heat. He lifted the fabric off her back and she sighed, and then she moaned in contentment as he lightly scratched at her delicate skin.

"I wish there was something I could do for you to return the favor, Dr. Murray."

Don't say it, do not say it, he told himself firmly.

"Thank you, Miss Farnham, but I am doing well." He'd stripped down to his shirt earlier, and she craned her head over her shoulder and said, "You men have such an easy time of it, your clothes are so simple compared to women's clothing.

"Of course, there is the dandy set," she went on. "George was like that. He would spend all morning with his valet, having his cravat tied in a style that would make a statement."

"What was the statement?"

She blinked and turned her body at an angle to look at him. "I do not understand."

"If someone spends an entire morning on something as frivolous as tying a neckcloth to make a statement, then what is the statement he is trying to make?"

She stared at him, opened her mouth, closed it, then opened it again.

"Perhaps the statement is that clothes make the man?"

"Do they, Miss Farnham?"

"They did for George. That is what he was known for— always being properly turned out and prepared for any social situation."

"Let me ask you a question. When you die, do you want people to remember your life by saying, 'She was always properly turned out and prepared for any social situation'?"

"I never thought about it."

"No, I imagine it is not a question that would arise in your social set."

"I think being shipwrecked is making you cranky, Dr. Murray."

"It does have that effect on me. Now, I suggest you try to rest during the midday heat. I will do the same, and then we will try to catch some supper."

"We?"

"This is a joint venture. You brought the equipment, I bring the skill."

He turned around to pull the canvas into a shape where it would shelter them from the sun without stifling them, while Miss Farnham made noises behind him that indicated she was wiggling out of her corset and putting on her night rail. When he turned back to her she looked modest enough, the long sleeved garment buttoned up to her chin, but the fabric was sheer, and he could see her shift beneath it, and beneath that, shadows of two nipples that he had not had the pleasure of seeing but if he had to guess, he would say they were rosy pink, just like the rest of her.

Focus, Alexander, he told himself. Letting his imagination run wild only made it worse.

"Give me your dress and I will put it on top of the canvas to dry out."

She passed him her dress, sadly faded and salt stained, and he spread it out to dry, pulled the canvas to the side for an impromptu awning and settled himself next to her. The dog wedged itself between them, which was probably just as well.

The heat of the day and the rocking of the boat combined with his restless night to send his eyes drifting shut. The warm body of the woman next to him, even with her cur separating them also relaxed him. Miss Farnham might not be the perfect companion in a shipwreck, but she was another soul adrift on the seas and her company was welcome. He had no desire to be like Robinson Crusoe, alone and friendless until he found his savage Friday.

"Whales."

He turned his head and saw her looking out from under the canvas. Her hands were clasped across her stomach, and a slight smile hovered around her lips, deepening her dimples.

"You see whales?"

"In the clouds. See, that one up there?" She pointed. "It looks like a whale, don't you think?"

He looked where she was pointing, over the edge of their toes. Her bare feet were alongside his, hers much daintier, the nails neat and smooth. Her foot had a delicate arch to it, and the toes looked…

If Miss Farnham's toes were looking like something he would want to nibble on, he needed to be sure he caught more fish this afternoon. "It looks like a cloud. Which it is."

She turned her head and looked at him. "Have you never lain in a meadow and imagined what clouds resemble?"

"There is no time in my life for such foolishness."

"Never? Not even when you were a boy?"

He wanted to tell her that some children grow up working and being useful, fishing for supper, weeding the kitchen garden, snaring rabbits. But there had been summer afternoons when he'd stretched out on the heather, looking at the blue sky above him and imagining the shapes passing overhead were ships and castles, dragons and mounted knights casting shadows on the hill.

"You have time now. What do you see in the clouds?"

He squinted and tried to remember what it felt like to see shapes up in the sky, rather than indicators of rough weather or smooth sailing.

"Sheep?"

There was a soft giggle to his right. Odd, that noise did not set his teeth on edge as it used to. It must be that he was now accustomed to it. Rather like becoming accustomed to a corn, or a callus.

"All clouds look like sheep, Doctor. Or sheep look like clouds. Surely you can do better than that."

He turned his head and looked at her. She was watching him, and her eyes were soft and dreamy, the thick lashes shading them from the bright sunlight.

Mere inches separated them, and all he would have to do is move his head slightly forward, maybe toss the dog over the side, angle his mouth over hers, and he would know if she tasted as luscious as she looked.

Madness. He was sunstruck and delirious from being out on the water to be even thinking such a thing now, with this woman.

Why the hell not? whispered a voice in his head. *Do you truly believe you'll be rescued?*

"I see a ship," he said abruptly. "A ship, in the clouds. See there? That one on the right? It looks like a sloop."

"What is a sloop? Did you serve on one?"

Instead of following his urges, Alexander told Miss Farnham stories of the ships he'd served on over the years, ever since becoming a surgeon's mate.

"So young to go to sea!" She watched him, her head propped up on her arm. "Was that your dream, in Scotland? To go to sea?"

"You knew I was from Scotland?"

"I can hear it every time you open your mouth. The way you roll your *rrrrr's* sounds...tasty."

Tasty—a most inappropriate word. He stopped looking at her and watched the clouds.

"My dream, Miss Farnham, was to become a physician."

"Why didn't you? You are a very clever man. I am sure

you could have read all the books they would give you to read."

"It takes more than a good mind to be a physician. It takes money to pay for schooling."

The scene in Janet Murray's neat kitchen was still fresh in his mind, his mother asking Fieldhouse for funds to send Alexander to Edinburgh.

"Funds for the boy's maintenance do not include schooling him at that level, madame. He is old enough now that he can apprentice himself to a surgeon or an apothecary and learn a suitable trade."

A bastard should not try to rise above his place in the world was the unspoken message.

"What about now, Dr. Murray? The war is over. You could go to school now and become a physician if you wished, couldn't you?"

"Aboard ship a surgeon also acts as a physician and an apothecary, through necessity. I physicked men and set their bones and dispensed drugs to them. It was my life for many years but now..." He let his eyes follow the fluffy shapes overhead, thinking that one looked like a dog chasing a ball. "Now I will set up a surgery on land."

"You sound certain we will make it to England."

"Of course we will. It will just take longer than anticipated."

He said this firmly, and with conviction, because that was what they both needed. He had survived other shipwrecks, they would survive this one. Both of them. "What of your dreams, Miss Farnham? Do you dream of hats and gloves and shoes?"

There was silence, and when he turned his head, she was looking up at the clouds.

"No. Hats and gloves and shoes are my life. They are not my dreams."

He looked at her but she had lain back down, her eyes were closed and the dog was cradled beneath her arm. He followed her example and closed his eyes, and they must have napped, for when he awoke the sunlight was coming off the canvas from a lower angle and the dog was barking.

"Look, Dr. Murray! A bird!"

Alexander sat up and saw her pointing over the bow. He was still muzzy headed from sleep and thought she meant a cloud, but the dog jumped up and barked again and he heard the cry of a seagull.

Seagulls meant land, and he moved so quickly the boat rocked dangerously, but he scanned the water looking for—

"There! That smudge on the horizon! Is that land?" she said

CHAPTER 7

"It is land, isn't it, Doctor?"

Daphne felt like laughing and clapping her hands. She was right to believe Dr. Murray would find a way to save them. He was so learned, he knew everything! Except how to find shapes in clouds. And he probably did not know how to tie his neckcloth into a Mathematical, but right now that was not as important as making it to land.

He was scanning the horizon, his hand over his eyes. A strong hand, she'd seen him bending the pins into hooks, a hand that was sure in its movements. A surgeon was like a carpenter or a cooper. He had to have capable hands and strong arms and shoulders for the work he did. The only other man she'd seen in his shirtsleeves was her late George. When she caught glimpses of his skin it had been the same pasty white as the fish pieces she'd eaten earlier, and instead of muscle there was…nothing. The idea of expending energy needed to build muscle would have made George shudder.

"Fitting into my coat in the morning is exhausting enough," he'd once said to her as he picked a minuscule piece of lint off his sleeve. "Do you have any idea, my dear Daphne, how hard it is for my valet to wedge me into it for the perfect fit?"

Daphne had sympathized since she was daily bullied by her dresser into a corset that would give her the shape gentlemen rhapsodized over. Truly, one had to suffer to be fashionable!

Dr. Murray really did not understand these things, but that was all right, because he thought about other things. Maybe there were some women who would want to be marooned with a handsome and entertaining fellow like George, but right now there was no one she would rather be with than dear old Dr. Murray. He knew how to fish with a hair net and signal with mirrors and perch off the bow of the ship. George would never have known how to do that!

Dr. Murray's face was shadowed by the growth of his beard, the hair glinting like a silvered fox's pelt in the sunlight dappling the water. It was a strong jaw beneath that stubble, and the column of his neck was as solid as the rest of him.

She swallowed and reached for her water flask. It certainly was warm during this part of the day!

He moved away toward the bow of their boat and she grabbed Pompom to keep the dog from following. He gazed out toward the dark line in the distance, following the seagull as it winged away from them.

"I believe you are correct, Miss Farnham. That looks like land."

"How will we make it there?"

He looked back at her and his eyes glowed in the sunlight. He did not smile at her, but his face was lighter, less strained.

"The current will carry us close enough that I can put the oars to use."

Daphne sat up straight, clutching Pompom on her lap.

"Are you sure?"

He shrugged, then looked back at the horizon. Was it her imagination, or was the line larger now, darker, more clearly defined?

"It is better to believe that will happen than to worry over what we cannot affect. In the meantime, we still have needs aboard this boat."

With renewed enthusiasm Daphne asked what she could do to help.

"I will prepare a line for you, Miss Farnham. Two fishermen are better than one."

She left her hat off as the sun was lower and she did not want her vision obscured. Dr. Murray needed her help, and she was going to be there for him. He thought she was useful. Or at least someone who brought useful items to a shipwreck.

"Be a good boy, Pompom, and Mummy and the nice doctor will catch you some supper."

She placed the dog in her valise, and he scratched around and grumbled as he tried to make himself a bed, finally throwing himself down with a heartfelt sigh.

When she looked up, he was watching her.

"Do you have indigestion, Doctor?"

"When you address your animal as if he were a baby it makes my stomach hurt."

"Oh. Would some of my ginger cure your pain?"

"A massive infusion of rum would cure this pain, but unfortunately that is not an option."

Poor Dr. Murray! Here he was doing so much to keep them alive and he was in pain. When they were on land she was going to make sure her father knew how much he had done for them. Papa would arrange a pension for the surgeon, and he could retire and rest after all his labors.

He prepared a line for her and put one of the small, glimmering fish from the bucket at the end of the line. Daphne winced, but she understood they needed to eat and the little fish would soon be gone.

"Make yourself comfortable in the bow, Miss Farnham. I will be here in the stern."

She made a cushion with her now-dry dress and set her valise next to her. Pompom poked his head out, realized there was no food or entertainment for him, and went back to sleep.

"What do I do? How will I catch a fish?".

"You never fished?"

Daphne giggled at the idea.

"Oh, Doctor, I can just imagine what my governess would say if I came in browned from the sun and smelling of fish. And I had no proper clothing for fishing." She frowned. "What does one wear for fishing? A morning dress? A walking dress?"

"One wears old clothes, clothing that can handle some soaking and contact with fish."

"Right there I would be handicapped. My maid always whisked my clothing away when it was worn, or past its season." She leaned closer to him. "Confidentially, I think she was selling the dresses as soon as she could."

He turned his head from where he was tying his line and looked at her. "You did not mind your maid taking your clothes and selling them that way? One could say it was close to theft if you did not give them to her. People are transported for stealing a kerchief, much less a gown."

Daphne blinked at him. "If Hattie did not sell my clothes, where would she find extra funds to support her mother and sister? Her sister was run over by a cart and has difficulty walking."

"Couldn't you pay her a higher salary?"

"My father would never agree to such a thing, and I could not simply give her money from my own purse. Hattie has her pride. It is the customary arrangement for women in her position to dispose of their mistresses' clothing when it is worn. This way she could sell it and earn more money."

Dr. Murray watched her for a moment longer as if she were some exotic species he had never encountered before. And perhaps he never had. By his own acknowledgment he admitted he was not used to drawing rooms or society or what occurred in the homes of the gentry.

The sun was much lower now, and it was cooler on the water without the rays beating down full on them. Daphne dropped her line over the side, maintaining a tight grip on it.

"If you feel a tug on your line, Miss Farnham, do not yank on it. Let the fish grab the hook firmly before giving the line a steady pull."

"Are you sure I can do this, Doctor?"

"I am sure you are going to try."

Daphne bit her lip, adjusted herself on the seat and watched her line. It floated in the water, nothing happening around it, but if he said she should fish, she was going to do her best.

It soon became apparent fishing was a dreadful bore.

"Do you think we will be at that island by tomorrow? What kind of towns will there be? I wonder if I can buy some shoes? Shoes would be nice. Oooh, maybe it is a French island and they will have the latest fashion journals from Paris! Maybe a hat, too, somethi—"

"Miss Farnham."

"Yes?"

"Cease chattering," he said mildly. "You will disturb the fish."

He wasn't watching her as he said this, concentrating on

watching his line in the water. So he didn't see her make a face at his back as she went back to being unutterably bored. She feared she would nod off sitting there with her line in her hand, but her fishing companion said something beneath his breath and moved back to the bait bucket.

"What happened?"

"It took my bait, but not the hook."

"You were hoodwinked by a fish?"

"Do not sound so surprised. It has happened to wiser men."

He re-baited his hook, returned to his seat, and silence reigned again. She looked to the horizon and the line looked darker, and longer. Perhaps there would be theaters at that island. Even if a play was in French she could still enjoy it, because after all, one did not go to the theater to watch a play, one went to the theater to be watched and commented upon. But who would escort her to the theater? The very idea of Dr. Murray in his rumpled coat and gray hairs escorting her made her giggle, a sound quickly stifled so she would not annoy him again, although why he thought her conversation would disturb anythi—

"*Eep!*" Daphne grabbed her line and held on with both hands. "Doctor! Something is happening!"

He rushed over and the rocking of the craft nearly caused her to lose her grip, but she clung to her line and braced her feet against the side of the boat.

"You've caught something."

"What do I do?"

"Do not panic and do not let go. Here, let me help."

He seated himself behind her and put his arms around her, grabbing hold of her wrist with one hand to brace it, while the other hand moved in front of where she gripped the line and held on. Daphne immediately felt the reassurance of his strength added to hers and anchoring them.

"You won't escape, fish!"

"That's the spirit, Miss Farnham, show him you are more intelligent than he is," he said right next to her ear. "Now, let me help you play him in."

Daphne concentrated, but when Dr. Murray shifted forward, his bristled cheek brushed against hers and she tried hard not to jump at the contact. The fish was important, but she was vividly aware of the strong arms wrapped about her, his body pressed to hers. He was still in his shirt-sleeves, and the thin layer of linen allowed her to feel the muscles of his chest against her back, her own body separated from his only by the material of her chemise and the night rail. His body was sun-warmed and his head blocked some of the light, shading her in the late afternoon.

Neither of them smelled fresh at this point but rather than be offended, Daphne found his scent oddly stimulating. It wasn't sweet like George's cologne, but smelled musky and male and she wanted to wiggle back farther into his lap, much as Pompom enjoyed doing in hers.

But there were fish to catch. Dr. Murray was speaking in low tones, his Scots burr more pronounced as he instructed her.

"Follow my lead. When I begin to pull, exert pressure and pull back with me, but in a steady movement, not jerkily. Be prepared to play out the line if I tell you."

"Wouldn't it be better for me to pass you the line?" she whispered, not wanting to alert the canny fish to their plans.

"Too much risk of losing him. This is your catch, Miss Farnham. You will bring him in."

His matter-of-fact voice soothed her, and she sat up a bit straighter, basking in the confidence he displayed in her abilities. It also moved her a fraction away from his distracting torso and allowed her to concentrate.

Dr. Murray's hand covered hers, his a much richer color,

and she felt calluses and roughness from where he'd gripped saws and instruments and the tools of his trade over many years. The only other times she'd felt a man's hand in hers, the hand had been properly gloved or smoothly pampered and manicured, not the sinewy hand of someone who worked hard at his craft.

His other hand was over her wrist.

"Your pulse is racing."

He played out some of the line as he said this, and Daphne felt the tug of the sea creature, unseen beneath the waves, but beginning to fight back against the humans.

"It is so exciting!" she said in a low voice. "I am catching a fish!"

"Do not fry your fish before it is caught. We still must be patient, and calm."

Daphne nodded once, but even as she followed his lead and began to pull on the line, she wondered what it would take for Dr. Murray to lose his composure and not be so calm and unruffled.

"Now, Miss Farnham, we are going to bring this laddie closer."

He began pulling on the line with a steady but gentle pressure and she worked with him. The fish fought back but they held on, even though the line cut into her hands and she knew she would not be able to hold the sea creature without assistance.

"Be ready. Whatever we've landed may be armed with sharp teeth. I need to take over at this point and you should slip back in the boat."

"What can I do?"

"I'll take the line, you hold my knife."

He released her wrist, and one-handed opened his clasp knife and passed it to her, and Daphne held on to it with a firm grip. Pompom poked his head up to see what the excitement was, and she set down the knife and with her free hand pushed him back into the bag and latched it—the pup would be safe in there for a few minutes, and not able to attack—or be attacked by—their supper.

Dr. Murray concentrated, pulling it in, his hands steady, and she saw a flash of movement beneath the surface.

"Now, Daphne!"

He pulled the line straight up and a fish jerked at the end of it, thrashing and bobbing in the air. Dr. Murray tossed it into the boat and said, "The knife!"

She passed him the knife, handle first, and he did something to the fish that stopped it from thrashing. She swallowed, but she could not keep the pride from her voice.

"My fish! What have I caught?"

He picked it up and put it on the seat and studied it. The fish was about eighteen inches long, its body an iridescent blue-green on the upper part, the lower body silver. It had spots on its side, splashes of bronze that gave it a festive appearance.

"I am no expert, but I would guess this is a member of the mackerel family."

She clapped her hands and laughed. "I caught a mackerel! I don't know anyone who has ever done that!"

"If you ever go fishing off of Cornwall you might catch another," the surgeon acknowledged. "Assuming when you return to Britain you wish to continue being a fisherwoman."

"It is a useful skill," Daphne said, hugging herself with glee. "Because of my efforts we will not go hungry tonight."

Dr. Murray looked at her and it was the strangest thing. He did not smile, she knew what a smile looked like, but nonetheless she knew he was smiling. At her.

It made her stomach flutter in a way that had nothing to do with the idea of eating raw fish again.

"Well done, Miss Farnham. Now you can tell fish stories at supper with the best of them."

She remembered when men dining with her father had told stories of the trout and salmon they'd fished for.

"Wait, before you cut it." She took her hands and put them on each end of the fish, measuring it, then held her hands up to see how far apart they were. "I want to remember how big this mackerel is for the retelling."

"I find that the size of the fish in question tends to expand over the telling."

"I have no need to exaggerate," Daphne said loftily. "This is a noteworthy fish all on its own."

There was a muffled noise from her valise and she remembered the third member of the crew and released her dog, who jumped over to sniff at the new item.

"Keep the animal away and I will clean this for our supper."

"I wish I knew how to do that."

Dr. Murray looked up from where his knife was poised over the mackerel, his eyebrows raised.

"You want to clean fish?"

"It is my fish. I caught it. I should know how to clean and prepare it."

"An admirable attitude. For now though it is better if I do it given our primitive facilities."

She was relieved but meant what she said. While the idea of cleaning a smelly, slimy, cold dead fish did not appeal to her, she enjoyed learning new things and if she was ever shipwrecked again it might not be with someone as knowledgeable as Dr. Murray and then who would people look to for useful skills? Daphne Farnham, that's who!

So she tucked her knees up beneath her chin and watched, humming to herself.

"Musical accompaniment with dinner, Miss Farnham?"

"I find that singing makes the time pass, Doctor. Not gloomy songs, but cheerful ones. Don't you know any songs? Isn't there some Scotsman named Brown, or Bowen who wrote some songs?"

He stopped cleaning the fish and looked at her with an expression of deep pain.

"Might you be referring to Rabbie Burns, the bard of Scotland?"

Daphne thought about it for a moment.

"That sounds right. He wrote a song about a red rose, and one about a hag." Her brow scrunched. "Though why someone would want to write a song about a hag is beyond me."

He closed his eyes, then opened them and looked at her.

"Not a hag, Miss Farnham, a haggis. A haggis is a dish enjoyed by the people of Scotland."

"Really? What is it?"

Dr. Murray described, with loving detail, the inner workings of the mysterious haggis. Daphne looked at him, speechless for a long moment.

"I would think raw fish a treat after that!"

He just shook his head and went back to the fish.

"Do you know the rose song?"

"'*My Love is like a Red, Red Rose*'? Yes, I know it."

"Will you sing it?"

"No, I will not," he said shortly.

Daphne tilted her head and rested it on her pulled up knees. She knew it was a most unladylike pose, but she was feeling cramped from being in the boat and it felt comfortable. And who would see her, except Dr. Murray, Pompom and the stray bird winging overhead.

"Why not?"

"It is a love song, Miss Farnham." He stopped cleaning the fish and looked at her. "There is a Rabbie Burns song I will sing for you, one more appropriate for—for our circumstances, you and I being who we are."

He set aside the knife and looked at her and started to sing. He had a pleasant voice, a baritone that did not hurt the ears. The song's lyrics were hard to understand in the Scots dialect, but she picked up on the repeating line, *"For a' that."*

She looked at him when he was done. He gazed at her a moment longer, and then went back to cleaning her fish for her.

"That's not a fun song," Daphne said in a low voice. She didn't know why it bothered her that he would not sing the rose song, but it did bother her. Maybe there was someone else he was willing to sing it to. Some girl who was clever. Or who knew already how to catch and clean a fish.

She wasn't feeling very pretty right now. Maybe this other girl, the Scottish girl, was prettier than her. For a time, Daphne had forgotten it was important to be pretty, she was so caught up in being useful.

What did it matter? He was only Dr. Murray, not somebody important. Of course, he was important now, here in this boat, but he would not be anybody in London. No one would bury him beneath invitations to the best dinner parties. No one would imitate his style of boots or repeat a witticism he made about another dinner guest.

She did not care that maybe there was some young lady who'd heard him sing a song more pleasant than a ditty about men being men and laughing at their betters or something equally uninteresting and incomprehensible.

"Now it is your turn."

Daphne raised her head, looked at the fish guts on the bench and swallowed.

"No, not your turn to clean the fish, your turn to sing."

He checked the offal for bones, then tossed the mess to the dog, who was thrilled with this treat.

"And after you sing for your supper, we will enjoy this fine mackerel you caught."

"Oh," Daphne said, scrunching her brow as she thought. She wasn't going to sing Dr. Murray a love song, not after he refused to sing one to her.

"I know! I will sing you a song that I learned from one of the sailors on the *Magpie*."

"Really? You intrigue me. Most of the ditties I've heard sailors sing aren't proper for young ladies to know."

Daphne giggled at the thought of singing an improper song to Dr. Murray. Her good humor restored, she said, "Please pass me the water flask. I will not take much, but I must drink some before I sing."

"I often find that drinking before I listen helps," he said, but did not take any of the water.

Daphne smoothed down the fabric over her legs and thought for a moment.

"Jacob was an American who signed on with the *Magpie* after the war, and he called this *'The Liberty Song.'*" She hummed for a moment and then began to sing:

——

"Come, join hand in hand, brave Americans all,
And rouse your bold hearts at fair Liberty's call;
No tyrannous acts shall suppress your just claim, Or stain with
dishonor America's name."

——

Daphne sang two verses and the chorus before she realized Dr. Murray was staring at her, and the only way to describe the expression on his face—there was no way to describe the expression on his face. She'd never seen anything quite like it before.

"There are more verses," she said helpfully.

"Miss Farnham!" He shook his head and started again. "Miss Farnham, that was the most treasonous piece of trash I have ever heard. Do you know what melody that is? *Heart of Oak! Heart of Oak*, Miss Farnham! I implore you, never, ever sing those lyrics around a navy man, for I could not answer for the consequences if you do."

"Oh!" Daphne put her hand over her mouth, her heart plummeting. "Why would Jacob teach me that song then, knowing I am an Englishwoman? Was he trying to make me look stupid?"

Dr. Murray looked down at the bottom of the boat where befouled water lapped back and forth, then at her.

"No, I'm sure he was only attempting to share with you something dear to his heart as a Yankee. They are a strange race, and he likely did not consider how it would appear."

He must have seen something in her face, because he wiped off his knife and closed it. He clasped his hands together, his forearms on his knees and he leaned forward.

"Who tells you that you are stupid?"

Daphne didn't want to say anything. What good would it do?

But Dr. Murray sat there, patiently waiting for her answer.

She mumbled something.

"I could not understand that, Miss Farnham."

"People. I hear people say it is a good thing I am pretty and rich, because I am very stupid."

He did not say anything, and she raised her head. "You think it, too, don't you? Do not deny it."

He looked away at the island, then back at her.

"I have spent two days with you in this boat. You are not

stupid. You are far too trusting, however. You seem to believe everything men tell you."

"Why would they lie to me?" she said in confusion.

"Have you not been told that 'Men were deceivers ever'? That's from Shakespeare, I did not just make that up. When men tell you something, you should be a touch more hesitant to believe them."

"What about you?"

"I will not deceive you. In addition," he said, passing her a piece of fish, "you are a fast learner and are becoming a useful person. I know some extremely intelligent men who are totally useless."

"Truly?"

"Truly," he said firmly. "They think deep thoughts but cannot put those thoughts into action, or even write about them in a coherent fashion so others may learn from them. What good are they? Far better if they spent their time catching fish, or matching hats to ensembles."

Daphne giggled, and took the fish from his warm fingers. She did not need help to eat it this time. Dr. Murray's eyes glowed almost golden in the afternoon light. He could be a nice man when he set out to be pleasant.

"You need a wife, Dr. Murray."

He choked on the piece of fish he was eating and she passed him the water flask.

"Are you volunteering for the position?"

She nearly choked on her own supper.

"Oh no, I meant you need someone older, someone closer to your age."

He looked at her for a moment and appeared about to comment, then stopped. He chewed a bit more fish and so did she. The mackerel had a different taste from the little sardinelike fish. Less oily. Eating raw fish might catch on if she could figure out the best way to serve it, which probably would not be in a boat with a smelly wet dog.

She picked up Pompom out of the bottom of the boat so he'd dry off, setting him atop the canvas. He perched there like a figurehead, staring out to sea, sometimes barking if a seagull flew by.

"A wife. Odd you should mention that, Miss Farnham. I have been thinking it is time I married."

"Really?"

"Indeed. The war is over, and I am returning to England. It seems like a reasonable thing to do."

He ate some more fish, then looked at her.

"Why do you think I need a wife?"

"Oh." Daphne thought for a moment. The idea of Dr. Murray taking a wife had just popped out of her mouth, but now that she thought about it, she was not as excited by the idea. He deserved just the right kind of woman. Someone useful, but it wasn't all he needed.

"If you had a wife, she would help you dress in the morning so you would look like a successful and prosperous man."

"A good valet could do that for me."

That was true. She took another piece of mackerel and thought about it.

"A wife would make your home comfortable for you, and entertain your friends and family, and pick out the right furnishings and wall coverings."

"That sounds expensive," he mused. "Perhaps I am better off just renting rooms. And hiring a valet."

"There are other things a wife could do for you, Doctor." Daphne said, exasperated. She thought he was brighter than this. But the man just sat there, sucking on a fish bone, and waiting for her to explain. "Don't you want children? And companionship? Your valet couldn't do that for you."

He looked ready to argue the point, but instead nodded sagely. "You are correct. A valet could not supply me with children."

"Or companionship."

"I don't know about that. Perhaps he would be a good conversationalist. A chess player would be appreciated."

"Not that kind of companionship, the kind of companionship that leads to children!" She peered at him in the soft light as twilight crept over the water. "Are you bamming me?"

"Perhaps, just a wee bit, Miss Farnham."

She was thunderstruck. Dr. Murray was teasing her? That did not sound like him at all.

"You may be onto something. I will consider what you say, though I admit I have not had good luck finding ladies to marry me."

"Really?" Here was a side of the doctor she never expected. But then, it was hard for her to imagine the man courting someone. Who would want to marry a gentleman who never smiled?

"Who were these ladies?"

"One was a young lady who rejected my proposal just a few months ago."

"She must not be intelligent, to reject a proposal from you."

"Your loyalty touches me, Miss Farnham. In actuality she was a bright young lady, but for some reason she preferred a pirate to a surgeon."

"Oh. That makes sense."

"It does?"

"Certainly," She said, tossing a piece of fish to Pompom, who caught it mid-air. "I imagine if she chose this pirate he did not just carry her off like booty. He offered the attractions of adventure and excitement, and I would also guess he presented a dashing appearance. She probably saw herself as Medora to his Conrad."

"You have read Byron's *Corsair*?"

Daphne giggled, covering her mouth with her hand.

"My father doesn't know I did, for he would forbid it. The book was all the rage last year and all the fashionable people claimed to have read it. I *did* read it and found it to be lively in parts, not so much fun in other parts."

"What else do you like to read?"

"You think this a terrible waste of time, but I enjoy reading novels. I know there is no value to them, but just think—for a few hours you are caught up in an adventure! You experience danger, and turmoil, and love, all from the safety of your own armchair. Do you ever read novels, Doctor?"

"I read journals, Miss Farnham, and exchange letters with other surgeons about situations they encounter, or new treatments they are exploring. And I do enjoy good poetry on a long evening."

"See there, we do have something in common," Daphne said. "We both like poetry. Who would have thought that?"

The sun was sinking now, and she looked out toward the line of land, but could no longer distinguish it from the surrounding water.

"Do you think we will reach that land tomorrow?"

He tapped the water butt with his foot and frowned at the sound. "We will deal with that tomorrow. For now, wash up and see to your animal, and we should rest."

Daphne did as he instructed, and once again the doctor pulled her alongside him to share his warmth and help cushion her as she slept. She snuggled next to him, Pompom wedging himself into a little nest of his own making among their limbs.

"This is nice," she murmured as her eyes drifted shut. "Goodnight, Doctor."

"Good night, Miss Farnham."

His voice rumbled against her ear where it rested on his chest. She knew tomorrow could bring more problems and even disaster, but at this moment she felt safe and secure in the good doctor's arms, and that was enough for now.

CHAPTER 8

*I*t was clear the next morning that land was in sight and the ocean was carrying them closer to it.

Alexander studied it as well as he could without a spyglass or even a true knowledge of navigation. While the island promised safety, the issue would be arriving in one piece. Most of the islands in these waters were surrounded by coral reefs. Even with its shallow draft their boat risked being torn up, dashing them into the ocean.

There was no sign of smoke rising over the trees indicating civilization. They might be looking at an undeveloped area, but the odds were just as strong the island was empty of inhabitants.

No fish were caught that morning. Daphne Farnham shared her small allotment of water with the dog when she thought Alexander wasn't watching, but even so the animal appeared lethargic and whined at intervals. It grated on his nerves, but he couldn't pitch the animal over the side. That would make Miss Farnham hysterical. And they might yet need the dog for sustenance.

Miss Farnham herself was looking far from the ideal of

English womanhood she'd been a few days back. Despite their best efforts, her nose was peeling. Her hair hung in roughly braided lanks in need of a good scrubbing, and there were patches of sweat darkening her salt-stained and faded dress.

He didn't need a mirror to show him he wasn't in any better shape. His face itched constantly from the beard growing in, and even his toughened skin burned. He could smell himself, though Miss Farnham had been too polite to remark on it, and the dog either didn't care or enjoyed the effluvia.

And yet, despite all these travails, Daphne Farnham's eyes were bright, her face full of belief he would keep them safe.

She had no way of knowing just how scared he was.

"What are you thinking about, Doctor?"

"The tide is carrying us to that island. We must prepare for a rough landing."

"What do you mean?"

He looked around at their scant supplies.

"My medical chest will float. I will attach lines to it, and if we capsize, grab onto it. Hold on to it and kick to shore. I can try to assist you, but we could be separated by the surf. As long as you have the chest and keep kicking, you will make it to the beach."

"What about Pompom?"

"He can take his chances in the surf."

"No." Her spine straightened and her jaw tightened. He saw a resolution in her gaze that had not been there before.

"I will not leave my Pompom to take his chances. I will wrap him up inside my shawl, up at my shoulder. If my head is above water, his will be also."

"He is a liability, and the extra fabric will weigh you down. You cannot concentrate on saving yourself if you try to save the dog."

"Pompom comes with me."

"I could throw him over the side now," Alexander said quietly.

"Only if you are prepared to see me follow right behind him."

She said this just as quietly, just as firmly. The giggling girl who stared at him worshipfully was gone, and the woman whose unwavering blue gaze reflected the water around them was a different person, one who would risk everything for a companion—even an animal companion.

For a brief moment he wondered what it would be like if she cared about him as much as she cared for that animal. A short time ago he would not have thought her capable of such depth of feeling and commitment, but he'd gotten to know Daphne Farnham better through their adventure. She would not back down on this, and there was no way he could follow through on his threat without knocking her unconscious.

The hours dragged on, the two of them not speaking any more than necessary. Alexander tipped the last of the water from the butt into the flask, giving it to Daphne to drink.

"Do not share it with your dog."

She ignored him, but only gave the dog a splash from her hand. Then she took a swallow and passed the flask back to him.

"You drink it," he rasped through lips cracked and stinging from the salt spray.

"If you do not drink some yourself, Doctor, you will not have enough strength to do what you need to do. We are in this together—all three of us."

He took the flask from her and tipped his head back. The water tasted like scum from being stored for so long and from the heat of the water butt.

They lay back in the boat beneath their canvas cover,

conserving their energy. The dog rested atop Miss Farnham's stomach, and her hand periodically would stroke the animal, soothing him.

Alexander lifted his head to check that they were still drifting in toward the island, but sometime after midday he saw what he'd feared.

"What is it?" She propped herself up on an elbow, shading her eyes and gazing toward their destination, shimmering now on the horizon like a green mirage. They were close enough that he could see hills rising out of the tree line, but there was still no smoke, no sign of humans, no hope of rescue.

"The tide is turning. I am going to row and bring us closer." "How can I help? Can I row also?"

He shook his head. "If you have never done it before, it will slow us down. We can be more effective if I row. Give me your night rail."

Without questioning why, she passed him the delicate fabric, wincing when he grabbed it at the neck and tore it straight down the middle.

"Now I could use your assistance. Wrap the cloth around my hands, each piece, and tie it off."

She put the dog down and it lay there, silently watching them, then closed its eyes. She sat across from him and took Alexander's hand in hers. Her hand was browned now, the knuckles skinned, the once smoothly manicured nails broken and ragged. Her head bent over as she began her task and Alex's other hand rose up and rested on her head for a moment, the hair sunwarmed beneath his fingers. She stopped and gazed into his eyes. Two lines were furrowing between her brows, and he moved his hand down, smoothing them with his thumb.

"No fretting, Miss Farnham. You will give yourself wrinkles. What a fashion disaster that would be."

"I did not think you cared for fashion."

"I do not. You, however, are in my care, and a wrinkle would distress you."

She favored him with one of her brilliant smiles, and he did not tell her that it brought out lines at the corners of her eyes. Or that he found those lines…endearing was not the right word, was it? Why would the sight of Miss Farnham looking more like a real woman and less like a porcelain fashion doll gladden his heart?

Why would the sight of her smiling at him tempt Alexander to lean forward and put his lips on hers?

He did not have long to ponder this conundrum, for her glance shifted.

"The seagulls are more distant, Doctor. We must hurry."

She bent to her task and finished wrapping his hands, tearing the end of the cloth to make a knot. She switched places with him and Alexander removed his coat, rolled up his sleeves and grasped the oars.

"You sit at the tiller and keep me on course."

"Aye, aye, Captain," she said cheekily, taking her place with her dog in her lap.

She watched while he rowed, sometimes directing him to starboard, or to larboard, to keep them aimed for the beach that he could see when he glanced over his shoulder. As they drew closer, she took her shawl and made a sling, putting the animal inside it, his head at her shoulder.

His shoulders burned, the overworked muscles protesting each sweep of the oars, but he kept up a steady rhythm until he could hear the pounding of the surf over the pounding of the blood in his ears.

"We are almost there!" she called out, "Not too much farther now, Do—"

The crash of the boat hitting the reef ended her sentence on a scream. Alexander whipped around and grabbed

Daphne's skirt just as her momentum was about to pitch her over the side, dashing her onto the sharp coral. He yanked her back and the cloth tore, but he still managed to pull her in, holding her tight as the boat shuddered from the impact.

Water poured in through the gashed hull.

The dog was barking but stopped at a sharp command from its mistress. Alexander looked at the two of them watching him for direction on what to do next. There was no choice.

"Look there—that beach ahead. Keep kicking your legs and you will make it."

He did not mention sharks, or rays, or riptides, or any of the other disasters that could occur in the short span of distance between the boat and shore. He had to concentrate on her landing in one piece and the faster she could swim there, the sooner that would happen.

She looked at him, her eyes wide, but only said, "Yes, Dr. Murray."

"Remember," he said in a gentler voice, "the chest will keep you afloat."

The chest was already floating in the seawater rushing in. In a moment she'd be stepping up and out of the boat as it sank lower.

"Go now, Daphne."

She seemed startled by his use of her name, and then she startled him by impulsively leaning forward and hugging him, earning a protesting yip from the dog squished between them.

"I will see you ashore, Doctor."

"Yes. Yes, you will."

Alexander went over the side, watching as she grabbed hold of the lines, holding onto the chest, her dog watching him from over her shoulder.

"Kick now, kick for shore." Alex grabbed hold of the

water butt floating empty beside him, and staying behind her, occasionally calling out encouragement to her. She was fine initially, but her strength began to flag. "Kick, Daphne, kick, blast you!"

Where cajoling was failing, his rough exhortation gave her a boost.

"Now, hold the chest! Let it carry you through the surf!" he called hoarsely, his voice almost gone. He'd swallowed too much water yelling and trying to keep her moving, and he saw black flashes at the edge of his vision.

If he could help her through the surf, she would be safe on land. That was all that mattered. She was too far ahead to hear him now, and he strained to watch, his grip slipping on the wet wood of the water butt. He watched, his heart in his throat as the surf tossed her and the chest, but then he blinked water out of his stinging eyes.

She was on the beach. Not moving.

"Daphne," he whispered, releasing his hold on the wooden barrel and kicking for shore. Just before the blackness overtook him, he had his last vision of her lying there, her hand stretched out to him like a silent supplicant.

CHAPTER 9

"I am not dead."

The words came out in a cracked whisper, but the act of saying them—and the pain involved in the effort—was empirical evidence Alexander Murray was still among the living.

"Dr. Murray! Are you awake now?"

He did not open his eyes, that would take too much effort. Hearing Daphne Farnham's voice eased the tension from his frame, and he lay there, silently thanking whatever powers watched over silly girls and grizzled surgeons.

He heard a repetitive yipping noise and realized the animal, too, had survived. He did not give thanks for that.

A shadow fell over his face and he felt a thump as a body settled nearby. Alex cracked one eye open, blinking at the soreness of its salt-crusted condition, amazed he still had enough water in his body to produce the resulting tearing.

"Are you weeping for joy that we're safe and not drowned?"

"No. Eyes hurt," he rasped. Her voice did not sound nearly as bad as his. "Water?"

"Yes! I found a shallow pool in a rock. Maybe it rained here. Can you walk?"

For a drink of fresh water Alexander would crawl if he had to. Since he preferred to walk under his own power, he sat up. His shirt was in tatters, pieces of linen fluttering like ribbons in the island breeze and his trousers were torn down one leg that he could see. He worked his gummy eyelids open and examined his companion.

Miss Farnham was not in much better shape. Her dress was missing a sleeve, and the other had a huge hole gaping under her arm. Without her stays, what remained of the dress hung oddly. Her hair was a curly bush sticking out in all directions and falling over her eyes. She was sitting on her knees on the sand, bare feet tucked beneath her, watching him with concern.

The only one of them who looked himself was the dog, who sniffed at Alexander's foot.

"Do you need assistance walking, Dr. Murray?"

"Try on my own first. Are you injured?"

She tried to look over her shoulder where her sleeve had been attached.

"I am scraped, I think. A slight headache, but the water helped. And I am hungry," she said as her stomach made a noise punctuating the sentence.

"My case, did it survive?"

"Yes!" she said brightly. "It is over under that tree."

She pointed toward a palm and there was his medical chest, and the sight of the familiar box eased something inside of him. Just knowing he had it with him gave him a feeling that he could weather any disaster.

Miss Farnham stood and walked toward the trees.

"Come this way, and I will show you the pool."

Alexander pushed himself to his feet, not without effort. The shirt was a loss, but he could use the linen for other purposes, so he pulled it over his head, wincing as the cloth chafed against his own scrapes and abrasions.

The pool was a shallow depression in the rocks, fed by a trickle of water from the hills. It was shaded by the surrounding trees and a heavy growth of ferns, and after he brushed the leaves off the surface Alexander stuck his face directly into the water, letting it soak into his salted pores and his hair as he gulped it down.

He pulled himself back from drinking too much, stopping before he became ill. When he brushed his wet hair back from his forehead, she was staring at him, her mouth agape.

"What?"

"You!" She pointed an accusing finger at him. "You are not old!"

"Were you knocked on the head when you were washed ashore? That statement makes no sense at all."

She ignored that, and was looking at him, at his bare torso, and her red face reflected anger and…something else.

"You are not old," she said again. "Your belly, it is not all wrinkled and saggy, it is…"

"Yes?" Now he was intrigued. He did not know where the conversation was going, but it was a glimpse into the strange workings of Daphne Farnham's mind, and that at least had entertainment value.

"It is firm, and there are muscles, and…" She stopped, flustered and at a loss for words.

"Miss Farnham, I beg you, spare my blushes," he murmured as he wiped his face with his shirt.

"You do not understand!" She stamped her bare foot on the ground in frustration. "When you were old Dr. Murray it was different. I could think of you like an…an uncle, or a, I do not know what! But now, it is all changed!"

"I am devastated to be such a disappointment to you. I cannot do anything about my age, but if it is any comfort to you, I feel older by the minute. And I feel positively ancient next to you."

"That's not good enough," she muttered. "We must do something about this."

She walked off, still talking to herself.

Alex almost called her to return, but he trusted even Daphne Farnham could not find trouble just a few feet from where he stood. He took advantage of the water in the rock pool to wash himself and thought about their current situation.

It was amazing how life could put things in perspective. After you have contemplated dying of thirst and exposure in the middle of the Atlantic Ocean, a tropical island, deserted or not, is a paradise by comparison. He and Miss Farnham appeared to be whole and relatively unscathed. There were birds here, and birds meant meat and eggs. He would build a fire. There was, most importantly, fresh water.

It could be much, much worse.

Alex hummed a Rabbie Burns melody to himself as he scrubbed his arms at the edge of the pool. When she returned, she stopped and whirled about at the sight of him and presented her back.

"This is terrible," she said, throwing up her hands in the air.

"This changes everything! We slept together!"

"We were on a boat in the middle of the Atlantic Ocean."

He could see her arms were crossed in front of her, her back stiff.

"Miss Farnham, we are both the victims here of false assumptions."

She did not turn around, but she stopped tapping her bare foot on the ground. "How so?"

"Think about it. You looked at me, and saw what you wanted to see, and perhaps what you expected to see. An elderly man. You made that assumption based on my white hairs."

"And on your demeanor." She sniffed, giving him a glance over her shoulder.

"I will grant you my demeanor may seem to you to carry a certain gravitas not found with many of your contemporaries. How old are you, anyway? Eighteen?"

She turned around and a smile tugged at the corners of her mouth. "I am twenty-five years old."

He stopped still. "You are that old?" She did not appear offended at his blunt assessment.

"I suppose you were fooled by my appearance, and by my demeanor. I do not have any—what was that word?"

"Gravitas."

"Yes. I am not a grumpy, dowdy, stick-in-the-mud who never smiles. But how does that make us both victims of false impressions?"

"You looked at me and saw a crotchety old man. I looked at you and saw a porcelain-headed fashion doll."

"I can see how you might think that about me, since you are so full of gravitas." She flashed her teeth. "But you don't think that now, do you?"

"We need to look for food," he said, looking around the glade where the rock pool was, and glanced up at the sun through the trees. It looked like mid-afternoon from the sun's position. This spot had possibilities.

"We must construct a shelter also—"

"Dr. Murray—"

"I suppose we can make a lean-to out of those palmettos. It won't be very adequate—"

"Dr. Murray!"

"Would you please stop babbling, Miss Farnham, this is important. We need to have shelter, and food. If you will leave me alone, I can construct something for us."

"Oh, very well. You stay here in your leaves. Pompom and I will sleep at the cottage."

He stopped talking and felt his head whip around, not a good feeling considering how battered he was from being tossed ashore.

"Cottage?"

"Yes," she said, looking annoyingly smug. "There is a building up there, through those trees. I explored while you were sleeping on the sand."

Alexander tried not to think of the things that could happen to a young woman exploring on her own.

"I had Pompom with me."

"That does not reassure me. Before we trot up there, was there anyone at this house?"

Daphne shook her head, her disarrayed curls bouncing about.

"It looks unoccupied. Come and I will show you."

Alexander followed her, along a path so narrow he hadn't spotted it earlier. It wound up through the lush foliage and trees, opening up in a clearing where there was indeed a cottage. He stopped just behind Miss Farnham. It was more of a wooden hut, actually, but it looked sturdy for all of that. The land in front of it was cleared, and there were scatterings of wood around the hut that gave him a clue as to its purpose.

"A cedar plantation."

She looked at him, an eyebrow raised.

"We might be in the Bermuda Islands, and someone is here harvesting cedar."

"Are they on the island with us?"

"Not likely. More often the owner will send over a crew once or twice a year to chop down the trees and haul them down to the beach. That hut is where the overseer sleeps at night."

"Do you think the owner will mind if we use his cottage?"

"I am not overly concerned with that."

The cedars had thick brown trunks, rising up into the air and awaiting their date with the axe. There had been some near the beach, their trunks twisted from exposure to the constant sea winds.

Miss Farnham walked around the empty cabin, lifting plants that trailed on the ground and examining them. Morning glories crept along the back wall of the hut, their bright blue bold against the verdant ferns and vines.

"There was a kitchen garden here. It's mostly gone wild now, but there are peas and corn, beans, and I think those are pumpkins."

"How do you know that?"

"Hah! I am not as ignorant as you think I am!"

"You have no idea how ignorant I think you are, Miss Farnham."

She looked at him sharply, no doubt wondering if she'd been insulted. "I am the one who explored and found us shelter. I located the food and water. Perhaps I should be in charge, Dr. Murray, not you! After all, it was different when you were elderly. I was willing to listen to you then. Now, maybe you should listen to me."

"That statement is so ridiculous as to not deserve a response." Alex left her fuming at his back and went to the hut. It was dusty inside and looked like mice had nested in one corner of the dirt floor. Ideally the dog would earn his keep by keeping the rodent population at bay. There was a table, and one chair. A scattering of cheap pottery dishes and metal implements sat on a shelf, candle stubs alongside them. There was also an earthenware pot sitting on a trivet.

No bed, no lamps, no other amenities. Only rough shelter from the elements.

It seemed like a castle after days in an open boat. He went

back outside and looked around. There was a line of sight down to the beach through the trees, no doubt cleared that way to help the caretaker keep an eye open for returning supply ships.

Or ships that did not belong on the island.

"I am going down to the beach to fetch my chest."

Daphne Farnham stood there, barefoot and ragged, her face red from the sun with no hat to shield her. He made a mental note to bring some of the aloe he'd spotted growing down near the shore, and try his hand at weaving palmetto hats for them. A seaman had demonstrated the craft when Alexander first shipped to the Indies, and he hoped he remembered how it was done.

But for all of that she looked approachable, in a way she had not when she was dressed up and properly turned out from head to toe. Now she looked like a woman, a woman whose lush, nubile body was exposed by her torn clothing, even her bare feet giving his head—and other parts of his body—new things to ponder.

A distraction was what was needed right now, and he knew what he had to do.

"Miss Farnham, after I check on my instruments I will see about finding us some supper."

"Will we have to eat raw fish again?"

"I hope not. I should be able to start a fire. You check the garden for other food."

"Oooh, that sounds heavenly." She clapped her hands together and strolled over to him, her dog following behind. Pompom paused at the sight of a blue-tailed skink sunning itself on a rock, his entire body stiffening. The two humans watched the dog, who was totally focused on the lizard.

"If he was only a little larger, Pompom could hunt for us, Dr. Murray."

Alexander started to say something snide about the animal, then stopped himself.

"Would he bring us a deer, do you think?"

She giggled, the soft breathy sound soothing to Alexander's nerves, because it meant she was happy, and not despairing about their situation.

"A deer? Do not be ridiculous."

"Well, perhaps some mice then," Alexander said with a small smile of remembrance that Miss Farnham did not see, because she was watching her animal. "You will be all right here, by yourself?"

She looked at him, her head tilted to the side. "I am not alone. I have Pompom. And you."

"It is good to know where I rank. If you need me, Miss Farnham, yell loudly. I should be able to hear you."

But Daphne wasn't watching him, her eyes caught by a bird flying overhead.

"Oh look, how pretty he is with his red head. Is that a woodpecker?"

The bird landed on a nearby tree and commenced hammering with its beak, searching out its own supper.

Alexander watched her, her face alight at the sight of the bird. He'd come to realize that she was not simple yet had an almost childlike ability to seize enjoyment from the moment.

He couldn't understand it at all. If he had been asked during the first few days aboard the *Magpie* to describe what Miss Farnham might be like in this situation, he would have said she'd be crying hysterically, and whining about how unfair it all was, and demanding he take care of her.

Daphne Farnham was doing none of those things. She was cheerful and cooperative and helpful, and it suddenly struck him how lonely it would have been in that boat without her, and how close he could have come to despair.

He might even go so far as to say he owed her his life.

"I believe it is a woodpecker, yes."

"I'm glad someone's having supper today."

At the word "supper" the dog barked and wagged its tail, and Daphne looked down at him ruefully.

"Oh dear, I should know better than to say that word around Pompom."

"If you will check on items growing around the cabin, I will see what I can do."

She smiled at him and said, "Come, Pompom, let's go dig in the garden," and Alexander watched them as they walked off, her bare feet placed carefully to avoid stones and stickers.

Down at the beach he took a moment to scan the horizon, hoping against hope that there might be a sail. But there was nothing. However, the beach itself held unexpected treasures. In addition to his chest, there was driftwood from their boat, one piece of which had Daphne's valise snagged to it. He opened his surgical chest, wincing. The velvet indentations holding his instruments were darkened by saltwater. More importantly the instruments themselves were wet and would rust if not cared for properly. It was a lesson he'd learned from his first days of cleaning up after his teachers, assisting them at their post-mortems and the dissections performed on the corpses stolen and smuggled into the schools— a surgeon's tools were an extension of his arm and must be always ready for use.

The rags of his shirt served to dry the instruments, followed by an oiling with the sealed bottle in the bottom of the case. He examined each item, giving the saw particular attention. While he hated to use it for this purpose, it was a tool of a different sort on the island.

He found a sapling of the right thickness and cut through its base, sharpening the end into a point. He set it aside. Once he had a fire going he could harden the tip in the coals. If necessary, he could lash one of his knives to the spear, but the idea of treating his instruments in that manner made him wince. Maybe the clasp knife, which had survived in his pocket as they tumbled through the waters.

"Fire first," Alexander said to himself. He was about to raise his voice and call for Daphne when she came through the brush, the dog at her heels.

"Just the person I need. Your valise is here, but it's half empty. It must have come unlatched in the surf. If you can leave it sit to dry, I could use your assistance gathering wood for the firepit in front of the hut." He paused and looked around the beach. Some holes in the sand gave him a clue as to their supper possibilities.

Daphne trotted off with her dog, and Alex took his case and some of the aloe spikes and went back to the cabin. From the bottom of his case he drew out his pistol. It was a necessary evil, especially during wartime. The ports of call of the Royal Navy were not populated by sterling characters. If it came down to his life or that of a brigand, Alexander was willing to shoot first and heal later.

Today the pistol would bring welcome heat and light.

He stepped outside as Daphne unloaded some dry wood. She'd pulled her skirt up to make an apron to hold more, and he carefully kept his eyes up on her face. He could hardly help but note, however, that her lower limbs were as shapely as the rest of her.

"Whew!" She wiped her hand across her forehead. "Is that enough?"

"No, I'm afraid not," he said gently. "We will need a goodly amount of fuel to keep the fire going long enough to cook our supper. Then we will bank it so there are coals in the morning."

"Oh." She looked dismayed for a moment, but then her

usual sunny disposition asserted itself. "I will look for more then."

"As soon as I am sure the fire is going strong, I will help you."

She flashed him a smile and turned back to the beach for more sticks. Alexander watched her go, then cleared the firepit of debris and prepared some kindling. He took his pistol and the tinder, and angling the pistol pulled the trigger, striking the flint against the steel and throwing a spark. After a few strikes, a wisp of smoke rose from the tinder, and he patiently nursed it into a flame.

Daphne returned with another load of wood, her face red from exertion.

"Drink some water, you do not want to become overheated."

"My arms are sore. Do people work like this every day?"

He looked up from the fire he was tending, but he did not give her a sarcastic answer. He could not expect Miss Daphne Farnham to understand how most of the world earned its daily bread. That would be like expecting the dog to start spouting Shakespeare.

"Yes, some people do have to work like this. Every day."

"I am glad I am not one of them," she said with complete honesty.

"I can understand why you feel that way. However, while we are here, we must imitate the working classes."

"I am being useful, then?"

The fire seemed to be going on its own, so he stood and joined her in gathering firewood.

"Yes, you are being most useful. If I were here alone on the island I would need to work twice as hard to fetch enough wood to keep the fire going."

"Imagine that," she murmured. "I am useful."

The thought put a spring in her step. After two more trips, Alexander pronounced himself satisfied.

"Tomorrow we will build that lean-to, a shelter for firewood. As the seasons change it will turn cooler and there will be rainstorms, so having a dry wood supply becomes more important than ever."

"But what about supper?" Daphne said, her hand pressed over her stomach.

"Were you able to find anything useful in the garden?"

"Corn, and some yams and beans. Tomorrow I will look again."

"Tomorrow we will also search out fruit and other plants growing here. Palms contain an edible core we can extract. Tonight we will put the yams in the fire to roast, and save the other vegetables for later."

He showed her how to cover the yams and put them at the edge of the firepit. Then hoisting the earthenware kettle onto his shoulder, he followed her down to the ocean. Alexander filled the kettle about a third full of seawater and carried it back to the fire, Daphne trailing behind.

"How do you know all these things? How to build a fire and how to cook?"

"I was raised on a farm, Miss Farnham, and we did not have servants to do things for us."

"Us? You had a large family?"

"No. Just my mother and myself."

"But what about your father?"

"I had no father."

She sat back on her heels and looked at him. "That is sad, Dr.

Murray."

"I learned to live with it. Now, we need to heat this water."

The pot sat atop the trivet, and when he was satisfied it

would not tip into the fire, he rose to his feet. Daphne was quiet, and when she stood, she was weaving on her feet.

"Hunger is making you light-headed. You sit here and—"

"Can you use my assistance?"

She was watching him steadily, and while he could have brushed her off, she deserved an honest answer.

"Yes. I could use your assistance. And I will need your valise."

He took his sharpened stick and the valise, and they walked back down to the beach. The sun was closer to the horizon. He needed to move quickly so they wouldn't be stumbling around in the dark. The last thing he needed was for one of them to twist an ankle or break a leg.

"See those holes?" He pointed to the sand. "Those are crab holes. Just as the fish are more active at sunrise and sunset, the crabs will come out looking for food. We will catch our supper here."

"We will?"

"Do not worry, you won't have to eat them raw. That's what the boiling water is for. Your task is to hold the valise."

"You are putting live crabs in my valise?"

"How hungry are you?"

"That is a good point," she acknowledged, and dutifully followed behind him.

The blue crabs were wily, but they were no match for two hungry and determined humans. There was some inevitable shrieking when one of the crabs made a dash for freedom from the open valise, but Daphne grabbed it with a fierce expression on her face and tossed it back in with its sisters. Hunger could spur people to amazing feats.

He carried the bag back up to the fire, and while Daphne winced and looked away when he dumped the live crabs in the pot, she did not protest.

"Please keep an eye on them. I'm going down to the beach for more water."

"What if they try to escape?"

He handed her his stick. "Bash their little heads, Miss Farnham. They'll behave."

She looked at him skeptically but took the stick. Pompom sniffed all around the valise, then flopped down next to her, eyeing the pot with his head on his paws.

Alex returned and added water to the pot, careful not to let it fall below a boil. Eventually, after some whining (the dog) and grumbling (Miss Farnham), he pronounced the crabs ready for consumption. He extracted the crabs by using his stick to flip them into the air.

"Catch them, Daphne! Quick, before the dog grabs them!"

Holding the valise open, she dashed about, catching the manna as it fell from the heavens. The dog barked and she laughed, and Alexander felt almost lighthearted.

He put it down to hunger.

She gave one more weak laugh and flopped down in the sand next to him. He passed her one of the cheap dishes from the cabin, using a broad leaf as his own plate. The dog tried to climb into his lap when he sat, but Daphne grabbed him and held him 'round his shoulders.

"Very soon now, Pompom," she assured him, giving him a kiss atop his head.

Alexander laid a crab out on the leaf, cracking it open. It wasn't the most efficient method, but it did expose the succulent white flesh, steaming in the dusk. He piled hot pieces atop her plate, and then cracked some open for himself.

"This could use some melted butter," she said wistfully, passing a bite to Pompom. "But it's tasty, and the yams are sweet. This is an excellent supper."

"Better than raw fish?"

"Isn't everything?" She shuddered. "I hope I never, ever eat raw fish again."

"But now that you have, Miss Farnham, do you not feel better for it?" He sucked some crab meat out of a claw while she looked at him quizzically. "You survived a shipwreck at sea and learned to adapt to changing circumstances. I daresay there are few young ladies of your acquaintance who would be able to claim such a breadth of experience."

"Oh! I am having an adventure! Maybe when I return home I will write a book about it."

"You would not be the first castaway to use the experience for gain. My own countryman, Alexander Selkirk, was one such individual. Some say he was the true Robinson Crusoe."

"You don't think it is a silly notion, someone like me wanting to write a book?"

"I admit, I would be astounded if you wrote a treatise on the circulatory system, but you could write a book about something you know about—fashion, hats? Maybe the care and feeding of small yapping dogs?"

"You are being harsh on poor Pompom, Doctor. He, too, is part of our adventure."

"Exactly. You could write a book about a young lady and her brave little dog, castaway on an island."

"Is there a surgeon full of gravitas in this book?"

"That would add nothing to the story. Fierce savages threatening to cook and eat the lady and her doggy might be a better way to go."

The sun was gone now, only the diffused light of dusk lingering. Daphne looked over her shoulder and inched closer to Alexander. Her eyes were large in the reflected firelight.

"Do you think there are cannibals here?" she whispered.

Alexander lowered his own voice and said, "If there are, Miss Farnham, I have no doubt your dog will dispatch them."

She looked at him a moment, blinked her lushly lashed eyes, then looked at Pompom. "I wish I had your faith."

He was tempted to string her along further but did not want to have to deal with the consequences if she heard a noise during the night and became hysterical.

"No, there are no savages on these islands. However," and he looked at her to make sure she was paying attention, "there are dangers. These scattered islands are used by all sorts of desperadoes. Some are simple smugglers trying to avoid tariffs, but others can be of a much nastier sort."

"You mean…pirates?"

"Try not to sound so excited. I assure you, the pirates found in these waters are scum who bear little resemblance to Byron's corsair.

"Tomorrow we will explore more of the island," he said, ending the talk of piracy. He'd earlier scouted out a suitable spot for them to use as a temporary privy, and he banked the coals while Miss Farnham went off into the bushes. She paused inside the hut on her return, then stood watching him work. There was enough light from the moon for him to see without stumbling about. He didn't want to light the candles in the cabin until it was necessary.

"Dr. Murray? May I ask a favor of you?"

He paused and looked at her, waiting.

"Would you please brush my hair?" Her voice caught, but she went on, looking down at the brush in her hands. "I know I should do it for myself, but when I try to raise my arms they hurt."

"You are not used to physical labor," he said gently. "I am not surprised your arms ache. And you were swimming ashore, too. It is perfectly appropriate for you to ask for assistance."

She came over and sat facing the coals, sitting cross-legged on the ground and Alex knelt behind her. Daphne's hair fell in a mass down her back that suddenly made him itch to plunge his hands into it and soothe whatever aches she had. The evening was still but for the sound of night birds hunting their own supper, the tropical paradise lush with the smell of the surrounding plants and their cedar hut.

He gritted his teeth and took the brush, starting first with the snarls at the bottom, patiently working his way through the tangles. His own arms ached from his pounding in the surf, but he was not about to tell her that because she might tell him to stop. He did not want to stop. He'd thought about doing this again since that first night when she'd asked him to help her, to teach her how to braid her hair.

There was a great deal he'd like to teach Miss Daphne Farnham, none of it good for his peace of mind. He experienced again the feel of her silken tresses sifting between his fingers, the curls that wrapped themselves around his hands like living vines. She'd rinsed herself in the pool earlier, washing the salt out of her hair and letting it dry in the warm air. He'd caught himself watching her as her hair dried, the locks lightening to their vibrant golden shade, flowing across her neck and down the torn arm of her dress.

"Would you like me to braid it for you to sleep tonight?"

"I usually prefer my hair unbound, but that might be best."

Was it his imagination, or was her voice lower, huskier than earlier? Whether it was his imagination or not, his unruly body responded to the aural cues. If he spread his legs and pulled her back, her rounded bottom would be snug against him, cradling the erection straining at the front of his ragged trousers.

Sweat broke out on his forehead as he tried to wrench his thoughts away from that direction. His efforts were defeated when he said, "Do you have a ribbon?" and she reached forward on the ground to fetch it, which brought her rump up, perfectly positioned for what he was imagining at this moment would be the ideal ending to this long, arduous day.

She trusts you. You cannot betray her trust.

That helped. Some. Not much. Especially when she looked at him over her shoulder, and he could see the gleam of her bare skin through the rent in her bodice, but he was pleased his hand was not shaking when she gave him the ribbon and she sat back on her heels, waiting for him to braid her hair.

He managed to separate the locks, braided them and tied off the end with her multi-colored ribbons, still wet from being rinsed in the fresh water.

"There. You are ready now, Miss Farnham. It is time for bed."

CHAPTER 10

The word "bed" hung between them in the night air, and Daphne pushed herself to her feet before looking at Dr. Murray. All she could think about what a surprisingly attractive companion the doctor was, not as old and decrepit as she'd suspected.

But he could still be grumpy and irritable, so she might survive this experience without embarrassing herself.

"Where will you sleep?"

"We only have the one room of the cabin. Tomorrow we may be able to work out something more comfortable, but tonight we will share that space. I cut some banana leaves earlier, and we can sleep on top of them."

She must have looked quizzical, because he added, "If we sleep on the bare ground it will drain warmth from our bodies. The leaves provide insulation and padding."

He gestured and she entered the cabin and she heard him vigorously shaking the banana leaves before he brought them into the cabin and arranged them on the floor.

Daphne gingerly lowered herself to the leaves and lay on her side, her head pillowed on her arm. Pompom curled up at her stomach, snuggling next to her for comfort as much as warmth, and she put her other arm around him, holding him close. He sighed and licked her hand. She did not look at Dr. Murray, who stepped out one final time. A bird screeched and she jumped, but she heard a gruff voice coming out of the darkness.

"That is only a petrel. You will become used to their night calls soon enough."

Then he was behind her, not positioning himself against her body like he had on the boat but lying alongside her. She could not see him behind her, but suspected he was lying on his back.

"Are you going to be able to sleep like that?"

"I am a surgeon, Miss Farnham. I can fall asleep anytime, anywhere."

"Really?" She rolled over to look at him.

That was a mistake. Her eyes were adjusted to the faint light coming in through the doorway. He lay on his bare back on the leaves, his hands beneath his head as he looked up at the roof. The position brought into detail the corded muscles of his arms and his finely defined chest with its light brushing of hair. She'd noticed earlier that the hair on his chest was a blend of silver and rust, like the hair atop his head.

Old, he's old, far too old for you, her mind told her, but her body sent her a different message.

"Oh dear, I just knew this would be a problem." She moaned, flopping onto her own back. She couldn't look at him. Pompom grumbled at the disturbance then, settled back down.

"What is your problem?"

"It is not you, Dr. Murray, it is me. I do not know if I can sleep next to you like this!".

"I promise not to ravish you in your sleep, Miss Farnham. I can control my appetites."

"You do not understand! It is my appetites I am worried about." She rolled over on her side, propping herself up on her arm. "You see, this is what I was trying to explain earlier! When you were an old man I could sleep next to you without worries. But now that I see how you really are, it gives me disturbing thoughts and I may want to act on those thoughts, and then where would we be?"

He did not say anything for a long time, then he cleared his throat.

"Disturbing thoughts?"

"I am not worried about you making advances on me. I know you are a scholar and a natural philosopher. You have gravitas. You would never, ever give in to your base passions. But I am only a woman, and one who..." How could she best phrase this? "One who has a passionate temperament, and when I see you, looking like you do, lying here next to me, I worry that I will do something that will give you a disgust of me and my base desires."

He cleared his throat again.

"So, you are saying it is up to me to ensure that you do not ravish me in my sleep?"

"Exactly! You must be strong for both of us, for I cannot assure you that I can control myself."

"Miss Farnham..." He stopped and said something beneath his breath she couldn't hear.

"I was afraid this would happen," she said sadly. "You are disgusted with me now. I will understand if you want to sleep somewhere else."

"I do not wish to sleep elsewhere. I am not disgusted with you. Far from it. Your frank honesty is exactly what we need in a situation like this."

"It is?"

"Of course. Now that I understand you are not attracted to me in any fashion other than at a base, physical level I am prepared to repel any untoward advances you may make to me."

"That's a relief," Daphne said, feeling lighter in her mind and much more at ease. "I will do my best to control myself, and you just…just be yourself."

She rolled over on her side, cradling the sleeping dog next to her again. "Good night, Doctor."

She couldn't be sure, but she thought he said something beneath his breath again. Her eyes were drifting shut when she heard him say, "Good night, Miss Farnham."

"And Pompom, too?"

"Go to sleep, Miss Farnham."

Daphne awoke the next morning to the cries and twitters of the island's bird population. Pompom had already awakened and slipped out the open doorway to take care of his needs, and she heard him out there barking at a bird or two.

She was not inclined to move. It was comfortable here, her head pillowed on a strong arm, his other arm wrapped around her and his body spooned against her, keeping her warm. She could feel his soft breath on the back of her neck, and lower down where he was pressing into her from behi—

"Hah! I knew it!"

Daphne scrambled to her feet and whirled to face her companion, who blinked at her dazedly. She put her hands on her hips and watched as he rubbed his eyes. He had no right to be looking good this early in the morning, his beard-shadowed jaw and the tousled hair falling across his forehead giving him a decidedly rakish air.

"Why are you screeching at me?"

"You, you…you man! You *are* like the others! Just look at you!"

She pointed in the direction of what had her screeching.

"Oh. That."

"Yes, that! What do you have to say for yourself?"

"Miss Farnham, that is a perfectly natural state for a man upon awakening. It has nothing to do with you."

"You are not blaming me for putting you in that state?"

He thought about it for a moment. "No. You may have contributed some to the situation, but I do not blame you."

He started to rise, but her next words stopped him.

"It isn't a life-threatening condition?"

"I beg your pardon?"

"I was told when men woke up like that it was something requiring immediate attention or a man could become crippled, or even die!"

He propped himself up on one arm.

"Who told you that?"

"Never mind," she muttered. "It is not important. I am glad you are not going to die, Doctor. And that I don't have to cure it for you."

He looked down at himself, then looked at her and for a brief moment he did look vaguely hopeful, but Daphne whirled on her foot and hurried out of the cabin, heading to the designated bushes to take care of her own needs.

When she returned, the doctor had gathered up the leaves and put them in the corner.

"We have a busy day ahead of us, it's best we start working."

Daphne sighed. "Work" was such an unpleasant word. She suspected what the doctor had in mind would turn out to be more exhausting than finding the right hat.

But they were companions in this adventure, and each experience gave her more to add to the book she was going to write someday, and that thought cheered her up.

"What do we do first, Doctor?"

"Each day we will need to gather firewood, fetch water

and food to cover our basic needs. If there's time remaining in the day and we're not too tired, we will explore our island."

"What about rescue?"

He frowned, thinking. "I am of two minds about that. Not that I don't want to be rescued, but all sorts of people ply these waters. If we light a signal fire we might attract the wrong ones."

"But if there is no signal fire no one will know we are here," Daphne said reasonably. "It's a chance we have to take."

He thought some more, then gave a small nod of agreement.

"You are correct. We cannot wait on the chance that the plantation workers will return soon. We have leftover yams and vegetables? Let's have them for breakfast, then you can gather firewood and I will fish for us."

"I saw a pawpaw tree when I was out behind the hut. We can gather those also. This way."

He followed her outside, Pompom sniffing the ground behind them. The slender tree was heavy with golden yellow fruit, and her mouth watered at the thought of the treat with breakfast.

She tried to grab the low-hanging fruit, but it was just out of reach. Dr. Murray had no difficulty plucking down a few for them, and they headed back to the cabin.

"Do not eat the leftover crab. You can give it to the dog."

She almost protested that it might make her precious baby ill, but she'd seen some of the things that animal was willing to consume, so she said nothing. If it made him sick, he'd disgorge it soon enough.

Dr. Murray went down to the pool and refilled their flask while she took the knife he'd left behind and sliced open the pawpaws, exposing the creamy flesh with its black seeds. Her stomach grumbled and she fetched the leftover roasted vegetables while waiting for the doctor. When he returned with the water it reminded her of something else she'd seen.

"There are calabash trees here, too. We can use the gourds for containers."

He looked at her with an odd expression on his face.

"How do you know all this, how to identify the trees and plants?"

"The house we rented in Jamaica had a garden, and the woman who cooked and cleaned for us tended it. Viola—that was her name—used to go with me to market and she showed me what trees and plants were being used or cultivated. Some of the same ones grow here." She busied herself slicing the vegetables. "I like growing things. It is rewarding to watch them change and brighten your life with color and scent, like flowers, or add to your enjoyment of a meal. And in Jamaica it helped distract me from… Well, it was good to learn new things.

"There!"

She'd arranged the servings neatly on some fresh leaves, making a pattern of the different colors and textures. There was no reason why a meal had to be drab, any more than clothing needed to be drab.

The doctor was still watching her.

"I do not think I have ever met anyone like you, Daphne Farnham."

She paused, suddenly feeling nervous. She wiped her hands on her skirt, looking down at her dirty bare toes. "Oh. Is that a good thing?"

She looked at him through her lashes. He didn't answer and he wasn't smiling, not with his mouth open and his teeth bared, but the expression on his face, in his eyes, made it seem like he was smiling, smiling at her. He took his food and sat on the dirt floor, leaning against the wall, leaving her the table and chair. After a moment's hesitation, she took her leaf and joined him, sitting on the floor next to him. He raised his eyebrows but didn't say anything.

"You think we are near Bermuda, but I thought Bermuda is an island."

"Bermuda is a grouping of islands, and most people live around St. George or Hamilton. Bermuda is an isolated area but it has its share of traffic from the ocean. We could be on one of the smaller islands. Since we have not seen any smoke rising anywhere else, I suspect we are the only ones here."

Daphne stopped chewing. "What if no one comes here? Will we be stranded here forever?"

He looked at her sideways. "I doubt that will happen. This appears to be a thriving plantation. Someone will come to cut down those trees."

She looked down at her torn and stained dress. "I could be in rags by that point."

"That's possible," he said, chewing thoughtfully. "We might find some goats like Robinson Crusoe did and make ourselves clothes from their skins."

Daphne shuddered at the thought. Goatskin dresses sounded hot and scratchy. And smelly.

"One crisis at a time," Dr. Murray said, rising to his feet and brushing off his hands. "Food, water, shelter, fire, these are the essentials."

He gave her his hand and helped her up, then frowning, turned her hand over. She knew what he saw. The skin was rough and her nails were ragged. They were no longer the hands of a lady.

"Tonight, take some of the aloe sap and lightly rub it over your hands at bedtime. It's not as effective as an emollient cream, but it will help."

He seemed almost reluctant to release her hand, but he did, saying only, "And be careful of splinters when gathering firewood."

He turned to leave the cabin but paused and looked over his shoulder.

"Come down to the beach with me and gather driftwood there. I will feel better if we stay together until there is time to explore."

That made sense to Daphne also, so she followed as the doctor fetched his sharpened stick and her much abused valise. Pompom trailed behind them and did not appear to be suffering ill-effects from his seafood breakfast.

Breakfast had Daphne thinking, and she stopped walking.

"Eggs!"

Dr. Murray turned and looked at her.

"This island is full of birds and where there are birds there are eggs, correct? If we can locate their nests we can boil eggs for our meals."

"Excellent suggestion, Miss Farnham."

"Do you know how to boil an egg?"

He looked at her again. "Don't you know how to boil an egg?"

"Why would I?" she said. "I never had to cook a meal for myself until last night."

"True. I forget sometimes who you are."

She wished he would forget that all the time. It was much more enjoyable just being the Daphne Farnham who knew how to find a yam in the garden or cut up a pawpaw. Today she wanted to be the Daphne Farnham who caught fish. Although it would be nice to wear shoes again, she thought, as she stopped to remove a thorn from her foot. Pompom romped ahead of her down to the shore, pausing to bark at a tern flying low to breakfast from the water. Dr. Murray peered into a grove of mangroves hugging the edge of the land and she joined him there, wading gingerly into the water. The sandy bottom squelched between her toes and she wiggled them, enjoying the feeling on her hot and abused bare feet.

"What are we looking at?"

"Keep your voice low, and look."

He pointed into the water lapping at the roots twisting through the shallow pools, and as her eyes adjusted to the shade of the trees and their tangled roots, she saw what he was looking at. Fish darted about and there were more crabs, all coexisting together, with one or another occasionally ending up as a meal.

Dr. Murray tapped her shoulder and pointed, and she followed the line of his finger. A nest was lodged in the low branches, and while she couldn't see up into it, apparently he could, for he leaned down and whispered in her ear, "Eggs."

She knew she should be concentrating on securing food for them, but she was distracted by his warm body beside hers, the puff of air as he spoke into her ear sending shivers down her spine.

He motioned for her to step out of the water and she followed him back onto the sunlit shore. His skin gleamed in the morning light, his back broad and solid. His trousers were sitting just above his hipbones, bones that made her wonder if this broad, solid man was solid everywh—

"Are you listening, Miss Farnham?"

Daphne shook herself with a start. There she went again, salaciously daydreaming when poor Dr. Murray was doing his best to stay out of her clutches. It was a good thing he would be strong for both of them, because her mind would ever move in low directions.

"I am sorry, Doctor, I was woolgathering."

"I said I will take a chance in the surf with my spear. Now that I know there's food available in the mangroves, I want to see if I can do this."

He did look rather like a youngster anxious to try out a

new toy. Daphne smiled to herself and said, "I have faith in your abilities, Doctor. I will gather the eggs you saw, then begin on the firewood."

"Tell me if you need help with the wood," he said, but he was already looking out at the water, bouncing the spear in his hand as if testing its weight.

Daphne moved back toward the mangroves and the nest. The mother bird was not nearby. When she raised her arm to feel inside the nest, the arm with the missing sleeve moved easily, but the other arm was constrained by the shape of the dress, its fit dictated by fashion more than practicality. She could fix that back at the cabin. In the meantime, she took her hand and felt around inside the nest. There were four eggs there, warm in their haven. She felt a pang for the mother bird and only took two, leaving the others in the nest. If they wanted more eggs, tomorrow she would look for another nest to rob.

She carried the eggs up to the cabin and deposited them in a cup, then craned her head over her shoulder. If she removed the remaining sleeve from her dress she would be able to move her arms more freely. Since this was one of the dresses Dr. Murray insisted she wear without his assistance she was able to remove it herself, and taking a knife from his surgical case she snipped the threads at the back of the sleeve, creating a gap under her arm that allowed her to raise her hands over her head.

"That's better," she said to herself, putting the knife back. As she set the tray back in its place she saw a flash of gold, and curiosity pricked at her. She felt around in the pocket where the metal's edge glinted.

It was a framed miniature, a portrait of a young woman. She had the look of a cheerful country girl and Daphne wondered who she was and what her connection was to the doctor. She looked at it a moment longer, then put it back in its pocket, sliding it deep so it would not fall out.

Pompom came in and nudged her leg, and she absently patted him atop his curly head.

"It is a good thing I have you, Pompom. Maybe when we return I will have your portrait painted so I have a miniature of you. Would you like that?"

The dog licked her hand, then wagged his tail and ran out the door. He at least seemed to be in fine spirits over their adventure.

Daphne followed him out into the sunshine. The day was advancing and there was wood to be gathered. Dr. Murray had pointed out the twisted driftwood on the beach as a good starting point, and soon she was dragging limbs up through the brush to their rough campsite, piling them near the firepit. It was work like she had never done before, hot, and hard, and all too soon her arms and hands were aching from the unaccustomed chore, but she kept at it. Dr. Murray would find no reason to say she was slacking and not doing her share. She sang as she worked, smiling as Pompom danced a few steps alongside her.

"Do you miss those days, sweetie?" she said to him and he wagged his tail. He'd been a sad case when she'd snatched him from that street performer. The blackguard was beating the pup with a leather strap because Pompom limped on sore paws instead of dancing as he was supposed to. The nasty man was set to make a scene, but Daphne's coins—and the sight of the two brawny footmen with her—convinced him to part with his dancing dog.

"Talking to your dog when you are stranded on a deserted island could be viewed as a sign of mental instability," said a voice behind her.

Pompom barked and wagged his tail, and Daphne turned with a smile. "I talk to Pompom even when I'm in the middle of civilization, Doctor, so that would be a false diagnosis on your part." He carried her bag, wet and dripping at the bottom. "Oh dear, should I ask what is in my valise?"

"Supper," he said succinctly.

"You speared some fish?" He nodded, trying to look modest, but she could tell he was proud of his hunting skill. For a wild moment, she was tempted to pat his tousled head and praise and coo over him as she would over Pompom if he brought her a beetle.

"Here, switch with me," he said. He passed her the valise and took the heavier load of firewood from her arms. Daphne wrinkled her nose at the condition of her bag. "I do not think I will be putting my clothes in here again."

"A sacrifice for the common good, Miss Farnham."

She hummed to herself as they resumed walking.

"I know that tune," Dr. Murray said, looking at her sideways. "You have an interesting repertoire."

Daphne giggled softly. "I like to sing and I would listen to the sailors singing their— what was it Mr. Lowry called them?"

"Shanties."

"That is correct," she said, smiling at him. "Their shanties. Mr. Lowry said it made the work go easier on the *Magpie* if the men sang while they were at their tasks."

She stopped so abruptly that Dr. Murray nearly ran into her. "Why did you do tha—Miss Farnham, what is the matter?"

Daphne looked at him.

"They are all dead, aren't they?"

He just looked at her and did not ask whom she meant.

"Mr. Lowry and Captain Franklin and Mr. Carr and all the sailors—they are all dead," she whispered.

"We cannot know for certain. We survived. They may have survived as well."

"Do you truly think so?"

"I have no evidence one way or the other, so I cannot draw a conclusion. Now, if you are ready to move on, there are fish to prepare."

Once again, his matter-of-fact words braced her in a way that sympathy or platitudes or pretty lies would not.

But she was no longer humming as they reached the cabin. Daphne set down her valise and straightened her back, rubbing it at the base.

"How are you going to cook the fish, Doctor? Are you going to boil it like you did the crabs?"

"We might do that at some point and make a fish stew, but I have a different thought for tonight. Are you up to some more labor?"

She knew what she wanted to say, but she also knew what the right answer was.

"Yes, if you need me, I can work."

He didn't say anything but looked at her with approval, and Daphne realized that for this man she was willing to push herself to do more than she would have thought herself capable of just a few short weeks back. Dr. Murray did not expect people to work harder than he did, but he had no patience with those who did not give their all.

"We need some flat rocks, about so big," he demonstrated the size. "Slightly smaller or larger is acceptable."

"How many?"

He looked at the firepit, then back at her.

"Half a dozen, maybe eight if they are small. Down by the pool would be a good place to start looking."

She was about to head out when she paused and turned on her heel. "Do not clean and prepare the fish until I return. I cannot always depend on you to feed and take care of me—not that you aren't dependable—but I need to know how to do things for myself. What if I am shipwrecked again someday? People may look to me, Daphne Farnham, to lead them and show them what to do!"

"You expect to be shipwrecked again?"

"I did not expect to be shipwrecked at all! But I am, so now I want to learn. You cannot let one bad experience stop you from learning and trying new things."

Really, she would expect a natural philosopher to know that. Sometimes she worried the doctor wasn't as intelligent as he thought he was, but he managed to muddle along with her assistance.

He was looking at her now in that strange manner, like she was a species of butterfly he'd never encountered before, but then he said, "If that is what you want, then I will gather the rocks with you and show you what to do."

He looked at the firepit and their wood supply and added, "I also want some green wood to make smoke. It is our best hope of rescue if passing ships see it."

The idea of rescue excited Daphne, but it also made her feel a little sad. Of course she did not want to spend the rest of her life stuck on this rock with only Pompom and dour Dr. Murray for company, even though Pompom was a great deal of fun and amused her with his antics.

But if she was rescued, she would go back to being Miss Daphne Farnham, young lady of fashion. It would be lovely to see what the latest trends from Paris were and set the fashion tone for others to follow, but it would also be lovely to know how to lead a band of shipwrecked castaways if she found herself in this situation again.

"I want to know how to start the fire, and boil an egg, and clean the fish, and you said you would make palmetto hats," she told her two-legged companion as they walked down to the pool.

"That is a lot to learn."

"Necessary to learn, I think," she mused. "Either I will use it if I am shipwrecked and people naturally turn to me because I know the most, or I will use it in my book when I write about our experiences here."

"You mean to make yourself the heroine who saves the day?"

"Think about it from a literary point of view, Doctor. Would people rather read about a beautiful, passionate and brave young lady, or someone who has no sense of humor, no fashion sense, and no finer emotions or sensibility?"

"I am not without sensibility."

"I was not talking about you. I was speaking in generalities. I read novels, and what makes them interesting is when people do not do the expected thing."

"Novels are a foolish waste of time for foolish people. Their time would be better spent reading improving material."

Daphne nodded her head at his statement. "You make my point for me. I enjoy reading gothic novels. You do not. Therefore, I know better than you what the reading public wants, and I am prepared to give it to them. If you were writing this story, it would be a dry recitation of facts that would act as a sleeping draught."

He stopped abruptly. "My writing does not put people to sleep."

"Oh dear, I have insulted you, haven't I?" She patted his arm. "I am certain the other natural philosophers find your work just riveting."

She moved ahead to the rocks, humming again. What an interesting day this was turning out to be!

Dr. Murray rather grumpily showed her the right sort of rocks and since they were both gathering them up, it only took one trip to bring them back to the cabin. He arranged them in the pit and then built up a sandy area next to them before stoking the fire around the rocks.

"Now we wait for the rocks to heat and tend to the fish. I need about a half dozen large green leaves."

"Banana leaves?"

"Those will do. And some vines to tie them. We are going to wrap the fish in the leaves and cook them on the rocks."

"I know you are learned, Dr. Murray, but how do you know all this?"

"When I visited Bermuda in the past, I spent time exploring, looking for plants that could be helpful in my medicine chest. And I have a great curiosity about my surroundings. I also watch the sailors at their tasks, and I learned from them."

"Many in your position would ignore the sailors and servants."

"Knowledge is knowledge. You are an excellent example of how one can learn from one's surroundings. You paid attention to what your housekeeper was doing in Jamaica, and now you are better prepared for life on our island."

He gave her his clasp knife and she went out to fetch the leaves. There were some small bananas on the tree, nearly ripe, so she cut those to take back to the cabin.

"I think there are some onions growing wild in the garden patch," she said when she stepped into the shade of the cabin. "They would go well with the fish, wouldn't they?"

"More yams, also, if they're there."

Daphne stepped back out into the light and winced. "You mentioned hats. Can you make one for me now? The sun is fierce out here."

He stopped what he was doing and walked over to her, turning her head to the light. "Your nose is quite red, Miss Farnham."

"It will turn brown and peel, won't it?" she fretted.

"Too late now, but the aloe will help. In the meantime, let me take care of the hat for you."

He cut palmetto fronds and after a few false starts remembered how to weave them into a hat. It was not nearly as well made as those offered by the women in the market in Jamaica, but it would keep the sun off her head and face.

When she put it on the corner of his mouth almost turned up in a smile. "Maybe you will set a new fashion."

"A returning fashion. In my mother's time palmetto hats were the height of style in London."

The hat smelled green and fresh and provided welcome shade for her eyes as she returned to her chores. It was late and she understood why Dr. Murray warned her the work would be nonstop just to stay fed and have heat and light.

"Now it is time to clean the fish," he said. He gathered the valise, the leaves, the vines and the onions and with her assistance carried it down to the pool, Pompom trotting behind.

At the edge of the water he took his clasp knife and showed her how to split and clean the fish, removing the guts. He did the first one, then let Daphne try her hand at the second. When she was done what she had bore little resemblance to the neat filets laid out by Dr. Murray.

"I destroyed my fish," she said glumly.

"Like anything else, you will improve with practice."

Birds alerted to their task swooped down at them, Pompom's barking keeping them from coming too close.

"Bear in mind that I have been cutting up creatures for many years," he said as he cleaned the last fish. "Now we lay the filets out on the leaves, add those onions you found, and wrap them into packages, like so."

He finished by tying them up with the vines, then stood to take them to the cabin until the fire was ready for them.

"If you would, take this trash down to the shore and toss it to the birds."

She gathered the offal into one of the leaves and, followed

by a raucous flock of birds, trotted down to the shore. She'd no sooner flung the leaf and its contents toward the water when the birds dived after it, making short work of the mess.

Something shiny glinted at the edge of the surf and when she went to investigate, she nearly shouted. More from their boat! One of her shoes, and Dr. Murray's jacket, its buttons gleaming. He would be glad to have it when it dried, and maybe she would not be so distracted by the sight of his muscled body if it was covered.

Daphne tilted her hat forward to shade her eyes and looked out to sea, hoping to spot more of their goods, but the ocean looked empty, and vast. She could now see smudges of land on the horizon, other islands. Were they inhabited?

Even if they were, they couldn't be as nice as her little island. Their island had a house, and a garden, and good food, and water, and Pompom.

It had Dr. Murray.

Humming to herself, she went to share the good news about his coat but paused. She should tell him about the neighboring islands also. She grinned as she saw in front of her exactly what she needed for more information, and then he would see just how useful she could be!

CHAPTER 11

Where had that woman gone off to? She hadn't passed him going to the cabin, so he went to the beach to see what kept her. The dog was there, sniffing at some seaweed, and Alexander felt his shoulders relax. If there was something wrong the animal would be agitated. He wasn't good for much, but he was protective of his mistress. The dog moved over to the base of a cedar, one growing wild at the edge of the mangroves, and lay down in its shade.

"Miss Farnham?" he called.

"Yes, Dr. Murray?"

Alexander looked around at the sound of her voice.

"Up here."

He looked up, a creeping feeling of horror growing in his chest. Daphne was in the cedar tree, her legs dangling from the limb where she sat high above the ground.

"Co—" his voice came out a hoarse croak. "Come down."

"But the view up here is spectacular. Look, I can see far out to sea. I can see other islands!"

She climbed higher and *stood* on the branch and Alexander feared his legs would crumple beneath him.

"Come down! At once!" he tried to shout, but his voice was barely more than a whisper.

Daphne peered through the branches at him. "Are you ill? You are pale as the sand."

"Please come down," he begged her, ashamed at the pleading tone of his voice.

She did not argue but shimmied down the tree trunk. He wanted to close his eyes—or vomit—but he kept watching her as cold sweat inched down his spine. She reached a branch about six feet off the ground, then swung down by her hands and dropped the remaining distance.

When he saw her standing uninjured, briskly wiping her palms together, Alexander put his face in his hands, shivers wracking his frame.

"Dr. Murray! What is wrong with you? Do you have the fever?"

Daphne came over and stood beside him, and he grabbed her by the arms, holding her, holding on to her because he feared his own legs would crumple.

"Do. Not. Ever. Climb. Again."

Each word came out on an exhalation of air.

She looked at him like he was insane, and he knew how he acted *was* insane, but she did not know, she had not been there, she had never seen someone die as he had seen it happen, the blood pouring out, the body twisted and misshapen from striking the ground, the ribs and organs crushed, punctured…

"Dr. Murray, you are hurting my arms."

He released her like she was afire and stepped away from her, because if he was standing next to her he would want to grab her again and make sure she did not move out of his sight. But instead of doing what any normal, rational person would do, flee the madman, she stepped next to him and put her hand on his forehead, her own brow furrowed with concern.

"You are covered in sweat. Are you sure you are well?"

She stood so close to him he felt the warmth of her body through her torn clothing, he saw the pulse at her throat, beating so strong, so full of life. The scent of her, a scent of woman and comfort, undisguised by perfumes or pomades, overwhelmed his senses.

He put his hands on her face, framing it, hearing the blood pounding in his ears as he pulled her to him and did what he longed to do since that night aboard ship when she smiled at him. That smile, which held all the sweetness missing from his sour life, all the warmth others received.

Her lips softened beneath his and she made a small sound, of surprise, or maybe pleasure, then her hand moved down to the back of his neck and she pulled him into her embrace.

The feeling of Daphne in his arms overwhelmed him. Her body fit his as if she'd been constructed solely for his pleasure. He moved his mouth across hers, easing her lips open and she moaned her approval, the sound reverberating in his soul. Her genuine and enthusiastic response, not the whores' practiced arts he was used to, fired his need like nothing else could. It would be so easy, so perfect to go to the next step, to pick her up and carry her into the shade at the edge of the mangroves and remove her dress.

Then the dog barked. Loudly and repeatedly.

Reluctantly, Alexander lifted his head and looked down at the bichon. It was crouched at his feet, growling, protective of its mistress.

The dog was brighter than he was. Someone had to think clearly, and it wasn't him. His emotions, so carefully tamped down for so long, were veering out of control like a runaway carriage.

He pulled himself away from Daphne, whose arm fell from around his neck as her eyes opened.

"Why did you do that?" she whispered.

"I don't know." He cleared his throat, the words sticking there because he did not want to talk, he wanted to kiss her again and discover if it was as sweet when she was not caught by surprise. He shook his head, as much to clear it as to tell himself no. "I must offer you my most sincere apologies. I do not know what came over me, to react in such an irrational fashion."

She dreamily smiled up at him and patted his cheek. When she touched him, all he wanted to do was pull her back into his arms and finish what they'd started, a notion his unruly body was very much in favor of.

"It is all right to be irrational every now and then, Dr. Murray."

He sighed and ran his hands through his hair, brushing it off his forehead. "No, Miss Farnham. I will not lose control like that again."

"Oh."

"Do not pout, this is for your own good."

She stamped her bare foot on the sand.

"I hate it when people say that to me! Why can I not decide what is for my own good?"

"To date, you have presented little evidence that your critical thinking skills are up to this task. If we let our emotions run away with us and do what feels good, we are asking for a great deal of trouble. Right now we need to concentrate on our survival on this island."

Her head was slightly tilted as she studied him. "I thought all sailors climbed those ropes on the ships."

"I am a surgeon, not a sailor."

"But you must have seen sailors climbing all the time

without wanting to kiss them. Why are you so upset about me climb—"

"My reasons are not the issue," he interrupted her. "Do not do it again."

He was pleased at the steadiness of his voice. He needed to remember which one of them was the rational, thoughtful one, and which one was the passionate, hot-blooded, lushly curved, full-breasted…

"Doctor? Are you returning to the cabin? Oh! I found some more of our things."

She headed over to the rocks at the edge of the beach and pointed.

"See? Your jacket washed up, and one of my shoes, and some wood from the boat. I put your jacket over there in the sun."

"Thank you for that."

He was glad to have a piece of clothing back, not just for protection from the elements, but because he knew that the more he could cling to the trappings of civilized life, the more he could keep his distance from her.

Daphne walked away and he could see the glimpse of ivory skin through the back of her torn dress, and he rubbed his hand over his face.

"You go ahead. I will be up shortly," he said.

*

Daphne marched up to the cabin feeling…what was that word her governess used? Disgruntled, that was it. She was definitely no longer gruntled, not after that kiss with Dr. Murray.

"Old Dr. Murray," she muttered. Ha! There was nothing infirm about that man's mouth!

The situation was bad enough before, but now that she'd

kissed him, it was a whole new box of troubles. How was she supposed to sleep next to him knowing that his kisses set her blood on fire? How was she supposed to watch him parading around half-naked and not think about what it would be like if his trousers were off and he lay next to her atop the banana leaves, those skilled hands of his stroking her body.

Why, she would wager he knew things about the human body that would make him a regular virtuoso of the bedroom!

Daphne remembered a trip to a sculpture gallery in London. She'd gone with other young ladies and their beaus. The girls were more interested in flirting than art, though they "Oooohed!" over a nearly naked statue of Apollo.

It wasn't that statue that stayed in her mind. Apollo was sleek and all that was handsome, but she was entranced by a statue of Hephaestus at his forge, his brawny shoulders and broad back, arm upraised over the anvil, hands that were not delicate for handling a lyre, but corded and sinewed as they clutched a hammer.

It was a statue of a hard-working god, not an aristocratic dandy.

Pompom, oblivious to the undercurrents, trotted alongside, following her when she detoured to the pool to stick her head in the cold water.

The rest of the afternoon she gathered firewood and when she made her third trip back to the campsite, there was a pile of green wood there also. No doubt Dr. "I am a natural philosopher and cannot lower myself to consort with an emotional ninny like you" Murray was doing his best to make sure they were rescued as quickly as possible.

That was a good thing, she told herself. The sooner she was back in civilization wearing proper clothes and proper hats and being courted by proper young men who knew what was important in life, the happier she would be.

Her stomach grumbled and she realized they'd worked through luncheon, but that, too, was just fine because it meant less time sitting across from that irritating man and looking at his lips. Of course, at that moment he showed up, his hair wet and slicked back, water gleaming on his body.

She realized she was staring when he said, "I went for a swim in the ocean, then rinsed off the salt at the pool. I also rinsed my coat in the pool and as soon as it is dry I'll put it on."

He looked at her sidelong, a bit tentatively.

"Are you ready for the next step in our fish preparation?"

Since she could not maintain being angry at someone for long, Daphne rose from where she sat on the cabin floor, dusted her hands off on her skirt and said, "What do we do next, Dr. Murray?"

He looked her full in the face at that and seemed relieved she was not going to pitch a fit.

"Come, and bring the fish packets. Please."

She followed him out, smiling to herself over that "please." She imagined it was a word he did not offer to many people.

He took his fishing spear and carefully maneuvered the rocks away from the fire and into a nearby hole in the sand, then taking the packets of fish, placed them atop the hot rocks.

"Now, Miss Farnham, help me scoop sand over this and bury it."

She assisted him, and soon their fish were cooking beneath a pile of warm sand.

"It is like you made an oven."

Maybe he was the cleverest man in the world. Certainly he was the cleverest man she'd ever known.

"I am so glad I am castaway with you, Dr. Murray. Not

that I'm glad we're castaway, but if I have to be stranded, I'm glad it's with you."

"You are the one who found the fruits and vegetables. We make a good team."

Daphne felt a warm glow spread through her chest at his words.

"We do make a good team, don't we?"

"In this we do," he said, looking at her steadily. "But you and I come from different worlds, Daphne Farnham. A ship's surgeon and a lady have little in common. In an emergency I might be called upon to treat your wounds, but I would not be welcome in your drawing room. Do not forget that, and we will muddle through this together."

His words extinguished the glow. She liked it when they were a team, working together. Even though she suspected that sometimes he was being rude to her, and other times she *knew* he was being rude to her, he still wanted her help. When it came to things she knew that he did not, like which vegetables were growing in the garden, he listened to her. Really listened to her and took what she said seriously.

It may seem a small thing, to be valued for one's knowledge of turnips and pumpkins, but at the moment it meant the world to her.

He looked up at the sun through the trees.

"In about an hour, as best as I can estimate, those fish will be ready to eat."

"The eggs!"

She dashed into the cabin and came out cradling her contribution to their meals.

"Can we boil them and eat them for breakfast?"

"An excellent suggestion. I will fill the pot and put it on the fire to boil."

When he returned with the pot Daphne watched it until it boiled.

"Hah! I knew that was just a saying," she said smugly. "But how will we take them in and out of the water?"

"I believe I have the answer to that," he said. He went into the cabin and returned with a grim-looking instrument.

"Is that from your surgical chest?"

"It was not just lying around the cabin. Yes, it is from my chest." He opened and closed the device, which looked like tongs. "Crowbill forceps, used to extract bullets from hapless victims. Tonight they will be put to a much gentler use."

She shuddered at the thought of that iron tool digging around inside a human body, but in Dr. Murray's hand it looked like an extension of his arm, something he was completely at ease holding.

When he judged the eggs sufficiently boiled, he extracted them from the hot water and set them on a leaf, then sat beside her in the sand.

"There you are, breakfast. Perhaps tomorrow I will snare a bird and we will enjoy fowl for dinner."

"Oh." Daphne thought about the lovely birds winging through the air. Today she'd seen one that had the longest tail feathers ever, and Dr. Murray told her it was indeed called a longtail. It swooped and dipped over the land, soaring with a freedom she could only envy. She did not want to eat such a special creature and said so.

"You would eat a chicken, wouldn't you?" he asked her with a raised eyebrow. He had one leg stretched out, the other bent at the knee and his arm rested over that leg. He looked relaxed and younger than he usually did. She tried to remember his question.

"Well, yes, I would eat chicken, but a chicken is not beautiful. It is only a chicken."

"Ah. Then the value of a creature lies in its beauty? An interesting concept."

"You are twisting my words, Dr. Murray. And you yourself said the value of a person lay in her usefulness, so you are also a judgmental type. You are just judging by a different standard."

"That is a profound statement, Miss Farnham."

"Try not to look so surprised it came from me."

He ducked his head and she looked at him suspiciously because for a moment she thought he had smiled, but when he looked at her again his face was as composed as ever.

"We should talk about how to organize our days to maximize our chances of rescue, and if it does not happen immediately, how to plan for our future needs."

He picked up one of the eggs and turned it over in his hand.

"I am still confident at some point someone will come to check on the cedar plantation. Until then we need to make sure we have enough food, and food of the right kind. People do best when their diets contain variety, so we want meat, vegetables, and the fruit. We need salt, but that can be obtained from the seawater. We can distill it through evaporation." He set the egg back down.

"I do not worry about us having enough fresh air and exercise, and at this point the insects don't seem too bothersome.

"Clearly, you are in charge of our garden, Miss Farnham. What do you think can or should be done to keep it going?"

The glow returned.

"Let me think about this a minute."

He was watching her, waiting for her answer. He did not rush her or grow impatient with her while she hummed and thought about how to best answer the question.

Daphne cleared her throat.

"The plants are surviving untended, and that is a good thing. It shows they're hardy. What I need to do is weed the garden, which will be difficult without a hoe, but maybe you can find me a pointed stick and I could use that. Some of the plants can be reseeded, but I hope we will not be here long enough for it to be an issue."

"Very good. That is a task for tomorrow. In the meantime, our fish is ready."

He used his stick to push the sand away from their supper, then took the forceps and plucked the packages off the rocks and set them aside. She ran into the cabin for a few bananas and some water, and when she came back Dr. Murray was snipping the vines with his knife.

"That crowbait is a handy tool."

"Crowbill," he corrected absently. "I should have thought of using it last night with the crabs."

He picked it up and turned it over in his hands, opening and closing it at the hinge. She sat across from him, cross-legged, and Pompom climbed into her lap. He liked this new way of sitting. She blew on a piece of the hot fish before passing it to her pup.

"Maybe it is good to see things in a new light, Doctor. You showed me how a hairnet can catch fish and keep us from starving. Tonight, you used an instrument that causes pain to help us serve supper."

He looked at her, a piece of fish halfway to his mouth.

"I believe this island sojourn is turning you into a philosopher, Miss Farnham."

"That's just silly," Daphne giggled. "Philosophers are old men with long beards."

"You will start a new fashion. Philosophers who dress in pink."

"And do not have beards."

They ate in silence, and after a few minutes she said, "This fish tastes wonderful. In fact, I do not recall fish ever tasting this good."

"Now I will wax philosophical. Your hard work today

gave you an appetite, and that is the finest seasoning. This fish is very fresh, and the onions helped give it extra flavor. I imagine you eat fish in London covered in preparations from some French chef who feels compelled to demonstrate his skill and imagination with the saucepan. Sometimes, though, simple is best."

Daphne nodded in agreement.

"It is like when you braided my hair. A simple style, but practical when one is working in the garden or fishing."

She wiped her hand on the edge of her skirt, then picked up the end of the braid snaking down her shoulder like a golden rope.

"It might be better if I cut it off. Less to fuss over."

"No! I mean, there is no need for you to cut your hair, Miss

Farnham. I will help you care for it."

"You don't mind helping with it?"

"Brushing and braiding your hair is not an…unpleasant activity. I do not mind."

They finished supper and cleaned up after themselves, and a long night still stretched before them. Neither mentioned going to sleep early.

Daphne felt keyed up and tense. She worked hard today, harder than she could ever remember working, and by all rights should be exhausted. But all she could think about was that kiss earlier, the one Dr. Murray regretted so much, the one opening a door she did not want opened. She had been congratulating herself on resisting her own proclivities once she realized what kind of man she was stranded with—one who was beginning to resemble the hero of the gothic novels she enjoyed so much. A strong man, capable and no-nonsense. He threw more wood on the fire and by its light cared for his instruments, sharpening them, checking them for damage. There was no hesitation in his movements, his fingers caressing the cold steel as if he felt affection for these instruments of pain.

A shudder ran down her spine.

"How do you do it? How do you know when to cut some-one? Do you ever hesitate?"

He paused, and looked at her across the fire, then resumed caring for his tools.

"The human body is an amazing machine, Miss Farnham. I have seen people survive horrific injuries and diseases, and in some cases live out a normal span of years. Whatever I can do to help someone survive, I do. Even if I must remove a limb to ensure that survival."

"My mother did not live out her normal span," Daphne said abruptly. She had not thought about her mother for days, but she knew even now, all these years later, her mother was a constant presence in her life.

"What happened to your mother?"

Daphne sighed. Pompom, sensing his mistress's mood, snuggled closer and licked her hand, and she patted his round belly.

"She died giving birth. The baby also."

He nodded, not offering sympathy or words of comfort.

"How old were you when that happened?"

"I was seven."

She remembered it so well. She was not allowed into the room, of course, but she hid outside the bedroom, in the hall, and watched the servants scurry back and forth. First her mother's abigail, then the midwife, and finally the man-midwife her father hired for the birth. The hours dragged on. While there were shrieks in the beginning, in the end there were only moans, and then silence.

Late that night, the servants came looking for her, and then her father came looking for her. He found her hiding behind the drapery, rocking back and forth and humming to herself, hoping that if she was a good girl her mama would call for her.

Her papa picked her up and held her tight and she'd felt his tears wetting the back of her neck. He carried her in to say goodbye to mama and to the little brother who would never grow to be a playmate for her. Her mother looked asleep, but pale, so very pale.

"Why do people die, Doctor?"

"Their hearts cease beating and they stop breathing," he said calmly. "If you are looking for a theological or philosophical answer, you will have to look elsewhere."

He set his saw aside and looked at her. "I learned many, many years ago, death is one of the few things you can be sure of in this world. We are all dying, all of us, from the moment we first draw breath. I cannot beat the Grim Reaper, but there are days I can hold him at bay."

Daphne thought about this. It explained why the man was the way he was. Dealing every day with death and disease, if he became emotional or hysterical or swooned at the sight of blood, it would be difficult for him to do his job.

It was comfortable sitting here in the night air in front of the fire, with Dr. Murray. They were talking about serious things, the kind of conversation no one wanted to have with her. Who knew how long they would be here together? The more she knew about the doctor, the better she would be able to deal with him.

"It occurs to me, Dr. Murray, that you could probably call me 'Daphne,' instead of 'Miss Farnham,' considering the circumstances."

"Would you then want to call me Alexander?"

"Why would I want to call you— Oh! That is your name."

"Your mind is unequalled," he said beneath his breath, but she heard him and smiled at his compliment.

"No, let us keep our relationship at a more formal level,

Miss Farnham. We shall be rescued soon, and the less conjecture there is about us, the better. Too much informality would only feed gossip."

Daphne blinked at him. She knew people thought her naive, but this…

"Dr. Murray," she said gently, "I ran off with George Tyndale. There is no way people will put anything but the worst possible interpretation on *our* being stranded together here. I will have to work hard to regain a place in society, a place amongst people who love gossip. They have nothing of real substance to discuss, other than fashion, of course, so they spend their time tearing down peoples' reputations. They're not like you and me, doing important and useful things."

"It does not sound like a pleasant milieu. I am surprised you choose to dwell in that setting."

"For now, it is where I am comfortable. I am used to it."

He cocked his head to the side and looked at her. "Where would you be more comfortable?"

"I like this," she said wistfully. She pulled up her knees and rested her head on them. "Not for the rest of my life, but I like being stranded here, away from people judging me and gossiping about me. Of course, I would also like to wear shoes and a proper hat, so I do hope we will be rescued."

"Did you just insult my handiwork? I believe that is a most excellent hat I made for you."

"You are teasing me. But I do like your hat. It is practical because it keeps the sun out of my eyes."

"Exactly. A hat should protect your head from the elements. It does not need fripperies to make it function properly."

"Those fripperies you dismiss make wearing the hat fun as well as functional. And there is nothing wrong with that," she said firmly.

"So you say," he said, but even in the firelight she saw the glint in his eye and the lessening of tension around his jaw that might be the most this man could conjure up in the way of a smile. It would do until he learned how to smile properly.

~

Alexander was enjoying himself. And that was a problem. It was one thing to avoid intimacy with Miss Daphne Farnham when he thought her a china-headed fashion doll. It was much harder when he saw her as a person, a person capable of involving him in conversation he found pleasurable rather than burdensome.

And he could not banish that kiss from his mind. It reminded him of when he was sixteen and everything, every passing thought, seemed focused on women and sexual relations. Bread rising on the kitchen table made him think of intercourse. Of course, at that age it had all been hypothetical. Now it was worse. The craving carried with it an idea of just how marvelous it would be to have her beneath him, responding to his caresses as she'd responded to his kiss earlier.

He could not count on her rebuffing him if he made advances toward her. Her response earlier was all he could wish for in a woman he wanted to bed.

That was part of the problem. Miss Daphne Farnham, society beauty and toast of London, wanted *him*, Alexander Murray, a Scottish bastard with few social skills and a lifetime of gore and disease in his wake. He was not an idiot, he knew his looks were at best passable. He did not flatter himself he was the answer to a maiden's prayer, but he was only human. Being desired by a beautiful woman was making it hard to resist doing something stupid.

She was no shy retiring damsel, her response to his kiss proved she was a young woman of passion. He feared if her fiery nature came into contact with his dry-as-dust sensibilities it would cause a conflagration of epic proportions. A true disaster. Which is why he had to resist looking at her and try not to think about the coming hours when they would adjourn to their little shack, and he would lie next to her voluptuous form, her skin in contact with his nearly naked body.

He stood abruptly and said, "Your pardon, I will be back shortly."

He knew walking about in the dark was a good way to trip and break a leg, but logic was overridden by the need to put some distance between them, at least for a few more minutes.

Eventually, he had to return. She was sitting with her arms around her knees, humming to herself, looked up at his approach and smiled at him as he sat across from her.

That was the thing. She smiled at him *all the time*. As if there was something about him worth smiling at, something that inspired in her feelings of warmth and…friendship? It could not possibly be anything stronger, not between the two of them. It was not just the difference in their status, it was that they were such different people. No doubt in a different place they would bore each other to tears. It was only here, now, without other distractions he was able to tolerate her. And vice versa.

He also had the proof of his own eyes that she smiled at strange men with little provocation. He'd seen it aboard the *Magpie*.

"Why do you smile at me?"

The abrupt question wiped the smile from her face.

"Because I like you?" she asked tentatively, as if unsure of her own feelings or his reaction. Then she rallied and said,

"Smiling is something people do, Dr. Murray. Some of us, anyway. I am not sure you know how to smile. Have you always been such a sobersides?"

"Yes."

"Well! When I have a little boy, I will smile at him all the time, so that he does not grow up into a big grumpy stick," she sniffed.

Alexander looked into the flames dancing in the firepit and remembered a russet-haired woman who smiled even when worn down by the cares of the world and the upbringing of a fatherless boy.

"You do that, Miss Farnham. Little boys need to be smiled at. Especially the grumpy ones. They need smiles the most."

She propped her chin on her hand and studied him. "Tell me about your family. I know you did not have a father, but did you have anyone else? Cousins?"

"No, there was just my mother and me," he said, still looking at the fire, and not the woman. "Mother had to leave home; her family did not want her living nearby."

"Oh. Surely you had friends?"

"Children are taught not to befriend boys who are bast— who do not have fathers." He was not inclined to say more, but the words kept flowing. "I did have one close friend, Jamie Campbell."

"Where is he now?"

"He is dead, killed in an accident when he was ten years old."

"He fell from a tree, didn't he?"

He looked at her across the low burning fire. Her face was unusually grave and it struck him again that she saw things with an acuity he would not expect from her, an ability to see deep into a person. It was disturbing, especially when he had his neatly ordered view of her where she resided in the compartment labeled "widgeon."

"Yes. We were climbing after the last of the season's apples. Jamie stood on a branch that looked sturdy enough but could not bear his weight. It snapped. He fell to the ground."

He took a deep breath, forcing himself to dredge up the memories.

"His organs were damaged, and he was bleeding internally. Bones poked—I sat there with him, paralyzed with fear, but there was no one near enough to run to for assistance."

"You could not save him."

"I know now no one could have saved him. But at the time, all I knew was how helpless I was, incapable of doing anything."

"Dr. Murray, this tragedy could just as easily have happened if your friend Jamie were climbing by himself, or with another boy, correct?"

He looked at her. Without her smiles, her face was the face of the grown woman she was, not that of a giggly girl. She was still every bit as beautiful but in a different fashion, the difference between Athena and Aphrodite.

"Yes, he could still have fallen and died."

"Then your being there accomplished something. You could not save him, but you were with him. He did not die alone."

Now it was her turn to look into the fire.

"When George was dying of his fever, he did not know me. He cried out for his mother, so I stayed with him, and held his hand, and allowed him to think his mother was with him at his last moments. The odd thing is, Dr. Murray, I know George's mother, and she is as frozen as one of Gunter's ices. I cannot imagine her interrupting one of her card games or dress fittings to stay with a dying man, even her son."

"You must have loved him very much."

She was silent for such a long time, he was not sure she'd heard him.

"No. I did not love him, but I was fond of him. He was fun, and fashionable, and he made me laugh. I did not need to marry for money, and I thought George was what I wanted in a husband."

"Is that why you ran off with him to Jamaica?"

She was sitting with her arms clasped around her knees, her bare toes peeking out in the firelight.

"My papa…" she swallowed and tried to speak again. "Papa arranged a marriage for me, a marriage I did not want."

She looked at him, and there was confusion furrowing her smooth brow.

"I told Papa over and over again that I could not marry Lord Bernard, that he was too old, and his breath smelled rank, but he would not listen. I knew I could not be happy with this man, but Papa said he knew what was best for me, and it was for my own good. I would be a countess, and I needed someone to take care of me, and that was what mattered.

"When George suggested we run off together, it seemed like the best idea. And it was fun," she said wistfully, "Until he realized my father was not going to give us any money and we were stuck in Jamaica, and then George became ill. My father sent Mrs. Cowper after me and you know the rest, Dr. Murray."

"Miss Farnham, were you actually married to George Tyndale?"

"Why do you ask?"

"It seems a reasonable question, since everyone calls you 'Miss Farnham.'"

She cleared her throat and clasped her hands tighter around her knees. "George said the captain on the ship would marry us, and he had with him what he said was a special license. It looked impressive, full of Latin and flourishes, and I saw both our names on it, and I believed him.

"Do you know what, Dr. Murray? It turned out that it was not a special license at all. It was a ruse! He was in such a hurry to hustle me away before my father married me off he was willing to lie for me! He must have really, really wanted to marry me."

Alexander thought it more probably he really, really wanted access to Miss Farnham's fortune. But Tyndale was dead and unable to defend himself, and she had had enough of her illusions about the good nature of people quashed like a butterfly beneath a boot. He did not need to add to the list.

She continued, "And I know now he had no funds for a special license. Then the captain said he would not marry us, that it would not be a legal marriage. By then I was with George in the middle of the ocean. He told me we were as good as married and we would make it legal in Jamaica."

She sighed. "You must think me a complete hussy."

Alexander opened his mouth, and closed it, and held back his first response. "I think you are a young woman who feels emotions strongly, Miss Farnham. And you are trusting." *And naive and credulous and gullible...*

"You know me so well. I like people! What is wrong with that?"

He did not need to interfere, but he felt compelled to say something. It was too easy to lead Daphne Farnham astray. Wave something bright and shiny in front of her, or tell her lies, and she would give you one of those heartfelt smiles and do whatever you asked.

"I suppose it is not a bad thing to like people. It has never appealed to me, so I cannot say for certain. However, it might keep you out of difficult situations if you learned how to be somewhat less trusting. Sadly, not everyone has your best interests at heart."

"I know that! I am not a complete ninny, you know."

There must have been something showing on his face—like utter disbelief—for she continued.

"No, really, I am not. But I worry…"

She looked around to make sure no one was listening, oblivious to the fact that they were on a deserted island. He took a drink while he waited to hear what worried her.

"I worry, Dr. Murray, that I have unnatural desires."

Alexander sprayed out his drink as he choked. Daphne Farnham pounded on his back until the wheezing subsided. She watched him anxiously.

"I shocked you. I was afraid that would happen, but I also thought…" She looked down at her hands, twisting together in her lap. "I thought since you are a surgeon I could talk to you. Remember on the boat when you said my parts were no different from any other woman's? I thought since you knew all about women's parts, you could talk with me about this."

He wiped his face with his hand, trying to collect thoughts which had blown up like a Congreve rocket. "Have you had a conversation like this with your physician?"

"Oh, heavens, no! Talk about this with Dr. Drummond? I could never!"

Alexander almost said, "Then why am I being blessed this way?" but after all, she trusted him. She was not the first person who had asked him to keep a confidence, though he was not yet sure her issue was a medical one or a moral one. But a surgeon heard all sorts of information in the course of his work and he could deal with this professionally. He hoped. She couldn't know that *all* he knew about women were their *parts*, that the last woman he'd spent any real time with had died tragically, that since then his relations were only with women who wanted his silver, not his opinion?

"I worry I am not normal, Dr. Murray. You know how women say they do not like 'that part' of being married? *I* liked it. I liked it a lot! I liked it in the morning, I liked it late at night, I liked it in the afternoon, after luncheon." She frowned. "I did not like it during luncheon, that was messy."

Sweat broke out on Alexander's brow as he tried hard not to think about Miss Farnham on the luncheon table, her skirts tossed up and honey drizzled across a belly as delectable as Devonshire's finest cream.

"Do you think I am normal to have these strong feelings?"

He cleared his throat, took a sip of water, and looked at her. She was gazing at him with anticipation, and he chose his words as carefully as he'd ever felt his way around a wound.

"Normal—" he started, then stopped. Did he have even the vaguest idea of what was normal, or was he going off halfcocked, without having evidence to back up his pronouncements? Hadn't he spent his entire life looking at symptoms and vital signs before making a diagnosis?

"Here is what I think," he said slowly, trying to sound like he knew what he was talking about. "You are a young healthy adult who was married. More or less. The amount—and types—of activity you engage in would depend on the abilities and desires of the two people involved, and based on what you told me, I cannot find anything abnormal in your behavior."

She leaned over and put her hand on his arm. "Thank you. I know you find me a sad trial, but I do enjoy talking with you. I will always remember these days and this island."

"Perhaps we should leave the island first before we wax nostalgic for it. I will build that signal fire in the morning."

"I have another favor to ask, Doctor. Would you show me how to start a fire?"

"You never started a fire for yourself?"

She looked at him as if he was the one who was not bright.

"Why should I? Every morning of my life, when I woke up a maid had lit the fire in my room. If I needed to light a candle or lamp, a footman would do it for me, or I could light a taper from an existing flame. I had no need to do it for myself."

Alexander was stunned that this woman in front of him, who came from the most civilized and privileged society, was incapable of performing one of the most basic of human tasks.

But as she said, why would she learn?

"Yes. I will teach you in the morning how to start a fire. It is something everyone should know, and it is important for you to learn it here and now. Something could happen to me, and you need to know how to light a fire to warm yourself and cook your food."

Daphne drew back in shock.

"Something happen? What would happen to you?"

"Anything could happen. That is the nature of life…and death. I could be hit on the head by a tree branch, or choke to death on a fish bone, or be punctured by a sharp stone and become septic."

"But…then I would be all alone!"

"Yes, you would. I am going to do my best to ensure that if anything happens you can care for yourself. You already learned some skills in food gathering. You would survive, with or without me."

"Oh, please, do not tell me that!" She clutched his arm, her eyes round in terror. "I do not want to think about being here alone! I would die! You need to stay alive, to take care of me!"

He knew he was being brutal with her, but it was better than giving her silly platitudes or making promises he could not keep. He leaned forward and put his hand on her other arm and felt her fingers digging into him, their contact a circle of comfort in the darkness.

"Miss Farnham—Daphne—listen to me. I do not expect any further disasters. Remember when I told you to pack your valise aboard the *Magpie*? It was a precaution, but you were ready when the ship went down. The officers prepared the boat by putting water in it. We might not have survived in the ocean had they not done that. This is just more preparation, and preparation and knowledge is always better than not knowing how to deal with a situation."

"You won't leave me here alone?"

"I will do my best not to," he said gently.

Daphne threw herself into his arms and clamped herself to him like a limpet, just as he'd done with her earlier in the day.

It was fear, he told himself, fear of being alone, fear of him not taking care of her, just as his response this morning had been the unreasonable fear of his boyhood tragedy repeated.

But his mind was telling him one thing and his body another. His hand hovered above her head, ready to burrow into that silken hair and clasp her to him. She was warm in his arms, and soft, and smelled of wood smoke and woman. It was all he could do to control himself, to not take hold of her and lay her down on the soft ground and bury himself within her welcoming heat. To forget his own fears for a handful of blissful hours.

Someone was going to have to be cool-headed and rational, and he was going to have to be that someone. Again.

He disengaged her arms from around his neck and held her hands a moment so she would not be hurt by his rejection. Though why he cared about whether her feelings were hurt was a mystery to be solved another day.

"Why don't you find your hairbrush and I will brush out your hair for—for you. We will deal with the rest in the morning."

He did not want to say "for bed" because the intimacy implied by that was more than either of them needed to be contemplating this second. She rose and fetched her hairbrush from the cabin, then settled between his legs. Neither of them remarked that she was now quite capable of brushing out her own hair. When he was satisfied, at least in the sense that her hair was gleaming and unsnarled, he said, "You go to sleep. I will be in after I tend to the fire."

"I need to learn that also, Dr. Murray."

"Tomorrow, Miss Farnham."

"Do you want Pompom to stay with you? He is good company."

Alexander looked at the animal sprawled on its back, legs up in the air as it dreamed doggy dreams.

"No, take him with you. He would miss you."

She gently awakened the dog and gathered him up in her arms, he watched her walk into the dark cabin, and not for the first time, envied the dog.

CHAPTER 12

"Do you have everything you need?"

Daphne looked at the items in front of her and ticked them off on her fingers.

"I gathered the driest wood and plant shreds I could find. Here is your piece of char cloth. I have my twigs ready and more dry wood. I prepared the firepit."

"Then stop humming and listen, Miss Farnham."

She couldn't help it. She was so excited at learning how to make a fire that the humming was springing out of her like the water burbling up to the pool. Why had no one ever realized how much she loved learning new things? Why had *she* never realized it? She vowed when she returned to England, she would make it her goal to learn one new thing each day. Maybe learn a new word like "gravitas," or how to build a fire, or how to help gruff surgeons smile.

That last one needed further work.

Daphne slanted him a glance from beneath her lashes. Dr. Murray had his jacket on today, the one that washed ashore. It was torn at the front and could not be buttoned, and his chest shone through the opening. If he thought by putting on the jacket he could redirect her into not dwelling on his body and the pleasures they could enjoy together, he'd failed miserably. The civilized coat combined with the uncivilized sight of his bare chest, as hard and solid and golden brown as the wood of the cedar tree behind her, was even more enticing than when he'd been completely bare.

"Pay attention."

"Yes, Dr. Murray," she said, squelching the musical notes leaking out of her.

"Now, we will prepare the firepit."

He motioned her closer, and she crouched down next to him, so close she could smell the salt on his warm skin.

"Stop looking at me and look at the firepit."

"I cannot help it. I like looking at you."

He turned his head and looked at her, his brows pulled together in a frown.

"You need to put your hat on. The sun is affecting you."

"No, it isn't. I do like looking at you."

He swallowed, and she saw the strong lines of his throat move. No wonder men wore high collars and cravats! She had no idea the sight of a man's naked neck was so enticing. It was a good thing men kept them covered most of the time, or women would want to do things like lean over and lick the little bead of perspiration trickling down into the collar of his torn coat.

"Stop looking at me," he said hoarsely. "You are only reacting this way because of proximity and our being the only two people on this island."

Daphne thought about this.

"No, I'm not. It is you. You make me feel this way."

She'd woken up this morning in his arms, her nose buried against his chest, and she lay there, feeling him, his body not stiff with the tension and tightly wound emotions he kept as far from her as he possibly could. Instead he felt warm and made her feel safe. She'd leaned back to see his face, and asleep he looked younger, even with his bearded stubble, the lines of care and worry smoothed out. Daphne also felt him against her belly, and now that she knew he wasn't going to die from being erect she found it rather…enticing. It made her want to rub against him, and stroke him, and see if he would feel as good inside her as he did outside her. It was all she could do not to kiss him awake, just to see what his eyes would look like when they opened and she was the first thing he saw. Would they light up with one of his hidden smiles? Would they grow dark with desire?

She was not to know, because he came awake with a sudden jerk, his eyes widening as he realized he was entwined with Daphne. He'd pulled away quickly, rose to his feet and left the cabin.

Now though they were sitting so close together, and really, what did he expect? It wasn't her fault that dry old Dr. Murray had turned out to be a very…what was that word? Virile. Very virile looking man.

"Miss Farnham. You are either giggling or humming. If you cannot refrain from making unnecessary noises, I will not be able to demonstrate fire making for you."

"Yes, doctor," she said, brought back to earth. He might be much better looking than he'd been aboard the *Magpie*, but he was still a grumpy stick.

She paid attention to the demonstration with the flint and steel from his surgical chest.

"Why do you keep fire making tools in your chest?"

"Because my chest is the one article I know I always have with me. And there are times when I need to start a fire to mix a preparation or boil water. Pay attention now."

He blew on the tinder to fill it with air, which he said would help feed the fire, then placed a piece of char cloth atop it. Holding the flint and steel at an angle, he struck the flint downward and a shower of sparks fell onto the prepared area. It took a few strikes, but he said, "See the glow?"

Sure enough, there was a spark atop the char cloth. He placed the tinder around it, and leaning over, blew gently onto the material until a wisp of smoke rose into the still air. Then he reached over with his fingers and pinched the fire out.

"Why did you do that? You had a flame almost started."

"I already know how to build a fire. Now that I have demonstrated, you will do it."

"I will?"

"Yes. Find fresh tinder and we will begin."

It took more tries than his efforts. First, she had to repeat striking until she found the right angle for the spark. Then she lost the spark by either smothering it with the tinder or blowing it out. Her back ached from leaning over, her tense muscles cramping up as she struck the steel again. This time she was rewarded with her own wisp of smoke, and following the surgeon's instructions fed it tinder, then kindling, and finally, small sticks until the fire was crackling along.

Dr. Murray stood, his knees making a noise that had him wincing, but Daphne felt invigorated.

"I did it! I made the fire!" She clasped her hands together as she sat back on her heels. "This must be how Adam and Eve felt in the Garden when they made fire for the first time."

"You did well," he said, smiling at her. No, wait, he was not smiling at her, not with his teeth, but his face! She could tell by that gleam in his eyes and the angle of his eyebrows he was smiling at her.

Pride washed through her as she took his hand to climb to her feet.

"I can build a fire. I can boil crabs and cook fish in leaves.

I can dig vegetables from the garden and cook and eat them. I can boil eggs."

"And you can braid your own hair. Yes, you are on the way to becoming a self-sufficient woman of parts, Miss Farnham."

She watched him closely, but for once he did not sound sarcastic. Maybe he was proud of her also.

He looked around where they were standing atop a hill. It had been a strenuous climb after breakfast, but he said, "Look out to sea. This may be the highest point on the island. Your fire will be our signal fire."

"Oh! My fire is important? Not just for practice?"

"Not just for practice. We need to gather wood, green and dry both. Your blaze will be a pillar of cloud by day, a flame by night, just like the one that led the Israelites out of Egypt."

"What if the fire goes out during the night?"

"Then you will restart it."

He said this matter-of-factly. Like he could depend on her. They trooped back down to the cabin, where the fish stew was cooking over a low flame. They'd worked on it together that morning, Dr. Murray supplying the fish, Daphne gathering the vegetables. She was keeping an eye on the garden to make sure there would be enough of the crops left for the future. It would not do to eat the seed corn.

When she said that, he looked at her with that odd expression he wore whenever she said something that surprised him. Surprised him in a good way.

"I grew up in the country, Dr. Murray. My father was busy in the city, so it was easier for him to leave me at Rawlings. One of my special friends there was the estate manager."

She had not thought about Mr. Branch and his wife Hilda for some time. It was funny. Whenever she thought about them and their snug little cottage, her memories were of it always being sunny, even though there were many rainy afternoons she'd sit curled up in front of the fire listening to Mr. Branch talk about crop rotation and silage and drainage and which crops to put in the next year and lambing season with its joys and woes.

"We may be eating this stew again for supper, Miss Farnham. There is more than I anticipated, even with your dog helping us consume it."

"I do not mind. I vow, after eating raw fish in the middle of the ocean, I will never again complain about a cooked meal."

"It does give you a new perspective," he agreed. "Do you know what I miss the most with a meal like this?"

Daphne blinked. They were having table conversation, just like normal people did. They were sitting outside the hut in the shade of the trees, on the ground, but it was almost like sitting at the table.

"No, what do you miss? Wine?"

"No, although that would be pleasant. Or ale. I am not much of one for spirits. No, what I miss with a meal like this is a good fresh loaf of bread," he said wistfully. "That is one of things I'd crave most when we were at sea. Light, fluffy loaves, hot from the oven, smeared with freshly churned butter, and perhaps a dollop of marmalade."

"I had not thought about it until you just said it, but you are right. I never realized how much good food was part of my life until now, though this stew is quite tasty."

"It is tasty because we are hungry and worked hard for it," he said.

"Do you know what I miss the most?"

"Your frivolous hats?"

"No, I mean food I miss. I miss my morning chocolate. I would have chocolate and a small sweet roll every morning when I arose."

"That is not a breakfast," he said dismissively. "Good hot porridge, thick enough so a spoon stands straight up in the center, with plenty of cream and honey, now, that is a breakfast that gets your bowels moving so you can start your day." His face grew red when he'd realized what he said to her, russet enough to match his hair.

"What I mean is that porridge is a better choice for your diet, Miss Farnham."

"I do not mind that you said 'bowels' to me. After all, did you not say that my parts were the same as anyone else's?"

She put her hand over her flat belly, looking down at those parts in question.

"I have lost weight, Dr. Murray. I can see bones where I could not before. Just as well my dresses washed away, since none of them would fit properly now."

"Won't you take in your dresses if they are too large for you?"

"Heavens, no! I will buy new ones."

"Sounds like an unnecessary expense when you could make do with your old dresses."

"La, but they would be out of fashion. And the lines would not be the same on them if I took them in."

He was looking at her intently.

"Yes, I understand you feel that way, but what would you do, if you did not have money for new dresses?"

Daphne looked at him, speechless.

"Not have money for new dresses? What else would I spend money on? Oh, hats and shoes, of course, but really, you need dresses to go with the hats and shoes. And gloves."

"Some people must spend their money on food and shelter and do not have any left over for new dresses each season."

"I know that, I am not like that French queen who told people to eat cake. I would have told them to eat meat and vegetables instead and buy cakes later. But that is not the point. Just because some people do not have money for new dresses doesn't mean *I* don't have money for new dresses."

"What if..." He looked down at the bowl in his hands, turning it around. "What if you married a man who had no money to support you in that fashion?"

"You mean like George? That would have eventually worked itself out. My father loves me, after all, and would not want to see me suffer. He would have sent money to us."

Then she remembered how her father tried to force her into a marriage she did not want. But that was then. Now that he knew she was serious about not marrying old Lord Bernard he would welcome her back.

"I hope you are right," he said, rising to his feet.

"I liked being married," Daphne said abruptly. "I would not mind having another husband, if he were the right man."

She looked down at the stones on the ground while she said this, unaccountably shy all of a sudden. She did not want to look at Dr. Murray to see his reaction to her statement.

"Matrimony is a natural estate for most adults, Miss Farnham, at least ones who are settled with enough income to support a family."

She looked at him now, through her lashes. He was looking out to sea.

"Most ladies would be pleased to marry you. Except..."

He looked back at her, one eyebrow raised. She knew his language now and answered his query.

"Dr. Murray, if you want a lady to marry you, you need to smile. Laugh, even!"

There. She'd said it. He could make of it what he would. And then he made of it pretty much what she expected he would.

"Ridiculous. A marriage is not about giggling and foolishness. A marriage is about shared values and compatibility and mutual goals."

"Oh?" she said loftily. "And do you speak from experience? Let me remind you that one of us has been married—more or less—and is the more knowledgeable in this area. You may know all about starting fires and cooking fish, but I know more than you about being married."

"Do you? Miss Farnham, the idea of taking your advice for something as important as how I'll spend the rest of my life, and with whom, fills me with dread."

"Scoff if you will, but if you are as intelligent as you think you are, you will listen to me. If I had a pencil and paper I would make you a list."

He leaned back against a tree and crossed his arms over his chest, then crossed his legs at the ankles. His feet were on the large side, which for some reason she had never noticed before, but now she did. George had small feet.

"Miss Farnham? You were going to offer me advice? I do not need paper, I have an excellent memory. You tell me what you think I need to know, and I will give it all the consideration it deserves."

"Very well," Daphne said. She sat up straight, her legs folded beneath her and her hands in her lap. Looking up at the surgeon leaning against the tree she was struck again by how she failed to notice so much about him aboard the *Magpie*. How his build was solid, but not heavy. It was the solidity of muscles earned laboring over men who needed bones reset and limbs removed. He was not overly tall, but his legs were long and, as torn as his trousers were, she could see those legs were excellently formed. The pared-down planes and angles of his face reflected his stony outlook, but it was not an unattractive combination. No, some woman would find his face attractive, she had no doubt, even with the wrinkles at the edges of his hazel eyes and the skin bronzed from the tropical sun and years at sea. In fact, some women might find him amazingly attractive, in a gruff and serious fashion.

Speaking of fashion…

"First of all, if you are going to attract a wife, you will need an entire new wardrobe when we land in England."

"All of my clothes were lost at sea. I will need an entire new wardrobe regardless of whether or not I mean to attract a wife."

"Exactly! You are presented with an opportunity, Dr. Murray, an opportunity to join the world of well-dressed men with good tailoring. No, don't pucker up at me! I saw your wardrobe on the *Magpie*. The best that could be said about your appearance was that you were clean and neat."

"Thank you," he said humbly.

"I am serious! We established this is an area of particular expertise for me, so you should pay attention."

"Yes, ma'am."

She looked at him suspiciously, but as usual his face gave away little. Even his eyebrows were at rest.

"Now then, your wardrobe. I noticed on the ship that you favor the color brown."

"It does hide bloodstains."

She shuddered.

"You will not be choosing your wardrobe based on what hides bloodstains, Doctor. I cannot imagine you will show up for a ride in the park or a morning call with a bloody knife sticking out of your pocket!"

He thought about this.

"Probably not, but I do always like to keep a tourniquet or two on my person. You never know when you'll need to tie off a limb."

"Dr. Murray, gentlemen do not show up in a lady's parlor bearing tourniquets! You are to show up with flowers or send them ahead of you. Really, you said yourself you were rejected for an *American*, for goodness sake!"

She stood, and briskly wiped her hands together. She needed to pace—and hum—while she was thinking. "We've established you like women—"

"Did you have doubts on that score?"

"Not the way you disdain fashion. Now then, on that note. You need colors and fabrics reflecting who you are, or more properly, who you will be by the time I am finished with you. The natural philosopher who thinks deep thoughts but is also capable of dressing appropriately."

"If that's the case, we are back to brown and bloodstains."

"No, we are not!" She nearly stamped her bare foot in frustration, but then she looked at him and realized he was laughing at her. Oh, he was not *laughing* laughing, that would be over the top, but he was amused.

And she realized one more thing—he was not laughing at her, thinking her stupid or empty headed, he was laughing because he was entertained by her.

That is what he needed. He did not realize it yet, but he needed a woman who'd take him out of his grumps, who would make him see more of the humor in life. Daphne could help with that. Once he was properly outfitted, she could introduce him to women who would be right for him.

She frowned at that idea. There was something about the idea of introducing Dr. Murray to other women that simply did not appeal. And to be honest, she knew few women of his class, women of the trade and merchant class.

But she knew dressmakers, and some of them were successful businesswomen in their own right, and if they were not looking for a man, perhaps they'd know a merchant's daughter or a tradesman's widow who was looking for a man.

She'd worry later about how the idea of Dr. Murray holding someone else in his arms at night bothered her.

"Do you not want to cut a dash in society? Never mind, I do not know why I even bother. If I said I needed a new hat you would say, 'You only have one head, why do you need more than one hat?'"

"I am perfectly willing to acknowledge you need a warm hat for winter wear and a straw hat for summer. This conversation is nonsense. I do not need to change my ways to catch a wife. I have money saved, and all my limbs and my teeth. I am a man of abstemious habits. I cannot imagine how having a waistcoat of daffodil satin would make a bit of difference in my prospects."

Daphne perked up.

"Now you are putting your brain to work!" She pointed her finger at him. "With your coloring daffodil satin would be a handsome choice. Not for a coat though, that would be a bit much. As you say, for a waistcoat. I had no idea you were taking fashion so seriously."

"I am not taking this seriously, for a very good reason. That statement about my wearing something as ridiculous as daffodil satin was meant to illustrate why this conversation is waste of time. I have no intention of drawing attention to myself that way.

"All I need is someone who can tend house, cook a meal, will not frighten the horses with her looks and who will care for her children. The more I think about it, the more I agree with you that I could use a wife. If I had a wife, I would not need to pay for a housekeeper or a cook, an economy I approve of."

Daphne was left speechless by his words, and it took a few moments to gather her wits together. Even George offered more to her than what Dr. Murray outlined in a spouse. George made her laugh and was entertaining. Now she felt sorry for the poor woman the surgeon would marry. An unpaid housekeeper and cook indeed!

In her stunned silence the surgeon pushed himself off the tree and began gathering up their dishes from lunch, rescuing the ones Pompom was licking clean for a more thorough washing.

Daphne had regained her equilibrium and could even smile as she envisioned Dr. Murray going to a hiring fair to find a wife, for that seemed to be his plan. She helped him carry the dishes to the pool and scrubbed them with sand before rinsing them for later use. Pompom took a drink from the pool, shaking his head and spraying her with drops of water when he was done.

"Poor Pompom, you are sadly in need of a good brushing also," she commiserated, but the dog seemed to care as little for fashion as the other male, and only barked and danced around her feet when she started back to the cabin.

She was not willing to let the subject of grooming the other male go by the wayside. Someday he would thank her for it. And if he did not, his wife would, no matter what he said. A flash of color in a palmetto gave her an idea.

"You are a natural philosopher, Doctor, and you observe the natural world. Do the males of the bird species not sport the brightest plumage? It attracts the eyes of their mates. Perhaps, sir, you would do well to add some bright plumage to your wardrobe."

"I have no desire to be a peacock."

"Maybe not a peacock, but even a robin sports colorful feathers. Your hair looks like autumn foliage, the bones of your face are strong, and your eyes are the color of..." She thought for a moment as they walked. "The color of sunlight and leaves together. A good combination for the earthen tones you favor. But for special occasions, a purple waistcoat would bring out the green of your eyes even more."

She realized she was walking by herself and turned around. Dr. Murray had stopped on the path and stared at her.

"What?"

"You see me that way, Miss Farnham? As someone whose physiognomy is all of that?"

"I do not know," she said. "What does that mean?"

"Physiognomy. My face. I believe it is the origin of the cant word 'phiz.'"

"Truly? Then I learned something else new today! Thank you, Dr. Murray. Physiognomy," she said beneath her breath, remembering the word. She would work it into a conversation at some point in London to demonstrate how much more learned she was than before she was shipwrecked.

She looked over her shoulder. He was following her, with an unreadable expression on his, she smiled, his physiognomy. Soon she would be sounding like Daphne Farnham, natural philosopheress!

After they put up the dishes, he said, "It is time to light our beacon."

"Do you believe it will draw ships to us?"

"I am more concerned about the sorts of ships it might draw. Unless it is a Royal Navy ship we will proceed with great caution."

Daphne looked down at her bare feet, scuffed with dirt and rough from walking.

"Will you be sorry to leave this island?"

When he did not speak, she finally raised her eyes, and saw him watching her intently. He took a step closer, then stopped himself.

"First comes rescue, Miss Farnham."

They walked in silence up to the beacon firepit. Everything was in readiness, the wood gathered, the conditions perfect—dry and only a slight breeze. Their fire would be visible for vast distances.

He passed her the fire making tools, and she stood there, looking at them.

"Think of all the hats waiting for you to purchase them."

She knelt down next to the pit, and after some fierce humming and a few strikes her fire started smoldering. It did not give her the same sense of accomplishment it had that morning, but he assisted her in laying the wood and feeding it, the green wood making her cough as the smoke rose up into the blue sky. They moved away from the smoke and watched it, a signal for all the ships at sea.

"It will burn until near sunset," he said. "Before it is too dark we will feed it again with the dry wood and hope for the best."

He watched her for some heartbeats, not saying anything else. Then he stepped closer to her, and put his hand beneath her chin, lifting her face up to look at him.

"Do not be downcast. We knew this idyll could not last, and we both have responsibilities and lives to return to."

She clasped his hand, so strong, so capable. "You will not forget me, will you, Dr. Murray? You will think of me sometimes, and our time on our island?"

"I could never forget you, Daphne Farnham," he said in a low voice, and his other hand came up, cradling her face. Her eyes fluttered shut and she wanted to stand there, forever, feeling the touch of his hands on her. He startled her then, kissing her on her forehead, a kiss of friendship, but she made a little noise deep in her throat and he stilled. She heard the far off call of a bird, and the snap of the wood smoking on the fire. Then she felt his lips again, touching delicately at the corner of her closed eye, her cheekbone, like the faintest brush of sensation, as light as smoke at the corner of her mouth, and her lips opened, seeking more of him, all of him.

She clutched at his shoulders, covered by his ragged coat, but that wasn't enough, not when his mouth was teasing hers, his firm lips caressing hers, his tongue seeking entrance.

Daphne opened for him with a hum of delight, her hands slipping inside his coat to feel his warmth, his back with the play of muscles beneath the skin, and she clutched him to her. It felt so good, like a fine wine trickling down her throat, the kiss opening up her senses to every other part of her body. She pressed herself against his bare chest, and her breasts, separated by only the thin layer of her remaining garment felt wonderful against his firmness, the nipples tightening and swelling against him. She could feel him against her belly, hard and erect, as solid as the rest of him and she wanted more. One hand held his head to hers, reveling in the feel of the crisp curls at the back of his neck, the other pressed against his hips, bringing him into contact with the place that needed his touch, that ached for him.

He kept an arm at her back while his mouth roamed over her face, her neck, down to the collarbones that showed through her ragged dress, and his kisses there made her shiver, his mouth making her feel—she had no more words left to describe how she felt, only that it was like flying. His other hand rested on her breast, so lightly she scarcely knew it was there until his fingers stroked her, at that point where she was swollen and aching, even as his mouth returned, his lips slanting across hers, his tongue stroking inside her. When she widened her stance to take him more fully against her, she hummed deep in her throat, a sound of contentment and satisfaction.

He broke the kiss and moved his head back from hers, his breath a harsh rasp. His hand moved off her breast to hold her head against his shoulder as a shudder wracked his frame. Daphne's hand fisted in the collar of his coat, not willing to release him.

"We should not—"

"Stop saying that!" she hissed, angry and aroused and not knowing if she should slap him or kiss him again. His chin jerked at the tone of her voice. She'd shocked him. Good.

"We are adults! I am a widow and not some chit who has never been out of the schoolroom. You are the one who keeps telling me we could die in the next moment from a coconut falling on our head—"

"I do not think there are coconuts here…"

She *was* going to slap him. Later. "I do not want a nature lecture, you ridiculous man! I want *you*! On top of me, inside of me, kissing me and…"

Whatever other commands she was going to give him were cut off as he groaned, his mouth coming back down on hers, his hands moving down her body to her hips, his arms holding her to him.

This was exactly what she wanted, was needing, after those nights sleeping side by side, the days spent together in closer companionship than she'd ever shared with another human being. She wanted him in a way she had never wanted any other man. She wanted his almost-smiles, his sarcastic remarks, his praise of her accomplishments, his willingness to treat her like she was something more than a beautiful frame on which to hang expensive garments and jewels.

Alexander's mouth moved fiercely across hers demanding her response, a response she was eager to offer him. His hands roamed over her body, and when she felt the heat of his palm on her thigh, she shivered in delight and pulled him closer to her, her hips beginning their own movement against his, craving what was hidden from her by the remains of his garments. She inched her hand down, across his bare chest, and her breathing hitched when she felt his heart beating fast beneath her hand, her explorations drawing another groan from deep in his throat. She was ready for more, she wanted more, and was moving to the buttons of his trousers when he grabbed her hand and gripped it, tight.

He brought their clasped hands up between them, where her heart was pounding a staccato rhythm, their joined fists separating them. He raised his head, his eyes dark and the harsh planes of his face stretched stark with need.

"We cannot do this."

"Aaargh! I knew you were going to say that! I just knew it!"

"This is not easy for me either! You are the most beautiful woman I ever held in my arms and you are so…" He stopped and took a deep breath. "I have a duty, Daphne, to take you back to your family in England. I cannot take advantage of our situation—"

"Yes, you can!"

"No, I cannot," he snapped. It was as close as he'd come yet to losing his temper with her. He was every bit as affected as she was by their mutual attraction, no matter how much he tried to deny it.

Ridiculous man!

He still held her hand but released her when she pushed against him, turned her back and stomped away, her fists clenching and unclenching as she tried to bring herself under control. When she could speak again, she whirled around and pointed a finger at him accusingly.

"I know you think I am some kind of strumpet, but I cannot help myself, Dr. Murray! You make me feel…" She struggled to find the right words, but they weren't there for her and her hand fell to her side, open and empty.

"You make me *feel*! You! Not someone else, not just because we are abandoned here, *you* make me feel this way! This is all your fault!"

"I know that," he said bleakly, looking down at the dirt. "I accept full responsibility for my actions."

He was so miserable that her anger at him dissipated, and she was ashamed of herself. He was just a man, after all, and he was trying to do what he thought was right.

"I am returning to the cabin now," she said, looking over her shoulder as she started down the hill, but he wasn't watching her. His attention was focused out to sea. She knew he was looking for rescue. From her, and from himself.

Their days settled into a routine where the work never seemed to end, but Daphne acknowledged it was work necessary to their survival. She loved it. She adored their strange, exotic life stranded on this tiny piece of earth where she awakened at dawn to bird calls and Pompom licking her face. She was still hoping for kisses from the other male on the island, but he kept his distance.

Except at night. They slept together and shared their warmth, curled like spoons with his arm around her waist. She sometimes heard him repeating mathematical formulae as part of his ritual to fall asleep. When she asked him if he did this every night, he said he only did it when he was sleeping next to her, which Daphne thought strange. Maybe she was distracting him from remembering all the important things he needed to remember.

Their days began with eggs from the many bird nests scattered about the island, and if there wasn't pepper to put on them, there was salt from distilled sea water. Dr. Murray rigged a piece of shiny tin from the flotsam washed ashore and showed her how evaporation would leave salt crystals behind. He explained the process to her, patiently answering her questions, as if she were a student in university and not a fluff-head.

After breakfast there was wood-gathering and food-gathering, and as they explored their island they discovered more of its treasures. Their little hut was decorated with flowers sitting in gourd vases, and seashells arranged outside the door. If they were gone when the woodcutters returned, they would be astounded at the changes. Daphne's greatest found treasure was smooth bits of colorful seaglass. She kept them in a flat shell and thought them as lovely as any jewels she'd ever worn.

They also discovered more of the bounty of their little Eden. A sweet bay tree and a patch of fennel seasoned their food, and Daphne took a hand at cooking. Dr. Murray used her one shoe that washed ashore to construct a sling, bringing down some ducks, of all things. That night they feasted on duck, which while gamier than the birds she was used to eating at home, were still a welcome change from fish.

"I wish we could net some ducks," he said as he passed her another piece of the succulent meat, roasted over their fire and seasoned with wild garlic and parsley. "We'd have a regular supply of meat and eggs."

"I was astounded when you brought down that bird, Doctor."

"Frankly, I astounded myself. It has been many years since I've hunted with a sling. It's good to know my skills haven't atrophied."

"Atro...?"

"Atrophied," he said. "A new word for you? It means a wasting away or decline, usually used in relation to a body part."

"Oh!" She couldn't help it, she looked down at that area of

her body that had not been used in a long while. "Am I going to be atrophied?"

He saw where she glanced and the color rose in his face.

"That is not a concern for you, Miss Farnham. Stop obsessing over…stop obsessing."

"You will make sure I do not become atrophied?"

"Have some more duck."

Well! If Dr. Murray was not going to see to it that she did not become atrophied, she might need to take matters into her own hands. So to speak.

He looked at her suspiciously when she giggled, but she concentrated on finishing the duck, which was excellent. Between the three of them, for of course Pompom had his share, they made short work of the fowl.

"I am glad we did not have to eat one of the beautiful island birds."

"I am sure this duck was thought beautiful by other ducks, but I agree with you. I wonder…" his voice trailed off as he thought. It was coming on toward dusk now, and Daphne was glad their chores were done for the day and they had this time to relax together.

"What do you wonder?"

"I wonder if I could rig a snare and capture a duck or two. Then we could build a pen for them and keep them caged for our use."

"That would be useful. It is too bad chickens do not migrate, because then we could have fresh chickens."

She smiled as she thought about flocks of Derbyshire Redcaps winging through the air to their little island. Daphne's arms ached and her back hurt and her hands were blistered and her feet were sore, but she would not trade these moments for all the gold in her father's vaults.

As long as she did not atrophy, it would all be wonderful.

"We explored most of the coast near our beach," Dr.

Murray was saying now. "If our chores are done early tomorrow, I would like to expand our exploration of the island. We can take some food and water with us and set out while it's still early. Those gourds you gathered are helpful."

He picked up one of gourds from the calabash tree growing near the beach and turned it over in his hands while Daphne basked in his praise. When it was dried out and carved it would make a utensil that had any number of uses. If they had fat or oil to burn it could be a lamp, or a container for food, or a means of carrying live coals for fire-starting.

"If I climbed I could gather more gourds, and some fruit also."

He looked at her sternly. "There will be no climbing."

Daphne stopped smiling and straightened her sore back, because she had been thinking about this all day.

"I am not sure I should have to always do what you tell me to do, or not to do, Dr. Murray. I know you are a natural philosopher and learned, but in America they let men vote equally, the stupid ones as well as the clever. Not that I am stupid, I am just not as learned as you are. While we are here on this island, just the two of us, we should be voting as equals, don't you think?"

He looked at her in astonishment, setting down the gourd.

"I am amazed, Miss Farnham, that a properly brought-up Englishwoman would take the riff-raff in America as her model for appropriate behavior. No, this is not a situation calling for some anarchic form of democracy. Your vote is not equal to mine.

"Our situation here is akin to being aboard ship where there is a commander. I am he. You are the loyal crew which offers advice and opinions when called upon to do so. Do not argue, you know you must acknowledge that I have more skill, experience and authority than you do."

"Not when it comes to climbing. If there was any climbing to be done, I'd be in charge."

"Miss Farnham, if there was an occasion where one needed to know which ribbon to use to trim a bodice, you would be in charge. Otherwise, I think not."

"I am in charge of the garden because you do not know a turnip from a tulip."

He thought about this for a moment and nodded, once. Grudgingly, she thought.

"You are in charge of the garden, that is correct."

"That is why I would also be in charge of climbing, because I climb and you do not."

"There will be no climbing," he stated again.

"But if there was climbing, I would be in charge."

"This is a ridiculous conversation," he said, rising to his feet.

Hah! She knew his ways now. When she was right, or when she disturbed him, Dr. Murray would run away. But she let him go without argument, feeling vindicated, for she knew she'd be the climber if it was ever needed.

After another night wondering whether she was in danger of atrophying, Daphne set out with Dr. Murray. She scratched at an insect bite through a new hole in her dress.

"Don't scratch, you will make it worse."

"The hole in my dress? I fear this garment is beyond redemption."

"I meant the bite. If you scratch it could become infected." She looked at her arms, bare, brown, and sporting a few bites. The insects here were not as fierce as in Jamaica but they were still annoying, and without cloth to protect her skin they had ample opportunity to feast on her.

"We need to figure out what to do about clothing

ourselves, Dr. Murray, or soon we will truly be like Adam and Eve."

The thought tickled her, both of them naked in Paradise save for a few strategically placed banana leaves. She knew the reality would not be pleasant, especially with the seasons turning to winter.

"I have been thinking about that, but I have no answers. There aren't any large animals we can skin and weaving plants into garments is beyond my skill."

"You made our hats."

"That covers the extent of my expertise in that area."

Daphne thought about this as she traipsed behind him on a narrow, barely marked path. The overgrown foliage alongside showed the lack of human activity, but a path down to the other side of the island gave him concerns he shared with her when they paused at a rivulet of water trickling down from the hills. It allowed them to refresh themselves and refill their gourds, and Dr. Murray tore a strip of cloth off her much abused shift to mark the spot.

"It could be why this path is here. I do not know. To date, we've seen no sign of life other than our absent woodcutters."

"Maybe there is something on the other side of the island the woodcutters needed? Some particular plants?"

He studied the ferns and fresh water while the dog lapped at a puddle at the base of a chinchona tree. He took his knife and carved off some of the bark, putting it in his coat pocket.

"Chinchona is used to treat fever. It's a good idea to gather Peruvian Bark while I can. It also makes me think that you could be correct about there being something on the other side of the island the woodcutters want. Native and slave crews have their own healers, and there could be herbs or plants for healing they want to access."

They set off again as the path wound down from the hills,

back to the shoreline. It ended at a patch of sand, which made no sense at all to Daphne.

"If they wanted a pleasant place to swim, why come all the way down here? The water is fine where we landed."

Dr. Murray looked out to sea, his hand shading his eyes, then turned and studied the hills. "If a boat put in here for water they would not find much from that freshet where we stopped. But it is a possibility."

He scanned the hills again, and the shoreline, and then stopped, staring at where the rocks and the sea met to the west.

"Look over there. What does that look like to you?"

Daphne followed where he pointed. The surgeon's hands were browner from their exposure. He would need to wear gloves when they returned to England if he wanted his hands to look like a gentleman's. Maybe some nice tan kid ones, she thought as she scanned the area, until she saw what he'd spotted.

"Is that a hole in the rocks?"

"I am thinking it is indeed a hole. One that leads to a cave." He looked at the area, and the surrounding plants and rocks. "It is above the waterline. If it is a cave, it could be used to store..." his voice trailed off. "Any number of things."

Daphne clapped her hands together, which made Pompom cock his head and watch her. "Do you think there is pirate treasure there?"

Dr. Murray stopped, looked at her, and raised an eyebrow.

"You dwell too much on pirates, Miss Farnham. Please rein in your imagination."

"Pirates are interesting," Daphne grumbled.

"Only to people who have no dealings with them." He looked up at the sky. "We have plenty of daylight left. Let's find out for ourselves if that is a cave."

"And if it has treasure!"

He sighed but trooped off and Daphne and Pompom followed. At the rocks she put Pompom in the shade with a command to "Stay!" Dr. Murray was impressed when the dog obeyed her.

"Pompom is the world's cleverest puppy, Dr. Murray."

"I would not go that far. I daresay you never saw a collie herding sheep."

"Pompom could herd sheep if he wanted to," she said loyally.

He turned and cocked an eyebrow at her.

"Maybe one small sheep." She paused. "Why is there one sheep and two sheep? Why aren't there flocks of sheeps?"

"I will not be able to sleep tonight for pondering that question."

She grinned at his retreating back, for she knew now when Dr. Murray was jesting. At least, she thought she knew. A catbird sitting in a twisted cedar gave its distinctive cry when their passage disturbed it, stirring up some bluebirds who took flight. All else was quiet though, no other human or animal marking their progress up to where he had spotted the opening in the rocks.

Daphne stumbled over a stone, but before she could fall, a strong hand had her, holding her, supporting her arm. Dr. Murray was watching her with concern in his eyes.

"I am pushing you too hard. You stay here and rest in the shade."

"I will not," she said indignantly, pulling her arm back even though it felt good to have him support her. "Did you not say I am the loyal crew in this adventure? How would it be if I let you go off by yourself without your crew to help you?"

He looked at her a moment, then his chin dipped in acknowledgment.

"I did say that. But a good commander also knows when the, ehm, men are being pushed too hard. I will not think less of you if you stay here."

"No," Daphne said firmly. "I am with you."

He looked at her again, then simply turned and continued climbing. She straightened her back and followed behind.

The path terminated at the narrow cave mouth, only about the width of Dr. Murray's shoulders, but he could squeeze in sideways and she had no trouble at all following him. He straightened up, careful of his head, and let out a low whistle. Daphne was speechless.

Someone was indeed using the cave to store goods. They couldn't see more than few feet in front of them into the dry cave, but they could see it was filled with parcels and bales and casks.

"It is treasure," she whispered.

"Maybe. Stand to your left there to let in maximum light. Good."

She followed his instruction and he began checking the casks and boxes they could see, while her eye was caught by three large and long parcels on the cave floor, tied with stout cord.

"Dr. Murray! I recognize this name. It is a mill near Manchester."

He joined her and they dragged the parcel closer to the cave entrance, into the sunlight. He pulled out his knife, slitting the cords on the package, and what spilled out was a bolt of fabric in a deep ruby shade.

"It's wool!" Daphne said with glee, caressing the tight weave of the fabric. She paused and fingered the cloth. "Not ordinary wool, but a fabric called 'the union,' mixing wool and silk together. It was all the rage in the dress shops a year or two back. I wonder how it ended up here?"

She noticed he had not said anything and looked up at him. He was looking at the other items in the cave.

"Spirits, goods from Europe and England, that looks like sacks of coffee beans over there and casks of molasses. My guess is it was placed here by someone who made off with it from other owners or is planning on smuggling it in to the islands or back to Europe without tariffs being collected."

"Pirates and smugglers?"

"Let us hope not," he said sternly. "You read too much bad literature, Miss Farnham. There is nothing pleasant or exciting about an encounter with pirates or smugglers. Whoever they are, they will come back for this."

"Our signal fire…" Daphne said, as the realization of what they might attract sank in.

"Exactly. We need to return to our camp and be prepared."

"We need this cloth also. We can use it to make ourselves clothing or wrap in it at night. We can figure out how to pay the owners for it later, can't we?"

He hesitated, then said, "You are correct, but right now we should return while there's still plenty of light."

"Let's check the other bolts to see what's here."

He pulled another parcel into the light and cut through the wrapping.

"Oh, Dr. Murray!" Daphne was struck speechless as she knelt down next to the bolt of cloth, her hand reaching out to caress the rich satin that glowed like the deepest blush of dawn, that edge of pink shading toward salmon that rose over the island in the morning. Her roughened fingers snagged the delicate gold threads shot through the fabric and she snatched her hand back, curling it in a fist in her lap, afraid to damage the fine material. It was so lovely. So unsuited to gathering onions from the garden.

The cave was silent, and then a warm hand rested on the back of her neck as she sat there, staring at the treasure.

"We will take this one with us today."

She turned around. He was looking not at the satin, but at her.

"Why? It will not keep us warm like the wool. It is pink satin for a ball gown. It is not useful," she tried to laugh, but it did not sound right and hurt her throat.

"We will need the wool also, but we will take this one now. It is silk, is it not?"

"Yes. Silk satin. Nothing takes color like silk does."

"Silk is a strong fiber," he said. "Remember your hairnet? This fabric could be quite useful. And it will make a practical garment, strong, yet cool in the summer heat."

"Practical?"

"Unless you see some dark brown silk that would hide bloodstains, this is our best option."

"I'll ruin it," she said, not looking at him, but down at her callused hands. She blinked her eyes, because her vision had gone blurred.

"Nonsense," he said briskly, and she heard him move behind her. "It will suit your purposes well, Miss Farnham. Come along now, we must leave here."

He gave her his hand to help her up from the floor, holding tight to hers, work-roughened skin and all. She thought he might have given it a squeeze, but that was likely just her imagination.

~

Alexander rewrapped the bundle and hoisted the cloth onto his shoulder, taking one last look around the cave.

"We can return for the wool. We know it's here when we need it."

"That is true," she said, glancing over her shoulder at him. Her step was light, and her normal good nature was restored. For a moment there he had been tempted to take her in his arms when he saw her distress over her rags, her work-roughened hands, things he did not think about, but that were upsetting to her.

"I feel better knowing we will not be reduced to wearing leaves or lizard skins or anything disgusting like that while we are here," she said, plucking at the rags of her dress. "Now all I need to do is figure out how to make a garment out of a bolt of cloth. Without shears or needles and thread or seamstresses or a dressmaker's form."

"In the Marquesas Islands—that's in the Pacific, Miss Farnham—the women wrap a length of cloth around themselves and fasten it at one shoulder."

He did not feel compelled to add that the style left a breast bare, but the image of Daphne Farnham wrapped in pink, one soft, rose-nippled breast exposed, a perfect complement to the blush satin, came to his mind and refused to leave him. He shifted the package on his shoulder and thought about the wool back in the cave. Thought about good, stout wool cloth and cold, damp Scottish winters. Damp, frigid, sleeting weather when you bundled up from top to bottom…and how wonderful it would be to peel off layers in front of a roaring fire, exposing ivory-hued limbs and a creamy white arse and soft golden curls hidden beneath cozy flannel undergarments…

He stumbled and caught himself, swearing beneath his breath. "Dr. Murray? Did you say something."

"I stubbed my toe. Keep walking, I wish to return before nightfall."

Daphne turned her head and flashed him a smile, which

did nothing to drive his mind back to a safer path. The sound of barking ahead of them drew her attention and her dog burst through the brush, wagging his tail and jumping up to try and lick her. She swooped the pup into her arms and it covered her face in wet kisses.

Lucky cur.

They paused at their water stop and Alex refreshed himself, shifting the parcel to his other shoulder. He ached from carrying the heavy bolt, but shook his head when Daphne said he could leave it behind and they would fetch it tomorrow.

"No. I can do this."

He needed to do this. There was not much he could do for his companion, stranded here with him through no fault of her own, but he could put a sparkle back in her eye by giving her this frivolous cloth. He put the cloth inside the cabin and the dog sniffed at it, but at a sharp word from his mistress let it alone.

"You go wash up. I can put supper on."

She said this with such pride in her voice that he paused from wiping his sweating brow and looked at her.

"Thank you. That would be greatly appreciated. When I return, I will check the signal fire."

"Is that wise?"

"We do not know how long that cave has been occupied. We are still better off taking our chances of rescue by some fisherman or naval vessel."

When he returned from the pond, wiping the water out of his hair, she was waiting outside their cabin.

"I want to go with you," she said, and he gave her his arm.

The late afternoon air was soft, but there was a hint of coolness as the sun dipped low. He was glad they'd found the wool cloth. They were going to need it.

Their fire was embers, as neither of them had been there

during the day to feed it. He threw some wood on and waited until it caught. He stood now, as he did each night before sunset, scanning for any sign of other humans. He took his time, methodically looking at all directions of the compass. Finally, he put his hand down from where it was shading his eyes and turned to his silent watcher.

"Nothing there," he said.

Was that relief on her face? Surely not. She'd been an amazingly adaptable companion—no, a partner in this castaway adventure, but she must long for a ball or a visit to the theater where she could dress in pink satin with gold trimmings, rejoining the world she was born into.

They walked down the hill, Daphne humming a merry tune, one he knew.

He did not realize he was humming along until she stopped and giggled, and then, all unexpectedly, took his hand in hers and they continued down to their little hut hand-in-hand.

~

*D*aphne prepared for bed still humming. The pink satin was propped up in a corner, nearly glowing in the firelight that came through the door. She hugged herself. Tomorrow she would make a dress, one unlike anything she'd worn before, and there would be no one to point and laugh and criticize or tell her it was not *à la mode*. There was just dear Dr. Murray and Pompom. Both males seemed to like her the way she was, calluses and dry skin and all. In fact, she almost thought Dr. Murray liked her better than when she'd been so careful with her appearance.

He was an odd man, but he'd found a special place in her heart. When she was with him, she felt a warmth she'd never felt with any other man.

Warmth was perhaps not the best word.

She wanted him to roger her within an inch of her life.

There! She'd said it! To herself, because she was too much of a coward to sit up and demand that Dr. Murray do what she knew he wanted to do. Even she was not that much of a hussy.

Not yet, anyway, but if they had any more wonderful days like today when all she wanted to do was throw herself into his arms and smother him with kisses, the silly man had only himself to blame for being so...so...rogerable.

And now he was returning from banking the fire for the night and once again she would lie down next to him and he'd put those muscled arms around her. While that was all well and good, and it was really quite delightful sharing warmth that way, it just wasn't enough.

Atrophy was becoming more and more a concern for her.

Daphne excused herself to take Pompom out one more time and scrub her teeth with the salt water and peeled twig as Dr. Murray had shown her.

He was so brilliant about so many things, and so utterly dense about other things. Between that denseness regarding rogering and his lack of fashion sense, she felt sorry for him.

When she was not feeling sorry for herself.

After the humans and the dog settled in for the night, Daphne found she could not sleep. She lay there on her back, her hands laced over her stomach, staring up at the rough ceiling that protected them from the elements. It was a good thing this cabin was here. They could be stranded for months and months until a ship and woodcutters came back. With the goods in the cave, some problems were solved, but others were still out there. The possibility of pirates, for example. Not the kinds of pirates in the novels she liked to read, but pirates like Dr. Murray's, who were not nice and probably did not bathe often enough.

"Go to sleep, Miss Farnham," rumbled a deep voice beside her. Pompom snorted in his sleep and snuggled closer.

"I can't fall asleep. I keep thinking about pirates and what our lives might be like if we're not rescued and we are here for months and months and maybe years."

He moved and she turned her head and looked at him in the dark. He was lying on his side, his head propped up on his hand.

"If I could build a boat I would, and then we could try to leave. But logic tells me that the woodcutters will return, and we are best off staying put here."

Daphne swallowed, her throat dry.

"I am frightened. I try not to be, especially because you are here with me, but sometimes I am afraid."

He did not say "Do not worry your pretty little head about it" or any of the other useless phrases she'd heard from men all her life. Instead, he sighed, and put his arm around her and pulled her up against his body. Her head rested on his strong chest and she heard his heartbeat, the steady thump of it a comfort to her, as much as the warmth and closeness of him holding her, and it was exactly what she needed at this moment. She needed to feel connected to him.

Daphne knew enough about men to know perfect heroes only exist in novels. Real men had stubbly faces and clothes they'd been wearing too long, and glum expressions. Once upon a time she thought that was what she wanted, that perfect hero, but now she knew better.

She sat up. "We need to come to some sort of agreement."

He looked at her, but she could not read his expression in the dark.

"What are you talking about, Miss Farnham?"

"How long have we been here? I know you are keeping track of the days since the shipwreck."

"Nearly a month."

"What if we are stranded here for six months? Or a year? I do not understand you! How do you sleep next to me, night after night, without wanting to—without—you know what I mean." He sighed and sat up alongside her.

"I am not a eunuch. That means—"

"I know that word, Doctor."

"As you know, I spent most of my life in the company of men. I tell myself that it is not unusual for me to go long periods of time without—is this conversation truly necessary?"

She put her hand on his arm. His very tense arm.

"Is that working for you, lying here, night after night?"

Daphne heard the frogs and birds outside, loud in the silence of a conversation come to a halt.

"No," he finally said. "It is not working."

"It's hard, isn't it?"

"Oh yes," he said, swiping his hand across his face. "It's hard. It's unbearably hard. It's harder than it's ever been. Painfully hard."

"Exactly! So this is what I propose. We endured a month of this painful condition. We must acknowledge though that we do not know when we will be rescued and will make decisions based on our needs here and now."

He was silent again, and she wished she could see his face. Then he dropped something into the conversation that startled her.

"Miss Farnham, are your menses regular?"

"My—you mean my woman's time?"

"Yes. Do you keep track of yourself?"

She thought about it for a moment, counting the days back to the *Magpie*.

"How clever you are, Dr. Murray! It will come in a day or two. Oh dear, I suppose that will be the end of wearing this shift. I will have to tear it up."

He sighed again, and when he spoke his voice was full of resignation, and maybe something else. "We will discuss this again after your courses are finished. If we agree to pursue this, that will be a safer time."

"Safer?"

"To avoid your becoming pregnant."

"Oh! I had not even thought about that."

"I assumed that was the case. Goodnight."

Daphne smiled to herself in the dark. Now that she had a goal, she could plan and make sure that everything was perfect when she and Dr. Murray finally fulfilled their mutual longings.

"Cease that humming, Miss Farnham, and go to sleep."

Daphne's days were even sunnier now that she knew Dr. Murray wanted to do more than hold her at night and recite formulae. Not that that was bad—the holding, not the formulae. She liked the cuddling. When her "flowers" came two days after that nighttime conversation, just as she'd predicted (and wasn't he the clever surgeon to remind her of that!), she did not mind the discomfort as she usually did because she had a special evening planned for when it was all over.

To that end, she'd put off wearing the breathtaking pink satin. With the doctor's help, and a small shears from his kit, she'd cut a length of cloth suitable for wrapping around her body. Sometimes she would see him watching her, when she was washing herself, or braiding her hair for their daily chores. The chores they did together, sharing their life here.

Now she paused from where she was peeling eggs for breakfast. What would a life with Dr. Murray be like away from here? She might have to cut back on her hat and shoe purchases, and perhaps there would not be as many theater evenings, but the rest of it would be wonderful. She would wake up beside Dr. Murray every morning. He would teach her new words and she would have a kitchen garden and teach him about vegetables. She would also help him with his wardrobe.

Daphne sighed. She was bright enough to know she was fooling herself. If she married him, she would be cut off from society and she did not know if his friends would accept her in their circle of natural philosophers. Assuming the grumpy surgeon had friends. Then she remembered that it could be a long, long time until they reached England. Much could happen in that time. Maybe they would not return to England at all.

"Dr. Murray, have you ever thought of moving to Canada? Or the United States?"

He gave her that vaguely confused look he sometimes wore when he was not following her conversations. Honestly, she expected a man with a brain as large as his to be quicker!

"Why do you ask that?"

She fiddled with the egg, rolling it to loosen the shell so she could avoid looking at him as she spoke.

"I was just thinking aloud. Sometimes people go to new lands to give themselves a fresh start. That's what George was trying to do when we went to Jamaica. Of course, he thought it would be a temporary stay and we would return to England, but I met other people there who were staying in Jamaica, building homes and raising families."

She pulled out another egg, trying to organize her thoughts to best say what she wanted to say.

"In a new place, there would be fewer issues standing between us. If you wanted to visit me, it would not be like your coming to my home in London and feeling as if you did not fit in except as a surgeon called to treat a patient. It is different in other places. I saw that in Jamaica. I hear that is even truer in the United States, and in Canada."

Her thoughts ran down and so did her speech, and she looked up to see him watching her in the steady, expressionless manner he had, and she wanted to bash him over the head with all the eggs just to see if he would respond with something resembling a human emotion.

"An interesting thought."

He stopped talking and looked at her and something shifted in his face. Daphne realized she was better at reading him, and the way he was looking at her now made her wish that it was tomorrow, and she was wearing pink satin.

"We are in a strange bubble out of time and place here, Da — Miss Farnham. We both need to return to London to pick up the threads of our lives, the lives we've been living for so long, because only then will we know..." his voice trailed off. "I do not know what will happen, but I do strongly believe our future lies in our homeland, not abroad. I need to earn a living, and there is business I must transact in London before I can determine where my future will take me."

"It was just a thought."

Pompom came running into the hut, a piece of seaweed draped over his ear. She knelt down to clean him off and fussed with the dog so she would not have to look at sober, businesslike, muscled Dr. Murray.

"I am returning to the cave for the other bolts of cloth. Would you care to accompany me?"

Daphne stopped petting Pompom and looked up at him.

"Why do you want me with you?"

He walked over to her and held out his hand to help her to her feet. He'd removed his jacket as the day was fast warming up, and she wondered if for the rest of her life she would always compare the men she knew to Dr. Murray and find them wanting.

"Your company is welcome. There are times I enjoy solitude, but I also enjoy spending the day with you."

Daphne's mood brightened. "I wager you would not have said that aboard the *Magpie*."

He said nothing to this but gave her a warm glance that made her feel even better about spending time with him. Maybe this was Dr. Murray's way of courting, after the fashion of a natural philosopher, spending time with her to study her and determine if she was appropriate? Entertaining? Rogerable?

She already suspected the last was a given, based on her experience with men, although Dr. Murray was a breed apart. No matter.

"What about the eggs?"

"We'll take them with us and eat while we walk. Fetch your hat and we will go."

Daphne grabbed her hat and the eggs and followed along beside him, Pompom dancing at her heels.

~

*A*lexander glanced over at his companion as they walked along, her mood bright again. There were so many things he wanted to say to her. He wanted to say, "You are the most beautiful person I have ever seen. You make my day brighter and my mood lighter and I care about you so very much."

But when he opened his mouth, what came out was, "Wear your hat."

It was just as well. He was already on edge in anticipation of his night with Daphne. Alexander was amongst those who sailed to Naples following the Battle of the Nile. There had been enough celebrating to gladden the heart of any navy man, and it was the surgeon's first opportunity to see a fireworks display. The illuminations dazzled the young Scotsman. He stood alongside his shipmates, many of whom were already roaring drunk and, as usual, roasting Alexander over his abstemious habits.

He ignored their banter, entranced by the entertainment in the sky. What could be more removed from his chilled, sober, frugal life than a show of lights and noise and color in a sultry climate, a show that produced absolutely nothing useful? Except joy in the heart of the beholder, a desire to say "Ahhh!" at each fanciful dragon and serpent and fire blossom created from the same substance that blew apart stout wooden ships and the men that sailed them? The colors burned their images into his eyes, and his brain, and there was no one there with whom he could share his thoughts on the illuminations, even if he had been able to find the right words.

That was how Daphne Farnham made him feel. She was fireworks, rockets, blossoms, filling the heavens with light and his heart with joy. And she was as much above him and beyond his reach as those explosions in the night sky. She'd mentioned her father trying to marry her off to raise her up in the ranks of society. Alexander knew Mr. Farnham would not welcome a bastard Scots surgeon as a replacement for an earl.

There were other reasons he would be all wrong for her. He did not know anything about women, not as a species. But how many men did, when all was said and done? Could any man truly know a woman's mind?

He smiled inwardly as he thought about how few of his colleagues who studied the heavens and the natural workings of their surroundings would be brave enough to consider making the study of women their life's work. They left that to the rakes, which was a shame when you thought about it. A rake was primarily concerned with his own pleasure.

Alexander wanted to make things as wonderful as possible for Daphne. He wanted her to have fireworks and explosions of colors.

She slipped her hand into his and he took it, relishing the human contact. Such contact was missing from his life for so long, he did not even realize it was lacking. Now he craved touch and warmth and he was not looking forward to going without it when they were rescued, as he believed they would be, eventually.

He resolved to find himself a suitable wife. He was sure he could find a woman who was sober and frugal and industrious and would consider marriage to a successful surgeon a social advancement of sorts.

He suppressed a sigh at the thought.

They returned to the cave without stopping along the way. Alexander built a fire far enough from the cave entrance that smoke wouldn't blow in, then lit brands for them to carry while they explored the cave's interior.

"It is a treasure house!" Daphne said in awe when they illuminated the cache. The treasures weren't gold and silver, but goods—coffee, salt, rum, tobacco, molasses, sugar—all highly saleable products of the Indies, and there were European goods desired in the islands, cloth and pottery and casks of oil and rice.

"We need a sledge."

Daphne looked at him in confusion.

"Some means of hauling other than our own backs. There is rope here, and wood. If we pry open the top of that long case, I can attach ropes to it."

"What a brilliant idea, Dr. Murray!"

She gave him that look that made him straighten his back, and he repressed the urge to strut and crow like a rooster.

They stepped back out, blinking furiously at the stronger light and stuck their torches in the sand. Alexander looked around for a rock he could use as a wedge to pry open the box, found one of suitable size, then turned to his partner.

"Look here. This one should do the—"

Daphne looked up from where she was scouting for her own rock. She said something, but he didn't hear her, his eyes frozen on the ocean that stretched out from their little paradise. Daphne came up beside him and in his peripheral vision he saw the concern on her face, then she turned and looked out in the direction of his gaze. When she drew close to him and slipped her hand in his he gripped it without saying a word, grateful for her touch.

"A ship," she said in a low voice.

He knew her mind now. She was frightened of the unknown, and his job was to reassure her as best he could. Even when he could not reassure himself.

She looked up at him, her eyes wide and questioning. Some hair came loose from her braid and fell across her forehead, and Alexander let go of her hand and brushed those stray locks off of her face. The silken strands snagged on the rough skin of his fingers, callused from his instruments and years of clutching the handle of the saw. Not a gentleman's hands, a reminder he scarcely needed as he resisted the urge to undo the braid and bury his hands in those curls one more time. Maybe one last time.

He looked back out on the water.

"Yes, it is a ship. Come, Daphne, we must prepare."

She glanced at him when he used her name but did not say anything. As they started walking back in silence she maintained her grip on his hand, and he held on to her, not willing to let her go a moment sooner than he must.

$\mathcal{A}$lexander stood at ease in front of his signal fire, the sky behind him painted in the clear blues of mid-afternoon. A breeze came up, wisping the smoke in his direction, then back out, but he ignored it as he watched the half-dozen men climbing the hill after rowing ashore from the schooner anchored in the cove. The vessel flew Spanish colors, but that didn't mean anything, not in these waters.

A weathered man with gray hair in a tight queue at the base of his neck led the sailors. They'd spotted him early on, but other than pointing and talking amongst themselves, did not hail him. Their leader, though, was watchful, scanning the hills as the men hiked, but Alexander knew he would see nothing odd.

At least he hoped not, recalling his last conversation with Daphne before climbing the hill. "You are to hide yourself and not come out, no matter what."

"They came because of our fire. They are here to rescue us!"

"Maybe. Maybe not. I will initiate contact and determine whether they are our saviors or our enemies. If anything should happen to me—no, do not interrupt!—if anything should happen to me, you will be safe here until the wood-cutters return."

Her hands flew up to cover her mouth in fright. He could not blame her, but the last thing he needed was Daphne distracting him. It had been hard enough earlier, when they took stock of their possessions in case they had to leave quickly. He also loaded his pistol and put it in his coat pocket. He banked the fire outside their hut so it would not draw their visitors, and when he stepped inside, Daphne stood there, wrapped in pink satin.

She looked like a present, like all the gaily wrapped parcels he'd spotted in the fine shops in London, shops that carried goods far beyond the reach of a struggling surgeon. He swallowed as he took the sight in. Her shoulders and arms, bronzed from the sunlight, glowed warmly against the gold threads of her improvised dress. She'd tied the cloth at her shoulder in a bow, and it draped itself like a classical garment, a sash of the same fabric tied around her waist.

"I wanted to wear it for you," she whispered.

For once, Alexander did not stop to think about conse-quences. He put the pistol on the table and stepped over to where she stood, her hands clasped together in front of her. He framed her face with his fingertips, memorizing each detail, the individual lashes of her eyes, the wings of her eyebrows. Her fine skin contrasted with his rough hands, but a tremulous smile moved up the corners of her lips, those lush lips like rose petals begging to be tasted one more time.

So he obliged her, touching lightly at the corner of her mouth, taking his time, exploring her jawline, her eyelids, the curve of her cheek, and finally returning to that soft mouth that opened for him, inviting him in, drawing him into her warmth and her embrace. His hands moved around to her back, sliding over satin that was no softer than the skin it covered, reaching up to bury itself in her hair.

He angled his head to explore her mouth more effectively and she drew up on her bare toes, her hands clasping around his neck, cradling him against her as his pulse raced with the sheer physical pleasure of holding her in his arms again.

She smelled like fresh air, sunshine, and woman, her beauty unmarred by cosmetics or perfume, purely her, all of it Daphne.

He wanted to unwrap her like the gift she was, but that part of his brain still functioning, that still had blood flowing to it, asserted itself and he pulled back. Even then he was unable to resist placing more kisses over her eyelids, the sensitive spot in front of her ear where her hair floated out like silken floss, the collarbone above the satin, and finally, the pulse at her neck beating fast, rapid with her longing and desire, desire for him.

He rested his forehead against hers while she sought to catch her breath. He knew she could feel him pressing against her, his need for her rampant, but she did not say anything. Her hands slid slowly, reluctantly from his hair and she fell back on her heels, stepping away from him.

Daphne took a deep breath, then looked up at him.

"Are we doing the right thing, Dr. Murray? Should we hide and wait for the woodcutters to return?"

He looked at her, drinking her in, wanting the moment to last forever, but he shook his head.

"We cannot risk being stranded if rescue is available. I will go to the signal fire. You will stay here."

He stooped and picked up Pompom, who wriggled and tried to lick his face as he passed the dog to her.

"Your task is to keep yourself and your animal safe until I return."

Now he stood remembering the look on her beautiful

face as he left. He was calmer knowing she was at their hut, away from immediate danger. It was prudent for any sailor to go armed in these waters, but the extent of the strangers' weaponry as they approached made Alexander glad he insisted Daphne stay behind.

The leader said to him in heavily accented Spanish, "Is that your signal fire, *señor*?"

"Yes," Alexander replied in English, "I hoped a passing ship would see it."

"You are English then," the man said in the same language, his voice reflecting his Liverpool origins.

"Scottish," Alex said, "I am Alexander Murray, late of His Majesty's frigate *Caeneus*, now castaway here."

"Yes, I suspected as much," the Englishman said dryly, looking at Alexander's bare chest beneath his coat, and his ragged trousers. "I am Horace Fuller, mate aboard the *Prodigal*, bound for…"

His speech was interrupted by a high-pitched yipping noise. Alexander's head whipped around to see the bichon burst through the underbrush and make straight for him. The dog planted himself in front of Alexander, lowered his head and growled at Horace Fuller, who looked stunned at this unexpected attack. Alexander swooped down and scooped the pink beribboned animal into his arms, where it began frantically licking his face and wagging its tail, no doubt pleased at having protected him from the intruders.

"Well now," Fuller said with a slight smile on his grizzled face, a scar at his jawline pulling up like a curtain string. "I can see you weren't alone here, Mr. Murray. What's your dog's name?"

Alex hesitated for half a second, but there was nothing for it.

"Pompom."

It took another half a second, and then the air was filled with the whoops of the sailors laughing their salty arses off.

"Pompom! Ooooh, what a sweet widdle name for a doggy!"

"Careful, Mr. Fuller, or Pompom might nibble on your toesywoesies!"

Alexander bore it stoically, even as he wondered why Pompom was not with his mistress.

"All right, all right, belay that, you lot," Fuller finally said, putting a halt to most of the tomfoolery, though a chuckle or two still drifted over on the sea breeze. He wiped his hand across his face.

"So, Mr. Murray, you are all alone here? Except for," a snigger leaked out, "your little friend Pompom?"

"What are you doing with my dog? And my doctor?"

Alexander closed his eyes and said a hasty prayer, but when he opened them and turned around he saw exactly what he feared he would see.

Daphne Farnham, looking like a sun-kissed Aphrodite in pink satin, her uncorseted form all too clearly outlined beneath her fine fabric, bounced up through the palmettoes. The sailors from the *Prodigal* were struck dumb to a man, their eyes wide with awe at the amazing example of pulchritude headed their way. She looked like every sailor's dream over a long voyage, and Alexander feared the situation would become very serious very quickly if he did not do something.

"By King Neptune's damp balls!" he heard one of the men whisper worshipfully. "Would ye feast your peepers on that?"

"Can we keep her, Mr. Fuller? Can we? Can we? Please say yes!" another sailor pleaded.

Fuller watched Daphne's progress, his mouth slightly ajar. He closed it with a snap and stared at Alexander.

"Does this woman belong to you, Mr. Murray?"

"Aye, for my sins."

"That woman, there, that woman coming up the path, is *your* woman?"

Alexander heard the patent disbelief in the man's voice and could hardly blame him. He couldn't quite believe it himself. However, it gave him an idea…

"Oh, Pompom, did these nasty men hurt you, my precious?" She snatched the dog from Alexander and glared at the men surrounding them, oblivious to the fact that she was on the receiving end of a glare as well.

"Didn't I instruct you to wait and not follow me?"

"I had to come after you! These pirates have my dog! And my doctor!"

"Always a comfort to know where I stand in your affections."

"Pirates?" Fuller said, not looking pleased to be labeled that way.

"This is my wife," Alexander said abruptly. He needed to regain hold of this situation, as best he could. "Miss Farn— the former Miss Daphne Farnham is my wife."

"I am?"

"She took a blow to the head during the storm that shipwrecked us here, and doesn't remember the shipboard wedding, poor dear."

"I was not hit in the head!"

"You see? She doesn't even remember the mishap that cost her some of her memories. It is a common result from such an injury. I have been addressing her as Miss Farnham while we are stranded here, hoping to ease her back into her memories of our marriage. Too much information too soon, forcing the memories of our deep connection and love, could cause a brain fever."

"It could?" Now she looked worried. "I do not want a brain fever, Dr. Murray."

"She even continues to refer to me as 'Dr. Murray' even

though I'm her own dear Alexander."

"You are?"

Fuller looked like he'd heard a similar tale around Banbury, but watched the two of them while the men stood silently, hands near their weapons, awaiting orders. He finally made up his mind.

"We'll let the captain sort this out. You're a physician?"

"A surgeon. Miss Farnham—Mrs. Murray likes to call me 'Doctor.'"

"A surgeon, eh?" He looked at him with new interest, and Alexander's heart sank. It was not unheard of for pirates to kidnap surgeons, keeping them aboard their vessels to tend to the wounded. But most of these incidents had happened long ago, so it was possible Mr. Fuller simply wanted his pox treated or to discuss his piles.

"We'll take you aboard the *Prodigal,* and see what's what," Fuller said. He instructed some of the men to start filling the water butts they'd brought from the ship. He turned back to the couple watching silently.

"Come with me, Mr. Murray and…Mrs. Murray. Do you have any gear you want to take with you? We will spend the night aboard ship."

Daphne moved close to Alexander and he put his hand on her arm, to reassure her, and to convince Fuller that she was indeed his wife.

"There are some items down the trail at the woodcutter's hut."

"I know where that is," Fuller said. "Paget!"

"Aye, Mr. Fuller?"

"You're in charge of this lot. I will meet you at the beach."
"Aye, sir."

Fuller followed the silent couple down the trail to the hut. His eyes scanned the room, resting on the bolt of pink satin.

"Looks as if you've been exploring, Mr. Murray. Take anything else for your use?"

"No," Alexander said. His question confirmed his suspicions that the *Prodigal's* crew was responsible for the cave of hidden goods.

"We had to take that cloth, Mr. Fuller. My clothing was just in rags! I know you would not mind a lady making use of those items you left behind."

Fuller looked at her bare shoulders above her pink satin wrap and patches of color stained the older man's cheekbones. It appeared even hardened pirates weren't immune to Daphne's charms.

"Well, miss—ma'am, I can see how you might need to make use of our goods."

Daphne smiled at him and he blinked, and looked for a moment as if he'd been whacked with a belaying pin.

Alexander cleared his throat, bringing the attention back to him, a safer outlet. "I have my chest and there's Daphne's bag, but nothing else of value here."

He looked around and saw that the colorful pieces of seaglass and some of the shells were gone, and he suspected they were in Daphne's valise. He said there was nothing of value, but then why did it feel like he was leaving behind happiness and joy along with battered dishes and pots?

Fuller picked up the bolt with its remaining cloth and the valise. Daphne took Alexander's free arm, Pompom following behind.

Fuller handed the cloth off to a man and directed his guests into the boat beached at the shoreline. Alexander had his surgical chest and Daphne had her valise, the only other item they brought with them from the island was Daphne's hat, which she wore now. She looked over her shoulder as the sailors rowed and the land receded in the distance, the smoke from their dying fire fading away.

"Regrets, Miss Farn—Daphne?"

She looked at him, her plush lips curling up, but only a slight amount. Not her usual smile.

"I will miss our island. It will always have a special place in my heart. Will you miss it?"

"Will I miss the insects, and the thorns in my bare feet, and hunting for enough food to survive one more day?" He looked down at the animal, who had somehow ended up in his lap for this latest sea voyage. "At least we didn't need to stew the dog."

"Dr. Murray!" she gasped. The dog, sensing he was the topic of discussion, licked Alexander's hand, the one absently scratching under the dog's chin. Pompom kicked his hind leg in doggy ecstasy at the attention.

Fuller hailed the *Prodigal*, and a ladder was lowered. Alexander popped the dog into Daphne's valise, giving it to one of the sailors to bring aboard. He took charge of his chest, slinging its worn leather strap over his shoulder before following her up the ladder, which she climbed with the same skill she'd assured him she'd bring to tree climbing.

The stunned silence as she ascended caused him to look over his shoulder and frown at the sailors staring at Daphne's trim ankles and calves and the satin drawn tight over her derriere as she made her way aboard, but there was nothing to be done for that now. When he saw the number of guns on deck he knew he was either aboard the safest merchant vessel afloat, or one that preyed on commercial shipping. Not many merchantmen would give up valuable cargo space to carry enough shot and powder for four four-pounders and a pair of swivels. The crew also wore more blades and jewelry than one might expect of merchant sailors. Usually, the only men who went around looking like that in port were those who were prepared for a fast fight and a faster getaway, wearing their wealth for a quick escape.

The other suspicious fact was the Spanish colors the ship flew, despite most of the men speaking English. He'd know more when he met the captain.

"You wait here with the lady, Mr. Murray," Fuller said, directing them to an area near the mast where an awning offered shade from the tropical sun.

"I would like to speak with your captain as soon as he's available," Alexander said as an answer, then helped Daphne to sit on a coiled hawser with Pompom on her lap, out of the sun.

Fuller nodded and went below. Daphne looked around with interest, humming to herself. After about thirty minutes there was the sound of voices and footsteps coming up from below, and Alexander helped her to her feet. She was looking over his shoulder and her eyes were as large as Delft saucers before a smile grew on her face that had Alexander turning around to see—

"Bloody hell," he swore.

The captain of the *Prodigal* stood on his deck, perfect white teeth flashing in his perfectly bronzed face with its cleft chin, the golden sunlight winking off his single earring. He was tall and lithe and wore a billowing white shirt, its laces unfastened to reveal a muscular chest. His hands were fisted on his hips, legs spread in a pose that drew all eyes to him. Alexander took this all in clinically as he studied the man. It was about as bad as it could be. From the top of his windswept ebon locks to the kohl-lined blue eyes, even bluer than Daphne's, to the red satin sash that girdled his waist, his legs encased in lovingly fitted buckskins, his feet in polished boots, he might as well have hung a sign around his neck saying, "Look at me! I am a dashing pirate rogue!"

And Daphne, poor impressionable child, she was eating it up like sugared custard.

"See?" She sighed happily. "I *told* you there would be pirates!"

At her words the captain strode over and took her hand, bowing over it to give it a kiss, then rose to say in a mellifluous voice, "Pirates? Dear lady, we are sea merchants here on the *Prodigal.*"

Alexander did not need to sneer at this absurdity as the crew was supplying the commentary for him with their collected snickers. A glare from Fuller put a stop to that, and the captain rose from his bow and, still holding Daphne's hand, said, "But I am so rude! You must forgive me, lovely lady, I have never seen such beauty aboard my sad little vessel. I am Robert St. Armand, captain of the *Prodigal Son.* And Mr. Fuller tells me you are a Miss Farnham?"

"She is Mrs. Murray," Alexander growled.

"I am?"

"Later, Daphne."

The captain turned smoothly to Alexander. "Ah yes, Mr. Fuller mentioned there was some…confusion…about the young lady."

"I am Alexander Murray. The young lady, whose hand you will release, Captain St. Armand, is my wife."

"Are you certain?"

"Not now, Daphne."

The captain listened to their conversation, his head cocked to the side. He did not release Daphne's hand from his own until Alexander glared at the offending body part. Pompom sniffed around the captain's feet, rejected the interloper, instead trotting back and lying down with his head across Alexander's bare foot.

Maybe the animal was more intelligent than Alex suspected.

Daphne, however, was acting exactly as he feared she

might. A silly smile was plastered across her face and a hum was slipping out of her while she stared at the pirate captain.

"We need to talk, Captain St. Armand, about your taking us to a port where we can obtain assistance."

"Come down to my cabin, Mr. Murray and…"

"Miss Daphne Farnham," Daphne chimed in, at the same time

Alexander said, "Mrs. Murray."

"I do not think that is quite correct," she frowned.

"Do not worry about that for now, m'lady," the captain said, which caused Daphne to giggle, a sound that once again irritated Alexander's ears. Maybe it only happened aboard ship. Or maybe it was because she was favoring another man with that giggle, a man who was younger and taller and leaner and was going to be missing vital body parts if he did not stop looking at her that way.

Pompom growled softly, which had Daphne swooping him into her arms. "Pompom does not seem to like you, Captain St. Armand…"

Alexander swore he'd give the dog part of his sea biscuit the next time they ate. Maybe all of it.

"Which is strange, because Pompom likes everybody. Even Dr. Murray, who threatened to stew him for our supper, didn't he, my widdle baby boy?"

To his credit, even St. Armand looked slightly nauseated at this dialogue, but he said, "Give your pup to Norton to watch while we go below and discuss your situation."

Without waiting for Daphne's approval, he plucked the dog from her arms and shoved him into the hands of a sailor standing nearby. The dog seemed to like the sailor well enough, and Daphne asked him to feed Pompom his supper and find him fresh water. Alexander headed off the captain and offered her his arm to escort her, a move that startled her, but she took his arm and they followed the captain below.

St. Armand's cabin depressed Alexander further. It was the most sybaritic seagoing suite he'd ever seen. An oversized bunk was buried under soft pillows in an explosion of crimson, amber, midnight-blue and even one covered in fur, all atop a deep mattress cushioning its occupant from the roughness of the seas. The bunk hung suspended by chains so the bed would move comfortably with the ship's motion.

He did not want to contemplate what other activities would made that cradle rock. He glanced sidelong at Daphne, whose eyes were shining as she took it all in—the bunk, the gold leaf adorning the woodwork, the giant mirror fastened to the bulkhead and positioned so that it reflected the bunk, the large stern window allowing daylight to stream in and light up the room.

Like a moth to the flame, she was drawn to the mirror, but when she looked into it she gave a shriek of dismay, "My complexion!"

To his eyes, the perfect grain of her skin was as fine as ever, the warm blush in her cheeks caused by sunshine and fresh air, not paint pots.

"I like you like this," he murmured, but no one heard.

"Do not fret, dear lady," Captain St. Armand said, coming up behind her, and he would have been at her back sharing her reflection if Alexander had not positioned himself in his way. St. Armand just favored him with a small smile, and Daphne never noticed the two men jockeying for position, as she was still absorbed with the ravages of her sea voyage.

She turned to Alexander. "Dr. Murray, help me! I need to fix this before we reach England."

He was going to dismiss this as nonsense, but when he saw St. Armand about to speak he jumped in first. For all he knew the pirate carried stock for a lady's dressing table aboard his vessel.

"You look fine," he snapped. "Wear your hat in the sun. I will give you some olive oil to rub into your skin at night and you will look just like a fashion doll in no time."

Which was not at all what he'd planned to say.

Daphne looked at him, startled and maybe a little hurt by his tone of voice. But then she smiled and said, "Poor Dr. Murray. I think all this has been a bit much for you. Do not worry. Soon we will be safe and you will not need to deal with me anymore."

Which was not at all what he wanted to hear.

He put his hand on her arm and eased her away. "Do not forget, Daphne, you are my wife—no, do not say anything. You are my responsibility and I will see that you are dealt with properly."

"Such touching sentiment! I am overcome at these outpourings of emotion. It is more than a man of my delicate sensibilities can handle."

Daphne turned to the pirate, a look of concern on her still lovely, sun-warmed face.

"Do not worry, Captain St. Armand. You should not let what Dr. Murray says upset you. Sometimes he is grumpy, but he cannot help it. It is just the way he is."

Before Alexander could refute this nonsense, St. Armand nodded gravely.

"I do understand, Miss Farn—Mrs. Murray."

"Oh please, just call me Daphne!"

"No."

The two beautiful people turned their heads and looked at him, almost as if they were surprised he was still in the cabin.

"We can discuss this later," St. Armand said easily. "Right now I imagine you are hungry. Mr. Fuller is freeing up his cabin for your use, and while he is doing that we will have some supper."

"This is such a fine vessel, Captain St. Armand. Far nicer than the *Magpie*."

"A woman of your beauty and breeding deserves nothing but the best, Miss Farnham. That dress you are wearing, that shade of pink looks lovely on you."

He walked to the door, stuck his head outside and called to the sailor stationed there.

"Tell Mr. Fuller to fetch the bolts of cloth retrieved from the cave, Simmons."

He turned his head and gave Daphne a warm smile over his shoulder. "The cloth will be yours to use, Miss Farnham. Sails can help you make dresses from it."

"What a lovely idea! Thank you so much. Maybe Mr. Sails can help dress Dr. Murray also."

The pirate looked at Alexander and his mouth twitched. "I do not think pink satin flatters Mr. Murray's coloring."

Daphne looked at Alexander and frowned in agreement. "True. Pink is not the doctor's color, not with his red hair. It would clash horribly."

"I defer to your judgment, Miss Farnham."

Alexander'd had enough of this foolishness and tired of correcting the pirate regarding Daphne's supposed marital status, but he did not want a discussion, not here and now. It could wait until they were in their cabin.

At St. Armand's invitation they seated themselves at his table, and he poured them each a glass of canary.

"Where are you bound, Captain St. Armand?"

"England," he said crisply. "This stop for water was my last before heading out into the open sea."

"Why, we were going to England also! What a coincidence!"

"A most fortuitous one, Miss Farnham, I can offer you passage."

"We need to go to St. George to let people know we are alive, and outfit ourselves for the journey."

"That is not going to happen," St. Armand looked at him steadily with no smile at all. "I am leaving these islands and it would not be convenient for me to return."

"Are you sure you are not a p-i-r-a-t-e?" Daphne whispered. Alexander wished she didn't sound quite so hopeful.

"Good heavens, absolutely not, dear lady!" the pirate said. "However, the islands are full of different governments and sometimes, through no fault of my own, there is confusion over cargoes, disagreements over salvage rights, that sort of thing. It is time for me to voyage to England. And I can offer you passage. Perhaps Mr. Murray would lend his skills to the care of the crew on this voyage? It would be most appreciated."

"You are English," Alexander said abruptly. Captain St. Armand spoke in the same cultured accents as Daphne Farnham. He was either of the same background, or a good mimic.

St. Armand did not confirm or deny his nationality, and before Alexander could probe further, there was a rap at the cabin door, followed by men bearing covered dishes that by their aromas were a far cry from raw fish. They were set before the captain and the covers removed, and Daphne whispered a worshipful, "Oh, my goodness!"

"I have an excellent seacook," the captain said, reaching for a dish of roasted chicken smothered in a sauce that carried a hint of ginger and cinnamon. He served Daphne, then passed the plate to Alexander, who found his own mouth watering at the delights before them. In addition to the chicken there was a rice pilaf, flatbreads, fresh vegetables and a round of cheese. The two castaways refrained from falling on the food like starving beggars, but they did justice to the *Prodigal* cook's efforts.

"This is an amazing feast, Captain St. Armand. Far better than the food we had aboard the *Magpie*."

Alexander grudgingly added his approval of the meal. "It is good. Have you had this cook with you for long?"

"No, Hill is working his passage to England, but he says he'll leave us there. A shame, really. Someone of his talents should be cooking for a duke or a king. Or me.

"So you see, I can offer you good accommodations and a fine ship for your voyage. As far as outfitting you, I am certain we have items in ship's stores that will take care of your needs."

Alexander had to admit there were worse ways to make the ocean crossing than in a comfortable, well-armed ship with an excellent cook. He would, however, vastly prefer being aboard a vessel with an older, uglier captain, one less liable to turn Daphne's pretty head. He'd given his word he would watch over her until England and he still intended to do that. Having her fall into the arms of a handsome pirate was not going to happen, not on his watch.

"I do appreciate your letting me make use of the cloth you have, Captain. Wherever did you find such beautiful fabric?"

"It fell off a boat."

"A frequent occurrence?"

"It does seem to happen when I'm in the area, Mr. Murray." He turned back to Daphne. "Some of the men are small and slender enough that you could fit into their clothing until we can make you some of your own. They would be happy to share with you, and Mr. Murray appears to be of a size with Mr. Fuller."

"After losing my clothes in the shipwreck, dressing like a sailor will be another adventure. I will put it all in my book!"

"You are an authoress, Miss Farnham?" He looked surprised and interested, and Alexander shifted in his seat.

"Not yet, but I hope to be published one day. Dr. Murray is helping me."

She looked at Alexander with that smile on her face he'd come to think of in a proprietary fashion as "his smile," and he felt some of the tension ease out of his back and neck.

"If there are quarters ready for us, perhaps Mrs. Murray could rest and then we will see about outfitting ourselves."

Captain St. Armand rose to his feet and stepped outside the cabin. Daphne started to speak, but Alexander brought his finger to his lips, signaling her not to talk, and for once she simply did as instructed. He had no illusions the rest of the voyage would be that easy.

St. Armand returned and said, "Mr. Fuller's cabin is ready for you. If you'll follow Conroy, he'll show you which cabin is yours."

He took Daphne's hand in his, bowed smoothly over it and said, "Until later, dear lady."

Alexander took another look around the cabin. With those fluffy, brightly colored pillows, the mirrors, the fondness for pink satin, the luxury…perhaps Captain St. Armand was of an inclination where he would not be a threat to Daphne's virtue. However, he had spent enough time at sea to have a good instinct in these matters, and he rather expected that the bold pirate would be a great deal of trouble indeed.

"Daphne—Miss Farnham—we must talk."

"We absolutely do need to talk! When were we married?"

"We are not married, it was a ruse—"

"Hah! I thought I would remember if we were married. I am tired of pretend marriages, Dr. Murray. They are not at all the done thing, I assure you!"

He looked at her with that expression of exasperation she suspected was the same look Pompom saw on her face when he'd chewed a slipper. What did the doctor expect? He said she was married to him, and did not remember being hit on the head, but now he said she was not really married to him. She had already been in one almost marriage and she was not about to do that again, thank you very much!

"A ruse to keep you safe," he continued, almost as if what she had to say on the nature of marriage was not important at all. "If this crew believes you are married to me, then I can protect you.

"And before you protest further, if Captain St. Armand does not believe we are married, he will not allow us to share a cabin. You would be too vulnerable alone. This is not the *Magpie*, and

these men are not the sort you are used to."

"Because they're pirates?"

He sighed and rubbed the spot between his eyes.

"Yes, because they're pirates."

"I knew there would be pirates," she said with satisfaction.

"That does not make our situation better, it makes it worse."

"It certainly makes it more interesting."

"Miss Farnham, I have been doing my best to escort you to England in one piece, but if you wish to arrive there safe and sound, you will pay attention."

He was looking at her again as he had aboard the *Magpie*, as if she were a nuisance or an unruly child, or worse, and Daphne felt something inside her curl up and wither like a frost-nipped rose. On the island it was different. When it was just the two of them, he looked at her like she was special, not like she was a chore akin to swallowing unpleasant medicine. It was the same look she'd received from Mrs. Cowper and Captain Franklin. The same look she received from her father when he was disappointed with her, which happened too often.

"I liked it better on the island," she said in a small voice.

He started to shake his head, then stopped, and said gently, "The island was special. But it was unreal, much like Shakespeare's *Tempest*. Now we must face the reality I warned you of. You will take your place again in society, I will make a place for myself amongst the laboring classes. This vessel is our best option for traveling to England, but I do not trust Captain St. Armand."

"Why not?"

"I cannot believe he is in the habit of rescuing stranded travelers," he said thoughtfully, placing his hands behind his back and pacing the small cabin. "Normally, pirates want to keep a low profile. He has his own reasons for taking us aboard. It may only be that he wants a surgeon on this voyage, but I urge you to be cautious, and let me deal with him."

Daphne couldn't argue with the logic of that, but she was also sure he had no idea how luscious the pirate captain was. His looks! His manners! His flair for dressing! It was a most entertaining display. She had spent her life being admired for her looks and grace and could appreciate those qualities in others.

Captain St. Armand did seem to bring out dear Dr. Murray's grumpy side, so she would work to smooth over relations between the two men, otherwise this could be an uncomfortable voyage.

And speaking of uncomfortable, she gave a small sigh as she looked around Mr. Fuller's cabin. It had none of the color or flair of the commander's quarters. The bunk was narrow and covered with a plain gray blanket, there was a drop-down writing desk attached to the bulkhead, one straightbacked chair, and no mirror. It did have a small port-hole, and that at least was a luxury anyone could appreciate, light and air in the cramped space.

"You will take the bunk. I can rig a hammock."

"I don't think the bunk is that narrow, Dr. Murray. I'm sure we can share it if we are very close—oh!" Her hand rose to cover her lips as she imagined how close they'd be in that small box.

"Exactly."

There was a knock on the door, and a sailor missing part of his left ear entered, Pompom cradled under his arm.

"Here's your doggy, Miss."

He scratched behind the bichon's ear, which made the dog wriggle in delight.

"He's a lively pup. If you like, I can rig a collar and leash for you to walk him around the deck."

"Would you, Mr. Norton? That would be wonderful."

Daphne smiled at the young man, who turned twenty shades of red.

"'S no problem," he muttered, not looking directly at her. "I do macramé and I can fix something up quick."

"Macramé! You make the pretty knotted strings? Will you teach me how to do that?"

Dr. Murray cleared his throat.

"We can discuss this later, Mis…Daphne. Why don't you let him return to his tasks now?"

Norton looked relieved to be released from her presence. He stammered out that he'd made a box for the dog to use near the head, but as soon as he said "head" he turned so red she feared he'd explode. He ducked out of the cabin before this could occur.

Pompom sniffed out every corner of the small space, then jumped on the bunk and pawed at the covers until he made himself a nest, turned around three times and threw himself down with a sigh. He'd had a difficult day, too.

"You said you did not trust Captain St. Armand, Doctor. Do you think he plans to rob us? We do not have anything of value except Pompom."

"I do not think robbery is what he has in mind," Dr. Murray said slowly. "I do not know what his game is, but for now I think we should be watchful and see what develops."

~

"Why are you dressed like someone from a theater troupe that wanders from village to village being paid in chickens and turnips?"

Robert St. Armand chuckled as he poured out two glasses

of rum, one for himself and one for his mate. Horace Fuller had gloomily predicted for years Robert would come to a bad end and was at his back in tough situations often enough that he deserved an explanation.

"You do not like my costume, Mr. Fuller? I assure you, it accomplished exactly what I hoped it would. Do I not look every inch the romantic pirate captain?"

"You look like a damned mountebank," Fuller growled, tossing back his rum.

"Oh, I don't know. I think this red sash makes the outfit. Regardless, there's a method to my sartorial madness. The name 'Daphne Farnham' meant nothing to you, but it did to me when you informed me of our unexpected guests. Miss Farnham is a famous heiress. When that girl made her debut it was all the talk of London. So beautiful! So rich! So brainless! Everything a man could desire."

"A lot of money?"

"Oh yes, enough to keep a man happy for many, many years. Think about it—what impressionable young woman is not in love with the idea of a bold buccaneer? A voyage across the ocean is just the opportunity I need to sway Miss Farnham to my side instead of Mr. Murray's."

St. Armand braced his arms alongside his mirror, looked into the glass and sighed with satisfaction.

"I am so damned pretty, Mr. Fuller. It is no contest at all. The girls at Madame Cornelia's fight to spend the night with me. The boys at Ganymede's Cup swoon over my face and form. Miss Farnham is no different, and I will soon have her bedazzled. It is inevitable. It is fate. Her money and I were meant to be together."

He smiled, admiring the teeth that were as white and shiny as ever.

"He says he's her husband."

"Murray?" St. Armand looked over his shoulder at his

unsmiling mate and snickered at the thought of his competition. If one could even call Mr. Murray competition. Which one would not, because the concept was so ridiculous.

"Then she'll make a lovely widow in need of comforting, won't she? A ship at sea is a dangerous place. People slip overboard, are struck by flying tackle, fall down into the hold, fall atop swords by accident. Terribly unsafe. I predict that if Miss Farnham is in fact Mrs. Murray, it will not be an issue by the time we dock."

Fuller grunted, taking this in stride as just another day's work aboard the *Prodigal.*

"Want me to remove him?"

Robert St. Armand thought about this while he looked back into the mirror. He adjusted his shirt collar open and tousled his hair to make it a tad more windswept. Much better.

"We could use a surgeon, so let's keep him around for a while. There is plenty of time over the coming weeks to deal with Mr. Murray."

~

Norton and another sailor named Conroy delivered clothing and other items to the *Prodigal's* passengers that afternoon.

Daphne's wardrobe consisted of trousers that were tight through the hips and cut off short at the bottom, showing a scintillating amount of ankle, and two shirts—one a knit that was made for an individual with a much flatter chest, and a sailor's blouse that laced up the front. There was also Captain St. Armand's red sash for use as a belt, sent "with his compliments, Miss."

Alexander's clothes also featured too-short trousers and a

too-loose shirt that Daphne said did nothing to enhance his appearance beyond covering him.

"I am surprised such a fashionable man as Captain St. Armand couldn't find more flattering clothes for you, Dr. Murray."

"I am not surprised."

There was another knock at the door, and Norton stuck his head in.

"Miss, Captain St. Armand says," he swallowed, the color rising again in his face. "Cap'n says you can take a bath in fresh water while we're here and this is the last opportunity you'll have to bathe before we set out," he gasped out in a rush. "It's in his cabin."

The door slammed behind him and Alexander wondered if the malicious captain sent this particular sailor just to see if he could make him die of blushing.

Daphne clapped her hands. "A bath! How wonderful, and how thoughtful of Captain St. Armand."

"Yes, he's all that is considerate."

She ignored his mood, humming happily as she gathered items from the goods sent to them by the ship's crew, including fine citrus-scented soap, no doubt the captain's own stock.

"Why don't you use the bath when I'm done, Doctor? You must admit, it is a wonderful luxury."

Alexander acknowledged a bath and the opportunity to shave would be appreciated, so he fetched his razor and his own borrowed clothing.

When they arrived at the captain's cabin it was unoccupied, but there was a slipper bath with steam rising from the water's surface. Alexander ushered Daphne inside, closing the door firmly behind her. He then took up a stance against the door, arms crossed over his chest, and was unsurprised when Captain St. Armand came down the ladder a few minutes later.

"Mr. Murray. I did not expect to see you standing outside my cabin."

Alexander nearly told the captain what he thought of his presence while Daphne was inside, humming merrily as she splashed in the bath, but he thought better of it. They were still at anchor and it would not be difficult for the pirate to arrange for him to accidentally be left behind when they were underway.

It also seemed a prudent time to remind the captain of a surgeon's value on the coming voyage.

"Is there space for me to set up a surgery while we are at sea? It would be best if I did not have to use my own cabin for examining and treating your men."

Captain St. Armand leaned against the wall opposite his door, his own arms crossed, and for an instant Alexander saw beneath the jovial mask to the man who commanded other pirates.

"I will have an area prepared for you. It will not be large but will serve once we rearrange the cargo in the hold. Are you a competent surgeon?"

"There are captains and commanders in the Royal Navy who would assure you of my skills," Alexander said without a trace of false modesty.

"You are no longer in the navy, are you?"

He shook his head, trying not to be distracted by the splashing and humming he heard coming through the door. He had an excellent imagination, and envisioned Daphne smiling happily, rosy nipples peeking above the waterline while she raised one long leg and soaped it, from her slender ankle all the way to her snowy thighs...

"Mr. Murray?"

"No, I am no longer in the navy. I am returning to England to deal with business and set up my practice."

"Having a lovely young wife by your side will surely be an asset to you," St. Armand said, smiling at him.

The man smiled too damn much. It was akin to a shark showing you its teeth just before it struck.

"What about you, Captain? Were you in the navy? Anyone's navy?"

"All that regimentation, the uniforms? Sailing at the orders of others? Leaving a port before I've the opportunity to experience all its delights? No, it's the rover's life for me, depending only on the wind, sailing where my fancy takes me."

"How poetical," Alexander couldn't help the slight sneer that crept into his voice. "It is a good thing we were there to keep the sea lanes open for, ah, merchants such as yourself."

"I am quite grateful to you and the navy for its fine work," St. Armand said cheerfully. "Mr. Fuller will organize the men so you can have a regular sick call each day, if that would suit you."

Alexander was listening with half an ear, distracted by the low singing coming from inside the cabin, a siren song luring him to open the door. His imagination went wild wondering if Daphne was using a sponge to cleanse herself, soaping it up, running it over her rounded breasts, her shapely belly, cleaning down around those delicate pink toes that had been bared to his gaze on the island.

Bare toes were generally not considered an erogenous area of the body, but he was always open to exploring new possibilities. Exploring Daphne Farnham's nooks and crannies and toes was taking a firm hold of his thoughts, so much so that he jumped when the captain snapped his fingers.

"Now that I have your attention again, I was asking about sick call for the men."

"Yes. We can do a sick call every morning."

Daphne sang now, a sea shanty about a ship's carpenter who'd smuggled two women aboard and was working at keeping both women satisfied over a long, rough passage…

"Captain St. Armand."

It was Alexander's turn to wave his hand in front of the captain's glazed eyes, eyes focused on the cabin door while a slight sheen of sweat glistened on his unlined forehead.

"I'm sorry, I was distract—where did she learn that song?"

Alexander ran his hand through his hair and felt a moment's empathy with the bemused pirate.

"Daphne makes friends wherever she goes."

"It must make life more interesting for you."

"It keeps me alert," he said, adjusting his stance before the door. "I would not want any of her friends to misunderstand her open and trusting nature and take advantage of her."

"No, of course not," Captain St. Armand said blandly. "It is good she has a mastiff along with her little dog to guard her."

Alexander had no reply to this because the singing stopped, thank heaven, and the tone of the water splashing behind him changed. He knew Daphne was standing up in the tub, water sluicing off of her like Venus rising from the sea, her limbs glistening with moisture, the hair between her legs slick and doing little to hide the delights within.…

"I said, I am somewhat concerned that you seem distracted. And you look fevered. Did you catch an illness on the island? I don't want it passed on to my men."

"No, I am not fevered. The air in here is close, that is all. Do not worry, Captain," Alexander said, tugging at his coat, which allowed him to also surreptitiously adjust his trousers, "I have enough experience to treat your men and weed out any malingerers who might show up. My greater concern is the damage my supplies suffered when my surgical chest was in the water. It would be best if we stopped in a port so I could restock."

"There is a medicine chest on the *Prodigal* and while it is not up to your standards, it will serve. Your presence aboard is a luxury. I am certain a man of your skill and experience will manage with whatever we have at hand."

"I will give your men my best efforts, Captain St. Armand, as I always do."

"Excellent!" St. Armand said, "In that—"

The door opened and Alexander nearly fell into the cabin but recovered himself. Daphne stood there, rosy and glowing from her bath, her freshly washed hair wisping around her face and falling down her back in a golden skein. She had toweling wrapped around her, from her armpits to her knees, but she might as well have thrown it open and stood there naked for the effect she was having, and a sidelong glance at St. Armand's face showed that the pirate wished she would do exactly that.

So Alexander slipped into the captain's cabin, pulling the door closed behind him and nearly smiled at the muttered curse he heard in his wake.

"Would you help me dry my hair, Dr. Murray? It will take forever to dry otherwise. Maybe I should cut it off after all."

"No!" He didn't know why he felt so strongly about this, except that it would be like damaging a fine painting, to snip off that glorious mass of gold simply for the sake of fashion or expedience. "I will help you, just as I have been doing."

"Oh good," she said, relieved. "I hoped you would say that. Now, where did I put that brush…"

"Miss Farnham…"

She turned and looked over one creamy shoulder at him. "Doctor?"

"Why don't you dress first and I will brush your hair."

"Oh." She colored rosily and looked down at those toes,

those bare, pink toes that were wiggling in the oriental rug in front of the captain's bunk. He stared at those toes and started to sweat and wondered again if he perhaps was suffering some kind of brain-fever after all.

"There are no undergarments to wear beneath my clothing," she whispered.

"Bloody hell," Alexander said, tempted to ram his head against the bulkhead to remove these latest fervid images from his mind. "Just…just put the clothes on and no one will know."

"I will know!"

"Just do it, Miss Farnham."

He turned his back to give her privacy, staring at the door, until she said, "I am dressed, Dr. Murray."

Her appearance now did little to help his equilibrium. It was abundantly clear that the knit shirt she wore was not designed for someone who was abundantly endowed. His eyes narrowed. The trousers flattered her in a way he'd never imagined a woman could look, clinging to her thighs and ending at the top of her ankles. They were loose at the top, but the captain's sash took care of that problem, and drew the eye to her narrow waist, which was, of course, St. Armand's objective.

Daphne looked down at herself and giggled. "I never imagined myself in such an outfit. La, if they could see me at Almack's dressed like this, I'd be barred for life."

What she said sank into her consciousness, and she looked up at him, her clear eyes troubled.

"No one aboard this vessel will be in a position to spread gossip about you," Alexander said, wondering why he even felt compelled to reassure her that she'd be able to safely congregate with other empty-headed fashionables in the rarified atmosphere of her little world. "They will not be conversing with your peers at Almack's."

She brightened at that, and then she clasped her hands together.

"That reminds me, Dr. Murray. I did not learn a new word today. I want to show all my friends how educated I've become. I already knew macramé, so that is not new. Do you have a word for me?"

I have lots of words for you, he thought. *Pulchritude, glistening, luscious, toothsome, resplendent...*

"I'll wager a pirate like Captain St. Armand could teach me any number of new words!"

...air-headed, feather-brained, nodcock, cloth-headed, ninnyhammer...

"You will leave the teaching of new words to me," he said crisply. "I have experience in this field, he does not."

"That is true. So, what is my word for today?"

Alexander thought about it for a moment. "The word for today is...ascariasis. It means to have intestinal worms, such as roundworms."

"Oh no! Do I have asc...ascar..."

"Ascariasis. No, you do not. To the best of my knowledge. But if you wish to use it in a sentence, you could say, 'Captain St. Armand appears to be infested with parasites. He likely has ascariasis.'"

"Ascariasis. Ascariasis. I will remember that, Dr. Murray, though I am not sure I can work it into polite conversation."

"You never know, Miss Farnham. I find words like ascariasis appear regularly in my conversations."

"I think you made a joke! Not much of one, but a joke, nonetheless. I believe this adventure has been good for you."

She beamed at him, which caused a funny jump in his pulse rate. He started to say something, he was not sure what he was going to say, but Daphne turned around and looked at the tub.

"Why don't you bathe while I return to our cabin, then you can help me with my hair?"

Alexander checked the passageway to make sure there were no lurking rogues and watched her enter the cabin and close the door behind her. The dog barked twice to signal his approval at her return, and Alexander felt secure enough for the moment that he could strip off his rags and take advantage of the *Prodigal's* tub.

He washed himself with the same bar of soap she'd used and the intimacy of the act struck him. Sharing a bar of soap was a very personal thing and when he smelled the scent on his own skin it would remind him of Daphne.

When he'd scrubbed himself clean he dried off and soaped up a brush to shave. As he looked in the mirror, his hand raised and soap dripping on the deck, he paused. The beard that came in during their tenure on the island was mostly white, and his face was seamed and drawn with a lifetime's worth of cares and sleepless nights watching over his patients.

There was nothing about him to appeal to a young lady of fashion. And why would he want to? He briskly covered the offending whiskers with shaving soap and started in on their removal. He did not need her giggles and her prattle and her soft lips and lush curves. He'd been doing fine without them in his life, and he would continue to do just fine without her. If he never had to suffer through another conversation about hair ribbons or whether clouds looked like dragons or why flowers had scent, it would not be a hardship. He would have his medical journals and his lectures and plenty of evenings filled with interesting discussions with other natural philosophers.

"Damn," he said, dabbing at a drop of blood where he'd nicked himself.

CHAPTER 17

*A*lexander accompanied Daphne and Pompom after they were dressed and Pompom was outfitted with a leash and collar, thanks to young Norton. They strolled the deck, careful to stay out of the way of the *Prodigal's* sailors taking the last of the water butts aboard as the men prepared the vessel to head out before full dark.

"Why is Captain St. Armand in such a hurry to leave?"

"I suspect he is unwelcome in these waters, and fears detection."

"Oh!" Daphne looked around and lowered her voice. "Because he is a p-i-r-a-t-e."

"Exactly," Alexander said, tucking her free hand into his arm and walking with her, careful to avoid the sailors busy at their tasks. A shout from above brought his head whipping about. One of the sailors slipped and was caught in the rigging, dangling from the mainmast.

Alexander froze, watching the man as his comrades scurried to assist him.

"Dr. Murray? Alexander?"

He pulled in a deep breath, his lungs aching, and realized

he had not been breathing while focused on the crisis above. He turned his head to see Daphne's eyes full of concern for him.

"It is all right. He did not fall."

Alexander was about to say something to reassure her when he saw Captain St. Armand watching him intently.

"Do you need assistance?"

Captain St. Armand glided over and Alexander shook his head, but Daphne spoke up.

"Dr. Murray is afraid of heights, Captain—"

"Daphne, that's enough!"

His words came out harsher than he intended, and both of them looked at him, Daphne with hurt, and St. Armand with satisfaction. The pirate looked up at his men, then back at the couple.

"All's well. Conroy did not fall and splatter himself like an overripe melon on the deck—are you sure you do not want to sit down, Murray? You look shaky."

"I am fine," Alexander said, as calmly as he could. He tugged at his coat, ill-fitting over the shirt the crew gave him. Captain St. Armand was also wearing a jacket now, this one a rich blue that perfectly matched his dark-rimmed eyes, the gold buttons gleaming in the light reflecting off the waves from the setting sun, the lines of it expertly tailored to his lean form.

They were both barefoot, at least they had that in common. He had never had occasion to compare feet with another man, but for some reason it made him feel better that his foot appeared larger than the pirate's.

The captain favored Daphne with one of his overly bright smiles.

"Is everything in your cabin to your satisfaction, Miss Farnham?"

"Oh yes, Captain St. Armand," Daphne said, but then she

glanced at Alexander sidelong. "You are supposed to address me as Mrs. Murray."

She was distracted from her thoughts by Pompom tugging at his leash. "Thank you for sending Mr. Norton to me. He has been most helpful with my darling Pompom."

St. Armand reached out a hand to Pompom, who bared his fangs, a low growl issuing from his tiny chest.

"Good boy," Alexander said to the dog. "He is quite protective of his mistress," he added for St. Armand's benefit.

"His mistress has nothing to fear from me."

Alexander was tempted to bare his own fangs but refrained. His goal was to make it to England in one piece, alongside Daphne. Then she could resume her life and if she made bad choices about men again, it would not be his concern.

Right now though, she was his concern and his responsibility.

"Come, Daphne, let us leave the men to their work."

Captain St. Armand favored them with a bow, but as they walked off Alexander could feel the pirate's eyes on his back.

The sailors were in a jovial mood, anxious to return to their homes. They raised anchor, the sails filled with a fresh wind, and he found himself at the stern, silently watching their island paradise slip away from them.

"I want to return some day," Daphne said in a low voice.

"Do you? Perhaps you will become a famous authoress and travel the world for your books."

"What a wonderful idea," she said, looking up at him with an expression that did odd things to his respiration. "If I am a famous authoress I will need a husband who understands my particular talents and desires."

Alexander looked at her and took her hand in his. When they returned to England he imagined she would begin a regimen of creams and lotions to smooth her skin out, but now her hands felt real to him, soft, but strong and capable.

"Do not ever forget that. You need a husband who understands you are your own person, unique and talented in your own right. Do not settle for less."

"I won't," Daphne said solemnly, looking deep into his eyes. He broke away from her gaze to look back at their island, disappearing into the dusk and the distance.

"If you were naming it, what would you call it, Doctor?"

Paradise. Heaven. Eden.

"I would give you the honor of naming this island, Miss Farnham."

"It seems so small, but while we were there it was just the right size, wasn't it?"

"You will make other homes for yourself. Your home is where you are content, and that can happen anywhere if you make it so. It can be in the middle of London, or on an island, or even on a ship at sea."

Daphne looked at him, her face serious in the evening air. The wind blew out strands of hair from her braid and he saw she still wore her colorful ribbon at the end, sadly faded now, the colors he'd woven for her running together. But she would not give it up, not even when Alexander offered to braid her a new one from the pink satin.

They stayed up on deck, enjoying the evening air. After the sailors took their meal they brought out an assortment of musical instruments to entertain themselves and their guests. One African whose face bore the ritual scarring of his homeland had a small drum, a sailor with a brogue coloring his speech had a tin whistle, and Conroy played the fiddle.

Daphne sat on a crate covered with a quilt to cushion it and she laughed when Pompom stood at her feet and began dancing to the music.

"I did not know your pup was so talented," Alexander

said, watching the animal pirouette and stand on its hind legs.

"I see one of your guard dogs dances, Miss—Mrs. Murray. Would you care to dance as well?"

Light-footed Captain St. Armand was standing behind Daphne, smiling down at her, but before she could answer Alexander said, "Mrs. Murray was about to favor me with a dance, Captain."

"I was?"

"Indeed you were," he said, helping her to her feet. She cocked her head to the side, listening to the music.

"That music is in waltz time, Dr. Murray. Do you know the waltz? It is my favorite!"

"Then it will be my favorite also."

Daphne looked up at him as he took her into his arms, a quizzical grin on her face. "What a charming thing to say! I vow, you are becoming quite the gallant."

Alexander said nothing to this, concentrating on the music. Yes, he'd waltzed when ashore. On occasion he'd been invited to balls and assemblies, even a surgeon being a useful man to have when the navy was expected to provide gentlemen at entertainments. But he'd never felt the music, the dance had never mattered so much until this moment, aboard this pirate vessel.

He saw Captain St. Armand out of the corner of his eye as he swung Daphne into the dance, a cynical smile playing about the captain's lips. He was competing with Alexander, and Alex wasn't about to back down from that challenge, not when the prize was his to protect.

And for the moment, the prize was his to cherish. Daphne felt so right in his arms, her face turned up to his, her soft lips slightly parted and beckoning in the lantern light.

"You are smiling, Dr. Murray."

"I do not believe I am, Miss Farnham."

"Yes, you are," she said dreamily. "I see smiles in your eyes."

They moved on the deck, drifting in and out of the lantern light as the music swirled over the water. The moon rose over the horizon, shining a silver ribbon along the waves and Alexander felt as if all his life he'd been waiting for this moment, this dance, this woman.

He lowered his head, wanting to taste those lips again, but a voice broke through his dreams.

"Play a livelier tune, Conroy, one we can all enjoy."

The music stopped, and Alexander stopped, and Daphne stopped and frowned, not at him, but at the captain who'd interrupted their interlude.

"May I have this dance, Miss Farn—Mrs. Murray?" he said to her now with one of those toothy smiles.

"You must to excuse me, Captain St. Armand. I am fatigued after our long day and wish to retire now."

Alexander offered Daphne his arm and they turned their backs on the pirate, but not before he saw the man's look of bemusement. He probably did not have many ladies rejecting his invitations as neatly as Daphne had.

~

Daphne smoothed down her dress, the pink satin warm beneath her hands. Shadows filled the cabin in the low light of the lantern near the bunk. When Pompom came over to investigate she sent him back to the ragged quilt folded in a corner of the small space for his bed.

She bit her lip now, watching the door. She hated being in a situation where she did not know the correct behavior. She wore her special satin dress that she'd promised herself she'd wear, but now she was unsure. How did one go about seducing a surgeon? Nothing she'd experienced in her past prepared her for her dealings with Dr. Murray.

Dr. Murray. Alexander. She liked that better. Such a noble name! And it matched his commanding presence, his air of competence. He looked like he could conquer nations, or diseases, or small tropical islands. When he'd stepped into their cabin this afternoon, his face clean-shaven and free of the white whiskers that covered him ashore, he was every-thing rugged and manly. It had been all she could do not to walk over to him and run her hands over the strong bones of his face, down his corded neck, across that wide chest and even lower to the trousers that were too small for him.

He was annoyed by that, she knew, but she found it delightful and mentally hugged to herself the image of him, the snug garment revealing his form in a manner that had her imagining all sorts of naughty behavior.

And he danced! Who would have thought grumpy old Dr. Murray waltzed? She hummed to herself the melody the sailors played, remembering it, cherishing it.

The door to the cabin swung open and Daphne stopped humming. She stood next to the bunk, staring at Dr. Murray, who silently watched her. He closed the door behind him, and it was quiet but for the night sounds of a ship under sail.

Daphne swallowed as an entire flock of butterflies took flight in her stomach. She'd made up her mind. She was not some weak miss to be tossed about like a rag doll, never taking charge of her own life. She was strong, and capable, and she knew how to boil an egg. She could do this.

Alexander still wore his shirt, his coat under his arm. The sailors had brought a hammock earlier and it was rolled and leaning against the wall, waiting for him to string it up, but that was not going to happen, not if she had her way.

He said nothing, still, as she crossed the tiny cabin that

felt suddenly as wide as the entire Atlantic, a journey of few steps filling her with trepidation, and excitement.

When she stood in front of him, so close she saw the gold and amber and emerald colors of his eyes, she reached for his hand and placed it on her breast, over the lush satin, where her heart beat so loudly she knew he would not need to put his ear to her chest to hear it. His hand was warm, and strong, and she put her own hand over his, holding him there.

"Miss Farnham, what is this?"

Her heart and all those butterflies fluttered down to her feet. "Don't you know? Dr. Murray, I thought you surgeons had to know all about parts of people!"

His eyes crinkled and his hand tightened slightly, which felt incredible.

"No, that's not what I meant—Daphne, are you trying to seduce me?"

"Yes. Is it working?"

He watched her a moment longer, but he did not remove his hand, not until he brought his arm around her waist, pulling her to him, and then he moved his hand to the back of her head, cradling it against his shoulder. She wrapped her own arms around him and inhaled, feeling delightfully warm and safe, his powerful arms around her, his heart beating in a steady rhythm.

And she could tell from where he pressed up against her that, yes, it was working. It was working wonderfully.

They stood there in the silent cabin, the noises outside of their little world reminding them that they weren't alone here as they were on their island paradise.

"You are not doing anything. Except holding me. Which is nice, but not as nice as when you kiss me."

"I am thinking."

He stroked her hair as he said this, the hair she'd unbound

and left loose around her shoulders and down her back. It felt so good, but she wanted more. Much more.

"Stop thinking and kiss me, Dr. Murray."

It was everything she wanted a kiss from Alexander to be. His mouth moved on hers, coaxing her lips open, enticing her into allowing him into her heart just as he was enticing her to open for his tongue, his hands moving on her satin-clad back, easing down to her hips, a move that made her shiver with delight.

He raised his head, and his eyes were heavy-lidded, the planes of his face harsh with the tension she felt in his body. She looped her hands behind his neck and looked up at him, and she felt a smile pulling the corners of her lips, but then he shook his head.

"I want you, Daphne Farnham, more than I want my next breath of air, more than I want life itself, but this would only complicate our situation and make it harder to say goodbye later."

Daphne moved her hands up through his thick hair, the silver and russet curling over her fingers, and he closed his eyes and a sigh seeped out from between those lips locked now in a grim line.

"Open your eyes and look at me."

He did, and he looked miserable, but he was still holding her, caressing her back above the satin fabric of the dress, a move that made her want to purr and rub herself against him.

"You are always insisting that anything could happen and our lives are short. I do not know what will happen tomorrow, and neither do you. But I know what I want to happen tonight. You promised me a night of passion on the island. I want my night."

She licked her dry lips and his eyes followed that movement, and she heard him suck in his breath, and felt his chest move. What a marvelous thing the body was! Daphne was glad to be alive, glad not to have a brain fever, glad not to be drowned in the ocean, glad this stern man was with her, sharing her adventure.

She tightened her grasp and pulled his head closer to hers, but he hesitated, a breath away from her lips. "How can you say no?"

He looked at her for a heartbeat, an eternity.

"I cannot," he whispered against her mouth.

This time when his mouth came down on hers it was with a force and a hunger that drew a moan from deep within her as he gave her a taste of the power leashed within him. A small guilt niggled at her that he would regret this later, but she had no intention of regretting anything, not now, not when his hand in her hair made her feel like it was as alive as the rest of her body, his fingers moving to her scalp to hold her in place for his mouth, stronger now, more demanding.

Her fingers brushed across Alexander's neck. That was who he was, her Alexander, for when he touched her like this, his rough hand cradling her cheek, his eyes gleaming in the near dark, he wasn't the gruff surgeon. He was the man she'd been dreaming of when she saw him washing at the pool, and standing in the surf fishing, and almost smiling at something she'd said.

She might be too silly for dry old Dr. Murray, but she appeared to be exactly whom Alexander wanted this night. His warm lips caressed her, his mouth, that mouth she'd studied so often while he taught her, his words steady and thoughtful as he fired her imagination, his mouth now was igniting fire of a different sort in her, a fire that swept through her from the hair he was stroking down to her toes.

He touched her in all the ways she dreamed he would touch her, his mouth on her neck, through the silk knotted at her shoulder, his breath a puff of sensation against nipples that were already almost painfully hard and sensitive through the light fabric of her dress. He drew her into his mouth there, though the fine cloth. Her knees went weak as she felt warmth, and wetness, and his tongue swirling around the erect peak. His hand beneath her back supported her as she arched even higher into his embrace, seeking more, asking him for more.

He swept her up in his arms and laid her on the bunk. He blew out the lantern, faint light entering through the porthole, starlight and moonlight guiding his hands as he unknotted her dress, unfolding the satin like she was a gift to be unwrapped, a gift for him.

"You are so fair," he said, his words low and hoarse with a Scots burr that sent a frisson of heat down her spine, the richness of his voice stroking across her like the satin. He reached down and traced a line from her neck to her naval and Daphne watched, waiting, wanting to know what he would do next. He pushed the pieces of her dress aside and she sat up, her arms crossed over her breasts as she suddenly felt self-conscious beneath his steady gaze.

"No, do not cover yourself. Your beauty shines in the starlight like…like…stars."

She bit her lip to keep her smile inside at his heartfelt attempt at poetic language. If the words did not trip off his tongue it was not necessary, because his skilled hands could speak for him, and his mouth was clever in other ways.

Alexander demonstrated that now as he laid her back down on the narrow bunk, his arm pillowing her head. He kissed her again, not rushing, taking his time to know her, to explore her, to experiment and determine what she enjoyed. The slight stubble returning to his face rasped across her collarbone, making her shiver in a delicious combination of sensations.

"Oh, yes," she gasped. "That is perfect!"

He raised his head and Daphne thought she saw the brief gleam of a smile on his face, but it was too dark to be certain, and it was of no matter now. She knew where his smiles were. They were in his eyes, and in his hands when he touched her with such care, and, most of all, they were in his kisses.

He paused to pull off his remaining clothing and toss it on the deck, then lay down beside her again, the two of them as close as the ribs of a fan in their space, which was fine with her as she ran her hands over his arms, his back, her caresses earning murmurs of approval from him as he responded in kind.

Her pulse pounded and she knew she was ready for more, until she reached down for him and stilled, holding onto what she had only felt against her before. He rolled atop her, but she put her hand on his chest, which made him pause. Daphne licked her dry lips.

"You are an intelligent man, Alexander, and there is a lot of knowledge in your head, but maybe not enough knowlededge. I do not want to stop, but I must tell you—this won't fit."

He buried his head into her shoulder where it met her neck and made a muffled noise somewhere between a snort and a laugh.

"It will fit."

"Doctor, I do not know if you have done this before…"

He pushed himself up on his arm and his face was strained and tense in the moonlight, but he took the time to rub his thumb across her lips before placing a soft kiss there, a reassuring move that eased some of the tension from her frame and made her feel safe.

"I have done this before, Miss Farnham. Daphne." He put his finger over her lips when she would have continued protesting, his voice rumbling from deep in his chest. "I studied anatomy. I know about women and their parts. Remember? You can trust me to know what I am doing when I say we will fit as neatly as your hand fits in your glove."

"You are certain?"

"I will prove it."

And he did, moving carefully, cautiously. He kissed her again, deep, drugging kisses that made her twine her arms around him and caused her legs to fall open, and he moved his hand down, across her belly, feeling the bones, the skin, watching her reactions and how she responded. When he touched her, finally, in that spot that was aching, he gave a noise of male satisfaction.

"Good girl," he whispered in her ear. "You are wet, and you will see how well we fit. Like this," he said, slipping one finger inside her. She gasped at the sensation and felt herself tighten around him as he withdrew his hand, but then he was back, two fingers easing inside of her body as her back arched. He watched her intently, gauging her reactions, and he was the one who gasped when he slipped a third finger inside and she cried out at the stimulation, her hips moving, seeking more.

Sweat covered his face and a bead trickled down his muscled arm where he was propped above her and she did what she'd been longing to do, turning her head and licking that droplet of salt from his hot flesh.

His mouth swooped down on hers again, one hand gripping her, holding her against the thin mattress but that did not matter because he was stroking her with his other hand. Then it was not his hand probing between her legs and she went still, adjusting, feeling more than she'd ever felt before, but he was true to his word and moved carefully until he was a part of her, his body rigid with tension when he propped himself up on his arms and looked down at her.

"Raise your legs, my dear—ah, yes, just like that. Perfect—so perfect," he whispered, his mouth returning to hers as his hips began to move.

And he was right, as usual. It *was* perfect, being beneath Alexander's solid bulk, feeling him moving within her, gliding out and returning in a rhythm that made her see starlight even though her eyes were closed now. Her other senses opened to the sound of them moving in the dark, his sweat-slick body gliding against hers, his hands holding her, gripping her as she arched beneath him with a cry of satisfaction, her arms wrapped around his back, and his name on her lips.

"Perfect," he whispered again, driving into her a final time before pulling out suddenly and spending himself on her belly.

There was little room to move in the bunk and she lay draped over Alexander, her back pressed up tight against the bulkhead.

"Why did you pull out?"

His hand stilled from where it stroked her hair, and he sighed.

"I do not want to risk getting you with child, Daphne."

"Oh." She suddenly felt chilled and put her hand over her flat belly. "I do not think that will be a problem, Dr. Murray. I was with George, and we never had a baby."

"Every man and woman together is a different story. There's always a risk."

"I wouldn't mind." She thought about it, cuddling a sweet, serious little baby with red hair. Maybe he would have a Scottish accent, too. It would be better than anything.

In the meantime, though, she was relaxed and sleepy.

"I am glad I did not atrophy," she murmured. "Don't hang the hammock, we can fit in here together."

"Only if you sleep on top of me."

He managed to maneuver them into a state where they could lie on their sides under the cover, with his arm around her waist to anchor her against him and keep her from falling out.

Daphne smiled to herself. There was a long sea voyage ahead of them. Plenty of time to see what could develop.

CHAPTER 18

"You look cheerful this morning, Mr. Murray."

Alexander glanced over at Captain St. Armand, who posed on his deck in a white shirt gleaming in the sunlight, the linen open at the neck to reveal too much of his tanned body. He comforted himself with the thought if the pirate kept dressing in that fashion he would develop a chest cold when they moved into cooler climes. Seeing him sneezing, coughing, and red-eyed might turn a young lady's attention to a healthier alternative.

The captain's long legs were in close-fitting buckskins which earned him a second glance from a sailor or two, but Daphne was not there to appreciate the fop. Alexander'd left her sound asleep in the bunk, her hair spread over the cover like a golden shawl.

They'd woken twice during the night to make love, and despite the activity and lack of sleep, he felt like the cock caged on the deck with the other poultry. Crowing seemed the natural response to a night like the one he'd had.

"In fact, one might say you look—smug," the captain continued.

"Nonsense," Alexander said smugly. "I look well-rested, having been rescued from being castaway."

Captain St. Armand looked around, a slight frown on his face. "Miss Farnham is not with you?"

"Mrs. Murray is resting. It was a stressful experience for her." "That explains why you are in charge of the livestock."

Alexander was trying his best to ignore the animal sniffing around his feet. Pompom had looked at him so hopefully when he awoke that he took the dog with him, making a stop first at the sandbox for the dog's use. And to fetch him some water and biscuit. And to put his leash and collar on him for a walk.

"Have you eaten, Mr. Murray?"

"Yes, I stopped at the galley earlier. Did you prepare a place for me to work?"

The captain nodded. "Follow me," but then he paused. "That animal of yours—is he a ratter?"

Alexander looked down at the fluffball at his feet. Daphne had washed him, thankfully after Alexander's bath, and combed him out, tying a ridiculous scrap of pink satin into a bow on the dog's hair. He looked ready to attack a dandelion.

"I do not know. He hunted lizards on the island, but I never saw him fetch a rat."

"He could earn his keep if he keeps the rat population down."

"You do not have a ship's cat?"

The captain looked away and mumbled something.

"I am sorry, I did not catch that."

"Cats make me sneeze."

This second mental image, of the pirate captain with eyes streaming tears and a nose swollen and red from sneezing, enhanced Alexander's morning stroll.

"Let's take the dog into the hold and see what happens." Fewer rats aboard ship would make his life easier as well.

~

*D*aphne awoke refreshed and ready to sing. What a glorious morning! Dr. Murray was, well, amazing was not too strong a word for him. Rogerable indeed! It must be all those years of studying the human body that made him so skillful. Clearly, none of *his* parts had atrophied from lack of use!

She giggled to herself, then called for her pup.

"Pompom?"

His leash and collar were gone, as was her dear grumpy doctor, so he must have taken the dog for his walk.

Daphne hummed a merry tune as she dressed in her sailor's clothing. It still felt strange to her. Wearing trousers was good for gentlemen, but it would never catch on as a fashion for ladies. Taking care of her needs was much easier when all she had to do was hoist her skirt, but she had to admit it was easier to move in the confined space of the ship and climb above in trousers. No doubt it would be easier to climb trees in trousers, not that she was likely to do that with Dr. Murray watching over her.

She found her way to the galley, where Hill fussed over her and fixed her an egg fetched that morning from one of the hens.

"Enjoy it, miss. Hens can be contrary on sea voyages and may decide not to lay any more until they're on land again."

He'd fried the egg and she savored it, along with excellent coffee. The galley was tiny, but neat as could be, and the cook chattered to her as he worked, about everything from fashions to cooking techniques.

"I am learning how to cook, Mr. Hill—"

"It's just Hill, miss," and he gave her a wink.

She smiled back at him. He wasn't flirting with her, she'd spent enough time with men of fashion to know when they weren't interested in women. He was a sweet fellow, but not a competitor for her affection.

"Dr. Murray showed me how to cook on the island," she said as she watched the cook wield his knives with skill. "I can make fish baked in leaves, and I can stew crabs and boil an egg."

"Well now," he said, putting down his knife and looking at her. "I would say that puts you ahead of most ladies then."

"Really?"

"Yes, miss. I grew up working in the kitchen of a fine house, and the ladies there couldn't even make a fire to fix themselves a cup of tea. Can you imagine?"

Daphne looked down into her own cup to hide her embarrassment. She'd been one of those useless ladies before she met Dr. Murray. He was so patient with her, and he wanted to teach her new things. She blushed, thinking of some of the new things he had taught her in the dark. She finished her tea and brushed off her hands, standing and returning the tinware to the cook.

"Thank you for breakfast, Hill. Have you seen Dr. Murray?"

"He was by earlier to fetch himself a bite, and some biscuit for your little dog."

That dear man! Taking such good care of her Pompom! She needed to find both the males in her life and wish them a good morning.

~

"*H*ere's another shilling on the rat!"

"I'll take that, Norton. That doggy's a bruiser!"

The crew lucky enough not to be at their duties were enjoying the action in the hold. Mrs. Murray's little pooch was proving to be a scrapper, and a valuable addition to the crew. Their voices rose as the betting became fierce, and Pompom seemed to love the attention. Perhaps it reminded him of when he'd been a working dog and not a lapdog, and that even fluffy furballs could be useful.

Alexander pulled a biscuit from his coat pocket to give the bichon another small bite for his latest prize. There were four corpses at his feet, their necks broken from a vigorous shaking.

Now the animal was staring down the king of the hold, a low growl rumbling up from his chest. The dog hunkered down, shoulders bunched, waiting for the right moment. He had scratches on his muzzle and his tail stood straight.

The rat looked near as big as Pompom. It crouched, beady eyes darting, not daunted by the cries of encouragement from the wagering sailors. The dog prepared to spring when a shriek tore through the space.

Pompom ignored this, leaping into action when the rat jumped, startled by the high-pitched sound. It was the last move the rat made as Pompom grabbed him and shook his head, snapping the rat's neck. The sailors—at least the ones who'd bet on the canine—cheered mightily at their champion's prowess.

"What are you doing with my precious baby? Dr. Murray, I demand to know what is going on here!"

All heads turned toward the ladder, where Daphne stood, perched on the lowest rung, her blue eyes narrowed in anger.

"Good thing she's your wife. You handle this," St. Armand said, slinking away.

"Dr. Murray!"

Daphne advanced on Alexander but was halted by her pup prancing up to her, tail high, a corpse clutched between his teeth.

"Oh, my darling, did you fetch that for me? What a good boy you are, what a fierce hunter!"

She crouched down to pet him, wincing at the fuzzy body dropped at her feet. Meanwhile, the pirates deserted the surgeon like rats fleeing a sinking vessel, easing away from the couple and mumbling excuses as they exited the hold.

Daphne looked up from where she was tickling Pompom under his chin and rose to her full height, tapping her bare foot on the deck, hands on her shapely hips. Hips that were outlined amazingly well by her garments, Alexander couldn't help but notice.

"Well?"

"It seemed to me the animal is less likely to end up in the stewpot if he earns his keep."

"Dr. Murray!"

She looked so adorable in her anger. Her protectiveness of her animal sparked something in Alexander's chest, a feeling that she'd be as protective of anything she loved, whether it was a dog, or a child, or even possibly a surgeon. He ignored the rats and stepped over to her, taking her by the elbows. She craned her head back to look at him, a frown putting lines between her brows. He put his thumb over the lines and gently erased them.

"Do not frown, Daphne. You don't want to end up all wrinkled like me, do you?"

"You are not so wrinkled, Dr. Murray. Just a little"—she thought about it—"weathered from being in the sun too much. Like a leather shoe left out by mistake."

"Exactly," he said. "It occurs to me, I did not teach you a new word today."

She sniffed, her delightful little retrousse nose making even that rude gesture endearing.

"That is because we did not see each other this morning. You, sir, have been busy corrupting my dog."

The dog in question sniffed hungrily around the rats. If midshipmen would eat them, then the dog was not above such behavior. Watching her precious Pompom devour rats would not improve her temper, so Alexander sighed, kissed Daphne on her unlined forehead and set her away from him.

"My word for the day, Dr. Murray?"

He scooped the animal up in his arms and scratched the proud pup behind his ear. He'd clean the animal's scratches so Daphne wouldn't rail at him again.

"Your word? I believe the word for today is…osculation."

She shaped it out with her mouth, which he watched with interest, then she said it aloud.

"Osculation…but what does it mean?"

"Never fear. I will demonstrate for you later."

~

"Mr. Murray! So good to see you survived your experience in the ship's hold."

Captain St. Armand was all smiles when they came above, and Alexander turned to Daphne.

"I need to speak with the captain about my sick bay. I will see you at luncheon?"

Daphne nodded, and it was all he could do not to take her in his arms and retreat to their snug berth, but duty called. He passed her the dog. "And wear your hat, Mrs. Murray. The sun is strong out here."

"Yes, Dr. Murray," she said with a sunny smile of her own. He watched her walk away, her trouser clad bottom drawing his eyes nearly as much as her tightfitting shirt did. He was not the only male to watch Daphne stroll, but when he turned back to the captain, the captain was watching him.

"I have concerns about my wife's safety aboard this vessel," he said bluntly.

"I run a tight ship. The men know the punishment would be severe, and likely permanent, if they offered Miss Farnham— pardon, Mrs. Murray—any insult. Ah, here is Mr. Fuller to show you your space in the hold. I will see you at luncheon."

With a nod the captain turned away, but not in the same direction as Daphne, so Alexander relaxed a fraction and followed the mate.

The space in the hold was cramped, but not impossibly so. Most of the room was taken up by a table in the center, and Alexander looked at it critically.

"I need restraints for this table, a brazier, and plenty of lanterns."

Fuller grunted his assent. "What else do you need?"

"Bring me Captain St. Armand's medicine chest and anything else you have aboard this vessel for dealing with the ill and wounded. I will inventory it. I'll also need bandages. Clean ones, and vinegar and soap."

He did a quick survey of the space, judging the size of the cabin against his need to be flexible in his movements.

"Finally, place a drop-down desk and a chair, and install a locked cabinet on the bulkhead."

"The carpenter will take care of it."

"Have you been with Captain St. Armand long?"

"Aye."

Alexander waited, but the man held onto his information about the captain as tightly as a spinster guarded her modesty. If he wanted information, he would have better success with the crew. Nervous men chattered, and a trip to sick bay was usually enough to make any strong man break out in nerves.

"Sick call will be after I eat my breakfast. I need journals to record information about the men."

"Sounds like a lot of bother," Fuller grumbled. "Never had a surgeon before."

"No, and I imagine there are dead or injured sailors who wished there had been a surgeon aboard. Who cared for the ill and injured?"

Fuller shrugged. "The cook, or captain, or sometimes the carpenter."

"I assure you, the men will be gratified there is a competent surgeon to deal with their ills, rather than the carpenter." He peered around at the space. It could use a good scrubbing, and he said so to the mate.

"There's not much here normally except cargo, so it isn't cleaned as much as the rest of the vessel," Fuller acknowledged, and said he would see that it was done before the next morning.

Alexander had to admit Captain St. Armand ran a tidy ship. No one was sitting around drinking, the ship was clean, the men appeared healthy, and even the rat population was normal for a vessel of this tonnage.

"I will begin tomorrow morning then. Good day, Mr. Fuller."

❧

Daphne breezed into the cabin on the heels of Dr. Murray, who was washing his hands when she entered. She set Pompom on the deck and her parcel on the bunk. The dog immediately ran to the surgeon, rolled over on his back, and presented his furry belly to be rubbed.

Now, if only Alexander would do that for her!

She smiled to herself at the thought, but clearly Dr. Murray had other matters on his mind, though he obligingly rubbed the dog's belly and asked how her morning was.

"Oh, lovely! I have been talking with Mr. Sails. He is

going to take fabric and make me up some dresses to wear aboard ship, and he found this coat for you in ship's stores. Look!"

It was a brown heavy weather coat. There was a hole in the chest with some rusty stains around it.

"Thank you, Daphne, that's a useful item. Though I believe I will have it cleaned and patched. That hole looks too much like a target."

"I knew brown was your favorite color, and the more I've thought about it, the more I believe it is a good choice for you. It flatters your coloring and hair."

"I am glad it meets with your fashionable approval. Speaking of which, what about you? What will you wear when the weather turns cold?"

"We took care of that. Mr. Sails will use the wool from the cave to make me a quilted coat that he says might not be the first state of fashion, but it will serve."

"I am not sure I approve of his measuring you for garments." She giggled, then walked over to put her hand on his arm.

"Dr. Murray, Mr. Sails was a tailor before he went to sea. We talked about clothing, and fashion and I assure you his interest in me is only as a form for his designs."

"You are sure?"

"This is an area where *I* am experienced. Yes, I am sure."

Alexander pulled out his surgical chest, saying he needed to return to his sick bay. Daphne sat on the bunk, playing with Pompom, tossing a red cloth ball for him to fetch. After Alexander left the cabin it was quiet, and she realized something was bothering her. It took her a few moments to put her finger on it, but then she figured it out.

She was bored.

On their island she'd been busy from sunup until sundown, but there was no place for her on this pirate vessel.

She was useless. An ornament, again, just sitting on a shelf like a china doll waiting to be admired. And that wasn't right. She was a different person than before the shipwreck. Butterflies were lovely, but sometimes you needed to be not a butterfly but a bee—busy, busy, busy.

A deep "Enter" was the response when Daphne knocked at the door that a sailor told her was the new sick bay.

Alexander looked startled to see Daphne inside his workspace, but he only said mildly, "I am glad I did not have a sailor in here with his trousers down. I was not expecting you."

"Would you say 'enter' if you were in the midst of examining one of the men?"

He thought about this for a moment, a frown creasing his brow.

"I spent so many years in the navy it would not occur to me to be concerned for the privacy of the men I treated. I see I will have to give new consideration to how I deal with patients when I practice in England."

"You see? I am being useful to you again. That is why I am here," she added briskly. "On the *Magpie* you insisted I help you in your sick bay. There is no reason why I cannot be useful here, rolling bandages or something."

"You enjoyed being useful," he said, and there was a gleam in his eye, and she thought he was laughing at her.

"Exactly!" She crossed her arms over her chest, trying for a stern glance. He did it so much more effectively. Maybe she just needed to practice more. "You are thinking back to our conversation, the one we had just before Mrs. Cowper passed on."

"You must admit, my dear Daphne, if one were keeping score of such things, then one would be forced to concede I won that argument."

"Good thing no one is keeping score, because then I

would need to keep track of all your fashion disasters just to keep the game fair."

He watched her still, and she'd swear the corners of his mouth were higher than they'd been a few minutes earlier. Alexander called her his "dear Daphne," which made her feel all warm inside, like she'd just had a drink of chocolate. He was looking at her chest where her arms were crossed, and he looked at ease as he talked with her—dare one call it bantering? She'd been dreading him returning to his old Dr. Murray ways once they were off the island. She relaxed as she realized their relationship was still a special one, even away from their paradise. "I do want a task. It will make me feel better."

"I think we can accommodate your needs and mine, Daphne. Do you write a fair hand?"

She clapped her hands together in joy.

"Yes! My former governess praised my handwriting and still mentions it when I write her."

"If that is the case, I could use someone to transcribe my notes on my patients into a more readable form. You could be my amanuensis."

"I would be a man?"

"No," he said with a shake of his head. "Amanuensis means one who takes down the words of another in writing. Like a clerk or a secretary."

She sounded out the syllables of the new word. "Amanuensis. Oh my, Dr. Murray, you taught me a new word. Now we can save osculation for later. You will not forget, will you?"

The corners of his eyes crinkled, matching that newfound curl at the corner of his mouth.

"Never fear, Daphne. I will not let us forget osculation."

CHAPTER 19

Daphne hummed to herself as she copied Dr. Murray's notes that afternoon and took down his words into the journals from the *Prodigal's* stores. She enjoyed this, keeping track of what Alexander was doing, updating lists, making notes. It was all so interesting! She assured her surgeon she would never discuss outside of the cabin what he said or wrote about the sailors, or what diseases he treated.

"They would be uncomfortable knowing you knew which of them were suffering from various ailments, especially the diseases of Venus."

She blushed at his words but also felt a secret spurt of satisfaction that he was conversing with her like an adult, and not like some fresh out of the schoolroom miss.

He looked over her work, and he appeared, not unhappy, but bemused. "Daphne, there are hearts dotting the *i's.*"

"Oh!" Her hand flew up over her mouth and she giggled. "That is my habit, Dr. Murray."

He turned his journal sideways. "Is it also your habit to decorate your work with…is that a rainbow? And a puppy?"

"I think a little decoration helps make the reading more interesting, don't you?"

"The only thing I expect to see pictures of in my journals are dissected organs. I suppose I can live with it."

Daphne stretched her cramped fingers.

"Here, let me see," Alexander said, taking her hand in his. His hands were strong, and when he held her hand she felt a feeling unlike any other. She loved his kisses and thrilled to their lovemaking in the bunk, but an act as simple as her bare hand in his felt—it felt like something that could last a life-time, not just a momentary flash of pleasure. He stood next to her, and she felt his warmth, and inhaled his scent—clean, and earthy, and real.

He caressed her fingers, opening them, flexing them, turning her hand over in his. He rubbed where a tiny callus was forming from holding the pen, then raised her hand to his mouth and kissed it, not on the back as a greeting, but at the wrist, at the pulse that she felt speed up beneath his firm mouth.

A gasp escaped from her own lips and he raised his eyes, dark and full of those emotions that did not show in smiles or laughter, but were kept only for her. It made her catch her breath and made her heart melt.

"Oh my," she said, as the realization of these new feelings struck her. She would have to think about this, but right now she was too distracted by what his mouth was doing to her.

Unfortunately, he stopped doing it.

Alexander stood straight and took a step away from her, wiping his hand across his brow.

"I—I did not mean to take advantage of the situation as I did. We must be careful and avoid further complications."

He could say that after the way he made her feel when she was in his arms? He wanted to stop, again? That was not going to happen, not if she had anything to say about it!

"Alexander, if you feel this way every time you kiss me, it is going to be a long and uncomfortable voyage. There is no going back, not after last night! That sheep has already left the barn!".

"Horse. That horse has left the barn, Daphne."

She grabbed him by the lapels of his coat.

"This is no time to be discussing the habits of livestock! Kiss me!"

So he did.

His mouth felt as delightful on her lips as it had on her wrist and she gave a little sound of satisfaction, and maybe even triumph when he opened for her, and his arms wrapped around her, pulling her close to him. She went willingly, eagerly, into his embrace. Now that she knew what she wanted—Grumpy Doctor Mister Alexander Murray—she was prepared to use every weapon in her arsenal of flirtation and a lifetime of coquettishness to convince him to see her as someone he'd let draw rainbows in his journals for years and years to come.

She knew he wanted her. He demonstrated that over and over again most effectively last night. She would not let him run away from her, not when she was working so hard to keep him.

"We should return to our cabin," she murmured when he pulled his lips away from hers and began tickling kisses down her throat, across the expanse of skin exposed by the wide neckline of her sailor's shirt.

"This cabin door has a lock on it," he said, his deep voice rumbling over her senses, that slight burr tickling her nerves much as his tongue sent shivers over her skin. "And there's no animal here."

"But this is the sick bay, Dr. Murray."

He straightened up and looked around, and when he looked back at her there was heat in those hazel eyes. "So it is. Which means it is an ideal place to give you a most thorough examination. Now, remove all your clothing. No giggling, this is serious business."

He was being silly, but he was also being, again, highly rogerable, so she stepped away to follow his directions. Besides, she liked it when he was silly. She suspected it was a side of him no one else in the world was privileged to see, and that made her feel special indeed.

"I need help out of my clothing," she said.

He latched the door, then looked at her sternly, arms crossed over his chest.

"You are not wearing a dress that fastens in the back, you are wearing men's clothing."

"Oh. Does that mean you won't undress me?"

He put his hand on his chin and rubbed it reflectively.

"I think you should demonstrate for me how you dress—and undress—yourself in these garments."

She almost giggled again, but as she *was* feeling overly warm, taking off her clothes sounded like an excellent idea. And he was watching her so intently.

She looked down at her bare toes that moments ago had been curling when she was being kissed so expertly. She'd been promised shoes by Mr. Sails, who said he could cobble something together before they were in colder waters, but for now her clothing was not complicated at all.

Nonetheless, she took her time, thinking about how to do this most effectively. She brushed her hand across the wide neck of her shirt, easing it away from her collarbones, then sweeping her hand down, slowly, across her breast, demonstrating just what a close fit the tight garment was. So close that when she moved her hand down she felt the point of her breasts, her nipples pulled tight and erect against the fabric. It felt good to touch herself that way, and the man watching her made a noise deep in his throat that sounded like he approved as well. She glanced at him from under her lashes. Oh yes, given the condition of his trousers he very much approved of what she was doing.

"This shirt is so tight," she said, her voice coming out soft and breathy. "I may have to wiggle my way out of it."

His eyes gleamed and, yes, that was definitely an upturned corner on that luscious mouth.

"You do whatever you need to, my dear. I am a patient man."

He said that, but he looked tense as he watched her take the bottom hem of the shirt and slowly lift it. There most definitely was wiggling involved to pull the tight shirt over her head, but she finally managed, and the look on his face said it was worth the effort.

"Now the trousers," she started, but he stepped closer, and put his hands on her hips.

"I can assist you with that," he said in a low voice.

"You don't need to."

"I think I do," he said, his hands brushing up across her ribs, down to where her waist curved in. They paused at the buttons, then moved up again to her breasts, enveloping her, cradling her. "You were beautiful last night in the dark, but to see you now, in the light, to see my hands on you, it is better than anything I could imagine."

His thumbs rasped across her nipples and she arched into those hands. Daphne put her fingers behind her neck, lifting her hair, lifting her breasts higher into his grasp, and she held herself still, bound by his touch as surely as if she'd been bound with shackles.

She braced her legs wider to balance as the ship soared across the Atlantic waters, bringing her closer to home, closer to all those problems that would appear when she was back in England. For now she was here, in this cramped space with this wonderful man, and she intended to seize every moment of happiness she could. People thought her shallow and flighty, but she'd had her share of pain in her life. It left her knowing happiness was something you grabbed. People you loved could die, or could be disappointed in you, which caused its own little death inside your soul.

Alexander cared for her. She saw it when she saw the smile in his eyes, when she felt his hands on her body, so careful, so capable, and she released her hair and wrapped her arms around his neck, bringing his head down to kiss her. She could spend all day in her doctor's arms, enjoying the feel of his mouth on hers, his tongue sweeping inside and causing her to rise up on her toes and hold him tighter, even as his hands finished with her trouser buttons and her garment fell to her feet.

He pulled her against him and she felt how much he wanted her, how his own needs overcame his constant thinking with that large brain of his. She approved, and let him know with her mouth, and her hands, and her own whispered words that what he was doing now, with his mouth on her breast felt like heaven—

"Mr. Murray? Are you in there?"

They both froze at the voice outside the sick bay. Alexander raised his head, his hair mussed and falling across his forehead and his eyes narrowed as he looked at the door.

"It's locked, isn't it?" Daphne whispered.

He nodded, but he was focused on the door and the passageway beyond. Now there was a second voice.

"What is it, Turnbull?"

"The door to the sick bay is latched, Mr. Fuller. I saw Mr. Murray in there a while back and I was going to ask him about this rash on my arse."

Alexander put his finger up over Daphne's lips when she would have said something. The latch rattled on the door.

Alexander sighed and leaned his forehead against hers.

"If we are quiet maybe they'll just leave?" she whispered hopefully.

"Pull up your trousers, Daphne."

The voices from the passageway continued to drift in, more sailors milling about as she yanked up her trousers. She was not happy about this, not at all! Didn't those sailors have a ship to steer, or sails to reef, or something else to do besides annoy her?

"Why do you think the door is latched?"

"I saw Mrs. Murray go in there with him earlier."

Daphne paused as the passageway went silent, the men out there no doubt mulling this latest development over in their little waterlogged minds. Alexander sighed again and ran his hand through his hair, giving her a vaguely apologetic look.

She stamped her bare foot and glared at the door. "I am receiving an examination from Dr. Murray! Go away!"

The silence was profound. Alexander gave her a look of disbelief, and in a moment she knew why.

"I think he's futtering her."

"Do you think she's a screamer? Or one of those who makes kinda squeaky noises?"

"Mr. Fuller, why aren't these men at their tasks?"

Now Captain St. Armand was standing there, too. Daphne gave up and pulled her shirt on over her head. Her hair had come unbraided, and was flying about, the curls springing to life in the sea air. Alexander put his own clothing to rights.

"The surgeon is in there with Mrs. Murray. And the door is latched," Fuller said gravely. "We are concerned, Captain. She says she is receiving an examination, but they may need our assistance."

"Mr. Murray? There seems to be some disagreement out

here as to what you two are doing in that cabin. Perhaps you could open the door and clarify it for us?"

It struck Daphne how ridiculous their situation was, and her giggles escaped.

"See? She's laughing. I think they're futtering."

"I don't like it when they laugh while we're futtering," one of the pirates said grumpily.

"You shouldn't take it to heart, Peanut."

"Mrs. Murray likes shanties, gentlemen. Why don't you sing something to help her pass the time during her examination?"

"Short-haul or capstan, Captain?"

There was much snickering at this, which made Alexander frown and say something under his breath.

The sailors took the captain's suggestion and started in, singing "Juliana" with enthusiasm, led by Norton, the shantyman.

"Ignore them, Daphne. Come, let me help you with your hair." Alexander efficiently braided it back up and tied it with an equally efficient bow. He looked down at her breasts, again covered by her shirt, and sighed before he tilted her chin up with his fingers and gave her a brief kiss.

"Later," he said before again running his hands through his hair and stepping over to unlatch the door.

Daphne peeked around his shoulder. The crowded passageway was full of sailors staring at them expectantly.

"It occurs to me, Captain St. Armand, that your men might benefit from a good dose of salts," Alexander said, which cleared the area of lingering crewmen.

Captain St. Armand just flashed Daphne a blinding smile. "I trust all is well with you?"

"I would be happier if your men had not interrupted us while Dr. Murray was giving me my examination, Captain.

He is a serious surgeon and should not be distracted from important tasks!"

Daphne looked at that serious man out of the corner of her eye, but his gaze was on the deck above them, lips pursed.

Captain St. Armand smiled again. He did that a lot. Maybe too much.

"I understand, Mrs. Murray. A man of the surgeon's years might not be able to perform up to expectations if he is distracted."

She tugged down the hem of her shirt, which brought both men's eyes back to her until Captain St. Armand spoke again.

"Is everything in your sick bay satisfactory?"

"For the most part, though I am short of medications."

"I hope that will be the only difficulty you encounter."

"Are you anticipating the need for battle surgery?"

There was a drawn out silence as the two men looked at each other.

"These are dangerous waters, Murray. You know that from your service with the Royal Navy. Even with the war over, there are still brigands loose who would attack merchant ships. Merchant ships such as this one. I am always prepared."

Alexander made that noncommittal noise which sometimes passed for conversation and turned to her. "Return to the cabin to see to your animal, Daphne. I will join you shortly."

"Will you come with me when I take Pompom for his walk? He likes it better when both of us are there."

"A pasha with his entourage?"

She blinked, then smiled. "That is exactly the way he is! See, you do care for my little puppy."

Alexander opened his mouth to say something, thought better of it, and simply said, "I will see you in the cabin."

She left the two men there and returned to her Pompom, but as she stood at the cabin door she glanced back over her shoulder. The men were watching her, and she couldn't help but contrast the two of them. Tall, lithesome, toothsome Captain St. Armand, his windblown piratical looks enhanced by his stylish attire. Then there was her rumpled, crumpled, worn-down surgeon in his hideous cast-off garments.

She smiled to herself as she closed the cabin door.

~

*I*t was awkward accepting the captain's invitation to dine with him and not having the proper attire. Daphne fretted to herself, thinking of the perfect outfits now at the bottom of the sea with the *Magpie*. A particular favorite was a lilac crepe with long sleeves laced with silver ribbons, with the most cunning silver *lamé* trimming at the hemline and neck. It had a matching lace cap with silver tassels and Mrs. Cowper would arrange her hair in a knot *a lá grecque* to show it off.

Mrs. Cowper had not been a pleasant person, but she had been good with hair.

Daphne tapped her finger against her lips as she thought about her limited options for dressing for supper with the captain. Very limited. There was the pink satin, but she hesitated as she reached for the shimmering fabric. No. She would not wear that for dinner with the captain. That dress was for Alexander. Captain St. Armand would just have to bear looking at her dressed in her too-tight sailor's shirt and trousers. It couldn't be helped.

Alexander was still wearing his own ragged coat, and his trousers from the island were washed so he wasn't forced into the sailors' ragbag wardrobe, and she thought he looked just fine and told him so. This appeared to amuse him, or at least relax the lines around his jaw.

"Thank you for the compliment."

"It is true, Alexander. You are a striking man no matter what you are wearing. Or not wearing."

He paused, his hand on the latch and turned to look at her.

"You called me Alexander."

"Do you mind?"

"Not at all. I don't often hear my own name. Usually it's 'Mr.

Murray, come quickly!' or 'Mr. Murray, I'm bleeding!'"

"Or 'Dr. Murray, you are being an old grump!'"

"That, too," he acknowledged. "I enjoy hearing my name on your lips, Daphne."

The look he gave her as he said this was quite warm, and she felt the color rise in her cheeks. He'd better not argue with her when they went to bed, not after leaving her so…so twitchy after their session in the sick bay earlier!

Daphne tugged down the hem of her shirt. "Shall we join the captain?"

He kept his hand on her lower back, the passageway being too narrow for him to offer her his arm. It was a short walk to the captain's cabin, but she appreciated the comfort of his touch. When other escorts offered their arms while walking, it was largely impersonal, a polite gesture of a polite society. When Alexander touched her, it meant something. He was not a man who wasted effort on social niceties, therefore every one of his gestures meant more to her.

Captain St. Armand rose to his feet when they stepped into his cabin. His new ensemble again evoked images of a bad boy at sea. Trousers hugged his legs and drew the eye down to hightopped boots gleaming with a careful polishing.

He wore no jacket, but had a leather vest over his shirt, gold scrollwork in a Turkish motif covering the front. The shirt beneath it was a deep blue silk that made his eyes glow like Ceylon sapphires in the lamplight. A gold and sapphire earring looped through his ear, the perfect accent for his exotic looks.

"Our cook was pleased to hear you would join us for supper and promised a memorable meal,"

"Us?" Alexander asked.

"Mr. Fuller will keep the numbers even."

The table was laid with elegant linen and an array of silver and dinnerware that would look at home gracing a Mayfair dinner party.

"My! You certainly know how to do things with style, Captain."

He gave her a smile that seemed more genuine and unrehearsed than his other efforts. "I believe one should grasp every bit of pleasure from life Miss—Mrs. Murray. Fine china and good silver showcase excellent food, as much as fine tailoring shows off a man."

"On our island we were content with eating off of leaves and drinking water," Daphne said as he poured her a glass of claret. "After being in the boat at sea it tasted heavenly."

"Having been forced to abandon ship myself on occasion, I cannot argue with you on that point, Mrs. Murray."

Daphne frowned a little. When Captain St. Armand called her Mrs. Murray it did not sit well with her, because she knew it was a lie. But if he called her Miss Farnham, or Daphne, it would upset Alexander. Little lies can cause big problems, something she'd heard her nanny say too often while she was growing up.

There was nothing to be done until the ship docked, and Daphne saw the wisdom in their pretense. Having made up her mind to push her problems aside and enjoy the meal, she looked around the cabin, marveling again at its lush appointments.

"Is your home decorated so vibrantly, Captain St. Armand?"

"Yes, where is your home?"

The question was asked mildly, but Alexander's eyes were sharp as he waited for their host's response.

Captain St. Armand poured himself some claret. He took a swallow and his eyes closed in pleasure as he savored the excellent vintage. "My home? I consider myself a citizen of the world, or the world's oceans. With a fine ship and a fair wind, I can go anywhere, see everything. Why tie myself down?"

"But you speak like an Englishman, Captain," Daphne said.

"*Quand je parle français, je parle comme un Français.*"

"Everybody comes from somewhere," Alexander took only a half-glass of wine for himself. "They start out in life owing allegiance to a king or ruler, or a nation. We just completed fighting a war over that, you may recall."

Captain St. Armand looked at him, and it was hard for Daphne to read his expression in the evening light.

"Allegiances can change, Mr. Murray. You are a Scotsman. Not so long ago your allegiance might have been to a Stuart king. The Americans will tell you changing allegiances can be a right and necessary act. As for me, my allegiance is to my men and my ship. If I find a land where I wish to settle, then I will determine to whom my allegiance is owed. Other than myself, of course."

"But what of your family? Surely you owe them your allegiance. Your father? Your mother?"

He topped off his wineglass and drank before flashing her a brilliant smile.

"A rover such as myself does not claim ties to family,

Miss Farnham—pardon, Mrs. Murray. Nor would they necessarily wish to acknowledge a scapegrace sea merchant."

Daphne dropped the topic, though she felt sorry for the poor man. Everyone needed family. Even when her own father looked disappointed in her, he was still her papa. She was not looking forward to the lecture she would receive when she returned from her adventure with George. And Dr. Murray. And pirates.

"Why the long face?"

"I am thinking of what awaits me in England, Captain. You are correct, sometimes families can be difficult when it comes to, as you say, scapegrace behavior."

Mr. Fuller joined them then, apologizing for his lateness. The supper was served, and it lived up to the captain's promise, as the cook sent out dishes ranging from stewed chicken with rice to a squash pudding, fried yams, and a brandied fig cake.

Captain St. Armand kept Daphne's wineglass filled and Alexander frowned at her as she giggled at the pirate's tale of climbing for coconuts on an island where they'd been short of supplies.

"I know how to climb, but Dr. Murray doesn't approve. He's afraid of falling," she said with a small hiccup. She covered her mouth and apologized, but another giggle leaked out. "Uh oh, I wasn't supposed to say that again, was I, Alexander?"

"It doesn't matter, but perhaps you've had enough wine? You don't want to awaken with a pounding head, do you?"

She frowned and looked at her glass. He was right, of course, because he was almost always right, which was annoying, and the wine truly was delightful. It must be magical wine because even Mr. Fuller was looking better.

A call from outside the door interrupted these soggy

thoughts. "Captain? That idiot Nash took a fall and broke something. Can Mr. Murray come take a look?"

Mr. Fuller rose, as did Alexander.

"We'll be right there, Conroy," Fuller said. Alexander paused and looked at Daphne.

"I must go. Let me escort you to the cabin."

"No need for that," Captain St. Armand said smoothly, pouring more wine into her glass. "Let the lady enjoy the rest of her meal, and I will be sure to take care of her."

Alexander looked like he wanted to say something to this, but Mr. Fuller said, "Coming?"

He just said, "I will see you later then, Mrs. Murray."

It was quiet after the men closed the door, and Daphne looked around again, her eyes coming to rest on the main piece of furniture in the cabin. The captain's bunk looked far more comfortable than theirs, and it was certainly larger. That same captain was watching her now, and she was reminded of the kitchen cat at Rawlings who used to sit just so, waiting for an unwary mouse to poke its head out and be snatched up.

He smiled at her, his eyes half-lidded, a look on his face making her feel decidedly mouse-like. If the wine was making even Mr. Fuller look good, it was making Captain St. Armand look absolutely scrumptious, so she did what came naturally. She smiled back at him.

~

Alexander hurried back to the cabin after wrapping Nash's wrist. He opened the door without knocking and found a glum Captain St. Armand sitting in his chair, his feet propped up on his bunk.

It is not a prudent thing to tweak the man who holds your safety in his hands, but he couldn't resist.

"Bored her to sleep, did you?"

Alone in the bunk, spread out like an offering to a pagan god, Daphne lay fully clothed and softly snoring.

"That's droll, you witty fellow. It was the wine, I suspect. She took a swallow and I barely caught her before she keeled over into the pudding. Your wife does not appear to have a head for strong drink. Or even moderately weak drink," he said as he rose. "How is Nash?"

"Only a bad sprain. He'll do, but I told Mr. Fuller to keep him on light duty for a few days. If there's nothing else, I'll take Daphne back to our cabin."

"Do you need assistance?"

Alexander looked down at the woman asleep with a smile playing about her lips in some wine-soaked dream.

"I'll manage. Goodnight, Captain."

He lifted Daphne into his arms and she mumbled something and went back to sleep. He maneuvered sideways down the passage, and a passing sailor opened the door to their cabin. Pompom jumped around and yipped but settled back down when he saw his mistress was asleep, jumping into the bunk beside her and watching her.

Alexander looked down at her, then sat beside her on the bunk. His rough hand hovered over her hair, then stroked down the braid with its curls insisting on coming loose and flying free, just as Daphne insisted on seeing the world in her own special way, complete with illustrations of rainbows and puppy dogs.

She opened her eyes.

"Doctor," she said owlishly, blinking at him. "Wine makes me drowsy. Did you know that?"

"I do now. How do you feel?"

"Thirsty." She yawned. "And sleepy."

He poured her a drink from the carafe in their cabin and helped her sit up.

"Slowly. You do not want to make yourself sick."

She drained the cup and then let him tuck her into the bunk, watching him with a look on her face that was hard to interpret.

"I may fall asleep again, Alexander, so lovemaking will have to…"

The last words slurred away as her eyes closed and she was out again. He watched her sleep, the gentle rise and fall of her chest. When they arrived and he returned her to her father's care, would her father be forgiving of her scapegrace behavior? Would he find a man for her to marry who would care as much for her as Alexander did? Would he try to mold her into something she was not or let her be uniquely Daphne? There was little room in the world for people who were out of lockstep with the rest of society.

The very thought of another man putting his hands on her, a man who would not treasure her, made his fists clench. The idea now of marrying a woman who would give him a stable, quiet, colorless life held no appeal. She would not fill the empty space in his heart with flowers and seashells and heart-dotted *i*'s and ridiculous dogs. She would not be Daphne Farnham.

His life was so orderly only a few weeks ago. He'd return to England. He'd take care of unfinished business. He'd set up his surgery, and he'd find himself a wife. Orderly, stable, predictable. No butterflies, no rainbows, no Daphne.

He rose and adjusted the lantern and settled in to work on his notes, keeping an eye on the woman in his bunk. She needed him. For now, she needed him more than she needed any other man in the world. The question was, what would happen when she no longer needed him?

CHAPTER 20

Alexander came up on deck after a morning of routine work in the sick bay, the usual assortment of men displaying sprains, boils, inactive bowels and the consequences of time ashore in the arms of women who'd been passed around like after dinner brandy.

Daphne had her own routine. She walked the dog in the morning while Alexander saw to the men, then she would join him for a cup of tea and she would take down his notes in, he had to admit, a clearer and more legible fashion than he would do for himself. He could live with the daisy borders and unicorns for the ease of reading later.

After luncheon she napped with her pup while he caught up on other tasks or strolled the ship to keep an eye on the men and their health. If he could order them into sick bay before they were in a crisis situation it made his life easier.

He pulled his heavy weather coat closer around him now as the wind whistled through the rigging. The day was bleak and even the normally sunny Captain St. Armand was on edge. He stood at the rail scanning the Atlantic when Alexander came alongside him.

"If we encounter trouble, Mr. Murray, are you prepared?"

"That is an unanswerable question at some levels, Captain. What kind of trouble do you anticipate? I feel as prepared as I can be given the supplies aboard this ship and the lack of a proper cockpit, but I've been on vessels with less."

"I do not know what kind of trouble," the captain said pensively, tapping his fingers against the rail. "It is a premonition, if you will. And I learned over the years not to ignore my gut in these situations, even when I don't know what to expect."

"Is it the weather?"

St. Armand shook his head. "There is another ship out there. I can feel it. I can almost smell it."

The words were no sooner out of his mouth that the lookout yelled, "A sail, Cap'n!"

St. Armand pulled his spyglass out of his coat and put it up to his eye. Whatever he saw restored his good humor.

"Mr. Fuller!"

"Aye, Cap'n?"

"Call the men to quarters! These lazy lubbers are going to earn their pay. It's time to hunt!"

A cheer rose from the pirates and Fuller bawled out orders to clap on more sail. Alexander turned to the captain and said, "Whose ship is it?"

"I hardly think that should matter to you. Your task is to go below and prepare your station."

He smiled as he said this, as usual, but there was a fierce look on the pirate captain's face that promised he would not be entertained by arguments from his passenger. He turned away from the surgeon to confer with the mate. Alexander shaded his eyes and looked out over the water where the mist was beginning to dissipate. He could see a ship but couldn't make out its flag or heading.

His years of naval service had his fists clenching in frustration. Pirates were the navy's prey, and to be a part of their marauding was unconscionable. What was more, for all he knew the other ship was also pirates on the prowl, making him dependent on Captain St. Armand's seamanship to survive this. Not a good situation, no matter what angle he studied it from, but his task for now was to prepare for casualties. And to keep Daphne safe.

The door nearly hit Daphne as he entered the cabin and she jumped back as the dog yipped.

"I was just about to go up to see what all the commotion is."

"Captain St. Armand is chasing a ship," Alexander said, his words clipped. "You must stay here when we engage them, so you do not come to harm."

"But who are they attacking?"

"Does it matter? I suspect the captain is not particular about whom he robs as long as the ship has gold or goods."

Daphne's eyes were huge, her face pale. Her dog whimpered and she stooped to pick him up, clutching him to her breast. "Where will you be during the fight?"

"I will be in the sick bay, dealing with casualties."

"Is it safe?"

He was about to reply that they were on a floating piece of wood in the middle of the Atlantic and nowhere and no one was truly safe, but that would do no good and a great deal of harm.

He stepped over to her, took her by the shoulders and said, "I have been through countless engagements at sea. This will just be another day of work for me."

"What should I do?"

He leaned over and kissed her on the forehead. "Stay here. I will return when it is finished."

He was still holding her shoulders, and she was still

holding the damned dog. He wanted to smile, to reassure her, but his face wouldn't move into the proper configuration. So she smiled at him, instead. It was a wan effort, but at least as good as anything he could produce.

"I know you are worried about me, Alexander. Pompom and I will be all right here."

"I am reassured that your guard dog is on the job."

"Don't joke, he can be quite fierce when he needs to be."

He took the fierce dog from her arms and put him on the deck. Then he took Daphne into his arms, holding her tight, his mouth near her ear. Her hair smelled of sunshine and soap, and it was a scent he tried to store away in his mind, in his memory, because he knew what he would be experiencing and smelling during a battle.

"Daphne, when the attack starts it will sound to you as if the world is coming to an end. The guns explode with noise and the ship shakes. You will be afraid, but that is normal. You are a strong and brave woman, and you will weather this, too."

She pulled back and looked at him.

"You think that of me, Alexander? That I am strong and brave?"

"I know it for a fact, because I saw you in action, afloat in a boat and building a haven on a deserted island. You *are* brave and strong."

And very precious to me.

Instead of telling her, he showed her how he felt about her by pulling her back into his embrace and kissing her, memorizing the taste of her as he memorized her scent, her shape, her feel in his arms, all the quirks and joys comprising Daphne Farnham.

She clung to him like a drowning woman, her arms around his neck, her hands fisted in his hair. But there was duty, even on a pirate ship, and he pulled back from her and looked into those eyes the color of the ocean on a sunny day.

In the silence as they stood there looking at each other they heard the shouts of the men above, even laughter, as they prepared to engage with the unknown vessel.

The dog whined, sensing the tension in the cabin. She stooped and picked him up, clutching him close as he licked her face, seeking reassurance. Daphne's eyes were on Alexander though as he backed out of the cabin and closed the door behind him.

~

Daphne thought herself prepared after Alexander's talk. She'd heard the guns when the men practiced their gunnery, but that was different. That noise hadn't been accompanied by screams, and shouts, and someone firing back at them. The crash of something smashing into the ship scared Pompom so much he had an accident on the deck. She nearly joined him, she was that frightened. So she cowered in her bunk, clutching the dog and wondering if this is what hell was like, the noise, the confusion, the smoke. How did Alexander stand it? How could he work under these conditions?

~

When the door to the sick bay opened Alexander looked up from what he was doing and he stared at her standing there wringing her hands. He was covered in blood despite the leather apron he wore. There was blood in his hair, blood on his face and his neck, he had his hand inside the person on the table and blood covered his arm up to the shoulder. He paused and raised one crimson-splattered eyebrow.

"Miss Farnham, if you faint, you will block the doorway. What are you doing here?"

His tone and the way he called her "Miss Farnham" brought her back to herself. Daphne swallowed, and regretted it, for that only intensified the odors in the cabin, an effluvia she tasted on the back of her tongue.

She clasped her hands even tighter, tempted to turn and run and lock herself back in her cabin with Pompom and resume cowering in the bunk. It was what people expected of her. It was what she would have expected of herself a few weeks back. That was then. Today, he said she was brave and strong.

"I want to be useful," she whispered. She cleared her throat and said it again, and while she tried to be that brave, strong person, her voice shook. Alexander stared at her, the man beneath his hands mercifully unconscious. He looked down at him, then back at Daphne.

"A useful person is always appreciated," he said mildly. But the look in his eyes told her much more and she straightened her back to be that Daphne, the one in his eyes.

"There are two rules for you in my surgery," he continued, doing something inside the poor man. "Rule one, you do everything I tell you without question. Rule two, you cannot vomit on a patient. Or on me."

"I will not vomit!" she said indignantly. That didn't sound like something brave, strong, and useful people did.

"Yes, you will. Just try to be discreet about it. One more rule—no humming. Come over here, I could use your hands."

"Yes, Dr. Murray."

She put her hand where he told her on the man, one of the pirates whom she knew in passing, a scruffy individual who had an amazingly beautiful singing voice.

"Will he live?"

"Put pressure there—yes, right there, harder. Good girl."

He continued to do something messy and seemed to be thinking about what she asked.

"Will he live? I do not know, but I am fairly certain he will die if we do not help him."

He said "we." Daphne hugged that to her heart and tried to focus on what he was doing with his hands but sweat was pouring down her forehead and she blinked her eyes to clear it out.

A splotch of red hit her arm, then another. Daphne looked up, blinking again as another splash of red hit her in the face.

It was blood. Dripping down from the deck above.

She swallowed the saliva pooling in her mouth, swallowed again, but it was no good.

"I have to—" she said, barely getting the words out before she lurched to the bucket and gave up the remains of her meal.

When she was done, she wiped her hand across her mouth, which was a mistake. The fresh copper scent of the blood assaulted her. Nothing in her life had prepared her for the horrors of the surgery. Her senses were bombarded much as the ship was, with smells, with sights, with sounds, all of which she feared would come back to haunt her in her dreams. All she wanted to do right now was turn around and run back to Pompom. How could Dr. Murray deal with this? How could any human being?

"Now that that's over with, come back here and get to work."

The astringent words jerked her upright, bracing her. She returned to him, and to her tasks. He gestured with a nod to a clean cloth on the shelf.

"Wipe your face with that, then wipe mine. Daphne, I am going to teach you a new word now."

"Osculation?"

His lips twitched but he didn't look up.

"No, I will wait for a more auspicious time to teach you that word. Today we will learn about the surgeon's tools, so that you may assist me. Hand me that tenaculum now, the instrument on the end."

He gestured with his elbow and she grabbed the wooden handle of the tool with a hooked end.

"Now hold that needle ready for me, the curved one. Yes, that's the one. Daphne, what was that novel you read aboard the *Magpie*?"

Blood was dripping on her, there was an injured sailor whose guts were being rearranged, and Dr. Murray was chatting with her as casually as if they were walking in Hyde Park.

Except, when she looked at him, he was anything but casual. He concentrated on his patient, his hands moving with a sureness that dazzled her. He wasn't just a grumpy surgeon, he was a grumpy surgeon who saved people's lives, and her breath caught as she realized he might be the most useful person she'd ever met. No wonder he had such high standards when it came to those around him! All of her acquaintances back in London, useless, the lot of them. Unless one needed fashion advice. And didn't many of them turn to her in that situation? Now she was being even more useful, expanding her skills. Why soon, she would be the person people went to for everything from how to boil an egg to—

"More pressure, Daphne, there. Yes, right there. No shaking now, I need your hands steady. Tell me about that book you were reading, do you remember it?"

She tried to think back to that night so long ago, when

she had clean clothes that fit her, and shoes, and a cabin where she was alone, and for a moment, she wondered if she'd ever be able to again sleep in a bed without a man who snored a little (though she'd never tell him that) sleeping alongside her.

Right now, she wanted to just come through the next hour without anyone blowing her up. There was the sound of the guns firing again and the ship lurching as it moved far too suddenly for her peace of mind.

"You haven't answered my question," he said evenly.

"Oh, the book. It was *The Mysteries of Udolpho*. You said reading novels contributed to my having a nightmare. You listened to my chest."

"Yes, that's correct. Move your body, not your hand, a little to your right so I have more light."

She did as he instructed and he continued working and there were squishy noises and smells she feared she'd carry in her memory for a lifetime, but she held her ground and her hand was steady.

"When you write your novel about your heroine stranded on a desert island—don't move, I am almost done here—I hope you will craft the sort of prose which will inspire, and not lurid scenes to cause nightmares in impressionable minds."

"Now, really! Who are you to criticize my writing—or other peoples' novels? You admit you do not read such books, so it hardly puts you in a position to be a critic. What is it I am doing here, anyway, Dr. Murray?"

She chanced a glance down, then looked away at the lantern until the black spots in her vision went away.

"You're keeping this man's blood inside his body, where it belongs. Thank you, I have it now."

She looked back at him, his hands moving with such surety. "Am I useful?"

He paused, and then the most incredible thing happened. In that room reeking of blood, and spilled guts, and emptied bowels, and who knew what noxious fluids, he smiled at her, that secret look. No one else would know the surgeon smiled, because they did not know him as she did. They did not see him in his various moods, they did not understand how a raised eyebrow could be a most effective form of communication, how a change in the look of his eyes or at the corners of that lovely firm mouth was as much of an expression of something wonderful as a full shout of laughter in other men. It was only she, Daphne Farnham, who saw Alexander Murray's amazingly expressive physiognomy, here, with the screams of the men and the shouts of battle and the boom of the guns.

The experience dazzled her so much that she nearly lost her footing when the ship lurched. Fortunately, she did not grab onto—who was this poor sailor?—to steady herself, but grabbed the table instead.

"Steady, Daphne, we are almost done here."

"Then what?"

"Then you will help me move him to the deck until his mates come in to carry him to his bunk. Give me that rum."

Daphne saw the bottle he gestured at and passed it to him. As the sailor stirred and moaned, then opened his eyes, Dr. Murray put his arm behind his head and allowed him to drink as much rum as he could swallow. Soon he was unconscious again, and she grabbed his feet and helped move him, which was not easy! People were a lot heavier than small dogs.

She leaned against the bulkhead, her legs shaky. When the door opened and the sailors came in with another wounded man, they looked startled to see her but didn't speak of it, following Dr. Murray's instructions for the unconscious man, whose name, it turned out, was Arnold. She didn't know if that was his Christian name or his surname. Then there was no time to think about it, because another wounded man needed care, and Dr. Murray needed her assistance.

The next hours—was it hours? was it days?—would remain a blur to her afterward. There was Dr. Murray's steady voice, patient with her and showing her what to do, there was cleaning burns and bandaging bleeding scrapes and mopping brows, including her own. She saw the crow-bill used for something other than cooking food, and she tried to stay cheerful and smiling for the men who were conscious. They seemed to appreciate that. If she was not petrified of something going wrong, then they would put a brave face on it. The men apologized when they saw her there in the sick bay, as if it was their fault she had to see their half-naked bodies and oozing wounds and have their blood splatter her.

Maybe in a way it was their fault, but she knew who was truly responsible. Captain St. Armand may be a pretty fellow, but she did not like the way he treated his crew, sailing them into danger in this fashion just so he could be a pirate. Though if they were all pirates, then they wanted to be in danger, didn't they? It was all too confusing.

"Daphne, you look ready to drop."

She jerked her attention back to her surgeon—then paused. It was quieter.

"No explosions."

He cocked his head, then nodded. "The guns are silent now. It's over, and given the cheerful demeanor of these men, I assume Captain St. Armand carried the day."

"That is good, isn't it?"

He paused in wiping his hands and looked at her.

"Since the alternative would be our death, capture,

drowning, or being hanged ourselves as pirates, yes, I would say that's good."

She almost smiled at the idea of anyone considering her a pirate, but then the door opened, and a real pirate walked in.

Captain St. Armand looked more rumpled than usual, but Daphne had to acknowledge on him it looked good. His raven locks were all disheveled and his shirt was soaked with sweat and streaked with blood. He clutched his arm where some blood leaked through his fingers.

"Who did we lose, Mr. Murray?"

The surgeon raised his eyebrow at the presumptuous question.

"No one yet, but Arnold might not make it. Time will tell. The others should survive."

The captain glanced around and noticed Daphne for the first time.

"Bloody hell! What are you doing here?"

"I am being useful, Captain St. Armand! And I would appreciate you not swearing in my presence," she snapped.

Both men looked at her as if she'd suddenly sprouted two heads, then Alexander glanced down at his instruments, hiding his expression. Captain St. Armand looked at the surgeon, then back at Daphne.

"I beg your pardon, Mrs. Murray," he said, giving her a small bow. "I was rude."

Daphne frowned at him. "Dr. Murray should look at your arm, Captain. You're bleeding."

"I can see that," he said dryly. "I know from experience though that it is just a scratch. But what about my face? I feel a cut, but I cannot tell how deep it is without a mirror. Will it scar?"

Alexander looked up then. There was blood on Captain St. Armand's forehead, but it wasn't pouring down.

"I'll tend to the captain, and since his wounds do not look severe, you can return to the cabin, Daphne."

"Wait," St. Armand said. "Turnbull is preparing a bath in my cabin. Go there and wash up. Your usefulness today is appreciated, by me and my crew, Miss Farn—Mrs. Murray. This is one small way I can show our appreciation."

Daphne smiled at him, and he blinked in that confused way men sometimes did when she smiled at them, then started to step toward her, but Alexander said, "Your arm?"

"Um, yes," St. Armand said, turning back to the surgeon.

Daphne exited the cabin and leaned against the door to regain her bearings. There was bloody sand on the deck, tracked out from the sick bay. Footprints in the blood went in all directions, but above her she heard the men singing and felt the ship moving as it ought to move, not tilting around and weaving back and forth as it seemed to during the battle. When she entered the captain's cabin Turnbull was pouring hot water into the tub. He paused and gulped when he saw her.

"Do I look that bad, Mr. Turnbull? Captain St. Armand said I could bathe in here."

"Don't look in the mirror, ma'am," he said seriously, his own face still blackened with powder and grime. "Wait, don't climb in the tub yet."

He brought more water and rags from outside the door, and an empty bucket. "Wipe yourself down first with this seawater before you climb in the tub so you're not sitting in that mess."

After he closed the door behind him—and she made sure it was latched—she followed his advice. She didn't know what to do with her clothes, or if they could even be salvaged, so she left them in a pile near the door. Of course, that left the problem of what to wear out of the cabin. There was plenty of toweling for her to wrap herself in but she did not want to parade that way around the ship.

Whatever happened, Daphne knew she'd think more clearly if she was cleaned up, so she wiped herself down, staining the seawater red, and tried to remove as much of the gore as possible before climbing in the tub. She was scrubbing herself vigorously with the captain's lemon scented soap when there was a rap at the door.

"Daphne, are you in there?"

"Yes, Dr. Murray. I am bathing."

"I have some fresh clothing for you. If you're almost done, I will wait here and pass it to you."

She hurriedly finished and toweled herself off, then opened the door a crack. "Quick, come in, Alexander. You can use the bathwater before the captain returns."

He didn't argue with her but entered the cabin, shucking off his own clothing while Daphne climbed into the sailor's outfit he'd brought her.

"How was Pompom?"

"Shaking, but the animal appeared well."

"Poor baby! I need to give him extra cuddles tonight after his scary day."

"Pass me the towel."

Daphne turned, and paused. Alexander was standing in the tub, and she did not often have the opportunity to admire him as nature intended him to be showcased. She put a hand on her hip and studied him.

"Do you know, Dr. Murray, the more time I spend with you the more attractive I believe you are?"

To her delight he blushed, and her blatant perusal of his physiognomy—and the rest of him—cause that reaction in his body that made her want to clap her hands in delight. Really, it was an even better trick than Pompom dancing on his hind legs!

Then he shook his head.

"I must follow up on my treatment of the men, and make sure they're being cared for properly. Do not pout; duty before pleasure."

The door rattled.

"Miss Farn—Daphne? Are you still in there?"

Before Daphne could answer, Alexander spoke up.

"Mrs. Murray is almost finished, Captain."

There was a silence from the other side of the door, then St. Armand spoke again.

"That answers the question of your whereabouts, Mr. Murray."

Alexander wrapped the toweling around him, and Daphne figured he would not be worried about the men seeing him nearly undressed. When he was decently covered, she opened the door.

Captain St. Armand stood there, a bandage on his arm where his shirt had been ripped away, and a scowl on his handsome face. There was a plaster on his forehead, but it did not detract from his looks. He studied the nearly-naked surgeon for a moment, smiled dismissively and turned to her.

"Join me for supper later—" He flicked a glance in Alexander's direction. "Both of you. We will celebrate our victory today."

"I do not know if I should, Captain St. Armand. Who was it you robbed?"

"Robbed? I robbed no one, madam!" the captain said indignantly. "That ship attacked us first. They are pirates and we were only defending ourselves."

"Truly?"

"Were you up on deck to swear otherwise?"

This was said in a soft voice that nonetheless sent a chill down her spine. She glanced at Alexander. He was poised as if he was ready to leap at the captain bare-handed, and Daphne knew she had better be the Daphne that Captain St. Armand expected.

"Of course, if you say they were pirates then they must be pirates! It was silly of them to think that they could take on a ship full of brave, strong men like you and your crew."

Captain St. Armand relaxed, but he wasn't the one she was worried about.

"Oh, Dr. Murray, I am so upset over everything that has happened today. Please, take me back to our cabin before I have nervous palpitations!"

"Of course, my dear."

Looking as dignified as the toga-clad statue of some dead Roman that Daphne had seen in a museum, Alexander gave the captain a nod before taking her elbow to usher her out. He used his foot to nudge their disgusting garments outside the door, telling her they'd be picked up and cleaned for them later.

CHAPTER 21

"Captain St. Armand is pretty, but he's a dangerous pirate, isn't he, Alexander?"

"Yes, he is. We must act so he doesn't believe we're a threat to him."

"I'm not good at pretending," Daphne said in a small voice.

"Just be yourself. Be sunny, and smile, hum, and Captain St. Armand will be friendly to you."

She looked at him intently. "In other words, act like a ninny, is that what you're saying?"

Alexander opened his mouth, then shut it. There were no safe responses he could make to that question, not and be honest. "If the captain does not feel threatened by you, he will not harm you," he said lamely.

"What about you? He knows you are not a ninny."

"I am useful to him. It's sufficient to keep me from harm's way."

"I hope so."

She pulled Alexander's coat closer over her sailor shirt as

they prepared for supper. They were in colder waters now and, barring catastrophe, would soon be back in England.

The day had been exhausting, and Daphne had been amazing. Out of all of the women in the world he might expect to be helpful and useful in his surgery, Daphne Farnham would have been at the bottom of the list. Hell, she would not have been on the list at all! Today she'd shown pluck and mettle worthy of the most stalwart of helpmates, soothing the wounded men, assisting him without dramatics, doing the filthy work of putting men back together when they'd been blown apart. He turned his head and looked at her. Truly looked at her.

"Is there a smut on my nose?"

"Let us join the captain. The sooner we finish supper, the sooner we can return."

The look she gave him made his own pulse race in response.

The captain's cabin was crowded with crates and boxes, some open and spilling out a collection of odds and ends—china dishes, wine bottles, silver.

"Pardon the mess," St. Armand said. "We're still rearranging the hold to store everything."

Tonight he was dressed casually, wearing a knit sailor shirt much as his men wore. His shirt was of a much finer weave and outlined his limber frame as if had been designed just for him. For all Alexander knew, it had been. The pirate's trousers were tight and cut high on the leg, revealing muscular calves and bare feet.

"Is that French writing on those boxes, Captain? Were they French pirates?"

"That is it exactly. French pirates. Fearsome creatures, but we routed them."

Fuller joined them then, and the crew brought in supper as they crowded around the table. Captain St. Armand apologized for it not being up to their usual standards, but the cook was pressed into service during the battle, the galley cold during the fight. They dined on slices of ham, served with hastily prepared rice flavored with island spices, and the last of their tropical fruit.

"Your help today was of great value to me, Mrs. Murray," the captain said as he passed her the rice.

"I learned so much, Captain! Dr. Murray even took the time to teach me new words, like ligature and trephine!"

"Do you intend to be a lady surgeon?"

Daphne giggled. "Me, a surgeon? That is just silly! Knowing what the word means is not the same as knowing how to do something as expertly as Dr. Murray does. He just enjoys teaching me new words."

"Does he now? How very pedantic of him," St. Armand said. "Now that you mention it, the surgeon does remind me of an elderly tutor I once had. Dried up stick of a man, but his head was stuffed full of knowledge."

Now it was her turn to look puzzled as she mouthed "pedantic," and Alexander knew he'd have to define it for her later.

"I will miss this in England," she said as she bit into a mango that was only slightly overripe.

"If the weather holds we will dock in a few days," Captain St. Armand said, "and you will be able to eat those dishes you haven't enjoyed since you left home."

Daphne frowned and put down her fork.

"So soon?"

His smooth smile that did not reach his eyes and he leaned over to pour her more wine, but she shook her head.

"Why Miss Farn—Mrs. Murray. I would think you anxious to return to England. Think of what you are missing. The fashions, the theater, the entertainments. No doubt your husband is looking forward to taking you to all of your usual haunts so your friends can see you and you can retake your place in society."

The words hung in the cabin like knives poised to strike. Fuller seemed oblivious and continued to shovel food into his mouth, but Daphne looked at Alexander and her face paled. Captain St. Armand sipped his wine, his eyes glittering as he watched his guests.

"I do not know—would you excuse me? I have a headache."

She jumped to her feet and ran out of the cabin and Alexander was on his feet a moment behind her, but a hard voice said, "Sit down."

He looked over his shoulder. Captain St. Armand was watching him, as was Fuller, whose hand was beneath the table, and Alexander would not be at all surprised if he pulled it out holding a pistol. St. Armand looked at the mate and said, "Leave us."

"Are you sure?"

A corner of the pirate's mouth twitched.

"I can handle the surgeon."

Alexander turned as the mate left and looked the captain square in the face. "I must go to my wife. She is ill."

"She has a headache. Women have survived headaches well enough without you. No doubt you've caused as many as you've cured."

Alexander leaned on the table still set with supper, looming over the pirate.

"I am not in the mood for conversation."

"If you attempt to leave, I will shoot you before you unlatch the door. Then who would take care of the lovely Daphne?"

"You would shoot me in the back?"

"I find it is every bit as effective as shooting people in the front. I'm surprised you do not know that, being a surgeon."

He sat. The two men studied each other in silence, St. Armand's too-pretty face wearing a supercilious smirk that made Alexander's hand clench into a fist below the table. He broke the silence first.

"Now that I have traveled with you across the ocean, and seen you and your men in action, do you not fear me giving testimony against you?"

St. Armand steepled his fingers and studied the surgeon.

"Not really, no. You could identify me and make all sorts of wild claims about me, but you are not that foolish. My crew aboard this ship are not the only men loyal to me. I have friends ashore you would not care to meet. If I came to harm through your testimony, you could find yourself in a dark alley missing your spleen. More importantly, they could mistakenly harm your lovely companion because of your stupidity, and that would be a tragedy.

"But enough of such gloomy talk. What do you and Mrs. Murray intend to do after this ship docks? Will you be returning her to her father's house?"

"Why do you ask?"

"Curiosity. Simple curiosity. I have come to care for my two castaway passengers over these past weeks and would want to know that you are safe and sound. In particular, I want to know what will become of Daphne Farnham… Murray. Such a sweet young lady."

"I fail to see how it is your concern, Captain St. Armand. Mrs. Murray is my wife and my responsibility."

"Is she?" the captain said softly, giving him a brief flash of teeth. "Forgive me if I am a bit skeptical. After all, there has been confusion in the past over her status."

Alexander studied him.

"What would it be to you if she is not, in fact, my wife? Do you think her father would favor a pirate over a surgeon?"

St. Armand smiled again. It was most aggravating. "A pirate? Maybe not. But I have other charms, my dear Mr. Murray. Let us be frank. I am the answer to a maiden's fantasies, particularly maidens who read ridiculous novels and fervid poetry. You…well, you are a handy man in a medical situation, but you cannot possibly compete in this arena. Not against me.

"Regardless, I can help you arrange transportation if you wish to travel to London. You will be without funds when you arrive, and I imagine you will not be able to put your hands on money quickly. I can advance you that money."

"Why in heaven's name would you help me?"

"I wouldn't. But I would help Daphne return home."

Captain St. Armand couldn't know that a canny Scot like Alexander always had a little something tucked away for emergencies, gold in a hidden pocket of his surgical chest.

He had thought long and hard about what would happen when he returned Daphne to her father. He did not delude himself that Mr. Farnham would offer a navy surgeon his daughter's hand in marriage in gratitude for taking responsibility for her. He couldn't imagine the pirate faring any better and wondered what his game was.

"I will keep your offer in mind." Alexander stood, then paused. "I spoke with Mr. Fuller about the wounded. Arnold is holding on, but I will know more about his condition over the next days—if he survives that long. I will keep watch over him."

Which meant Daphne would sleep alone. It wasn't the first time Alexander spent the night at a patient's bedside, but he'd seldom done it with such regret.

"You are more of an asset on this voyage than I anticipated, Mr. Murray. I am relieved nothing happened to prevent you from fulfilling your duties."

"What would happen?"

St. Armand looked at him, a tad regretfully. "The usual mishaps. Falling over the side, accidentally getting yourself stabbed, that sort of thing. No matter. What's important now is finishing this journey and returning your companion…"

"My wife."

"If you say so—returning her safely to England."

~

The lantern was turned low, but when the door creaked open Daphne opened her eyes and favored Alexander with a smile.

"I did not drink too much wine tonight."

"I noticed your abstemious behavior." He sat on the bunk beside Daphne, who looked sleepy and tousled and delicious. She also looked deliciously bare beneath the covers pulled up to her naked shoulders. He took her hand in his.

"Today's work in the surgery was only part of the job. I need to stay with Arnold, and to check on the other men overnight."

"Is it always that way?"

"It is for me."

"Must you leave right now?" she asked with a plaintive note in her voice. He brought her hand up to his mouth, the small, delicate hand which had assisted him so capably, and he turned it over and kissed her at the pulse at her wrist. "The crisis usually comes deep into the night. It is early yet."

"So you will stay with me?"

"For a little while."

"I'm glad," she said.

He caressed her wrist, content to sit beside her for a moment, smelling her sweet fragrance, healthy and strong and womanly.

"Are you feeling my pulse?"

"I am, actually. It is something I do almost without thinking about it." He brought her wrist up to his mouth again, felt the steady beat as he rested his lips there. He caressed her with the tip of his tongue, which made her lips part on an indrawn breath.

And made her pulse race a touch faster.

Those lips were an invitation no man with blood flowing in his veins could resist, and Alexander gave in and put his mouth on hers, enjoying the taste of Daphne, the sounds of Daphne as she responded and put her arms up around his neck. When they broke apart, her eyes were dreamy and half-closed.

"You never finished your examination."

He looked deeply into her eyes, then nodded. "You need an intense, thorough, and probing examination, Miss Farnham."

"Dr. Murray! You made a rude joke!"

He leaned back, as if affronted, but used the opportunity to shrug out of his coat and pull his shirt over his head.

"You know I never joke. I am a natural philosopher and have a reputation to uphold," a statement at odds with his actions as he kicked off his trousers and hopped into the bunk alongside her.

She turned on her side to accommodate him and propped her head on her hand, her hair spilling over in a golden waterfall that gleamed in the low light.

"About this examination," she said huskily, running her finger down his arm.

"We will continue to monitor your pulse, Miss Farnham. Arterial palpation of a heartbeat can tell me a great deal about your general health. For example," he said, putting his hand on her neck, "the carotid artery, here, can be a noticeable indicator of your state. Unless you are wearing something high-necked, it is easy to touch and see your pulse."

Her eyes glowed like dark sapphires as the pupils expanded to accommodate the low light and her emotional state. The delicate lids were heavy, not with sleep now, but with arousal, and he kissed each lid, fluttering like butterflies beneath his lips, before running his fingers along her jawbone to highlight the location of her facial pulse, a sensitive spot that made her gasp and arch her neck. Since that area responded so well to stimulation, he felt he had to experiment again—because, as he explained to the woman in his arms, that was what a serious natural philosopher did— and kissed her at her temple, seeing if he could locate the superficial temporal artery with his tongue. That experiment, too, was a success and spurred him on to rove down and check the pulse at the artery in her neck.

"One has to be careful with the carotid artery, Miss Farnham. Too much pressure can cause unconsciousness."

"Why, Doctor," she whispered. "I am not a surgeon, but I suspect if you used your lips and not your fingers, I might yet swoon."

"There is only one way to find out," he murmured against her neck.

He did use his lips, and his tongue. The light sheen of moisture on her delicate form, her heightened respiration, the flush of excitement spreading through her skin, all signs telling him what she experienced. His own body responded to those signs, his cock growing so hard that it was almost painful. Daphne, clever girl, took matters in hand and demonstrated for him her own technique, which made all the blood rush from his brain into other regions, and for a brief instant, he feared *he* would be the one swooning.

He refused to be distracted from his task, delightful as that distraction was. After using his lips and his tongue to check her carotid artery, he demonstrated with his fingers for her edification how the veins and arteries moved down to her heart, that organ beating now beneath his hand.

"Dr. Murray, this is fascinating," she murmured. "I never knew the study of anatomy could be so stimulating! Tell me more."

Rather than tell her, he demonstrated, which meant she had to unhand him, to his regret, as he moved to the posterior tibial artery behind her inner ankle bone.

"I thought my posterior is where I sit?"

"It is, and it is magnificent. But there are more posterior parts to Daphne Farnham than just that one. And this is not the only spot at your lower extremities where I can check a pulse."

He rested his fingers on the top of her feet and she giggled when he rubbed his thumbs over a spot there that was ticklish.

"Why are you doing that?"

"You have a spectacular dorsalis pedis artery, my dear."

"Another artery? They are everywhere! I had no idea!"

"I will show you the popliteal next, but for that you should roll over."

She did as he requested, and he sat back, studying the form before him on the narrow bunk. He sighed with satisfaction.

"It is a truly magnificent posterior."

She looked over her shoulder and giggled at that, and again when he demonstrated the location of her popliteal artery, behind her dimpled knee, an area needing special attention.

"You feel how I compress the area here, where the skin is especially soft?" He then leaned down and kissed her there. "And fragrant, also."

She was so sweet smelling and healthy and delicious that he had to give her a most thorough examination indeed, though like a child hoarding a sweet he'd saved the best for last.

"Roll over onto your back again."

She giggled again at the formal tone of his request, which, he'd admit, may sound odd coming from a naked man, but she did as he asked. He knelt between her knees, his hands easing her legs apart until they were at the edges of the bunk and a shiver ran over her frame.

"Are you cold?"

"Just the opposite. I fear I am fevered," she said throatily. She ran her hands up her body, cupping her plump breasts.

"I feel swollen and especially sensitive, here," she said, circling her taut nipple with a slender finger.

He sat up, his hardened member twitching, and he feared he'd be reciting mathematical formulae again if he wanted to bring this exam to its proper conclusion. He clenched his teeth and focused his attention even as beads of sweat dampened his hairline.

"Let me see…does it hurt when I do this?" He licked his thumb and forefinger and clamped her rosy nipple applying gentle pressure. Her back arched off the bunk and her eyes went wide.

"No! Yes! Not sure, try again!"

So he did, and then repeated the motion on the other orb.

"Your right side is more sensitive than your left."

"Are you certain? Perhaps you should check again. Oh yes, more of that, right there. Dr. Murray, this is the best examination ever!"

He wanted to agree with her but found himself incapable of talk, only action, the action of tonguing her rosy tips until they stood up like rubies above her alabaster flesh. She writhed beneath him and wrapped her arms around him to pull him closer. He had to brace one foot against the deck to maintain their balance in the cramped bunk, which brought him so close to her entrance that he almost gave in to the temptation to thrust himself into her and never release her.

But he held back, wanting to make this as perfect as possible for her. Their castaway dreams were ending, and they'd soon return to civilization and their former lives. Their proper lives. If he could not hold Daphne forever in his arms, he needed to imprint himself on her, make these memories so strong that she would never forget their magical time together.

He knew he would never be free of this woman who was the sunshine to his clouds, the light in his life that lifted him out of the darkness of death and disease, lonely nights stretching into a bleak future without color or brightness. His urge was to clutch her to him and tell her all those things he dared not say with their separation looming. Instead he showed her, reveling in these moments of laughter and love-making, a respite from their troubles.

"Do you still feel feverish, my dear?" he asked, propping himself up on one arm.

"Yes, Doctor, I feel my heart racing and my body is so overheated, I do not know what to do!"

He arched an eyebrow at her, running his finger along her mouth, and a moment later her tongue peeked out to lick those lush lips, a gleam of wetness that made his muscles clench. But he would not be rushed, not now when he was so close to completion.

"I happen to have a sovereign remedy for that fever, Miss Farnham. It will restore all your humors to their proper balance."

He leaned forward, and instead of kissing her on her soft mouth, moved down her body, his tongue tracing a path over her shivering belly, detouring briefly to her navel, and then lower still.

"You have another spot, yes, right here," he murmured against her groin as he tongued her femoral artery.

"Another pulse?" she whispered.

"An important one, my dear. It is beating strongly, carrying blood through your body," he said, raising her leg and licking along the softness of her inner thigh, the musky fragrance of her body calling to him like the sea calls to a sailor, and he moved closer between her legs, and did what he'd been longing to do for so long, separating the golden curls with his trembling fingers, then taking her thighs and spreading her wide before lowering his head to take her into his mouth.

Had he not been holding her she might have jumped out of his hands. Clearly this was a new experience, and he felt a fierce rush of satisfaction that he was the man to show her all the delights her body could hold. He tongued her again, and she made a throaty noise and tugged at his hair.

"Alex—is that allowed?" She gasped.

He paused from his task and raised his head.

"Trust me, I'm a surgeon."

"You are a scoundrel!"

"The two are not mutually exclusive. No more talking now, I am busy."

She stopped talking, but the noises she made as he licked and sucked at her let him know what she was experiencing and feeling. He used his tongue and his teeth and finally his fingers, tasting all of her, feeling all of her until she rose up off the bunk with a cry, her trembling body hovering there before relaxing in his grasp.

He had no intention of letting her think that was all he could offer. Kissing his way up her curves he positioned himself over her and with one hand braced on the bunk, he guided himself to her slick opening.

She encompassed him, enfolded him, welcomed him into

her body, and as he glided home he knew it was not enough, memories alone would never be enough. For now, he took his cue from his woman. He lived in the moment, feeling her embrace him with her arms while other muscles tightened around him until he nearly lost his rhythm and his mind. It took every ounce of determination to hold back, to watch Daphne's eyes close, her mouth open, the whispering cries he drew forth from her as he thrust himself deeper, again and again, until finally she clenched around him and went still, the muscles of her neck standing out with the force of her climax, her fingers digging furrows into his shoulders. He barely pulled out in time, fighting every instinct within himself, to spend on the sheets rather than in her womb.

He stroked her hair as her breathing returned to normal and fought his own desire to close his eyes and sleep in her arms. He still had work to do and a long night ahead of him.

"Alexander?"

"Hmmm?"

"Is there a word for—for that thing you did? With your tongue?"

He smiled, though he knew she could not see it, and kissed her atop her head.

"As a matter of fact, there is a word for that. It is Latin."

"Ha! I should have known the Greeks would invent such a thing."

"Romans, not Greeks, Daphne. And while they may not have invented it, they did give us a name for it."

"It is too bad you already taught me my new word for today, Alexander, otherwise you could teach me that one also."

He started to reply that he could teach her that word, but she rolled in his arms and put her hand over his lips, her eyes twinkling.

"No, not now. Wait until tomorrow. Why, I would wager

there is a word that goes along with your Latin, *Dr. Gravitas*, that illustrates what would happen if I did that to you. You could teach it to me." She frowned. "Not exactly the same way, of course, because your parts are different, but you know what I mean."

He took her fingers in his hand and kissed them. "There is, I shall, and we will discuss this in the morning."

"Good," she said, yawning hugely. "I am sleepy now. You come and fetch me if you need me during the night," but the words were no sooner out of her lush lips than he heard a soft snore, and he carefully disengaged himself from her and exited the bunk, pulling the covers up over her.

He spent a long, precious moment watching her sleep before he sighed, pulled his clothes back on, and returned to his duties. Alexander paused in the doorway, ready to blow out the lantern, and looked over his shoulder at the woman he now knew he loved. At least this night, for one more night, he would not return to a cold and empty bed.

CHAPTER 22

*A*rnold was alive the next day, though Alexander knew the greatest danger still lay ahead if the wound became septic. In the meantime, he monitored the man's progress and diet and administered to the other wounded pirates. He taught Daphne more Latin, to their mutual delight, and talked with her late in the evening. He never raised the largest issue on their minds, the question of what would happen after landfall.

They were lying now in the bunk, but at opposite ends, Daphne braced against the bulkhead while he held her foot in his hands, massaging it, rubbing out the soreness from her ill-fitting footwear. Sails's efforts kept her feet covered and warm but wouldn't win accolades for style or comfort.

"I never truly appreciated the pleasure of soft kid slippers made to fit my foot. Oh, that feels so good." Daphne sighed in satisfaction. "I am looking forward to ordering many new shoes when I return home. Soft, pliable, shoes. With rosettes."

He knew it was just idle chatter, but it stabbed him like a needle. She took for granted all the things her money purchased for her. In his world there were sturdy work shoes, not kid slippers with rosettes.

He bent his head over his task.

"What do you want when you return to England, Alexander?" *"You"* hovered unspoken in the air between them.

"I want to set up my surgery, perhaps in London, though I am not averse to living in the north."

"You still want to be married, don't you?"

It was said calmly, but when he looked up from the foot he caressed he saw the tension at the corner of her eyes, the stillness as she waited for his answer. He owed her the truth. After all they'd been through, there was much he could not give her, but he could give her the truth.

Daphne pulled her foot back and leaned up on her knees.

"I can be that wife, Alexander." She ticked off points on her fingers. "I can boil an egg. I can cook fish stew. I can start a fire—and that is important for your wife to know. I can scrub pans clean with sand. I can keep a garden. I know words like physiognomy and gravitas and atrophy," her voice dropped, "and some other Latin words."

Her hands twisted in her lap, and she looked down at them. "I know the man is supposed to ask, but you know I do not always do the proper thing. Will you marry me, Alexander Murray?"

Time stopped, though the rigging still creaked overhead and the men shouted to one another. He had heard the tenor of the commands change, about two hours past.

She still looked down at her hands, her head bowed, the golden curls reflecting the lantern light, and it made his heart ache to see her so. But he needed to be strong, for her and for himself. Alexander put his fingers beneath her chin and lifted it so he could look into her eyes.

"Land was sighted, Daphne. If the weather holds, we will be in England tomorrow."

She looked at him, and for once he could not read her face, the face that was normally as open to him and as easy to read as a picture book.

"You didn't respond to my proposal."

"It is a dream, a dream only suited to desert islands or pretending on a pirate ship. It is not real, not for the two of us."

He said it as gently and calmly as he could. Why did it feel like hearing a pronouncement of a terminal disease, a disease that would eat at his heart until there was nothing left of him but the husk of a man? Someone who walked, and talked, and moved through his day, but was as soulless as a wind-up automaton.

He did not want to be that man, dead inside, but if he truly cared for Daphne, he would put her first. She might think she would be happy as a surgeon's wife, living off of his carefully invested prize money and what he earned at his craft, but it would not be enough. The first time there was disappointment in her face when she could not buy kid slippers with rosettes because the money was needed for rent and food would be the beginning of the end for them. Only fools believe that love alone will sustain them. He'd been out in the world enough to know better. He'd seen it, living with Janet Murray and her shattered dreams.

Alexander's mind flashed back to a bleak evening when his mother sat at the scrubbed kitchen table by the sputtering flame of a rushlight. They could not afford candles. The stipend she received each quarter was small and becoming smaller as the years passed.

He was consumed with the self-righteous indignation of an adolescent who feels life is not fair and has not been out in the world enough to know that "fair" and "life" do not go together.

"Why? Why did you give yourself to that man without marriage so now we must live on his charity?"

She'd looked up from where she'd been gazing at her care-worn hands, at the empty finger of her left hand. Her white hair combined with the lines of worry made her look far older than she was. He longed to erase those lines from her face, but the words kept tumbling out of his mouth, the anger breaking free.

"You should not have done it, Mother! To give in to your passions that way…"

Janet's soft eyes looked on him with love, despite his anger and words that made him wince inside to recall now.

"My passions brought me you, Alexander. I can never regret that. It is not always a bad thing, to feel. To love."

"Better I had not been born than you should be shamed this way! Taking the stipend from Fieldhouse, bearing the insults of these people who think themselves better because they hide their sins before they go to kirk! I will not give into my passions, Mother. I will control myself!"

"Will you now?" Janet had said, looking at the scraped knuckles of the hand he ran through his hair, disarranging the careful combing. A hand bearing the marks of his latest fistfight with another boy who called his mother names. "Then I feel sorry for you, my Alexander. For without some passion, what is life? Nothing but one empty day following another, without joy."

"I will spare myself the pain and suffering you experienced," he swore.

Those memories gave him the courage now to do what needed to be done, for Daphne's sake.

"You know it is the right thing to do. You belong in your own world, in London, not with me."

Her eyes narrowed in anger and her hands, fisted now in her lap, trembled.

"You think you know everything, Alexander Murray, but you do not! I am sure you can tell me all the pieces of my heart, the names in Greek and Latin, but you only know parts of me. Your head is stuffed full of natural philosophy and it has squeezed out the rest of your gray matter, the important bits about butterflies and flowers and love! You do not know my heart and you do not know your own heart! I love you, Alexander, and I know you love me, too, even if you will not say it."

She was so sure of what she was saying, but what did she know? She had always been sheltered from the cruel ravages of the world around her, first by her father, then by Tyndale, then by him. That is as it should be. A woman like Daphne needed to be cared for and pampered, not made old before her time by too much work and too little money.

The dog barked then, scratching at the door, and Alexander was grateful to have their painful conversation interrupted. "See to your animal. He needs you."

She looked at him, then shook her head. "At least Pompom knows what he needs in life and is willing to say so."

She rose from the bunk, wincing as she put her rough footwear back on in the silent cabin. Grabbing her cold weather gear, she took the dog's lead and carried him out.

Alexander followed soon after, going to his surgery and looked around the narrow cabin. He took comfort in knowing his skills had been needed and appreciated. If it was a far cry from a Royal Navy third rate, it was still his domain. He sat and took out his tools, cleaning and polishing them, sharpening the blades. The space around him smelled of vinegar and sulfur and blood, the sweat of scared men and the salt of the ocean. Soon he would have a workspace that didn't shift and move, and a proper cabinet to store his instruments, but the battered surgical chest would always hold a special spot in his home and in his heart.

He pulled out the miniature of Moira, and looked at it for a long, long, time before putting it back. She, too, would always have a place in his heart, but it was no longer the nut-brown girl he saw in his dreams at night. The boy's love had been trumped by the man's soul and passions.

～

The *Prodigal Son* docked at Portsmouth flying proper British colors. There was no hue and cry of "pirate!" from the docks, all the paperwork was in order, and Captain St. Armand came ashore to see his passengers off at Portsmouth Point.

"I hope your voyage with us was everything you wanted it to be, Miss Farnham."

Daphne was looking not at the pirate, but at Alexander as she replied, "Yes, Captain St. Armand, I will never forget this trip."

Then she did turn her face to him, her hair blowing around her eyes as it came loose from her braid, the braid still tied off by the now sadly faded ribbons Alexander made for her so long ago. She brushed a piece of hair out of her face. The day was blustery, with clouds scudding across the sky, and the light moved in and out as the sun hid itself, then reappeared. She hugged her ugly but serviceable coat closer. There was something to be said for function over fashion, but really, there was no good reason she could not combine the two, was there? Maybe now that she was home, she would work on changing the fashions for ladies to make them pretty, but more practical.

"So I must take my leave of you now, my dear Miss Farnham…"

"Mrs. Murray."

The pirate looked at Alexander, a long assessing look. Then he turned back to Daphne.

"It is time to stop pretending, is it not? You are safe in England once again, not on the high seas. You are returned to your home, Miss Farnham, where you belong. *Au revoir*, lovely lady."

She jumped when he took her hand and bowed over it to kiss it, and instead of kissing the air above like a proper gentleman he *licked* her, and she frowned at the forward fellow. He simply smiled a cat-like smile, eyelids heavy over those pretty blue eyes.

"Goodbye to you also, Murray. You were a valuable asset on this voyage and I was glad to have you aboard."

"Not *au revoir*?"

"I hope not. But if I ever need a skilled surgeon, I will look for you first."

"You will need a skilled surgeon if you do not release her hand."

The pirate let go of Daphne's hand and Alexander tucked it into the crook of his arm, holding her close to his side.

She made sure Pompom's leash was secure. He was so excited to be back on land, sniffing everything and leaving his mark to let the world know he'd returned to England. He trotted by her side as she and Alexander strolled along Broad Street, and she clutched at the surgeon's arm. "I feel like I am falling over!"

"You need time to regain your land-legs. Do not move too quickly, you will adjust soon." He looked into her eyes. "I will make sure you do not fall. Stay close to me, for this is not the most savory area of town."

She looked at him as the traffic of the busy port bustled around them. Then a startled guffaw of laughter whipped her head around.

"You are correct, Jameson, that is the most amusing thing I have seen today."

Two tulips of the ton emerged from a noisy tavern and were watching them, one peering through his quizzing glass as he took in their mismatched, mismeasured, and mixed-up wardrobes. Daphne wore her quilted coat, lovingly sewn by Mr. Sails to keep her warm on the voyage. Her palmetto hat sat atop her head, faded and battered from the elements, while her braid snaked out from beneath it, the worn ribbon resting on her chest. Her sailor's trousers were in sight at the bottom of the coat, and her stiff and ugly shoes covered her feet in their men's heavy wool stockings.

Alexander fared no better in his worn coat with its stains and holes, his too short trousers, his bare head. The surgical chest hanging from its strap looked every bit as battered as the rest of him.

The beaus having a laugh at their expense had put a great deal of effort into their wardrobes. One wore a Polish style redingote with a rich fur collar and cuffs, full-skirted and trimmed with braid on the front and back, Hessian boots and a beaver hat. The other had sacrificed comfort for style, appearing elegant but chilled in a sky blue frock coat with outrageously padded shoulders over a primrose waistcoat, and sported yellow Cossack trousers. He was the one using the quizzing glass to study Daphne and Alexander.

"Good heavens, Jameson, is that Daphne Farnham? I heard she was dead!"

"If it is the soiled daffodil, better she be dead than be seen dressed in that fashion. Did I say fashion? Clearly I misspoke."

"No, Alexander, do not do anything!"

Daphne gripped her companion's arm, not for support, but because he'd taken a step toward the young men, and the look on his face froze her blood. He shook her off and she panicked, throwing herself into his arms, there on the public street as bold as a dockside strumpet, holding him back, digging her heels in as Pompom yapped and wrapped his lead around their legs. Passersby laughed at the dog's antics but Daphne ignored them, clutching Alexander, her face buried in his coat.

"Do not, they are not worth it," she whispered, her limbs shaking as she held onto him.

The dandies moved off, still laughing, and after an eternity, Alexander's hand rose and rested on the back of her neck. He took a deep breath, held it, then let it out.

"You can let go now."

I don't want to, but she did as he said.

He took her arm and walked with her, his face as calm and placid as ever, but his eyes tracked where the fops disappeared to.

"I know them," she said dully. "Randolf Jameson danced with me often, and I thought him a witty fellow. His companion, Conrad, sometimes made up theater parties with us. I thought they were my friends."

He did not offer her sympathy, false or real, or any words of consolation over another bit of her sheltered life shattered like a teacup dropped on the cobblestones.

"Do you know, Dr. Murray, I believe I now prefer the company of Norton, and Mr. Fuller, and even poor Arnold with his guts hanging out than I do those two."

"Arnold *was* more entertaining."

Daphne giggled at this, the tension of moments before dissipating, though she still clung to his arm. "I have developed a strange sense of what is amusing, and I suspect it is your fault."

"I will accept the blame for that one, Miss Farnham. Spend time with naval surgeons and your idea of what constitutes humor will undergo a sea change for certain."

She hugged his arm and straightened her back, not caring who might see her. Let them talk! She was not the same girl who'd left their company so many months back, she was a new person, a stronger person, a useful person.

She was loved as well, she knew that, even though the words had never been said. That gave her strength like nothing else did.

Their inn was far enough from the water to be less attractive to the roistering sailors and their doxies, but it was still a seaman's haven. The aroma of roasting meat filled the space and set Daphne's mouth to watering.

"Dr. Murray!" the man behind the counter wiped his hands and stumped out on a leg and a peg to greet his guests. "This is your missus? Who would have thought I'd ever see the day when Dr. Murray would settle down."

Daphne would have corrected the man regarding her status, but Alexander spoke up first.

"This is indeed my wife, as I mentioned in my note, Daphne Murray. My dear, this salty dog is Nick Pyle, a fine gunner but an even better cook. His salmagundi was the talk of the fleet and made our vessel the envy of others."

"I had to become a good cook, didn't I, if I wanted to stay afloat?"

Pyle was a big man, built like one of the barrels at the back of the taproom, his sandy hair still tied back in a tarred queue. He looked at her now and didn't seem at all fazed by her odd wardrobe.

"Heard you was shipwrecked, missus. My old woman and my gal said they'd take you to the shops, get you outfitted so you can get underway."

"I don't want to be a bother."

"'S no bother at all. I owe Dr. Murray plenty." His voice lowered and he pointed at the length of wood poking out at the bottom of his trousers. "I begged him to splice me instead of dock me aboard the *Caeneus*, but he said this was the only way if I wanted to see my wife and gals again."

"Have you been well since then, Nick?"

"Aye, that I have, Doctor," the big man beamed. "And the old lady don't mind none at all. Says I can't run from her so fast now that I'm on timber. Scares me to death, she does."

The "scary old lady" emerged from the kitchen then, and Daphne hid a smile behind her hand. Mrs. Pyle only came as high as her husband's chest and it would take three of her to make one of him. And she was not old, though her face bore the marks of years waiting for her man to come home from the sea. She smiled now at Dr. Murray, and the introductions were made.

"Rosie will show you to your room. Will the dog stay with you, or do you want him outside tonight?"

"Pompom stays with us, Mrs. Pyle. He will be no trouble at all."

"Very well, Mrs. Murray. After luncheon my girl will take you to the shops. I sent word ahead based on Dr. Murray's notes, and the seamstress should have something there you can take with you."

She leaned closer.

"You're not the first lady to show up without her bags, and Miss West keeps some frocks on hand just needing alterations to be sold."

Daphne wanted to eat lunch in the public room, full of people and lively discussions, but Alexander insisted they eat in their room, explaining once they were in there and the door was closed.

"I've arranged for trays, Daphne." He stood with his hands clasped behind his back and looked at her sternly. "The less people see you before you're returned to London the safer it is for you and your reputation."

His look softened then and he took her chin in his hand.

He was watching her face as if he hoped to memorize her features.

"You don't want your father to receive rumors of your rescue and not know for certain, do you? It is probable he thinks you drowned, and your returning could be a massive shock. This is why I bought passage on the mail to London, so we can travel to town as quickly as possible."

He looked down at the dog.

"Will Pompom stay in your bag during the trip?"

"Of course," she said, scooping up her fluffy companion. "He's my darling widdle boy and I know he'll be good for his mum-mums."

"I'll tip the coachman extra just in case," he muttered, then ran his hands through his hair. He paused, looked around the room, then back at her. "Will you be comfortable here? It is just for one night."

Daphne looked around at their lodgings. The bed was covered in worn linens that smelled clean and sunshiney, not mildewed like ship's linens. It wasn't a large bed, but it was larger than their bunk, and a table with two chairs sat beneath the window. A fire burned in the grate and Pompom made himself comfortable, stretching out on the hearthrug. Sounds from the busy streets below filtered up through the window glass, but Pyle assured them that it was quiet enough at night.

"This room is perfectly splendid."

"I know it's not what you are used to."

"You are correct. It is not a cramped ship's cabin or a hut on a desert island or a surgery or a pirate's den, but I believe I will do well enough here."

He gave her that smile that wasn't really a smile, except to her. "You are becoming pert, miss."

"It must come from spending time with pirates and surgeons."

"Low company indeed. On that note, I'll be purchasing clothing of my own while you're out this afternoon, so I do not frighten the other passengers or the coachman."

A thought suddenly struck her. She hadn't had to think about such things, not since she ran off with George, but now she was reminded again of her status.

"Is there money for all of this, Alexander?"

Thank heaven he did not say, "Do not worry your pretty little head about that," like her father, and George, and every other man she'd ever known. He simply nodded and said, "Yes, I have coins with me, and funds in an account I keep here in Portsmouth."

There was a knock at their door and a young woman huffed in carrying a heavy tray with delicious smells. Pompom barked once, then sat on his haunches knowing he'd be fed first.

"Here's your lunch, missus. There's cabbage soup and roast beef and my father's own home-brew and potatoes and fresh bread and butter and cheddar and apple pie my ma baked this morning. If that won't keep you, we also have a shepherd's pie I can bring up."

"It all sounds wonderful," Daphne said. "I believe this will keep us, but if I can have a pot of tea that would be perfect."

"Coming right up," the girl said, and went back to the kitchen. Alexander uncovered the dishes and set out plates and silver, and she took a small wooden bowl thoughtfully sent by Mrs. Pyle, gave Pompom a drink of water, then refilled it with some choice pieces from their lunch.

"I do not want to wrestle that animal for my meal," her less furry companion grumbled, but Daphne just smiled and put the food down for dog. When she was seated, Alexander filled her plate and they ate in silence, giving Mr. and Mrs. Pyle's fare its due.

The good, plain English cooking helped lift her spirits

until he said, "I imagine you were accustomed to much finer cuisine here in England."

Daphne put down her fork and leveled her gaze on him. "Sometimes you are just silly. Do you think my days were filled with only eating fairy cakes and sipping champagne? There were those theater suppers with oysters, yes, but you forget I grew up mostly in the country. Even in London my father preferred to keep an English cook rather than a French chef like many of his friends. I am quite used to fare such as this and enjoy it."

Alexander raised his brow at this but said nothing further. Daphne was puzzled. It was as if he were looking for things to distance himself from her, rather than looking for things which would bring them closer, like making fires together, or how they each loved Pompom so much.

"Is it satisfactory that Rosie Pyle accompany you this afternoon?"

"I had rather hoped you would want to spend the day sorting through fabrics and ribbons and dresses with me." She giggled at his look, then took pity on him. "I was jesting. I never thought I would say this about you, Alexander Murray, but you are useless, at least in this matter. Your helping me pick out clothing would be like me doing a surgery on you."

"I do not think the two situations are comparable, but I will defer to your knowledge of this area."

"I wish I could come with you. I could help you pick out better clothes than you would pick out on your own. When you return to London, you should see a tailor who will dress you as befits your being a successful surgeon. I could help with that," she said, toying with her pie.

"Finish up, Daphne. Rosie will be back for the plates."

She sighed, and set down her fork just as there was a knock at the door. Alexander told Rosie to enter, and the girl said she'd return after she took the dishes down to the kitchen. Daphne shrugged back into her coat, refilled Pompom's bowl, had a promise from Dr. Murray that he'd walk the pup, and prepared to go out.

"Wait."

He came over and retied her ribbon on her braid, then held the length of gold in his hand. "I am glad you did not cut your hair."

Daphne blinked because her vision had gone blurry, but Alexander did not see as he pulled a purse from his coat and carefully counted out coins.

"I made arrangements for Miss West to be paid, but here's something for any incidentals you might need, ribbons or what not."

Daphne looked at the coins in her hand. "For a few weeks, Dr. Murray, everything we had was not valued in pounds and shillings."

"We are back in England, Miss Farnham." He closed her fist around the coins and held it. "Here, wealth and birth are what matter."

Then he released her hand and the coins felt cold and hard inside her fist.

"Go now and take care of your errands. We both have a busy day."

Daphne nodded, fearing she couldn't speak because there was a large lump in her throat. She turned and walked out without looking back but felt his gaze upon her back.

CHAPTER 23

Daphne breezed into their room followed by Rosie burdened down with enough boxes to make Alexander wince. "I thought I said only buy enough to travel to London?"

She looked at him in amazement.

"These are all necessary items, and much of what I purchased will be on my back tomorrow, so you have little to fear."

"We'll see," was all the comment he cared to offer on that issue.

"Until now, I did not know you could buy ready-made dresses," she chattered on. "It is not a very efficient system, if you ask me. There is less opportunity to find exactly the right cut or color, and if a dress sits in the shop long enough it will be out of fashion."

She shivered at this frightening scenario, then untied the string on her parcels.

"I must say, though, the frocks Miss West had were quite attractive if one has to resort to such methods. And she said triple Vandyke ruffs are all the kick this year. Can you imagine such a thing? She also said plaid scarves are the fashion. I would look positively Scottish in one, wouldn't I?"

Daphne pulled out a cloak of deep blue wool, similar in color to the coats the naval officers wore, but pedestrian in its form and fashion. She ran her hand over the material and frowned slightly, then shrugged.

"I wish it were pink, but Miss West said pink is an impractical color for a cloak. She found this for me though," Daphne said rummaging through a box and pulling forth some headgear. "Look! It's a cottage bonnet with cornflowers and a pink ribbon. Not the latest style, but I find it just adorable. And I was practical also, Alexander. I did not buy a bonnet so large it would poke you in the eye as we ride in the coach." She waited, apparently expecting him to respond.

"Good girl?" he said tentatively.

That earned an eye-rolling response from his companion.

"I am not Pompom, you know. Never mind. As I feared, you are useless at this. What about you? Did you find clothing?"

"Enough to carry me to London," he said. "There are tailors here whose clients sometimes ship out before they can pick up their clothing, or men selling their garments at secondhand stores, and I found what I needed. I even found boots that were barely worn."

"I look forward to seeing you in your new—well, not new, but new for you—garments."

She unwrapped more parcels and held up a frock of a faded rose color that had a discreetly repaired rip at the arm.

"I never truly thought about what happens to my clothes when I am done wearing them," Daphne mused, looking at the dress. "Now, see, this is a finely-made garment. I imagine it might have belonged to a lady, some years back. Speaking of that, Miss West gave me the latest Ackermann's Repository so I can see how fashions changed while I was gone."

Given how much Alexander authorized for this shopping foray, throwing in a periodical gratis to such a free-spending customer seemed only reasonable. His thrifty Scots heart stuttered as each furbelow and frill was revealed, but oddly enough, he found he was also getting pleasure from seeing Daphne happy with her purchases. Maybe this is why men bought fripperies for their wives—to share in their happiness. After all, didn't he enjoy purchasing a new, finely made lancet?

She unwrapped more linens, and a corset which he thought unnecessary, but Daphne said, "Stick to your surgeries, Dr. Murray. A corset is needed for the proper fit from my garments."

"If you say so. I would rather see you out of your corset than in it."

"Of course you would." She giggled. "You're a man."

By the time their supper arrived, a cold collation which was all they desired after their substantial luncheon, Daphne pronounced herself quite fatigued from the day's events.

"We have an early start so going to bed now is a prudent thing to do," Alexander said. "Pyle will wake us in time to catch the coach."

He'd considered sleeping on a pallet on the floor but rethought that as he watched her brush out her hair, each tug of the brush through the silken strands a tug at his heart. He squeezed his eyes shut, trying to still the voice inside that told him he could have her and her money and live happily ever after with rainbows and butterflies and unicorns.

"'But to see her was to love her, love but her and love forever.'"

"Did you say something?"

He opened his eyes, drinking in her face, her form, her love, the joy radiating from her. They only had one night left together. He'd be a damn fool and worse if he did not use this time to its fullest advantage.

"Daphne, you did not remind me to teach you a new word today."

She paused from where she'd been about to braid her hair for bed. He walked over to her and sat beside her, the soft featherbed giving way beneath him.

"Leave it loose," he said, his voice as rough as his fingertips as he caressed the gold. He worked both hands into it and arranged it on her shoulders, falling over the thin gown she wore, soft from repeated washings.

"Rosie gave me the night rail. There were none at Miss West's shop."

"It looks quite practical." His fingers moved down from her hair to where the linen stretched across her bosom, tracing the form beneath, memorizing it with his touch. So many years of his hands being used for painful, dirty work, but he'd always taken pride in his ability to feel inside a wound and remove debris, to stitch torn vessels and mend flesh. Now he thanked whatever forces blessed surgeons with skilled hands, for he wanted to use those hands tonight to pleasure this woman who meant the world to him.

First, there were other things they could do.

"Let us remove our garments so they do not interfere, because it is time for you to learn your new word for today."

"It involves taking our clothes off?" she said in delight.

Daphne's comfort with her nudity, her willingness to learn new things—was there ever a more perfect woman? And yet, this could be their final lesson. The cold thought nearly stopped him as he tore off his own garments but seeing her sitting on her knees on the bed, her skin dewy and flushed with excitement helped him stay focused.

He sat beside her and cleared his throat. "Your word for today, Daphne, is...osculation."

"Finally!" she sighed, clasping her hands together. "I wondered when you were going to teach me that one." She looked down at her bare bosom.

"And I had to take off my clothes? No wonder you did not want to teach me this word during Arnold's surgery!"

"No, that would not have been a good time," he agreed. "However, you've known the meaning of osculation for ages, but you did not know the word."

He leaned in, brushing the hair back from her shoulders, moving it behind her ears. She smelled like fields of flowers, but beneath the scent of her soap and creams he smelled Daphne, only Daphne.

"Dr. Murray?"

"Do not be impatient. This must be done with skill and not rushed for you to understand the concept properly.

"Osculation is…" his voice lowered so that she had to lean closer yet to hear him. "Osculation is a term used in geometry, Miss Farnham."

Daphne leaned back, surprised.

"Geometry? Isn't that when you study a globe to see where countries are located?"

It was a testament to his current relationship with this amazing woman that her question did not ruin the mood for him. Rather, it almost made him laugh, but he suppressed the urge and took her hand in his.

"No, dear, that is geography. Geometry is the study of measuring the earth, or studying relations between points and lines, curves and surfaces."

He illustrated his definition by running a finger from the point where her nipple stood up under his careful touch, following the curve of the surface, drawing a line up to her neck, which made her giggle, and then down to the other, matching curve, which made her sigh and squirm.

"I like this science, Dr. Murray. I like studying relations, also!"

"I knew that," he said, but in a distracted voice because he, too, had never thought about how much pleasure one could get from the study of geometry, especially when it applied to the planes and surfaces of such a delightful subject.

"But what about osculation?"

"Ah yes," he said, drawn back to his lessons. "Osculation. It is a Latin word…"

"Ooooooh, I like Latin!"

"I knew that," he said again, moving his hands and lifting her so she straddled his lap and she put her arms around his neck to steady herself. He looked into her eyes, deepened to a shade that called to mind the sky at gloaming, just after sunset when one can see the first stars and the blue is the blue of mystery and that which is hidden.

There was nothing hidden with Daphne. All her love, all her feelings were in her eyes, open to him just as her lips were open, parted on a breath as she waited for him to instruct her further.

"In geometry, osculation is a contact of two curves at which they have a common tangent. For example, you have a curve here," he outlined her lower lip, "and a curve here," he outlined her upper lip and moved in closer, bringing his arm around her back so that more of her curves came into contact with his planes and angles.

"Now, imagine these curves," he tapped her lower lip lightly, "coming into contact with other curves at a particular point."

"How does that happen?" she whispered, her breath a puff against his own lips.

"Like this."

He cradled his hand around the back of her head, tugging her into the contact of the curve of his lower lip, and her own mouth opened on a sigh as he pulled her tighter, his hand buried in the sunshine of her hair, his tongue exploring her, tasting her, teaching her even as she had taught him about love and passion.

Her lips were moist and full when he pulled his head back, her eyes dreamy.

"Osculation is kissing, isn't it?"

"Osculation is a perfect contact, my love, and your mouth was made for osculation."

"Oh, Dr. Murray, you say the most romantical things! I like this contact," she whispered.

He rocked his hips against her, stroking her, simulating the act of completion they both longed for but were willing to forestall to stretch out this magical time together, to heighten the feelings and sensitivity nurtured by their passion.

Nurtured by their love, though he would not say the words, even now, even with their sojourn together coming to an end. He could not say those words and then walk away from her. But he could create more memories for the two of them. He knew it was not likely either of them would marry for love. Not in their worlds, not in their circumstances. Would it be so awful to pull out one of these memories in later years, like a secretly hoarded treat, and remember a brief period when they were just Daphne and Alexander, not Miss Farnham and Dr. Murray? If it was a sin, he would gladly brave hell's fires. He would not think about tomorrow, and the tomorrow after that. He would revel in this one night, a final night, with the woman he loved.

Then she pulled his head back down to continue her lessons, and he let himself be carried away by the physical world, the wonder of Daphne in his arms.

"So much to learn," she said breathlessly when she broke that perfect contact.

"One can also osculate upon other curves," he whispered into her neck.

"Show me!" she demanded.

"My pleasure." He put his lips to the curve of her breast, following it with his mouth down to the point at the center of the warm, fragrant globes, their spherical shape demanding further exploration and, of course, more intense osculation. Daphne clutched at him and writhed in his arms, her sheer joy in the moment, her responsiveness filling his heart. This woman fit him as ideally as two halves coming together for a perfect sphere, like a shimmering drop of rainwater falling through a sunlit sky. She taught him so much. He never knew lovemaking could involve laughter before he met Daphne Farnham. "Would you like to learn some more geometry?"

"Oh, yes!"

"This," he said, taking her hand and moving it down to his groin, "is a rod."

He heard her huff out a laugh in the dark.

"I knew that. Now you are bamming me, Dr. Murray!"

"I would not do that, Daphne, not about something as serious as geometry. Here, feel."

She did, and he kept his hand over hers, stroking up and down. He was so hard he ached and nearly lost his ability to continue the lesson, but he gritted his teeth and tried to concentrate, not think about how her warm, soft hand felt as it moved up and down his...

"Shaft!" he gasped. "A solid, three-dimensional cylinder is a rod, or a shaft, or dear heavens that feels exquisite!"

"I wonder if rods and osculation go together?" she murmured.

Mindlessly he followed her instructions as she climbed over and knelt between his legs and put her Latin skills to work. Daphne cradled his balls in her hand while the other worked him in a perfect rhythm with her skilled tongue and mouth, and he clutched the bed linens and could not think about geometry, trigonometry, calculus, or any cold numerals but only the sensation of the wet heat enveloping him, how her tongue snaked around the tip of his rod, stroking the sensitive spot behind the crown that forced a sound of delight from deep in his chest.

She paused then, and pulled all the way off of him, and he sighed with regret. Until she eased forward again, lifting him with her hand and he felt her wet mouth on his ball sack while her hand worked him. And then…and then…

Dear heaven, he would never complain about her humming again!

When he stopped seeing stars behind his closed eyelids, and his breathing returned to normal, he turned his head and saw the succubus lying next to him, her head propped on her hand and a smile that must be termed smug sitting on her pretty mouth.

Sweat darkened the curls around her face and he brushed one away from her eye.

"I did not want to finish without you."

She looked down at his relaxed member. "Are you done for the night, Dr. Murray? I thought you navy men were made of sterner stuff."

He pushed himself up on his elbow.

"Are you challenging me, Miss Farnham?"

She just smiled at him, and he pulled her into his arms and kissed her, tasting himself in her mouth, tasting her. If the reputation of the Senior Service rested on his ability to rise to the occasion, he must be prepared to give his all.

"I have not finished instructing you, Miss Farnham," he said sternly, which elicited a coo of delight from his student as he positioned her across his lap. She shivered in the cool air and he pulled the covers around her but knew better ways to warm her up.

"The mouth, my dear Daphne, is an amazing organ, as you just demonstrated so skillfully. Your ears hear." He took one soft lobe between his teeth and pressed down, which caused her to gasp and clutch his arms.

He moved his fingertips over her soft eyebrows and he felt the lashes flutter down like butterflies coming to rest on her cheeks, then he kissed each lid.

"Your eyes see, but your mouth, Daphne, your beautiful mouth can do so much more. It can lick." And he demonstrated against her neck as he laid her back on the bed.

"Bite." He nipped at the juncture of her neck and shoulder, and she licked her own lips, parted now on her panting breaths.

"Suck." He showed her, demonstrating on first one breast, then the other, her nipples engorged and hard as she encouraged him to do more, and he moved down her body to accommodate her, until he came to the place where she was ready for his attentions, honey flowing from her core. He felt a wholly male and primitive burst of satisfaction that he was the man who aroused this woman to this level, where she was begging him in that breathy little voice of hers to demonstrate osculation to her complete satisfaction.

So he lowered his mouth to her, and with his tongue, and his lips, and his skilled knowledge of anatomy he licked, and bit gently, and sucked, and caressed her until her back bowed off the bed and she cried out at the completion of his lesson on osculation.

By this time he was ready to move from geometry to more practical applications of mechanics, demonstrating the insertion of a rod into a cylinder, not as a cold mechanical device, but the complete joining of two individuals in a timeless dance of love and satisfaction.

In the faint light filtering in through the window he saw her watching him as he rose over her, her mouth relaxed and full, her eyes heavy-lidded as her desire built again, and when he finally slipped into her welcoming heat she continued to watch him, as he watched her, silently sharing their love as their bodies said what he could not say aloud.

At the end there was no way he could keep it inside him, any more than he could stop the rush of his desire for her when he felt himself tighten and strain to be part of her forever.

"My love, my love," he whispered into her hair as she climaxed, crying out his name.

"You will see," she said afterward as she dropped off to sleep. "Everything will work out for the best."

He knew that. He would do whatever was necessary to make sure Daphne had the best life she could. And it would not be the life she'd have married to an impecunious surgeon.

He held her in his arms, stroking her hair until she fell asleep. When the dawn began to lighten the room, he was still awake, staring at the ceiling.

~

The trip to London was mercifully uneventful as the scarlet wheels turned and turned, taking Daphne home. At first, she chatted with the other passengers, a curate of middle years who did not appear at all interested in the latest fashion trends, and a motherly woman engrossed in her knitting. Mrs. Nealy *was* interested in hearing about the new bonnets being worn by London ladies, but acknowledged she came to town not to shop, but to assist her daughter in childbirth, hence the need to finish the garment growing beneath her clacking needles.

"Taking the mail was more dear than I planned, but it's my Bessie's first, and I wanted to be there with her."

"What a fortunate girl, to have her mother with her," she said, and couldn't keep a note of sadness from her own voice. Her hand rested on her own belly. She did not think there was a baby growing in there, but how wonderful it would be if there was! She must learn to knit so she, too, could make darling little jackets and blankets to keep her baby warm.

Daphne had never traveled by mail coach, of course. When she traveled to the country with her father it was always in his well-appointed carriage, with plenty of stops along the way to rest and refresh oneself. The mail coach was not nearly as comfortable, but it went so quickly! When the coach took its brief breaks Pompom jumped out of her valise and took care of his business before taking a drink of water and climbing back in. Her darling was an experienced coach traveler and was no trouble, though she saw her surgeon slip some extra silver to the coachman and the guard to ensure they would not fuss over the animal riding inside.

It was not Pompom who worried her, but Alexander. He did not talk to her as the mail coach flew down the road, but stared out the window, his arms crossed over his chest, lost in his thoughts. Maybe he was thinking about how he would introduce himself to her father and ask for her hand.

He kept talking about taking her home, but was the mansion in London still her home? Was her home on a desert island, or on a pirate ship, or in a seaside town? No, home was where her surgeon was. Daphne knew in her father's house she would want for nothing, nothing that could be bought with gold. With Dr. Murray she might have to forego a bonnet or two, or another pair of kid slippers, but she would be with Alexander and that thought warmed her more than any fur-lined cloak or swansdown muff could ever do.

Any suspicions she had that Alexander meant what he said about not marrying her, because of his foolish belief that he could not make her happy, were suppressed. She would not dwell on that, not now, not when she was so close to seeing her papa again and rebuilding her life, a life that would most definitely have Dr. Alexander Murray in it!

The courtyard of the Swan With Two Necks vibrated with noise and chaos, but it was an organized chaos befitting a bustling coaching inn. The passengers on the mail gratefully climbed down to the cobblestones, stretching cramped muscles, or in one furry passenger's case, poking his head out of the valise to bark at a duck risking feather and limb searching for oats left behind by the horses.

"No, Pompom, stay put!" Daphne said. "I vow, Dr. Murray, that was fast, but I feel as if all my bones are bounced to pieces!"

"Our journey is almost ended."

He led her to one of the hackneys ready to transport people to and from the inn. He stiffened when she gave him the location of her family's house in Mayfair, and she felt a chill, as if he was pulling his warmth away from her, even though they were sitting in a small space. Once she would have found the grime and smell of the hired vehicle disconcerting, but now she ignored it, watching the man with her as if she could hold him with her glance alone.

They were silent as the hackney rolled through the

streets, streets that became cleaner and wider as they moved away from the inn, and Alexander withdrew deeper into himself and Daphne found it hard to breath, her stomach cramping as they neared her house. Pompom whined, feeling her tension, and tried to lick her face.

"Stop! Stop here, at the park!"

He looked at her sharply. "Are you ill?"

"Stop, please!"

He gave the order to the driver, helped her alight from the vehicle and took their valises and his surgeon's case. She released Pompom, who sniffed around the grass at her feet.

Alexander watched her, concern on his face, but Daphne looked behind him to the house she knew so well. Her father would not be home yet from his warehouses, but she saw lit lamps and knew the servants would be there, preparing for the master's return.

She swallowed, worried for a moment she would indeed be ill, but then straightened her shoulders and grabbed Alexander's hands.

"Do not leave me, Alexander."

His bleak face paled further, but he shook his head.

"We do not have a choice, Daphne."

"Stop saying that! We do have a choice! I can choose to be miserable, or I can choose to stay by your side."

"Daphne, if you marry me and leave your world behind you *will* be miserable."

"There will be bad days, I know that! But I am also sure, very sure, there will be many days where we will not be miserable, and when we fight we will make up, and when we love, it will be a love that will carry us through the difficult times. That is what love is, Alexander! It is a shield against despair, and against poverty, and against the feeling life is happening to you without your being able to choose or to control it at all. You think you know everything, but you do not! I may not have a head stuffed full of knowledge, but I know what love is!"

He smiled then, a small smile, barely a lifting of the corners of his expressive mouth, but it lifted her heart and she began to smile in return.

"I know you know what love is, you taught me that. It is because I love you in return that I must leave you now. You deserve the life you were born to, and you cannot have it with me. I love you too much to watch you fade away in genteel poverty."

Her own smile washed away like a watercolor left in the rain. She reached up and held his head with its rumpled curls of silver and red between her hands. She looked into his eyes, eyes lined by years of thinking too hard and tending too many men who died no matter what he did. She said the words she needed to say, the words from her heart.

"Alexander Murray, you are the stupidest man I have ever met."

He opened his mouth, but she put her hand across his lips and he stopped but cocked an expressive eyebrow at her. She was not about to be intimidated by a caterpillar-looking bit of hair, not when she had things to say to this fool.

"Do not argue with me. I know stupidity when I see it, believe me. You have a chance at love, a chance at happiness, and a life with someone who loves you. Me. And you are throwing it away, you big looby. Sometimes it takes stupid people longer to figure things out. I understand that, and I am willing to give you time to become more intelligent."

She took her fingers off his mouth because she could not kiss him with that in the way. When she was done kissing him, and tasting the sweetness of his love for her, because she knew he loved her, even if he was stupider than a box full of rocks, she squared her shoulders and picked up her bag.

"You know where to find me, Dr. Murray. I will not wait

forever, because I am a useful person and I need to move on with my life. I will not sit around moping and longing for an idiot. That would be you," she clarified, just in case he was as dense as she suspected he was. "Come, Pompom!"

Pompom whined and tried to stay with Alexander, but she gave a tug on his leash. She walked away without looking back, because she did not want him to see the tears rolling down her face, not after that fine, brave speech. Oh, they were a pair of fools, they were! No wonder they suited each other so perfectly.

~

Alexander watched as his world moved away from him, the center of his universe leaving him for the stately home across the park. He watched as the door opened and the footman gave a shout of surprise followed a moment later by a crowd of servants rushing to the door and hustling their mistress into the warmth and light within.

He pulled up the collar of his coat and continued watching. He watched as a footman went running out of the house and soon, gratifyingly soon, a carriage pulled up and an older man jumped out and dashed up the front stairs, stumbling in his haste.

Even from where he stood across the park he heard Farnham joyfully shout, "Daphne!" when the door opened. He could not see the reunion of father and daughter, but Mr. Farnham was obviously excited and eager for a glimpse of his only child.

Daphne would be welcomed back into the bosom of her comfortable, wealthy family. They would cosset her and care for her and dress her in silks and satins, just as she deserved. It was good. It was the right thing for her. She would find a young man and forget about him.

Alexander doubled over gasping for breath. Pain wrenched through him and he wondered if everything he knew about medicine was wrong. Maybe one *could* die of a broken heart.

When he could breathe again, he picked up his valise and his surgeon's chest and started walking through streets that became narrower and darker and grimier as he left Mayfair behind and made his way down toward the wharves. He found himself standing in front of a familiar address. Like the house in Mayfair this one, too, had lamps that shone welcoming warmth through the windows, but the window frames could use a coat of paint and there were cracks in the steps leading up to the worn door. The steps were swept clean though and the knocker on the door gleamed. A middle-aged woman opened the door, putting her hand to her throat in shock at his appearance.

"Mr. Murray! Come in at once, and warm yourself in the parlor! We'd heard you shipwrecked and drowned, but you're not the first sailor the sea's tossed back ashore."

Mrs. Hayworth, herself a sailor's widow, bustled about him in the parlor, exhaustion weighing him down as he stared into the small fire in the grate.

"Do you still have a room for me?" he asked the landlady without looking at her.

"Aye, your regular room, Mr. Murray. Your gear is in storage for you."

That was good, he thought hazily. He would not need to buy clothes after all. Mrs. Hayworth's remark about him surviving reminded Alexander of his original purpose a lifetime ago in making this trip to London. When she excused herself to build up the fire in his room, he went to the writing desk where the landlady kept paper and pens for her boarders and scratched out a note, sealing it and setting it aside. Mrs. Hayworth returned carrying a tray.

"You stay here and eat your stew and have a good cup of tea while I fetch the bedding for your room."

He nodded without speaking, and she said nothing as she arranged his supper. That was one of the reasons he liked to stay at Mrs. Hayworth's. She was a woman who appreciated that sometimes a man did not want to talk about bonnets or butterflies or what bows would be decorating pelisses this winter.

He set aside the untasted stew when she returned and, digging a few coins out of his pocket, gave her the letter to be carried by a messenger in the morning.

"Mrs. Hayworth, is there a bottle of brandy here?"

"I have better than that for you." She fetched a dusty bottle from the back of the house. "It is yours, all the way from Scotland. You left it on your last visit and I kept it in case you returned."

She fetched him a tumbler and left him there. He rolled the bottle back and forth in his hands. It sloshed heavily. He'd barely made a dent in its contents last time, for the whisky, while excellent, fogged his mind.

He filled the tumbler until it overflowed onto the table.

$\sim$

*A*lexander opened his eyes or tried to. They'd been fastened shut with some kind of adhesive while he slept. He tried again, and the gummy eyelids finally worked, but it turned out to be a poor decision as the light in the room stabbed directly into his brain, setting up a pounding akin to someone using his skull as an anvil.

No, the pounding was external. On the door of his room. He dragged himself from bedding reeking of an excess of liquor and sweat and clinging to the wall for support made his way to the door.

Mrs. Hayworth stood there, arms crossed over her ample chest. She sniffed, then said, "It is time you were up, Mr. Murray! A message arrived for you."

He blinked at her blearily. She no longer pounded on the door, but there was still a pounding in his head, and something had built a nest of dust and twigs in his mouth while he slept. He reached up a shaking hand and felt bristles and dried drool on his face. "Wh—" He swallowed and tried again. "What time is it?"

"It is past noon. On Thursday."

He gripped the door harder. "Thursday? That is not possible."

"It is entirely possible when one drinks a bottle of that Scottish poison!" She sniffed again. Then her demeanor softened and she shook her head, sending gray wisps of hair bobbing from under her cap.

"You seamen are all the same. Come ashore and it's wine, women and wildness, isn't it? I knew that when my Samuel was home, but I have what will fix you and put you back on your feet. After you put some clothing on—fresh clothing—come down to the kitchen."

She turned to stomp away but paused and reached into a faded apron tied about her waist. "Oh, I nearly forgot. Here is your message."

Daphne! His heart sang out, but the missive was in an unknown hand with a strong, masculine slant. He opened it carelessly.

"Bad news?" Mrs. Hayworth said, hovering with interest. She loved a bit of gossip, did Mrs. Hayworth. Not in a bad way, but simply because news of other peoples' lives seemed so much more interesting than her own.

"Not bad news," he said, frowning down at the paper. He tapped the letter on his hand and looked at her.

"I will need a bath, and some coffee, and your excellent

remedy for men who consort foolishly with alcohol. Your other tenants spoke well of it in the past."

"A bath will be coming right up as soon as the water's heated. In the meantime, you come down and eat and drink something— something good for you. It will help you feel more yourself."

"What if I am not pleased with who I am?" he murmured, but she was already walking away from him.

Alexander felt more like himself when his visitor was ushered into the parlor later that afternoon. Mrs. Hayworth closed the door behind the man and Alexander rose to his feet. Stephen Childes bent over a silver-knobbed cane, his back twisted by age. He resembled a cricket, skinny and hunched, eyebrows bristling like antennae, but the eyes behind his spectacles were sharp and studied Alexander in a fashion that made him slightly uncomfortable.

"Please, Mr. Childes, have a seat."

The older man sat, carefully, and rested his hands on his cane. He declined the refreshments Mrs. Hayworth set out.

"I was stunned to hear you were alive, Mr. Murray. The last I heard you were dead in the wreck of the *Magpie*."

"It was a near thing," he acknowledged. "I was able to make it to land and recently returned to England. I was traveling home because of the letter you sent me."

"So many months ago," Childes said, and a shadow passed over his face, then was gone. "Do you know why I contacted you?"

"You mentioned a bequest, but you did not offer more information."

"Indeed. I could not share more information with you until I met you and saw you with my own eyes." He cleared his throat, and took some papers from a leather portfolio, looked at them, then adjusted his spectacles.

"What is your name?"

"Alexander Murray."

"Your full name, please."

"Alexander Archibald Murray."

"What is your mother's name?"

All of Alexander's senses sharpened. When the solicitor mentioned a bequest in his letter, he thought it might have had something to do with his naval service, not his life in Scotland.

"Why do you ask?"

"Please, Mr. Murray, just answer my questions, then I will explain all to you."

"My mother was Janet Murray."

Childes continued with his questions, asking Alexander about specific points of the village where he'd been raised, his schooling, his naval service. Then he separated a sheet of paper from the others and held it out, covering the bottom half.

"Do you recognize this letter?"

"Yes, that is the letter I sent you saying I would return to England."

"One final item, and then I tell you why I contacted you. Would you fetch the pen and ink I see on that desk and bring it here? Good. Now, please sign this piece of paper with your signature."

Alexander picked up the pen, dipped it and signed his name on the blank sheet of paper, then passed it back to the solicitor, who compared the two signatures, the one from Alexander's letter and the one on the paper.

Childes removed his spectacles, polished them, put them back on, and cleared his throat.

"I have a bequest for you from your father."

It took a moment for the words to register in Alexander's brain. He stood so fast his chair tipped over behind him. "I do not want it!"

Childes sighed. "Do not be tiresome. Sit down and hear me out. Did your mother never tell you who your father was?"

"My mother barely survived on the pittance sent each quarter by my *father*, Mr. Childes," he said through clenched teeth. "She had expectations I would go to school, to university, and those expectations were quashed by my father's agent, Fieldhouse. No, she did not tell me who my father was, and at this point in my life I do not care."

"Yes, you do care who your father is," Childes said. "Any man has a natural desire to know his origins. Now, I will speak and you will not interrupt me, for I am an old man and could pass on at any moment."

"You look healthy enough to me."

The solicitor inclined his head.

"Thank you for your professional opinion. Nonetheless, it is easier for me to tell this tale in its entirety." He removed his spectacles again, went through the polishing ritual, then put them back on, adjusting them before he spoke.

"I met your father many years ago when he came into his own inheritance, and over the years, I conducted much of your father's business for him. I was also one of the few people who knew he sired a son on a trip to Scotland.

"Your father, Mr. Murray, was Hugh Blackborne, the Earl of Rycroft. He could not marry your mother but made what he thought was adequate provision for your upkeep and maintenance. He did not realize until it was too late that his agent, John Fieldhouse, was robbing him, and you. I do not know if it is any comfort to you at this point, but Fieldhouse will spend the rest of his days in New South Wales.

"Rycroft wanted to contact you and tasked me with finding you. I found you, but your father was dying. He at least had the satisfaction of knowing you were coming home to England, but he did not live to meet with you as he desired so strongly."

The solicitor's face showed the weariness of a lifetime of losing too many people to age and disease.

"Before he died, your father wrote you a letter, and as I said, left you a bequest." He reached into his portfolio and withdrew a folded document. "Please read the letter first, as your father wished."

Alexander took the letter with an unsteady hand. There was a part of him wanting to throw it directly onto the fire, but Childes was correct. A man longed to know who he was, where he came from, and Alexander was no different from anyone else in that regard. He needed to know. The letter felt heavy in his hand, and there was a seal on the back stamped with a device. He heard the sounds of the traffic outside in the poor neighborhood with its shops and peddlers, its sailors and serving girls, but all of that faded as he broke the seal and began to read.

—

My dear son,

I hoped to have this conversation with you face to face, but that is not to be. My life is full of regrets, none greater than my failure to take care of you and your mother.

I did not contact you over the years because it would have distressed my wife. At the time, I thought I made the right decision, and had provided sufficiently for your welfare. I learned I was wrong.

Not being able to see my only child grow into a man has been the lasting sorrow of my life. Your mother was very dear to me, and not a day went by I did not think of her. The all too brief time I spent with Janet was the happiest of my existence.

I cherished the reports I received of your growth and achieve-

ments. By the time I learned the money I spent to further your education was stolen by my agent, it was too late to make amends. Even without my assistance you made much of yourself, and I am proud of you, and proud of your service to King and country.

I hope yet that I will be able to say these things to you in person, but my physicians tell me it is unlikely. I have delegated Childes to share with you my wishes, and I hope you will take this bequest and think well of me, despite everything.

You are the son of my heart.

———

The weakness of the letter's author was evident in the shaky scrawl at the bottom. The clock in the parlor ticked away the minutes as Alexander looked down at the document in his hands, then carefully folded it and put it in his coat. He did not know exactly what he was feeling at the moment, but regret was part of it. Regret for his mother's shame and suffering, regret he never had that face-to-face meeting, though he did not know what would have transpired. Perhaps it was better this way.

"Do you know what he wrote?"

"He dictated it to me," Childes said. "By that time, he was too wasted to write it himself."

The solicitor gave Alexander another moment of silence, then briskly opened his portfolio again.

"Your father wished to make amends to you. He could not, of course, leave you the entailed estates, but he had other properties."

The older man adjusted his spectacles again and looked over the documents in his hand. "Specifically, you now own a townhouse in London, a house and land in Kent, a substantial share of a mill in Lancashire, a portion of a shipping venture, and funds. I must tell you the Kent property was sorely neglected. Part of the problem is the poor harvests of the past year and lack of oversight, but if you put some effort into it, there's no reason it cannot again be a prosperous and attractive holding."

Alexander very much feared his jaw gaped open. "I am wealthy?"

"You are at the moment. Of course, you could gamble everything away, neglect your property and not manage your funds well, but you do not strike me as a profligate person. Do you still want to turn down your bequest?"

His jaw snapped shut. "No, but not for the reasons you think, Mr. Childes. There is a young lady—"

He stopped because he could not imagine why he would be sharing personal information with this man, except that the shock of the events was overridden by one over-whelming thought. He could approach Daphne's father now with his head high. A man of property, with funds, the son of an earl—even if he was a bastard—could compete for Daphne's hand where a poor surgeon could not.

"Yes, I would say you became an attractive marriage prospect in the last thirty minutes," Childes said dryly. "I wish you luck."

He slowly rose and gathered his things. "I suggest we make an appointment to meet again so I can go over with you in more detail what you now own. You are, of course, free to hire your own solicitor if you wish."

"I will be in contact with you."

"In that case, I will wish you a good day, Mr. Murray."

Alexander nodded absently. He finally had something to offer Daphne Farnham besides his battered self. Not a title, and not the kind of wealth with which she'd been raised, but he could keep her comfortably. And he could offer her his love.

If he was not too late.

aphne was bored and frustrated and feeling out of place and out of sorts. Of course, there were fittings for a new wardrobe, exhausting fittings, and training Betsy to take the now-married Hattie's place, and walks with Pompom, but none of that was enough to take her mind off of her Alexander. What was he doing? The foolish man was no doubt pining for her, because who else wanted to learn a new word every day from a grumpy surgeon? Who would he snuggle next to at night and practice Latin? She frowned at that thought as she tied the tapes on the second-hand dress Alexander purchased for her in Portsmouth.

She marched down into the kitchen and the conversations came to a halt. Mrs. Webster was directing her underling on the finer points of chopping carrots just so, and a footman rose hastily to his feet and slapped on his wig, crookedly, while her maid, Betsy, stared at her charge.

"Miss Daphne! Whyever are you wearing that old thing? You should have called me to help you dress in your new merino, that one delivered yesterday."

"I cannot be useful in those new dresses, Betsy. This garment is much more suitable, and I like it."

When Daphne said "useful" she thought she heard a snicker or two. Mrs. Webster frowned at the other servants. She had been with the family since Daphne's father's marriage and knew her exalted place in the Farnham universe.

"Useful, Miss Daphne?" the cook asked calmly, wiping her hands on a spotless apron, her broad face flushed with the heat from her soup pots.

Daphne looked around the room. She was being judged by people who'd spent their entire lives being useful, just as Alexander had. It did not matter that she was the daughter of the house. At this moment she was in their territory, and she must prove herself or risk being banished. Gently, politely, but banished.

She took a deep breath and wiped her damp palms on her skirts. "I can build a fire and I can boil an egg. Oh, and I can cook fish in leaves."

It was probably best to start small before offering to help with wounded pirates who needed their guts rearranged or limbs removed.

Mrs. Webster's basilisk stare froze anyone who might have giggled or snickered.

"Boiled eggs are an important part of breakfast, Miss. For lunch, however, I planned on a custard. Can you help with that?"

"Yes!" Daphne said, her tense facial muscles relaxing as her smile sprang out. Out of the corner of her eye she saw the footman start to smile back, but Betsy saw that also and elbowed him in the side. "Custard is just another way of cooking eggs, is it not?"

Perhaps she would track down Alexander and leave him a custard. Wouldn't he be surprised!

"Custard is eggs, milk, a few other things, but yes, it is cooking eggs. Betsy, fetch Miss Daphne an apron. If she likes that dress she will not want to spill anything on it."

She hummed to herself as she followed cook's instructions on how to properly scrape the tiny seeds from the vanilla beans to obtain the most flavor. The aromas filled the air around her and she chatted with Betsy about the remaining alterations to her new ball gown. The ball gown was similar fabric to the pink satin she and Alexander found. No matter that it was being sewn by the finest French modiste in London, it would never be as dear to her as the bedraggled cloth lovingly tucked away in a corner of her wardrobe. Last evening she'd taken it out and inhaled the cloth and thought she could smell the salt of the sea on it, a fragrance that brought back memories and brought tears to her eyes.

She was fast running out of patience with that man. If he did not show up on her doorstep in the near future, hat in hand and contrition in his eyes, she would need to take matters into her own hands. Daphne had dealt with shipwrecks and pirates and sea creatures who did not wish to be eaten. She was not going to let a surgeon block her path to happiness!

"What is the meaning of this?"

Everything came to a halt as the kitchen staff turned to stone at the sight of the master of the house standing in the doorway. Cook was whitefaced. Betsy actually trembled.

Daphne straightened her shoulders and faced her father. "I am cooking. I insisted Cook teach me how to prepare a custard. I am being useful, Papa."

"Useful?" He frowned at her.

"Yes." She twisted her hands together in her apron. "Now I will prepare your luncheon and it will be good, you'll see."

The kitchen servants and cook turned and looked at her as if she'd sprouted another head, but she held her ground. Her father silently watched her, a bemused expression on his face. Her insides were all aflutter, but if she could face down grumpy surgeons and pretty pirates she could prepare a luncheon for her father, who loved her very much.

After a moment that stretched itself out forever, he gave her a nod and said, "As you wish, daughter. Bring my luncheon to my study when it is ready."

He started to turn to leave, then paused.

"Bring enough for two. You will dine with me, Daphne."

"Yes, Papa."

～

"*E*nter."

Her father's command on the heels of Daphne's knock made her take a deep breath. Behind her, the footman, Prentice, whispered, "Chin up, miss," and she smiled to herself and entered her father's sanctum with as much dignity as she could muster. Prentice set the tray on the table and arranged it, then exited, closing the door behind him.

Daphne looked around the study. She had not spent much time in here over her life. It was her father's domain, while hers, he'd made clear, was the ballroom and the parlor.

The study was lined with books and she thought to herself how much Alexander would enjoy a room like this, a room filled with books and serious pursuits. Daphne's father came out from behind his desk, a desk covered with papers and more books and some maps. Her father, she knew, was a most useful person.

But he was still her papa, and there was a smile on his face now as he said, "I am anxious to taste this luncheon you prepared for me."

"Cook made the leek soup, but I made the sauce for the ham. A pirate taught me how to make the sauce. And this is my first custard."

Her father paused from where he was lifting the cover off of the soup tureen.

"Pirates? I believe it is time we talked about your adventures,

Daphne."

"Yes, Papa."

It was raining outside, but in the study Daphne felt nothing but sunshine, warmed by the cozy fire burning in the grate, cook's soup and her father's regard. She could not remember spending time with him like this since... She could not remember ever spending time with him like this.

He was always busy with his ships and his meetings and his investments and newspapers.

In addition to the leek soup, there was ham with a spicy sauce made from jam. Hill the cook had showed her how to prepare that. There was ale for her father, tea for her, and for the dessert, her custard.

After the first bite of custard, her father, who'd been eating silently up until that point, raised his brows and looked at her. "It is tasty. All of it is quite excellent, Daphne."

Daphne turned away from his regard to look out the window, where the view was only rain sheeting down. She saw a glimpse of white from the corner of her eye and picked up the handkerchief her father passed to her, then dabbed at her eyes.

Her father cleared his throat.

"You learned how to do this while you were gone?"

"Yes, Papa."

"Will you tell me now about your adventures? We do not spend time talking, do we? Yet here we are, in the same house— you always seemed to be flitting from a party to morning calls to dressmakers."

"You were at your warehouses and in your study, Papa. But I always knew you were there for me."

He blinked his own eyes, then cleared his throat again. He studied her, as if he had never seen her before. Perhaps he had not, not really seen her, not since she was a little girl and her mother died. His eyes, so much like her own, crinkled at the corners.

"Pour me a cup of tea, daughter, and tell me about Daphne Rose Farnham. I would like to know more about this intrepid young lady."

Daphne poured him a cup of tea and added the sugar, just as he liked it, then poured herself another cup. The fragrant steam rose around her, tickling her nose, and it made her smile.

"There were many mornings on the island when I wished for a cup of chocolate or tea just like this one. I believe I enjoy it more now, because of that."

So Daphne told her papa about her adventures. Some of them, anyway. How she'd learned to garden, and cook an egg, and start a fire, and a few carefully selected words she'd learned. Finally, after taking a deep breath, she told him of assisting Alexander in his surgery during the battle aboard the *Prodigal Son*.

"You were not afraid?"

"I was so afraid! Petrified! But I asked myself, how could I sit alone in the cabin with just Pompom when Dr. Murray needed my assistance?"

Her father leaned back in his chair and laced his fingers across his stomach.

"These pirates, they did not harm you?"

"Oh no, Alexander protected me, always."

"Alexander, is it?"

Daphne blushed and looked down at her tea cup. She did not feel it necessary to explain the sleeping arrangements aboard the *Prodigal Son*, and thankfully, Papa did not ask.

He did, however, sigh loudly.

"I was hurt and worried when you ran off with George Tyndale, Daphne. I wanted to marry you to a stable, mature man, one who would take care of you, not a useless fribble. You are an heiress, daughter, and that means you bear great responsibilities. Responsibilities to yourself, but also to those people who depend on me for their livelihood, and who will depend upon your husband and your guidance some day."

Daphne looked down at her lap, for she knew that her father was right, and yet…

"Papa, I cannot marry a man I do not love. I made a

mistake with George, I know that now. I do not know a great deal about business, but I can learn. I need to get advice from people who know more than I do. I know that, but I also know I need someone I can trust by my side to help me, and I had no trust in the man you picked for me. I had no feelings at all for him, so how could I learn to trust him?" She looked up at him and said what should have been said months past. "You never asked me what I wanted, Papa. I will tell you now I am a woman grown, and I learned things over this past year about myself, and about others."

"You are more like your mother than I ever suspected," he said, almost to himself.

That brought tears to her eyes again, but she blinked them away because he was still speaking.

"This surgeon, Murray. I would hardly consider him a good marriage prospect for you."

Daphne thought about it before opening her mouth to defend Alexander. She needed to pick the right words to impress her father.

"You would like Alexander, Papa. He is mature and he is full of gravitas."

"Gravitas?"

Daphne nodded her head.

"Yes, it means—"

"I do know what that word means, thank you. You care about this Scotsman, don't you?"

"I love him, Papa, and I trust him," she said simply. "Even though he is not very intelligent."

"How do you mean?"

"I told him I loved him and wanted to marry him and he told me I needed to come home to you so that I can marry some peer." She shook her head at this foolishness.

"But wouldn't that make you happy, to be a fine lady and go

to the finest parties?"

"I like parties, I won't deny it. But many of the people I see there? I hate to say this about them, but they are useless! I would rather be with people where I can be useful. With Alexander I am useful. And he listens to me."

Her father picked up his teaspoon and tapped it on the table, thinking. Daphne sipped her tea, though she wasn't tasting it.

"Maybe you should go to the country for a fortnight or two, Daphne, to rest and recover from your adventures. There was talk after you ran off with Tyndale, unpleasant talk. If you decide what you want is to re-enter society, we will discuss the best way to accomplish this. I can see how your time away helped you in many ways, but society will not look at you as I do. In the meantime, you have given me a great deal to think about and we should not rush headlong into making decisions."

Daphne was about to protest but held back. She did not want to rusticate, not while Alexander Murray was loose in the city. He might do something foolish like ship out to sea thinking it was best to not be around where he would tempt her like a new bonnet with flowers on it, flowers like the pretty little purple ones that grew in the shade on their island...

She pulled her mind away from bonnets and focused.

"Give me a few days, please. I still have fittings left on my dresses, so I must stay in town for now."

"Very well," Mr. Farnham said, rising to his feet. "But I trust you not to do anything foolish while you are in town, Daphne Farnham."

"I am done with adventures, Papa. You can be sure of that."

CHAPTER 25

Alexander took one of his new coats from the tailor's hands and tried to shrug himself into it, grimacing at the snugness through the back and shoulders.

"Look at this, Quinn. I cannot freely move my arms. How will I wield a saw with this fit?"

"Dr. Murray, if you wear one of my coats during your surgeries I will hunt you down and perform a surgery of my own," the tailor said mildly. "Now, hold still, please. These coats are for social occasions, not for the cockpit. You are a gentleman of substance now, and your valet will help you into your coat for the best fit and appearance. You wish to look fashionable, do you not?"

"Must this have velvet at the collar? I look like some useless popinjay."

"Popinjay? No, sir, I would say more like a Scottish grouse, but one who looks quite presentable."

"Fine feathers do not make fine birds, Quinn."

Henry Quinn raised his brows at that ridiculous assertion. He was a tailor who'd had an unfortunate encounter with a press gang and ended up on the *Caeneus* during the war. He left the sea just as soon as he was able and with his prize money opened this fashionable shop on Jermyn Street. He was also grateful to the man standing in front of him. It was in no small part because of Dr. Murray's skills that Quinn survived in one piece to come back to his tailoring. He peered now at Alexander over his spectacles.

"I would not tell you how to treat chilblains, so please do not presume to tell me my trade. My role is to ensure that when you wear my coats you make both of us look good."

"Damned foolishness. Do you have any idea how many coats I could buy in Glasgow for what you are charging me at your London rates?"

"And each of them would look like it came from Glasgow. Now, hold still, and let me adjust this cuff."

It was amazing what women could drive a man to do. Alexander wanted to rush to Daphne's house immediately following the meeting with Childes, pound on the door and demand she marry him, today!

He did not do that, of course. He was a reasonable and prudent man. While he did not need Mr. Farnham's approval or his money, it would help Daphne regain her footing in society if he accepted her bridegroom. Showing up on Farnham's elegant doorstep looking like he could afford to keep Daphne comfortably would further his case.

Alexander glanced at his shabby brown coat, thrown across a chair and looking as out of place as he felt in this elegant establishment. In the pocket of that coat was tucked a special license—and wasn't that an expense to chill him to his bones! But knowing the paper was there, ready for him, ready for her, comforted him and, he admitted, gave him courage.

"Will these coats be ready for me by the end of the week?"

"Once again, they will be ready for you, as I promised." Quinn looked up and his eyes gleamed. "If anyone had told me you would be standing here as full of nerves as any bride-groom I've ever seen—well, I would not have believed it of our Dr. Murray."

"Nonsense. I am not full of nerves," Alexander insisted, shifting from foot to foot.

The door to the tailor's shop slammed open. He had only once glimpsed the man standing there but recognized him immediately.

"Mr. Farnham! Daph—"

"Where is she?" Farnham yelled, his gloved fists clenching and unclenching. "What have you done with my daughter, you bastard?"

Quinn stepped back but looked at Alexander. "Should I fetch help?"

Alexander raised his hand to silence Quinn, his attention on Farnham.

"What has happened to Miss Farnham?" he asked calmly.

"As if you did not know! Where is she? Is she in your rooms? By god you will tell me or I will have the law on you!"

"I have not seen her since I escorted her to your home."

"Then explain this!"

Farnham's blue eyes were amazingly like Daphne's, though seamed at the corners with lines. Those eyes narrowed as he thrust a paper into Alexander's hand.

He read it and felt his eyebrows go up. "Miss Farnham did not write this, or if she did, she wrote it under duress."

"Of course Daphne wrote it! You are all she has been talking about, 'Dr. Murray this' and 'Dr. Murray that'! It is clear to any fool you are the man she loves!"

That warmed his heart, but right now it was not as important as finding Daphne. He looked at the note again.

———

Dear Father, I have run off to be married to the man I love. Do not follow us, please, for this is my true desire. I will contact you after the wedding and sea you then.

——

"Her maid went to fetch her for luncheon and found this," Farnham said, but his voice held more desperation than anger now. "I just want her to come home, I do not care what she has done."

"She is not with me," Alexander said, tamping down his own fears. "She has been abducted and the longer you argue with me the farther away her captor will be."

"Abducted? Who—what—"

"This note is not from Daphne, or not written of her own free will. Look here—where are the curlicues and rainbows, and hearts over the *i's*? Did she take her dog with her? No? Then obviously she went under duress, for she'd never leave Pompom behind. What's more, being the highly intelligent woman she is, she has given us the identity of her abductor."

"Intelligent? Daphne?"

Alexander yanked off his new coat, ignoring Quinn's wince as a basted seam ripped away. He pulled his old worn coat on, turning to Daphne's father.

"Clearly, you do not know the same Daphne Farnham I do. She is an intelligent and thoughtful person, and there is no time for further discussion."

"Now, see here, Murray—" Farnham started to say, but then he stopped. "I am beginning to believe there is a great deal I need to reconsider, but finding Daphne is most important of all."

Alexander was already moving toward the door, but he stopped now and looked at the older man. "I will find Daphne, and when I do I will marry her and I will keep her safe."

"How can I help?" Farnham said simply.

"Have a horse waiting for me at my rooming house. I can travel fastest by myself."

"You know where she is?"

"I know how to find out. Quinn, you're with me."

~

$\mathcal{H}$orace Fuller was a prudent man. When he exited his favorite dockside tavern and was yanked into a piss-smelling alleyway, he held quite still, that being the prudent thing to do when a surgeon has a knife pressed up against your throat.

"Mr. Fuller. Do you have any idea how quickly you would bleed out if I sliced your carotid artery?"

He did, actually. He'd seen men die of such injuries during battle. He'd even inflicted a few himself a time or two. "How did you know I was here?"

"My friend over there knows the docks better than I do. You and your captain are known in these parts."

Fuller looked to the other end of the alley, where a thin, well-dressed man lounged against a wall, blocking that exit. Fuller sighed. "I told the boy it was a harebrained thing to do, but he never listens to me."

"That was too bad of Captain St. Armand and if you do not tell me where he has taken Miss Farnham, it will be too bad for you, too. Unless you wish to die to keep your captain's secrets?"

The surgeon was a few inches shorter than Fuller, but the grip on the mate's shoulder was solid as Gibraltar and the look in the man's eyes—it was disconcerting to hear someone speak so mildly when his eyes burned so hot. Fuller cursed the young fool who put him in this situation.

"If I tell you where he is, do you promise not to kill him?"

"Mr. Fuller, you should be hoping I do not kill *you* before our conversation is finished. I make no promises regarding St. Armand."

So Fuller told him about the abandoned mill on the road to Portsmouth.

"He said he didn't grab her right away because he needed to know she'd still be her father's heir, otherwise she's no good to him. Once he gets her alone with him for a few days she'll be more eager to…urk!" Fuller rose up on his toes and sweat broke out on his forehead as the blade pressed a fraction deeper.

"When I find them, if a single flounce of Miss Farnham's dress is undone I will hunt you down and remove vital parts of your anatomy."

"Careful with that sticker!" Fuller gasped. "Didn't you swear some kind of oath not to harm people?"

"Physicians swear oaths. Surgeons carry knives. You'd be wise to remember that."

CHAPTER 26

"You ought to be ashamed of yourself, Captain St. Armand! I don't think you meant it at all when you said you would shoot Mr. Fuller if I did not write that note. Mr. Fuller left us just as calmly as you please after you bundled me into your gig."

Captain St. Armand looked at Daphne with amusement as he uncorked a bottle of wine.

"Miss Farnham, of course I would not shoot Mr. Fuller. He's my mate and an old friend. My dear, you have a soft heart. I approve. I think my wife should have a conscience. It's a good thing for one of us to have."

"I am not your dear anything! Being carried off by pirates and forced to marry only happens in silly novels. Besides which, you made me leave my darling Pompom behind. You are not a nice man, Captain."

Daphne smoothed down her azure gown, taking a moment to admire the blush pink and lilac rosettes adorning the overskirt. It was a lovely new walking dress and now no one would see it because she'd been kidnapped by pirates. And here she'd promised Papa no more adventures! She

389

looked at her captor from under her lashes. He held the glass of wine up to the candlelight, admiring its color, then brought the glasses and the bottle over to where she sat at the table. Captain St. Armand had bound and gagged her when he had hustled her into his gig but untied her as soon as they were outside of London and on the road. She did not like being tied up. Though there was that one evening with Alexander…

But that just made her angrier, this not-nice pirate thinking he could marry her. He gave her a glass of wine now and sat opposite her at the table.

The building where he held her was an abandoned mill, and she had to admit Captain St. Armand went to lengths to make it a comfortable prison. There were cushioned chairs and hampers of food and wine, and a crackling fire warmed the room as the wind picked up. He'd given her privacy to wash up, but he locked the door behind him when he left the room.

She tried not to notice the bed that dominated the space. It was large, smothered in silken pillows and satin covers in scarlet and gold. It looked inviting, but she had no intention of climbing into that bed, not unless the pirate was firmly on the other side of that locked door.

"I will not force myself on you," he said now as he took a sip of wine.

She turned back from frowning at the bed. St. Armand was not dressed like a pirate tonight, except for the small gold earring winking in the firelight. He wore a superbly tailored coat of bottle green, cut to show off a striped waistcoat in a cream satin with stripes of a darker shade, over a fine linen shirt. The coat, his trousers, and his boots were from London's finest shops, she'd stake a custard on it.

He leaned back in his chair now, crossed one booted ankle over his knee, and gave her a smile, the one she'd come to recognize as his "I'm a dashing pirate rogue" smile, not the "If you don't obey me, I will remove your intestines" smile he sometimes used aboard ship.

"I have no need for force, Daphne. Spending a few days locked in here, a few nights in my company, it will be enough to convince you. I am quite confident of the outcome."

Daphne shook her head, marveling at the man's foolishness. "You are not only not nice, you are not an intelligent man, Captain St. Armand."

He raised his brows at that insult, but it amused rather than angered him. "Why do you say that?"

"Because you do not realize the trouble you created by snatching me away. You do not believe me? Let us examine the evidence: the note you made me write says I ran off with the man I love. Who do you think my father will think of first? Not you, certainly. My father will go to Dr. Murray, who, being clever, will deduce I did not leave with you of my own free will. He will come after me."

He smiled condescendingly at her. Like she was a foolish girl, or a useless person.

"That's unlikely, since he has no idea where we are. You should hope your Dr. Murray does not meet up with me again. As you pointed out, I am not a nice man."

~

*A*lexander pulled his coat closer around him as the wind picked up. Clouds scudded across the moon, turning the nightscape into a chiaroscuro of silver and black, but it was enough light for him to stay on the road, following Mr. Fuller's reluctant instructions. Amazing how much information a man would offer up with a knife at his throat.

So here he was, riding like young Lochinvar to claim his bride. It was an image that under other circumstances would make him snicker, but he wasn't feeling amused. Poets and authors and even philosophers had written about what he was feeling. He'd thought he was above it all, that a good mind and a calm disposition could take him through life.

He'd been wrong.

How could he have ever thought he'd be able to live days, much less decades, without someone who adored fluffy dogs and pink frocks and, most amazingly, him?

He pulled up on the reins of the gelding when he saw the light in the tower, an abandoned mill, Fuller said. Alexander tied the horse and approached on foot, his pistol by his side. He saw no guards, only a shed with two animals stabled for the night and behind it, a carriage. He led his horse there and saw to his needs while thinking through the best course of action.

No guards were necessary because the door to the mill was bolted from the inside. It was thick oak, unbreakable without a battering ram. Alexander walked around the structure, looking for gaps, for other entrances, for some way in. There was nothing, only the window up at the top of the mill where lamp light filtered through shutters.

He pulled his coat tight around him as he looked up at that window, so far from the ground, the hard ground that could shatter him like a dropped wineglass. It was not the weather that sent a shiver down his spine. There was only one way he was going to break in to that dark tower looming over him like a monster from a fairy tale. There was a princess in that tower, a princess who kept special smiles for him, and held him in her arms and thought him worth those smiles.

He took off his coat, rolled up his sleeves and set his fingers into the bricks of the mill, his sensitive fingertips capable of finding veins and arteries and tiny fragments of shrapnel, now searching for crumbled mortar and precarious handholds.

His princess needed him. Alexander began to climb.

～

"Marry me, Miss Farnham, and I will take care of you. You can spend your entire day shopping for hats and trying on new frocks. Wouldn't that be fun?"

Daphne pulled on her hand, but Captain St. Armand had it in a firm grip, and stroked it with his other hand. He was a most persistent pirate!

"You and I are so well matched," he continued. "Think of what a beautiful couple we will make, at the opera, at the theater."

"Alexander says it is more important to have brains than beauty."

The pirate snickered.

"I do not care about your brains, I am dazzled by your loveliness! Forget Murray. We would make a much more handsome couple, you and I. I would be your Apollo, Daphne. With Murray, you would be Beauty and the Beast."

"You are beautiful, but it is my dear doctor's physiognomy which appeals to me."

"His what?"

"You see? You do not know enough to be my husband," she said loftily. "I want a natural philosopher, a man who is coolheaded and rational, who always thinks through a situation before he acts and isn't swayed by passion and emotion."

The shutters burst open and the wind howled in, but the tempest was nothing compared to the demonic creature flinging himself through the window, blood oozing down his face, sleeve torn at the shoulder and fluttering in the wind.

393

His hair was blown about like a madman's and his breath poured in-and-out like an overworked bellows. Steam rose off his sweating skin.

"Get your hands off my woman!" he roared.

Daphne smiled happily. "You see? That is the man I want. Good evening, Alexander."

Captain St. Armand rose to his feet. "This is…unexpected."

"Daphne, has he hurt you?"

"What kind of a monster do you think I am, Murray! We were only chatting."

"Move away, Daphne. I do not want any of his blood to splatter you," Alexander said, advancing into the room.

"What is wrong with his face?"

"He is smiling, Captain. Dr. Murray is happy to see me."

Alexander's fists were clenching and unclenching, and "insane glee" came closest to describing the expression on his face. He looked like a Bedlamite. He looked like her own dear surgeon.

Captain St. Armand looked worried. He held his hands from his sides. "As you can see, I am unarmed."

"Excellent! It will be easier to rip your head off!" Alexander bellowed, rushing at him.

Daphne sighed, and grabbed the wine bottle off of the table. Alexander was sweet, but he really wasn't very bright. Captain St. Armand was lying, he was a pirate, for heaven's sake! He pulled a knife from his boot and watched Alexander rush at him. He did not watch Daphne, a tactical error as she smashed the wine bottle down across the pirate's wrist, causing him to yelp and drop his knife.

～

"*S*he is the wrong woman for you, Murray! Use your brain! Think, man!" St. Armand said, trying to salvage the situation as he moved around the table.

The noise Alexander made in response to that was closer to a snarl than something coming from a human throat. It was all so simple. He was going to rend his enemy's limbs apart. Then he'd roger his woman within an inch of her life. There was no thinking involved at all.

Alexander moved fast and grabbed St. Armand, slamming him up against the bricks of the mill.

"See? I warned you, Captain," Daphne said, sliding out of harm's way.

St. Armand landed a punch that made Alexander's ears ring, but it didn't matter. The younger man landed another punch that made Alexander grunt, but he didn't loosen his grip. His arm flew forward and he heard, and felt, the satisfying crunch of cartilage being rearranged beneath his fist. St. Armand howled and threw his hand over his face, blood streaming out from between his fingers.

"OW! You boke by dose!"

"I can fix that!"

St. Armand tried to scramble away, but Alexander was faster, twisting the broken nose back into shape, eliciting another howl from the wounded pirate. Alexander grabbed a fist full of his shirt and pulled him up, shaking him like Pompom shaking a rat.

"You will never, ever put your hands on my woman again, you scum! Do you understand me?" He didn't wait to hear the reply but dropped St. Armand like a bag of dirty laundry and turned to Daphne. She was looking at him like he was, in fact, "So daring in love, and so dauntless in war."

"Oh, Alexander!" she gushed, clasping her hands together.

"You climbed up here! You are the most wonderful, bravest man I have ever known!"

He strode over to her and pulled her into his arms, and she threw her own arms around his neck, gazing up at him adoringly, ignoring the blood, sweat, and grime covering him.

"I knew you would come for me!"

He ached in every bone from the long ride, from climbing the damned mill, and from the pirate's blows. He'd never felt better in his life. He kissed his woman with all the passion of a man driven to the brink of despair and back. Then he set her from him and gripped her shoulders.

"You are never to worry me like that again, Daphne Farnham!"

"Yes, Dr. Murray," she said demurely, but her eyes glowed like sapphires, making him suspicious of her meek response. Then she turned her beautiful face up for another kiss and all of that was forgotten.

Out of the corner of his eye he saw St. Armand twitch, and he reluctantly broke away. Then he saw the bed against the far wall and that bestial sound escaped from his throat once again.

Daphne grabbed his arm.

"Nothing happened, Alexander. Other than abducting me, tying me up, and making me write lies, Captain St. Armand was a perfect gentleman."

She was clutching his arm and he was trying to pull away to remove St. Armand's head from his neck, as promised, but the pirate was prudently inching toward the door. His face was swollen and his eyes were blackening, and Alexander felt a rush of satisfaction. The pirate would not be so pretty in the future.

The satisfaction must have showed on his face, for St. Armand wiped his still streaming nose across his sleeve—

gently, wincing—and said, "Didn't you take an oath to do no harm?"

"A common misconception. Physicians swear oaths, surgeons carry knives. And sometimes, pistols," he said, pulling out the weapon he'd tucked into the waistband of his trousers. "Daphne, gather your things, we are leaving."

"Go, go." St. Armand waved his hand at them irritably, the hand that was not holding a stained handkerchief over his swollen nose. "I will not follow. She is all yours. You two deserve each other."

"Isn't that what I said all along?" Daphne said. She took Alexander by the arm and smiled up at him. "The doctor and I complement each other like…like my new morning dress and my delightful Huntley cap, the primrose satin one with three rows of blond lace.

"I would have said we're more like a tenaculum and a crowbill forceps."

"Oh please, would you two leave so I can suffer in peace? You nauseate me."

Alexander felt his lips pull back in that unfamiliar fashion that meant he was smiling. He was sure the feeling would pass, but right now the idea of pounding St. Armand into jelly continued to appeal. However, victoriously leaving with the lovely prize felt even better.

"Come, Miss Farnham, let us leave him to lick his wounds."

"Yes, Dr. Murray. Goodbye, Captain St. Armand!"

She'd brought nothing with her but her cloak, so he put it around her shoulders and held her arm as they navigated the stairs down to the front of the mill. He put his own coat on, hitched the horses and tied Mr. Farnham's gelding behind. St. Armand could crawl to Portsmouth for all he cared.

"There is an inn a few miles back. We will spend the night

there and leave for London in the morning. We will say we are husband and wife."

"Another pretend marriage? Dr. Murray I am so tired of that! I want a real marriage!"

"That is good, Miss Farnham, for I happen to have a special license in my pocket." He turned and looked at her, her face shining in the moonlight. "I bought it before any of this happened, because I was coming to you, Daphne. I was just waiting until I had the proper wardrobe."

Daphne giggled, a sound warming Alexander's heart. He wanted to hear that soft sound of joy every morning for the next ninety or one hundred years.

"Silly Dr. Murray, you did not need fashionable clothing to court me! Don't you know I would take you in nothing at all? In fact," she said in a low voice, "I prefer you in nothing at all. I was waiting for you to come for me."

Even now, when he looked at the stunning creature seated next to him, glowing like a pearl in the moonlight, he could not believe she wanted him.

"I do love you, you know," she said softly, as if reading his mind.

"I cannot imagine why. You were right all along, Daphne. You are a clever woman—thank you for that 'sea' clue about Captain St. Armand—and I am an idiot."

"You are just saying that to make me feel good."

"No. I'm an arrogant ass, thinking everyone should be like me. You think differently, but not stupidly. Why you want to marry me is a mystery."

"Alexander, I love you for lots and lots of reasons! You have strong shoulders and a deep voice, and you make me feel special, but not like the other men do. They like my face and form. However, none of them bothered to teach me new words or talk to me about things that are important. Important besides fashion. You do. You love me for my mind!"

"I do? I mean, of course I do."

"I knew that." She gave him a smile that had him blinking and turned up the corners of his own lips. This smiling business was becoming habit forming.

"You are correct again. I do love you for your mind. Yes, you have a beautiful face and a form that would tempt a monk, but I love the way you make me think in a new fashion, see things I have not seen before, or have not appreciated for far too long."

"You've changed, Dr. Murray."

"You haven't, Daphne."

She pulled back from him, affronted. "Yes, I did change! I am a useful person! I learned how to make custard, and my father said it was excellent. I can read important books and become more intelligent if that is what you want."

He pulled up on the reins. The road was empty at this hour and if he did not take this woman into his arms in the next minute, he would not answer for the consequences. She moved into his embrace with a sigh of satisfaction, her luscious mouth opening beneath his like a summer flower. By the time he was done kissing her she was sitting across his lap, her arms about his neck and most of the tapes of her frock undone.

"Daphne, there is absolutely nothing wrong with you. You were always useful and intelligent, but in your own way. Not about fashion, but about making people smile, and feel better about themselves, and laugh at life rather than consider it a gloomy journey to an inevitable end. You taught me so much, Daphne Farnham. I need you to keep teaching me to laugh and to take joy in each day. I need you to remind me life is not about enduring, but about living. Most of all, I need you to love me."

"I can do that."

"I know you can," he said, and kissed her again.

"You are smiling," she said dreamily as they broke apart, her finger tracing the outline of his mouth.

"You taught me how to smile," he said gently. "That is far more important than making a custard. Though I confess, I am fond of custard and I hope you will cook some when we are married."

"We must marry immediately, Alexander. I cannot wait to make custards for you! And I am learning how to cook a chicken stew also, in case we cannot hire a cook."

"Ah. About that, I have something I need to tell you. It seems I am a wealthy man. I can afford to keep a cook."

"And buy me bonnets?"

"At least two. One for summer and one for winter. More than that would be an extravagance. You only have one head, after all."

"You made a joke, Dr. Murray!"

"I never joke, Miss Farnham," he said sternly. Then he felt his lips move upward again. "Sometimes, though, I sing."

And he did, singing, "My Love is like a Red, Red Rose" in the moonlight to the beautiful woman who sat next to him as the horses carried them down the road to their future together.

ABOUT THE AUTHOR

Darlene Marshall is an award-winning author of historical romance featuring pirates, privateers, smugglers, and the occasional possum. She loves working at a job where business attire is shorts and a shirt festooned with pink flamingos and palm trees. Marshall lives in North Central Florida, a convenient location for researching sites of great historical significance, which also happen to also be at the beach and serve *mojitos*. Her books have been published in English, German and Estonian.

You can learn more about Darlene by visiting her website:

https://darlenemarshall.com

Want more of the pirate St. Armand? Read **The Pirate's Secret Baby** **(High Seas #3)** *New England Readers' Choice Award, CRW Award of Excellence—On sale now in ebook and print:*

The captain of the Prodigal Son *has a deserved reputation as the deadliest (and best dressed) pirate in the Caribbean, but Robert St. Armand's totally at sea when it comes to "Marauding Mattie", the daughter he never knew he had. How in the world can he deal with the littlest pirate, one who prefers knife-throwing to arithmetic lessons, and who'd rather be keelhauled than eat her beets? He needs help!*

Lydia Burke is living a safe, respectable life, separated from England by an entire ocean. It's exactly what she needs and she's not going to risk her boring, but secure, position as a governess to consort with pirates, especially one who's too pretty for his own good or her peace of mind.

Robert didn't fight his way to the top by letting small obstacles like scruples stop him. If he can't hire Lydia Burke, he'll steal her and take her to England with them, certain he can charm her into his bed along the way as an added bonus on the voyage.

It will be a true voyage of discovery for the pirate and the governess, as one learns to navigate the rocky shoals of parenthood while the other tries to keep deadly secrets hidden, and both will find that while it's a child who initially brings them together, the growing passion between them offers the greatest temptation.

facebook.com/DMarshallAuthor

twitter.com/DarleneMarshall

instagram.com/darlenemarshallauthor

bookbub.com/profile/darlene-marshall